BROKEN WIZARD

A novel
by Colin Dodds

Copyright 2011 by Colin Dodds

This is a work of fiction. Names, characters, places and incidents either are products of the author's imagination or are used fictitiously. Any resemblance to actual events or locales or persons, living or dead, is entirely coincidental. No part of this book may be reproduced without written permission of the author.

**This book is dedicated to the memory of Joseph
Earnest Martin
May 25, 1977—May 25, 2007**

Part One—Out of Hand

Several other nearby towns seemed to have better prospects than Worcester. Fitchburg, Southbridge, Oxford, Webster, Rutland and Charlton all had superior water sites. The Brookfields boasted more desirable land. Westborough and Northborough had better potential access to the coast. Yet it was Worcester, with none of these natural assets, that developed the manufactories that produced goods and wealth in amounts sufficient to attract thousands of immigrants from all over Europe. It was Worcester that, by 1980, had become the second largest city in New England.

Nothing came easy to Worcester. It had to develop its early industries without the help of major waterfalls. Since it was not on a navigable waterway, it had to build, at great expense, a canal along the Blackstone River all the way to the sea. Since it had no natural access to Boston, it had to build a road, including a bridge across Lake Quinsigamond. In its search for energy sources other than wood, it could only find an inferior type of coal to mine.

In some ways, the rise of Worcester to its current metropolitan and industrial status is not easy to explain.
—Margaret A. Erskine
Heart of the Commonwealth: Worcester

1.
Tuesday, December 23

Traffic was heavy, and a thick fog rose from the melting snows on the highways between New York and Massachusetts. It was two days before Christmas and a week before Dad's surgery. I was driving up for the holiday and the surgery, and planned to stay in Massachusetts for longer than any time since I was seventeen.

The drive up had the quality of a voluntary return to prison. I paid the toll and left the Mass Pike, following the highway into Worcester. I had no idea what was coming next. Not for my dad, my old friends still in town, or for myself. Still, I punched the rental car radio hard enough that the green digital display went black. I didn't know a thing about death, and held to the story that the trip would be a routine interruption in my life. Still, I sought to dawdle, and took the long way to Westborough, going through Worcester.

Driving down Interstate 290, the city of Worcester came up fast, everything full of memory. First came a Polar Cola billboard above the warehouses and silver tanks full of soda. Usually, a big inflated polar bear smiled at the traffic from the billboard. But it wasn't there that day, and I hoped it wasn't gone for good. Then the highway shimmied in an S-curve around the Holy Cross football stadium, where I'd played Thanksgiving football games in the cold mud.

Past that was a gap. There used to be a sign: *Every Great City Has At Least One College. Worcester Has Ten.* It listed all the schools. They'd painted the sign on a derelict warehouse with cork insulation in its walls. And a few years back, a pair of derelicts burned it down. The fire took a handful of Worcester firefighters with it. It was a big tragedy, and I guess it still is.

On the radio, Bruce Springsteen sang *Born to Run*. He'd opened a big tour at the Worcester Centrum when I was a kid. Some national magazine wondered aloud why he'd chosen to open the tour in "a burned out mill town." I remember people in Worcester being angry at the description back then.

Worcester's unheralded skyline came around the curve, dominated by a big, glass bank building and a high-rise apartment building that never quite caught on. I took the Vernon Street exit, by a leprechaun hat the size of a shed, and I called Joe.

2.

"What the fuck is your problem, dude?" one of them shouted back across Highland Street.

"You're an ugly fucking pussy is my problem," Joe shouted.

"Fuck you, faggot," the guy across the street shouted back.

The yeller had two friends with him, neither of whom looked particularly riled in the orange parking-lot light. The guy was just reading from a script written for him when he was eleven or twelve. And Joe was reading from a script written by the better part of a liter of Jack Daniels.

Before I could interrupt, Joe was walking his six-foot-two, 250-pound self across the street. I had no choice but to follow. Joe's ponytail bobbed with the spring in his step. The situation wasn't new. Sometimes I could defuse it. Sometimes, too drunk to know better, Joe was also too drunk to fight. Then I'd just break it up after he hit the ground a few times. Sometimes I'd have to throw and take punches.

It was too cold for this shit and we were too old for this shit, I muttered. The offending parties waited in a parking lot that Chinese takeout place shared with a three-decker. Joe seemed sober enough to handle himself, though drunk enough to fight on a whim. One of the guys in the parking lot gave a short shout—someone's name. And as we crossed the sidewalk, a door above the parking lot slammed and a big, bald guy with a long, red goatee came bounding down a flight of outside stairs to the parking lot. The bald guy was ready to go, readier than any of us, bouncing on the balls of his feet with his hands up, like a prizefighter.

"What the fuck, huh? You got a problem with my boys? You ready? You want to get fucked up?"

"What? Huh? No, man, no, there's no problem," Joe said, backing right down, laughing at himself. The guys in the parking lot seemed relieved that it wasn't going to happen.

"Hey, I'm Joe, Joe Rousseau. What's up?" Joe said, putting out his hand to the bald guy. The bald guy bounced for a moment, then decided not to press the issue. Then we all started laughing at the absurdity of the fight, and of Joe.

The parking lot guys introduced themselves and started talking with us about people we knew in common, places we'd hung around, high schools attended, and a dozen other connections implicit in Worcester. After five minutes, amity settled over us. It made a kind of sense. Joe's unfocused rage was common as the air in that town, and his wild audacity broke up the monotony. He was a friend the parking lot guys could appreciate. The almost-fight had already become nothing more than an anecdote about a crazy drunk, and a scary bald guy in a parking lot. And me, I wouldn't figure much in subsequent retellings, except as the guy with Joe Rousseau, the crazy drunk.

Joe and I said glad good-byes to the parking lot guys and went into Tortilla Sam's to get on with our plan of using chicken wings to transmute drunkenness into sleep. Most people had the next day off, and the bars had been full. The faces in the bars each had the history that hangs around everyone who hangs around long enough.

At one particularly noisy bar, I yelled an apology to a guy named Gabe I'd picked on rather viciously in junior high school. I bought him a drink and he forgave me for my abuses. I told him about my life in New York. And he fed me a line of shit about how he, a now-obese guy in a motorcycle jacket, had become a world-class martial artist who dominated the secret cage-match circuit until he chose to retire—a decision which the highly displeased crime bosses of Tokyo had no choice but to accept. Gabe hadn't changed much since the eighth grade. I excused myself before I did or said anything that would undo my apology.

"He was a cage fighter about the same time I was Surgeon General," Joe said, talking about Gabe. "I see him all the time. I think he graduated Worcester State last year. He's a bouncer sometimes at Irish Times."

"I'm just glad I got that off my chest. I always hated how I treated that kid."

"Remember that school trip, when you punched him in the face because he was crying because I put bug spray in his sleeping bag and then said he pissed it?"

"Yeah. I think that was included in my apology."

"You sure were a prick."

"Hey, we can't all be saints like you."

The waitress brought wings. One by one, Joe put a whole wing in his mouth, closed his mouth over it and pulled his head back. His knuckles turned white and his forehead veins bulged as he wrestled the meat off the bones.

Joe was part French Canadian and part Iroquois. The latter part dominated his face. His nose was broad and his eyes big. He couldn't grow a beard if he wanted to, and his mouth seemed too big for his face, especially when he smiled his wild, open-mouthed smile.

"Hey, what happened to the big Polar Cola polar bear over 290?" I asked.

"The Holy Cross kids must have taken it. They usually do it this time of year."

"Oh, good. I was afraid the Polar Cola people took it down."

"The big bear? They would never take that down."

"You never know. I mean, look at Spag's. That place was an institution, and now it's gone."

"It's still open," Joe said, pulling chewing chicken meat and cartilage.

"But not as Spag's. When I was up last summer, I saw they even painted over where his name was written in roof tiles. I can understand them taking the neon picture of Spag's face off the front of the store. Changing the name of the store might even make some sense. But why bother painting over his name on the roof? Did it confuse anyone? Did it upset anyone?"

"It just doesn't belong to Spag anymore," Joe said, shrugging.

"See? That's what I mean. People don't need a good reason to get rid of something. So my fear that some callous corporate vizier of a regional soft drink dynasty had removed the big inflated Polar Cola polar bear was not totally out of whack."

"Fine, my brother, I pronounce you not totally out of whack. You may go in peace," Joe said, making the sign of the cross in the air with a chicken bone.

"Speaking of out of whack—that guy who attacked you here, with the chair, what happened to him?"

"Who, Matt O'Brien?"

"Yeah, your latest nemesis …"

"Yeah, I hate that fucking guy. I heard he got out of jail around Thanksgiving. He was away for about a year. I told you about that, right?" Joe said and I shrugged. "It was this guy from down in Great Brook Valley—O'Brien carved his initials in his face at a party."

Since we met in the fifth grade, Joe always had an arch-enemy in his life. It gave a shape to the days. But in the fifth grade, his nemesis was just a popular kid on the soccer team.

"And they let this guy out?" I asked.

"I guess he pled it down to simple assault or something."

8

"This was the same guy you kept calling at two in the morning to tell him he was a worthless pile of rat turds?"

"I know, right?" Joe said, and started laughing. His laugh was staccato and out of control, like a happy seizure. It rolled over him and then me until my face and stomach were sore.

"You really know how to pick a nemesis," I said in between laughs.

"Do you know what he's doing for a living now that he's out?" Joe choked out.

"No."

"He *holds horses' mouths open* for a living, for veterinary dentists. And it gets even better," Joe said, talking, laughing, eating chicken wings and half choking from the effort of doing all of them at once.

"You mean better than beating you into the hospital with a chair, carving his initials into some guy's face and holding open horses' mouths for a living?"

"Yeah, it's nuts. He has '*You're Dead*' tattooed on his lower back."

"Who is that even addressed to?"

"I guess it's for whoever is sodomizing him in jail."

"At least he was thinking ahead," I said, and Joe laughed until his head touched the table.

We finished the wings and then drove down to Main South to an afterhours place. Joe was looking for this black girl he emphatically wanted to sleep with. She wasn't there, but we stayed for a few whiskey shots out of tiny plastic cups. Under the unmoving and unlit disco ball, I watched Joe hit on a hefty Irish girl. The depth and breadth of his libido was always impressive. Eventually, her friend, a bedraggled looking Spanish girl, dragged her away, but not before she had given Joe her phone number.

"She used to be the hottest girl at Burncoat High," Joe told me upon returning.

"I keep forgetting how long ago high school was."

"I always wanted a piece of that. Angela Murnion."

"Well, it looks like she's got pieces to spare nowadays."

A drink later, we were the only ones left, except for the Spanish guys whose basement it was. Joe drove us back to his apartment off Lincoln Street, up by Green Hill Park. We were drunk, but still awake. Joe broke out the chess set and we played a sloppy game. I won it, so we were playing best of three. I won that, so it was best of five. He won one, then I won one, so it was best of seven.

"Man, I'm beat. I think I'm just going to crash."

"So you're forfeiting the tournament?" Joe said.

"No, I'm not forfeiting, I'm beat, and I told Dad I'd be at his place by noon."

"If you're not forfeiting, then let's play," Joe said, getting a sinister smile on his face.

That smile meant he wasn't going to budge. More than chess, or any competition I can think of, Joe loved to argue. He could go for hours, days, even weeks. It was his sport, and it had no rules except the ones he made up.

"Sure, fine, I forfeit, whatever," I said, knowing an indifferent abdication would take the savor out of his bullshit victory.

"So you lose?"

"Sure, if that means I can go to sleep."

"You're an asshole," he said, smiling.

"That's Mr. Asshole to you."

Joe had two big mattresses laid out on the floor in his room, making an enormous bed. It was big enough for us to lay at right angles to each other. I got the mattress by the window, which was winterized with a taut sheet of plastic.

"So what are you going to do?" Joe asked.

"I guess that after Dad is back on his feet, I'll go back to New York, and get another job. I had an interview last week. It just sucks because there are a lot of guys like me looking for work right now."

"A lot of guys like you—that's a scary thought."

"I mean a lot of guys with my level of experience who are looking for the kind of job I am. It's fucking discouraging."

"Want me to ask around Worcester?"

"No, that's alright. I have the severance to tide me over. Things have to turn around eventually. Then I'll get something, work up the ladder, to sector analyst. Maybe from there to research head somewhere," I said. The story, with its slideshow of summer timeshares, watermarked bonus checks and new imported suits, had been reflexive since the layoff, a bedtime prayer against lengthening shadows of uncertainty.

"So that's the plan?"

"For now. How's your job?"

"It's okay. I have to figure out a way to get out of there. I got written up the other day."

"What for?"

"This dumb girl parked in the staff lot. And they gave her a ticket, as they should have. So she calls me and says she was only there for a minute and had to park there because she had to get in a paper or else she wouldn't get credit for this class and wouldn't be able to transfer out of Worcester State. So I'm like, 'that's too bad, but the officers here never give out tickets unless the car has been there for a *while*. You got your paper in on time, so just consider that the price.' So she says she can't afford to pay the ticket. I say then she should have parked in the students' lot and walked the extra hundred yards. So she yells at me 'it's not fair,' and starts crying. I say she should call back when she's ready to be rational, or better yet, just pay the ticket and not call back at all."

"So what did you do wrong?"

"That's exactly it! I didn't do anything wrong. But she called my supervisor, still crying, and said that I was abusive on the phone. I got chewed out and now I have this bullshit written warning on my record. Not that I care. But the job just isn't getting it done. I want to get some money together. I'm thinking about moving some coke."

"Is that a smart idea?"

"I have to get out from under this nine-to-five bullshit."

"But is that a good way to do it? What happened to getting your degree?" I asked.

"That's a few years off, more than a few, at the rate I'm going. It'll happen. But I need to get out of this job first."

Staring at the pale streetlight that had seeped through the curtains onto the ceiling, I felt the pull of an old drag. No matter how obstinate Joe was in the face of a fight, an argument, even a friendly disagreement, he was still baffled by the faceless opponent presented by long, otherwise empty hours. Those hours had already won too many battles, wrested too many plans from him—plans to become a pilot, a lawyer, a chef, and so on.

"But, I mean, coke? Isn't the saying that you sell weed with a handshake and cocaine with a gun?"

"It depends on how you do it. But I think I have it locked down. I'll only sell big amounts and only to my friends, people I've known a long time, people who I know I can trust. I just have to be disciplined. And I'll only do it for a little while."

I opened my mouth. None of the friends Joe could sell cocaine to were trustworthy. And Joe liked cocaine a bit too much to be in business with it. He was my oldest friend and maybe I should have said more. But it was late, and I honestly didn't believe he'd follow through. And I didn't feel like arguing. I closed my eyes and hoped for a few solid hours of sleep.

3.
Wednesday, December 24

Joe was still snoring when I left. It was cloudless outside, but the December sunlight was a thin gruel. The gray-brown landscape was soggy from melted snow. The sand on the street crunched under my sneakers. Bracketed by low snow banks, I drove to a Dunkin' Donuts for coffee. The roads were busy, but I didn't spot a single out-of-state license plate in all of Worcester's traffic. I found Route 9.

Route 9 rose and fell over the hills like a ribbon waved by a restless hand. It was an old turnpike, built back before the railroad and the internal combustion engine, to connect Worcester and Boston. Now it's a state highway lined with an unremitting string of restaurants, car dealerships, shopping centers and apartment buildings. Since the divorce, Dad lived in one of the apartment buildings. Mom lived in another.

The Mass Pike handles most of the East-West traffic to and from Boston now. But the Worcester mill owners jobbed the Pike so it gave quite a wide berth to Worcester, the second biggest city in New England. The story is that the factory owners didn't want to compete with Boston wages. As a result, it takes a little more than an hour to drive the forty miles from Worcester to Boston.

That day, Route 9 was mostly empty. The shopping plazas were half alive with last-minute shoppers.

It's only about fifteen minutes from Worcester, but Westborough is a very different sort of town. Worcester's heyday came in the first half of the last century, with hundreds of workshops, mills and factories humming along its streets, canals and railroads. Westborough's boom began in the early 1970s, as suburbs cropped up around the hi-tech companies and government contractors that filled the office parks along the newly laid I-495. I knew those office parks by their logos—Data General, Memtech, Raytheon, Wang—which loomed over the highway, and announced themselves on the business cards on my dad's night table. Those companies brought my parents to Central Massachusetts before I was born.

The Fountainhead apartments beat the future to a punch that was never thrown, and look out of place. Three modern concrete slabs enclose the main lawn of the complex. The huge fountain in the middle of the lawn was turned off for the winter.

Dad had been in the westernmost slab for about a year and a half. And things had been going well enough for him, until a doctor found a lump, close to his heart. The surgeons would have to crack open his sternum to get a good look at it. I pulled into the Fountainhead parking lot, grabbed my bags, buzzed up and he buzzed me in.

The corridor to the elevator was low-ceilinged and utilitarian. Some of Dad's neighbors put down welcome mats in front of their doors, or taped up their kids' school work. On the door next to Dad's was a drawing of a lopsided pair of people, with squiggles around the phrase "I IM SPECIAL." I coughed, something between a chuckle and a shudder, and knocked on Dad's unadorned door.

We embraced and looked at each other, blue eyes in broad, ruddy faces. His face had gotten older, with folds and sags here and there, like luggage that hadn't been put away. He had lost weight since the divorce. We said merry Christmas, his rough cheek scraping against mine. On the side of his door, I could make out the dozen or so coats of paint that had been applied over the decades. We sat down at his new kitchen table, a lightweight thing that wobbled too easily under our elbows. It sat in contrast to the dark wood bookcase behind it. For the dozenth time since the divorce, I was struck dizzy at seeing familiar pieces of furniture from childhood flush against strange walls. Dad was comfortably lost in big a white wool sweater. He was happy to see me—so happy it made me uneasy for a moment. It had been like that since the divorce. Well kid, you wanted a close fatherly relationship for all those years.

"Sorry I'm a day late. I just figured I'd catch up with Joe before the holidays started," I said, wondering why warm welcomes always trail apologies.

"It's no problem. We're going to see too much of each other before too long. How was the drive up?"

"It was a typical holiday mess, jammed up most of the way."

I put my bags in the room I used when I visited. Then we watched the football recap show on TV. The couch and TV were also from our old house. They seemed too big and too nice for the apartment with its wall-to-wall carpeting and bare walls. Even after a year and a half, Mom's and Dad's apartments, like all apartments in the suburbs, set off alarm bells in my head. At best, they looked like a shabby exile.

"So, how are you feeling?" I asked, breaking the silence the TV demanded. Dad muted it.

"I'm okay, I'm looking forward to the game Sunday."

There we paused and let the rest of conversation go unspoken.

"Thanks again for coming up to help out," Dad said.

"No problem. It worked out well, with the holidays and this time out of work."

With that, I started my own silent prayer of clichés: *It fell to me; It was the right thing to do; You regret the things you don't do more than the ones you do; He was all alone in that sad apartment in the suburbs and so on and so forth.* It helped me combat urge to flee.

"Yeah, it did. You'd think they'd have a better way of doing it. They have to crack open my ribcage, sever the pectoral muscles, then …"

Over the phone, Dad had already explained the procedure to me several times. I don't think he forgot saying it to me. He just needed to keep saying it, to keep what was coming within the understood boundaries. We were sitting in the shadow of a nasty question mark. And the less certain we were, the more certain our answers had to sound.

He continued: "… meanwhile there's the risk of all sorts of infection. They say this surgeon is one of the best in the state. But what I want to know is: what about the anesthesiologist? He's the one that will kill you. After that, though, with the drugs they have and the rehab techniques, it should only set me back a few months. I'll be back up to speed by this time next year. It's the sort of thing they do all the time now."

"Yeah, it's routine," I said by way of an Amen to his personal Catechism.

I appreciated him putting on a brave face. It was a courtesy, if nothing else. We drank Diet Cokes in the silence demanded by the TV, while the light faded through the big glass door in the living room.

"I thought we should to go out to eat. I know a good place that should be open tonight. Sushi sound good?" Dad said.

"Yeah. Do you want to do presents now or when we get back?"

We exchanged presents. I got him a DVD player that played the new kind of DVD and a new hardcover, both presents with an eye to the long, boring recovery that lay ahead. He gave me a set of speakers I wouldn't be able to use until I got home, and some shirts.

4.

The sushi place was in a shopping center in Westborough, though the proprietor had done all he could to make it seem otherwise. We entered through a zigzagging hallway of pale wood that sequestered the low-lit dining room from the vulgarity of the big plate glass window and the parking lot beyond it.

An obsequious Japanese man sat us in the main dining room. Dad rattled off the names of fish and beers to the waiter. The beers came fast and Dad finished his before I knew it. He ordered another, taking me for a designated driver. I took a long swig of my own just to stay competitive. The fish came on wooden blocks. Dad eyed the robe-wearing men behind the wooden sushi bar.

"A lot of these places out here, they're run by Chinese people. But this place—they're actually Japanese. That's what makes the difference. That, and they get the best fish."

Sushi was always our thing. When I was a kid, we'd go for sushi when Mom was out of town. Back then, the one sushi restaurant in Worcester was a big place next to a roller rink. It was where Dad paid me a compliment for the first time, when I was in high school. I had to go into the bathroom to hide how choked up I got over it. Sushi always made me think of him, of knowing him as my dad, and having the good fortune to know him later, as a friend.

"How's the job hunt?" he asked.

"I had that second interview last week."

"The one at … what was it?"

"Farragut Ward."

It was a big bank in Manhattan. I'd already started counting the money and planning my excuses to Dad—*I'm sure you'll be okay. It's just this new job. I'll try to come up on weekends, once things settle down.*

"It went smoothly at first. The human resources lady liked me well enough. And I seemed to impress the guy who would be my boss."

"That's good. What was he like?" Dad asked.

"He was the head of equity research, a decent guy—more intelligent than ambitious. He knew what he was doing, and we got along well enough. That part was fine. But then I met his boss, some senior vice president of something or other. He got my name wrong and seemed to do it on purpose—kept calling me Tim, even after I told him it was Jim. He was one of these guys with perfect teeth and a tan in December. He just seemed shifty."

"I know the type—senior management with an MBA from Bally's fitness. Just smart enough to pick the right tie and screw the other guy."

"Pretty much. So he starts asking me how long I've been out of work and how I lost my last job. I tell him about the layoffs at Bigelow Spencer, which he had to know about. They were in the papers for a week. But he wanted to see me squirm, I guess."

"I've been on interviews with bastards like that. They make senior management and think that makes them a Pharaoh or something."

"So this guy asks me if I saw the problems coming, the ones at Bigelow. And I said no, that I wasn't doing research for the part of the company that fucked up. Then he asks me if I should have found out. And I said that, with all the Chinese Walls at Bigelow, I couldn't have found out without breaking the law. Then he *stares* at me like he's waiting for me to confess the real truth, that I had been behind the problems at Bigelow and had come to his office to infect his firm. It was bizarre."

The waitress came by with more fish and more beer.

"Then it got even worse. He asked me why I was laid off when Bigelow was purchased, instead of the equivalent guy from Numera Partners, the guy who made me redundant. I explained that they canned my whole team from Bigelow. So he does another one of those staring pauses, again, like I'm lying to him. Then he says 'Now, I don't know you, Tim. We just met. But what I want to know is, are you loyal?'"

"*Loyal?*" Dad said through the sushi in his mouth.

"Yeah—loyal. I swear, I wanted to jump over the desk and kick his fucking Chiclet teeth down his throat. So I took a breath, and I asked him what he meant by *loyal*. Did he mean loyal to my employer? And he said yes, mostly, but also loyal in general. And I tried not to lose it, but I said 'Well, was Bigelow loyal to me? After a few bad quarters, will Farragut be loyal to you? I mean, pay me what we agree on and I'll do my job the best I can. I won't steal or complain. But *loyal*? I don't see where loyalty figures into it."

"What did he say to that?"

"He did the staring pause for another minute, then just said it was nice to meet me and he'd hold onto my resume."

"The kiss off."

"Looks like it."

"Loyalty? Obviously, this guy wanted you to say something," Dad said and gestured for another beer.

"Yeah. I don't think I gave him what he was looking for."

"Sometimes it pays to stand up to a bully. But I don't think this was one of those times."

"I think you're right. I'll see what comes in after the holidays."

"Loyalty. I heard a lot of bullshit in my day, but I never heard that question before. He must have really gotten burned."

"I thought I had all my interview answers down pat. I guess my bullshit isn't as cutting edge as I thought."

"My last job before the one I'm at now—they were like that. We'd have these 'culture conventions' every month or two with this consultant and talk about our feelings, about what the company fucking *meant* to us. The company meant a goddamn paycheck. But some people would just go on and on with this absolute horseshit about *community* and *personal growth*. After a couple meetings, I just scheduled sales calls for those days."

"It's like that scene in *The Natural*—'you pay me to hit baseballs, not listen to some headshrinker.' Why can't I just show up, do a good job and go home? Why do I have to buy into 'core principles,' and so on?"

"Then you buy in, and they lay you off at the first sign of a drop off. I was saying the other day, your generation has it so much worse than mine did," Dad said, drinking from a fresh Ichiban. I motioned for one.

"Tell me about it. I just hope that the market will come back sometime soon," I said.

"It's an absolute mess out there right now. If we didn't have the government contracts at Aerovan, we'd be in real trouble. I'm almost totally out of the market right now. What are they saying down in New York?"

"There's not much to say. A few million people lied to each other for a decade or so until someone called out 'bullshit,' and everyone ran for the exits. I guess a pipeline of empty promises isn't the best way to run a world. Go figure. It's just shameful. And it's a shit time to be out of work, that's for sure."

I took a breath, ate some fish, drank some beer.

"Anyway, you look good. How much weight have you lost?" I asked.

"About sixty pounds."

"That's great. You're putting years on your life with that."

"I just have to make it through this next month. Once they cut out this thing, I'm going to live a long time."

And there, Dad paused and looked right at me. He wouldn't imagine a scenario in which the mass wasn't benign. He was an optimist, come from nothing much, fought in a war, gotten a college degree, and made his way to the upper middle class, for a while anyway.

"I'm going to live long enough to piss on your mother's grave," he said.

Thanks Dad.

Half drunk and full of sushi, I drove us back to the apartment. Dad and I talked, then let the TV do it for us. Sometimes even a whole lifetime together isn't enough to come up with something to say. We switched between sports shows, history shows and the news. Then he passed me the remote and went to bed. I called Serena and told her voicemail I had gotten in safe and to have sweet dreams.

Then I went into the room where my father kept the miscellanea of his divorced life—his computer, golf clubs, big cases of toilet paper and coffee. I inflated my bed.

5.
Thursday, December 25

I guess if my folks had split up at a younger age, I wouldn't find the process of leaving one to visit the other so uncomfortable. My stomach squirmed and I had trouble swallowing. I guess the divorce still bothers me. Those are the words I had to go with the sick feeling.

Mom lived in Framingham, a half hour to the east, also on Route 9. The trip out there was a long reminder—the furniture store that used to be a nightclub, the Chinese buffet that used to be a barbershop, the Brazilian steak house that used to be an Italian restaurant, the liquor store that was always a liquor store, the Starbucks that used to be a hillside. Home is a place you can never see with fresh eyes.

Even Dunkin Donuts had closed for Christmas day. But the stucco blob that sold Honey-Baked Ham, according to its sign, was jammed. The place never made much sense to me as a business. On Christmas day, though, it even had a cop directing traffic. Up the hill from the ham-hawker was the yellow-beige brick apartment complex where Mom had lived since the day she packed up her things and left a note on the kitchen table while Dad was out golfing.

The guard at the gate waved me through with all of his impatience and resignation at having to work on Christmas. From the parking lot, I could see the two of the biggest shopping Valhallas of Route 9, whose parking lots were empty that day, eerie and ceremonial as archaeological sites. I gathered my breath and Christmas presents.

I buzzed Mom's apartment and she buzzed me up. After negotiating the door numbers, I found hers. Like Dad, she had lost weight and had dyed her hair since the divorce. I kissed her cheek on my way in. Her face was resuming the proportions of old photos, but with extra skin now hanging loose on it. She seemed very small. We sat down at the old wooden kitchen table, which took up too much of the apartment's dining area. She was glad to see me. Maybe not as glad as Dad. But then, she wasn't staring down the barrel of major surgery with no family in the world.

It was warm in the apartment, but Mom wore a fleece jacket just the same. She followed me as I dropped my bags and jacket in her spare room. It was clear that my presence threw her usual apartment routines into disarray. She offered me lunch, then breakfast, then a snack. I bargained it down to a soda and we sat down in front of the TV in the living room. Her apartment was clean and colorful. The pale sunlight did the best it could there.

"So how are things with you?" she asked.

"Well, I'm back here for a month, or more, for the surgery and the recovery. I'm not thrilled to be back that long. But I don't have a job. So I guess it is what it is," I said, quoting from Bill Belichick's defiantly bland press conferences.

"The surgery, is it serious?" Mom asked.

"It's just a mass they have to check out in his chest."

"Is it cancer?"

"I don't know."

"What do they think it is?"

"They wouldn't do the surgery if they already knew."

"But do they have an opinion of what it might be?"

"I just said I don't know."

"I'm just asking …"

"And I've told you all I know. If you have more questions about Dad or his surgery, you can call him yourself," I said. The hair bristled on my head.

"I'm just asking basic questions."

"Yeah. And I just told you all I know."

Mom shifted in her chair.

"I'm sorry you got stuck with this. It can't be easy."

"It is what it is," I said again.

The phrase said the same thing as the shrug of the shoulders that often accompanied it. One more thing you can't help, don't want and can't avoid.

"I'll be okay," I said, reminding myself to be glad that Mom knew enough and cared enough to worry.

"Okay," Mom said tentatively.

"It is. It's okay," I said, nodding my head, pursing my lips and widening my eyes to say 'enough already.'

Things went silent for a long minute. Mom asked me if I still liked my apartment in New York, and we were back in a safer conversation, something that fit the low-ceilinged apartment and the wooden bowl of potpourri in the middle of the kitchen table.

"And how's Serena?" Mom asked.

"She's good, busy. She'll probably come up one of these weekends."

"You already told me, but sometimes you seem so rushed on the phone, how was Thanksgiving with her family?"

"It was good. It was a little stressful meeting them for the first time. But they were really nice, very laid back."

Serena had saved me from a Thanksgiving of doing the divorced-child math of split holidays. I had just been laid off, and the prospect of meeting her parents seemed less draining than seeing my own. It was only the second Thanksgiving since the divorce and I was eager to dodge it.

"You said they were hippies?"

"Yeah, more or less. They live up by Woodstock and all that. Her father is a software engineer and her mother is the principal at a Montessori school up there."

"I didn't think that Montessori schools had principals."

"Maybe not principal, but something like that."

"So was it fun?" Mom said. I don't know exactly how she intended the words to sound. But a knife was indeed twisted.

"Yeah."

"Do you want to watch TV?" she asked.

Mom was just trying to be accommodating. I know that. But it was hard to hear. The TV is how my kind—the white folk from the suburbs—gently ignore each other. And in our limited Christmas together, it seemed like a hostile act, or at least a depressing one, to watch TV. But I was too tired to do much else.

"Yeah. I think there are some college football games on."

Mom put some fish cakes and stuffed clams from a nearby seafood market into the oven. The sunlight poured through big glass doors that opened onto a tiny concrete porch. We ate and talked—not about the divorce, or Dad's looming surgery, or the way everything you rely on for safety and comfort can vanish in the bat of an eye. We talked about my cousins, about my job prospects, about the winter. It was a courtesy. I couldn't tell if it was hers or mine. And I couldn't tell if I was grateful for it.

We ate and unwrapped presents in front of the muted TV. She gave me some dress shirts for the job I didn't have, and trinkets—a deck of Patriots playing cards and a Red Sox yoyo. I gave her another fleece jacket and a couple new hardcovers. Then we drove out to Newton, to see a movie. Newton was how far east you had to drive to see a foreign or 'art' movie. We saw something about how people in another country (it doesn't matter which, but it was Lithuania) have it tough, but still manage to find the beauty in everyday life. On the drive back, Mom steered the conversation from how pretentious the movie was, to the subject of sleep apnea, and what a shame it was that they'd found a cure for it.

"All those people who used to just die in their sleep, what will they do now? People used to say 'Oh, she died in her sleep. She didn't suffer.' It was easy on everyone, especially the people who died," Mom said, blowing her cigarette smoke out the rental car window. "Now they just want to keep you alive so the hospital can take every last penny."

Mom's morbidity was nothing new. When I was six, she told me that if she ever got to be as forgetful and generally decrepit as her own mother, I should kill her. I remember wondering whether I'd still go to jail if I had her permission.

"I guess you have a point there, Mom. But what are you going to do? Kill yourself?"

"With some of these lingering diseases—Alzheimer's, terminal cancer—you really don't have much choice but to kill yourself."

The lights of the closed businesses blazed on in the cold vacuum of night. Dick's Sporting Goods, Legal Sea Food and Starbucks gleamed above the pitted and shrunken snow banks. The signs reconfigured the landscape into a dormant, scrambled message.

"Mom, I advise you think of your only son, who won't get the insurance payout in the event of a suicide."

"Actually, with my policy it doesn't matter if it's a suicide."

"Really?"

"Really. You just have to hold the policy for five years. And I've had it for more than that, so it doesn't matter."

Thanks Mom.

And with that last unthinkable thing, we climbed the hill to her apartment building. Mom said it was past her bed time, and our Christmas concluded. Sometime around ten, Serena called. She was upstate, with her parents. She had gotten stoned with them, so the conversation stopped and started as her attention wandered. I guess my attention wandered too, sitting so close to the mad antics of the muted TV, and so far from her. But the conversation eventually found its holiday rails—the many faux pas of older relatives, the food, the good and bad gifts.

"… But at least the squash and cheese potatoes came out okay. I just can't believe it's been three years since grandpa died," she said.

"I know—unbelievable," I said, then realized I'd never met her grandfather. Serena and I hadn't yet been together a whole year.

"Unbelievable, huh?"

"Sorry babe. I mean, you know."

"Man-robot speaks."

"At least he's polite."

She giggled and I laughed, glad for an awkward moment of connection in the phone call.

"I miss you," she said.

"I miss you too. I'd invite you up to stay at Dad's apartment, but the hospital is probably where I'm going to be for most of next week. Maybe after that, when things get more settled, I'll get us a hotel room for a weekend. I have a car. I could show you where I grew up."

"That sounds like fun. I'm actually a little scared of it, after the stories you've told me."

"Don't worry. The dangerous part is easy to avoid," I said.

Just a week before, Serena and I got into our first real fight. She was mad I'd be away so long for Dad's surgery. And I was mad I couldn't avoid the situation, and that she wasn't more sympathetic. But we'd talked through it, and things were putatively okay. Serena had a way of saying that everything was okay. She helped me tell myself, almost thirty with a career if not a job, that I was doing okay. Still, it took longer than I'd like to say good-bye.

Then it was quiet. Not wind-through-the-trees quiet, but near-the-highway quiet. The occasional truck tore by, just down the hill from the apartment. A six pack of Sam Adams from when I'd visited in the summer was still tucked into the bottom compartment of the refrigerator door. I cracked one open and tried to imagine Mom's empty hours in the apartment, between the end of the workday and sleep. She had wanted her solitude without a false face on it. And here it was.

I stayed up late drinking and letting the TV tell me all about money I had and the money I didn't have, the man I was and the man I wasn't. It took a while. Mom and I crossed paths as she woke for the next day.

6.
Friday, December 26

In the afternoon, Mom and I waded into the holiday shopping crowds at Shoppers World and *The Natick Collection*. There really wasn't much else we could think to do in Framingham, and I had to return some shirts. The stores were jammed with dazed shoppers exchanging yesterday's gifts to harried retail clerks. It was a headache. I called Joe from outside Filene's Basement.

"What's up, brotha?" he answered, sounding ready to roll.

"I don't know. What's on tap?"

"Thinking of hitting some of the bars—and there might be a party later."

It sounded good. With three days until Dad's surgery, there was air I still wanted to breathe. Back at her apartment, I said good-bye to Mom and hit the road.

Riding the bumper of the car in front of me on Route 9, I could hardly breathe from the frustration. An eagle held a tractor trailer in its beak on the sign for a trucking company. It read "Eagle is better than par!" The sign frustrated me. So did the other signs: Dent N' Scratch, Monarch Spring and Wireforms, Home Depot, Lighting Showcase, Bed Bath and Beyond—men like me had moved the earth for these things. We had given our lives, forty hours at a time, for these things. And now, how could we say anything except that we were satisfied with the result?

Crossing into Worcester, I started to breathe more easily. At the Lucky Dog Music Hall, Joe was drinking by the door, in a black rayon shirt illustrated with a dragon fighting a tiger. He was talking with the owner, Erik. They liked Joe at the Lucky Dog, liked him enough to fire and then rehire him more than a few times. Joe introduced me to Erik, who let me in without paying the cover. I ordered a beer and Joe told me how had been fired the last time around.

"I was bartending, and I over-served myself. Like, I was out past the last boundary fence of anything even resembling sanity. So this guy orders a beer."

"And that's all he did—order a beer," Erik interjected.

"Exactly, by all accounts a perfectly reasonable guy. And I remember thinking I didn't like his face. So I said I didn't hear him, and he leaned in to order, and I punched him in the face. But by the time I hit him, I realized that it was the totally wrong thing to do. And Erik is like, right there," Joe said, punctuating the story with his laugh.

"So Joe just looks over at me and says 'I know. *I know.*' And he takes off his apron and leaves. It was the easiest time I ever had firing anyone," Erik said, cracking up along with us.

People forgave Joe. For all the dumb, destructive things he did, he was never malicious for very long. And he had a way of inviting even the people he'd wronged to laugh along. They mostly did. After all, he he'd given them a good story. And that was worth something.

The Lucky Dog was peppered with faces I had known and half forgotten in the last decade—people from little league, from keg parties, from high school, from McDonalds' parking lots, friends I'd

24

willingly or accidentally lost touch with, an ex-girlfriend I'd say hello to, and one that I wouldn't.

"Jim fucking Monaghan, how the hell are you?" said Terry something, emerging from the crowd and offering me his hand.

Terry looked pale in his black leather jacket and weathered Red Sox cap. We'd played little league and gone to high school together. I hadn't seen him in at least a decade. We did the recap. Now he taught high school in Shrewsbury and had a daughter who lives with her mother. I gave mine, leaving out that I was unemployed, that my folks had split, and that Dad was days from surgery. It's funny how you can live ten, fifteen years, but can't be bothered to discuss it, can't get excited about the story. It amounts to a line or two, careful to sound content, careful not to boast. It wasn't that I didn't like Terry—he'd never been anything but nice to me. But there was no place where our lives intersected, except in time and space. We drank a shot together and I excused myself to go to the men's room.

The night's first band started tuning up. Erik told me it was a hardcore band, which meant an angry wall of sound fronted by a fat guy with a shaved head and possibly a goatee. He would scream, gesture angrily and rock violently back and forth. It seemed like every third guy in Worcester was in a band like that. Erik, Joe and I drank and joked around until the band started screaming, thrashing and so on. After a few songs, the music got on my nerves, and Joe knew the unattached women at the bar too well to want to stay. We left and I followed Joe's white Buick Skylark across town to Ralph's.

7.

Along with the birth-control pill, liquid-fuel rocket, monkey wrench, smiley face and barbed wire, Worcester is the birthplace the diner. And an old green diner fronted Ralph's bar and diner. I followed Joe around an old mill building remade into a furniture showroom, past Ralph's spastic green neon sign, and down a crumbled concrete stretch that wasn't exactly a parking lot and wasn't exactly a street.

The stretch was Friday-night crowded, so we parked in the shadows beside Ralph's. In the darkness I could see I-290 atop a palisade of shadow in the distance. The city light reflecting off the clouds made the sky pink. No one had ever spoken or wrote or sang of a pink night sky. It had once made me believe I was dealing with a totally new experience.

Inside Ralph's, Joe knew too many people to list. It was a series of exuberant, cursory hellos. Upstairs, another hardcore band was playing, but you could only hear the roar of it when the jukebox paused between songs. We ordered drinks and Joe found an Italian girl who was spilling out of her jeans and low-cut shirt.

"Tina, you know you're the hottest girl here, don't you?" Joe said, his mouth agape with a wild smile.

"Joe, don't start. You do this every time you get drunk," Tina said, clearly enjoying her opportunity to abuse him.

"Me? Drunk? Maybe drunk on your utter hotness."

"How's the leg?" she asked.

"My leg is great. How's Theresa?"

"Theresa's fine."

"Not as fine as you."

"Later, Joe," Tina said and walked off to the pool table.

"She's Theresa's best friend. I guess she's not in love with me. Not yet," Joe said, gulping his whiskey through the ice cubes.

"How is Theresa?"

"She's alright—works over at the mall. I see her now and then. We say hi. We're pretty friendly, considering."

"That's good. It's important to get past that stabby phase in a relationship."

Theresa was Joe's ex-girlfriend from a few years back. She buried a steak knife in Joe's leg after he called her by another girl's name at a party. According to legend, she said nothing before or after—just stabbed and left. I remember Joe dropping his pants on the sidewalk to show me the fresh scar. Even now, the incident brought on Joe's machine-gun-like laugh.

"Stabby," Joe said between guffaws.

Joe tried to order us some shots, but the laugh took over, bending him until he emerged inspired, saying, "Man, let's get fucked up tonight—what do you say?"

We did shots of something that made my throat open negotiations with representatives from the land of vomit. The drinks and the laughs kept coming. Before long, Joe and I were in a bathroom with a skeletal Irish kid named Tommy, doing key bumps from a baggie of powder. It cut the worst of the drunk and kept us in the game. Last call came at 1:30, and cop cars waited near the door to make sure we left without incident.

On the way to our cars, two big guys started throwing punches in the shadows beside Ralph's. Their friends joined in, and it became a nasty scrum. Shadow legs kicked and shadow arms reached out from the mass and reached back in with vicious speed. The cops took their time getting over there, to give the fighters time to wear out. The big guys, winded and bloody, made a show of yelling at each other as their more peaceful or law-wary friends separated them. The smaller guys acted like they wanted to keep fighting, but didn't honestly struggle when their own more sober and less bloodthirsty friends pushed them apart.

In the end, there was just one guy who really wanted to keep fighting—the smallest guy. He was around five foot four and couldn't have weighed more than a hundred thirty pounds. He was covered in blood. He fought off all peacemakers and went after one of the original big guys—the bigger of the two. When a bouncer went over to block him, the little guy ran around him. Passing into the light, you could see that the little guy's blue winter coat was ripped and covered with blood from his badly abused face. But he kept on, cursing at people he could hardly see. Finally, two big, friendly looking guys smothered him.

With no fight left to join, the little guy approached Joe and I in the milling, post-fight throng. He was distracted and distraught. His heavy breathing made little blood bubbles swell and explode out of his working nostril. His coat, jeans and sneakers were all covered in blood to some degree and he only had one open eye. Joe gave him a cigarette. The little guy spat blood into the darkness between puffs. One of the cops came over and Joe walked away. The little guy tried to do the same, but the senior of the two cops grabbed him. The cop was a burly Italian guy made burlier by his bullet-proof vest and winter coat. He shone his flashlight on the little guy's face humanely, at an angle.

"Hey, let me see," the cop said.

The little guy tilted up his chin at the cop. Most of the blood, I could see, came from his nose, with some flowing from a cut over his closed eye.

"You want to go to the hospital?" the cop asked.

The little guy shook his head and spit more blood off to the side.

"Was it a fair fight?" the cop asked.

The little guy nodded, scowling at the cop.

"Okay," the cop said. Satisfied that they wouldn't have to file a report, the cops wandered off. I walked back to the car and met Joe and Tommy.

The sky over the I-290 was still pink. But the scene, for all its apparent wildness, seemed precedented as hell. It was written, sealed away and forgotten already. And us too-mortal folk, with our desires well-handled by the bars and the cops, had been dispatched to oblivion. I gave Joe forty dollars, which he gave to Tommy for more blow. Tommy agreed to meet us back at Joe's place by Green Hill in about an hour.

8.
Saturday, December 27

Joe drove his Skylark past Plumley Village and I followed in my gold rental car, to the walled school. They hadn't put the chain in front of the driveway, and we drove in. The place gave me a shiver. In the middle of the parking lot, Joe got out of his car. I did the same, closing the car door as quietly as I could.

"Remember your plans for this place?" Joe said.

"Which one?"

In the frigid air, my breath made satisfying little clouds. The school, convent, and gymnasium-auditorium-church building, surrounded the parking lot on three sides, all of them made of that tan-yellow institutional brick. Coked-up and half drunk, we stood at the granite feet of Rosa Venerini. She stood as unsmiling as the sisters who followed her, book in hand, rosary beads slung from a rope belt.

"The racquetballs," Joe said.

"That's right. It was either turn it into a crack house or fill it with racquetballs. I'm just waiting on the money to do it."

"You would still do it?" he asked, lighting a cigarette with a preternatural focus.

"Man, I don't know. I know that the kind of torment they served up here is the kind that all sane, successful adults are supposed to forgive, supposed to say was for our own good. But I promised myself I'd do it. I feel like I owe that miserable kid I was that much."

"I actually don't mind the place. I have fond mostly memories."

"That surprises me. It's not like they treated you much better."

"It was St. Johns I really hated. That fucking place. No girls, forty hours of homework, fucking asshole teachers."

"Yeah, St. Johns was grim. But what wasn't grim?"

I stopped myself before I said the rest: *What wasn't grim in Worcester?* An attack on the town always felt like an attack on Joe. He had stayed, made the best of it, fought the good fight to keep it interesting. I'd fled, and didn't feel right acting superior, not to him.

"One of the best days of my life was when I quit St. Johns. I told Mr. Hood I was going to join the ten percent," Joe said.

"Ten percent?"

"Yeah, he had this theory that every society has a bottom ten percent that accounts for all of its crime, its unemployment and so on. So on my last day, I said 'Mr. Hood, I'm off to join the ten percent.' Mr. Hood was not amused. But he shook my hand and wished me good luck."

The ten percent invited Joe just before high school. He got stoned and lost his virginity to a blind-drunk girl at a party that summer. And a world waited for him there—a parade of girls made available by drink and smoke, new friends who had sloughed off homework and other hassles, and wild, violent nights that refuted the evidence left by the day.

Venerini was where Joe and I became friends in the fifth grade. We paused to take it in. That night's booze and cocaine, along with all the time passed together made the moment feel special.

"I remember our last day at this place, throwing cold cuts behind the lockers," I said.

"That must have been the one thing we didn't get caught doing," Joe laughed and threw away his cigarette.

"Like when you got suspended for laughing at that girl's funeral?"

"That's not fair. I didn't laugh at the funeral. I laughed because I was about to laugh. And I was only about to laugh because I thought of how bad it would be to laugh during her funeral. And I only thought of laughing because you elbowed me in the ribs during the mass."

"I was just elbowing you back."

"I seem to remember you starting it."

We argued the point until Joe suggested we head back to meet Tommy. Across Belmont Street, through the side streets by the hospital and up the hill, Joe drove slowly, as if nuns still peered over his shoulder.

9.

In Joe's kitchen, we sat around a gray Formica table on hard, mismatched kitchen chairs. Tommy put two small jars of coke and a little baggy with just a trace of powder in it on the table. Tommy asked Joe if he had any beers.

"No, just tap water and this rum that doesn't taste right. But you're welcome to it."

"Weird rum, huh? Golly, I guess we'll just have to do a pile of hard drugs then," Tommy said, his eyes bugging out for comical effect.

Tommy tapped a portion from one of the vials out onto a CD case and handed it to Joe. He cut the lines with exaggerated precision.

"Jesus, they took less care drawing up the Peace of Westphalia," I said.

Joe's laugh started silently, just pursing his lips with an alarmed look on his face. He had the presence of mind to put down the CD case. From there, the laugh began its progressive convulsion, infecting all of us. Eventually, Joe collected himself and began cutting the lines again, which reminded him of the joke, which made him laugh again, which made us laugh again.

Finally, Joe carved the lines, took a deep snort and passed me the CD case. I took a line and passed it to Tommy. I sniffled for a few minutes, knowing it was stupid to be snorting coke, but too drunk and already high to give an honest damn. I wondered if any of my prospective employers would require a drug test, and did another line. The stuff was strong, filling my mind with World War Two stock footage.

"How you feeling, Jim?" Joe asked.

"Good. Great. Let's invade Connecticut."

"I know, right?" Joe said, breaking into another wild round of laughs.

"Those fuckers are soft, they're ripe for it."

We did more coke and more still. Things got funnier, but meant less. I never really liked coke that much. I think Joe liked to see me get high. It let him think I hadn't grown the pretensions that would separate us. I liked it for the same reason. I did another line.

"This shit is alright. Where did you get it?" Joe asked.

"Walshie's," Tommy said in a powerful exhalation.

"How is that guy? I feel bad. I haven't seen him since the night he lost his hand."

"Walshie is alright. But that fucking hand always gives me the creeps. It's just this pink stump, and he doesn't cover it or anything when you go over there. But he's still a cool guy," Tommy said, sniffling and widening his eyes.

"Jim, you met Walshie. We bought a sheet of acid from him during that summer you were back from college," Joe said.

"The guy over by Rotmans?" I said. I actually said it more like *ovah by Rowautmans*, as the drugs, booze and atmosphere made my accent resurface.

"Yeah, him. It was nuts. Last winter, he had this party with a ton of booze and a ton of, well, everything. It was just supposed to be some close friends, but word got out. I was there until they made me leave. I guess I got a little rowdy and broke some things."

"This isn't the time you stole a car from outside Dunkin' Donuts, is it?" I asked.

"Actually, it was. But after I left, these kids from Kilby Street show up at the party to rip off Walshie. So Walshie's roommate, his best friend, gets out a shotgun to scare them off and ends up shooting off Walshie's hand."

"Shit," I said. The coke made me wonder if I'd said it solemnly enough.

"No shit," Tommy said, excited as hell to carry the conversational torch. "He has this big steel door now. It must weigh about three hundred pounds. And he says he's stopped drinking, doing coke, everything but weed. He says he's going to go to Clark once he gets the money together for tuition," Tommy said.

"That's a plan," Joe nodded.

It seemed like everyone Joe knew in Worcester had a plan, to go to school, to move to Rhode Island, to fake an injury to their union, to buy land in Maine, to rob a sporting goods store, to work at their girlfriend's father's Ford dealership, to buy clothes at the Salvation Army and sell them on eBay, to learn carpentry and become a contractor, to grow and sell pot at their stepmom's house, to open a restaurant, to get a Canadian law degree by mail, to work on a fishing boat.

"What's that?" Joe asked, pointing to the little baggy.

"Walshie said some guys at WPI made it. It's got some fucked up name like R2D2 or something. He says it's nutty stuff, pretty trippy. He says this little baggy is enough for three or four guys. I'm into it if you guys are," Tommy said, holding up the tiny ziplock bag.

"You up for it, my brother?" Joe said, giving me his maniacal smile.

Before I say I snorted it, I would like to state that I do know better. I knew I had a career and an apartment and friends and responsibilities back in the city in which I had chosen to live. I knew that a functioning brain was essential to all of that. I knew that, especially since the divorce and the layoff, I didn't have much of a safety net in the world. And I knew that if something went wrong, no one would even be able to tell the doctors in the emergency room what drug I had taken.

But Joe had a way of making you not give a damn. It was one of his best qualities. Tommy shook the fingernail's worth of white powder onto the CD case and cut it up into miniscule lines. The teensy-tinsy line of powder burned my mucous membranes. Tears rushed to my eyes and as I blinked, the air filled with jovial patterns.

The patterns congregated into autonomous forms that judged us, then flowed on into fresh patterns, with fresh judgments. Joe's and Tommy's faces poked through the web of patterns in vivid colors. Tommy waited until Joe and I had stopped blinking, resumed breathing, and appeared to be happily fascinated with the activities of the empty space in front of us. Then he did his line. We all sat there a minute, regarding the strange scene strangely.

"Oh shit, I am tripping like Gerald fucking Ford," Joe said.

It summed up our situation well enough. Joe started to laugh, then got distracted. I stared into the silvery, undulating ocean of the Formica table surface. After an indeterminate period lost in similar pursuits, we decided that our place in this world wasn't under the fluorescent light tubes of Joe's kitchen, but out under the stars of a wider world.

"Be quiet, my neighbor's a cop," Joe said, whisper-giggling as we walked down the hallway of the apartment house.

From there, we crossed the street to Green Hill Park. The frozen grass crunched under our feet as we crested one of Worcester's seven cardinal hills. The sky spread itself about as wide as it ever did in that town.

"I remember sledding on this thing. After an ice storm, we used to fly down it," Tommy said, licking his lips as he looked at the hill. "See you guys at the bottom."

Tommy ran down the hill, first jogging, then sprinting, then leaping into the air with his arms spread. On his third or fourth leap, he landed badly, going down face first and rolling to a stop. The ground was cold and hard, but we could hear him laughing and whooping near the foot of the hill by the wilted remains of a snowman.

"I think I'm just going to walk this one," Joe said.

"I'm with you. How long does this stuff last?"

"What? This stuff we've never done before and don't know the freaking name of? Either two hours, or forever," Joe said, laughing.

The laughter made the patterns in the air swarm about us like giddy, ugly angels singing our unknown names. We laughed until the cold air burned our throats. It was twenty degrees out, and the park was empty—even the cops wouldn't bother cruising by. The drugs flushed the exposed skin on my hands and face with blood, so it didn't feel too cold. Tommy was quiet on the ground when we got to him. He stared at the parting clouds and moved his lips, like a movie character on the verge of prophecy.

"The stars are coming out. But not when you need them. It's just that there's never enough. That's the only way you even know you're here. The light never comes all the way through," he said, locking his eyes on Joe.

"Come on, we'll go to the light," Joe said, offering down his hand and pulling him up.

The light in question shot up from the foot of the hill, onto a series of rough-hewn granite slabs. In darkness broken only by dirty orange street lights, the bright white memorial lights stood out like the supernatural itself. On closer examination, the slabs listed the names of the young men from Massachusetts killed in Vietnam. We three men, young during another unpopular war, on drugs we didn't recognize, wandered past the names of the dead. It should have been more sobering, I guess. But long years of Catholic faith and middle-class anxieties had made solemnity a hard sell for Joe and me. And Tommy was just too high to care. He sat on the freezing concrete and took in the view.

"Your dad was in Vietnam. Was he fucked up by it?" Joe said.

"I don't think so. He doesn't talk about it too much and he doesn't talk about it too little. It definitely wasn't a good time, to hear him tell it. Mom said he used to get rattled when helicopters flew by."

"He got shot, right?"

"In the leg. They almost had to amputate it," I said.

"That's fucking crazy," Tommy said.

"What does he say about it, about being there?" Joe asked.

Joe had never met his own father. And he was scared of my dad as a kid, but also fascinated. Sons are always on the prowl for some idea of how to live. Dad never much liked Joe. But it was touch-and-go even with me, his own son, for a while.

"Yeah, he's funny about it. One time I asked him why we never went camping. He said, 'because I spent two years in the jungle being shot at, that's why.'"

"Most of these guys died," Tommy said.

"I think all of them did," Joe said.

"Really? You think?"

I wandered away from the memorial, to the darkness where the grass and the concrete met. I looked out over a pond and the golf course rising on the hill beyond it, to see what the drugs would make of it. Poised in hallucination, I lost the thread of the conversation. I thought of Joe, how he spun gold out of ordinary things—petty arguments or trying to get laid or getting high or holding a grudge or drinking— simply by taking them too far.

"… It was the Domino Theory. We couldn't let Communists take over the little countries and we couldn't really go all out, because of the threat of nuclear annihilation. So we were painted into a corner, kind of," Joe was saying.

"What's going on?"

"Joe was just telling me why we didn't win Vietnam. It fucking sucks. It's sad," Tommy said.

"Yeah, trying to get our way while being careful as a long-dicked dog in a room full of rocking chairs, basically," Joe said

Unfortunately, the drugs brought the image to life. I rubbed my face and blinked until it faded.

"That's great, Joe. Now I won't be able to watch CNN without thinking of dog dicks smushed on a wood floor. Thanks a bunch," I said.

"Fucking dog dicks!" Tommy yelled into the night.

"Oh man, don't think about dog dicks. I was just talking about mutually assured destruction. Think about that instead."

"Great, that's just great. Thanks, man."

"Dog dicks!" Tommy barked.

"Tommy …"

"Dog dicks!"

"Enough dog dicks …" I started, and then trailed off.

Things were still weird, but not as surprising anymore. The peak had passed. We walked back up the hill, which seemed about five times longer and twice as steep as he one we'd come down. Back at Joe's, Tommy got in his car and drove home. He made it, I hear.

Joe and I took our positions on his sprawling plantation of a bed. I set my cell-phone alarm and closed my eyes, praying for a little sleep. Coming down from the cocaine and mystery drug was a dose of hell.

"What's up?" Joe asked into the darkness.

"I'm just figuring out tomorrow, writing e-mails, sending off resumes, helping Dad around the house, stuff like that."

"I am going to sleep for twelve hours, then eat two Dunkin Donuts' egg sandwiches and watch some movies at my mom's house."

"Well, then I have to say, having thought it over, screw you."

"Jim you Mick yuppie bastard, you're my oldest friend, I love you," Joe said.

"Back at you, you froggy, last-of-the-Mohicans nutjob."

9.
Sunday, December 28

Dad had his season tickets since the early nineties. Back then, the Patriots were one of the worst teams in the league, playing in a stadium where you rented seats to clip onto the aluminum bleachers. But lately, they'd won a few Super Bowls and built a new stadium, with working seats, plentiful urinals, an alert security force, and even a shopping center outside of it.

It was only around ten in the morning when we pulled into the dirt lot outside the stadium. We parked under a pine tree and I went to work unfolding a table and chairs and setting up the grill. Dad sat down and I poured him a beer. The shouting drunks and the Patriots flags hoisted from trucks and campers at the edge of the trees made the Foxboro parking lot feel like the encampment of a Gothic tribe nearing the gates of Rome.

I cooked cheeseburgers on the grill. Dad criticized how I handled the spatula, how long I cooked the burgers and how much cheese I used. But when it was done, he grunted in praise. Hot and bloody, held in cold hands, surrounded by trees, camaraderie and washed down with beer, the burger didn't have to be perfect to be damn good.

The game was Dad's last hurrah before his surgery. The next day, he'd start his pre-operation fast.

Police and news helicopters cruised the sky above us. The game was one more chance for Massachusetts to matter, and everyone was excited. Among the fans, a few had dressed for attention, with body paint and costumes. One strolled the parking lot in a new Arizona Cardinals jersey screaming "Let's Go Cardinals" at the top of his lungs and otherwise taunting the fans who milled around their grills and coolers. Greeted by jeers and insults that included most of his family tree, he went on screaming in blinkered rage, cheering on the opponent.

"What's the story with that guy? He was here last time I was up, rooting for the Dolphins," I asked.

"He's here for all the games. He's always wearing the other team's jersey and shouting up a storm. He must have season tickets."

"And hate the Patriots."

"Something's wrong with him. Even if he doesn't have tickets, he'd have to pay for parking. And those jerseys aren't cheap," Dad said.

I could hear the guy scream that the Cardinals would sexually humiliate the Pats, and the fans in the row of cars behind us cursed and mocked him. Anger was part of our excitement for the violent game ahead. But anger is hard to focus, hard to limit. And it's hard not to be changed by it. The begrudged man kept on screaming against the Pats, until he was out of range.

We finished off the burgers and the beer. I packed up the car and we walked up the hill, toward the stadium. Though early, the sun was low. With thousands of edgy, half-drunk fans, we crossed the bridge over Route 1, past thousands more drinking beers, roasting meat, throwing footballs, shouting over each other and laughing.

The new stadium was state of the art. The seats were intact and clean, the concessions varied and pricey, the field synthetic and vivid green. I bought a pair of beers, left one with Dad, and walked down to the field to watch the big men warm up. Millions of dollars rode on the shifting of their shoulders, the strength of their thighs, the durability of their ankles and the sureness of their hands.

Dad and I stood and sang the national anthem along with the local celebrity. The clock by the scoreboard clicked down as she sang about rockets and bombs. It was zero by the time they got the microphone off the field.

The Patriots were favored by more than a touchdown. But as the big, fast men from all over the country ran toward the kickoff, fear took hold. The fear said me and my kind weren't worth a damn, that we were trash, whom history had passed by and would soon regret. But there was still a chance, and the game would decide the matter. It held me rapt until the Cardinals kickoff returner was tackled at his own eighteen-yard line. No billionaire owner, Nevada bookie, professional athlete, or scout, my interest was the irrational interest of a fan. And the game below was only more of that vast and mysterious exercise called entertainment. I yelled until my voice was hoarse from phlegm and blood and beer.

Anyway, the Pats killed them, 38–10, holding our worst suspicions at bay for another week. The stadium lights were on and the sun was setting by the time the clock struck quadruple zeroes. And we the faithful thousands streamed back to our cars, warmed by victory and beer. There were still fights in the parking lot, though.

Dad drove back to Westborough with the same careful drunk-drive he taught me. We passed the maximum security prison and the historic Massachusetts towns along Route 27, down the silent Sunday night streets, listening to the sporting opinions of the drunk, the mad, the lonely and the dull on the car radio.

Back at the apartment, I cooked up a pair of sausage sandwiches and we watched what was left of the four o'clock game. Dad went to bed as the 8:15 game started. Torn between a lackluster late game and the amorphous promise of the other three hundred channels, I flipped around and tried to convince myself that I was tired. Then Joe called.

10.

Joe sounded distracted when he invited me over. But I was glad to be free of my obligation to watch TV and go to sleep. I wrote Dad a note, pulled on my shoes and cut through the night in my rental car.

At Joe's, it didn't take long to realize that something was wrong. The apartment he shared with his roommate Marissa was in disarray when I arrived. The furniture sat at odd angles from the walls. There was a fresh hole punched in the sheetrock a few feet in from the door, with a big smear of blood by it. Joe offered me some rum and then excused himself to take a shower. Then Marissa came out of the other bedroom. She and Joe had been friends since high school, when they used to play hooky and get stoned together.

"I thought I heard something, what's up, Jimbo?" she said. I never liked being called Jimbo. I think she knew that. Being a pain in the ass was part of Marissa's charm. "How's New York?"

"It's alright, could be better. I'm just hunting for a job right now."

She pulled up a creaky wooden chair across from the couch I shared with a small pile of dress shirts and textbooks. She crossed her legs and leaned forward. She somehow managed to have a tan in December. Always pretty, she never pressed that point. Not with me, anyway.

"Looking for work sucks. The place I'm at is looking for waiters."

"Thanks, but I think I'm just going to stay in town until my dad gets past his surgery."

"Okaay," Marissa said.

She said it like she might humor a recovering alcoholic who said he just wanted one little drink.

"I have some interviews lined up back in New York," I lied. "I think I'll stay around there a while longer. What's up with you?"

"Just working, spending time with little Angelica, and partying."

"How is Angelica?"

"She's good. Her dad has her most nights, until I put some money away and get my own place. That should be soon. I'm going to get better shifts at the place I work. I'm banging the night manager."

"Well, there you go. You can't keep a good woman down."

"That's what I'm saying," she said, lighting a cigarette.

"What happened here?" I asked, nodding toward the hole in the wall, the blood and the general disarray.

"What? The bloody hole in the wall? This is Worcester. Most apartments have that," Marissa said, a devilish smile spreading, like a child who'd put something on your chair.

"It's a nice touch, really. But what happened?"

"The apartment is just the beginning of the mess Joe made. I had to spend most of today cleaning the place up just so it would look like this. That's what happened," she said, rage suddenly animating her features.

"That's bullshit, Cravesi!" Joe yelled at Marissa, leaning out of the bathroom in a towel, his wet hair hanging down by his shoulders.

"Fuck you, Rousseau! I was cleaning all fucking day."

"You did maybe half the cleaning, and it only took a few hours. *And* I bought lunch."

"One grinder for two hours of work? Yeah, you're the fucking dictionary definition of generosity."

"So what the fuck happened?" I interrupted.

Joe walked out of the bathroom, wearing jeans. An unfinished tattoo of a samurai warrior covered his chubby midriff. The tattoo artist had illustrated every fold of the samurai's robe, but hadn't gotten around to filling in the colors, so the picture looked more like a map of the Balkans than anything. Joe paused next to the couch and picked up a pack of cigarettes.

"Marissa, can I have a cigarette?"

"Fine. But admit that I did most of the cleaning for your dumb bullshit."

"Okay. Even though you didn't do most of the cleaning and I paid for lunch, I admit it," Joe said, lighting the cigarette with a level of focus that seemed like overkill. Then he shoved his pile of shirts and books onto the floor and sat down next to me.

"Enough already. What the hell happened?" I asked.

"Fucking last night got out of hand in a big way," Joe finally said, laughing.

"*Out of hand* doesn't really express it. I might have to move back in with my parents," Marissa added.

"You know Sully?" he asked.

"From up on Burncoat?"

"No this is a different guy, from Main South, by The Pickle Barrel. Well, me and some of my friends almost killed him last night."

"What the fuck, Joe?" I said, looking at the hole in the wall.

"I know, right?" he said, laughing his convulsive machine-gun laugh. It took a minute for Joe to gather himself back to a storytelling condition.

"So I had some people over. There was Smitty, Burger and Rich Papadopolis and a bunch of guys. And we're just hanging out and drinking. We do the coke that's left over from the night before, then someone gets the totally original idea to score some more coke. So Smitty starts calling around, and I remember this guy Sully, who I used to buy from. But Sully is a real prick. I think he stole some CDs at a party I had here in the summer, and he just generally acted disrespectfully when he was here. Nobody likes him. But he always has coke, because he hangs out with these thugs from around Main South."

"Okay, let's just stop there: Main South, plus the fact that he sells cocaine, should tell you that he has friends who can fuck you up," Marissa said to me, angry at Joe and amused by the danger all at once.

"So I tell Smitty, Burger and Vietnam and them about Sully."

"Vietnam?" I couldn't help but ask.

"Yeah, you don't know him. Vietnam is just his nickname. You want to know why? Because he's Vietnamese! Are we clever or what?" Joe said, taking a break from his story to laugh at the snowballing absurdity. "Anyway, we're drunk and coked up and pissed off. So I call Sully and invite him over. I'm all nice on the phone, just calling to invite him over and I say we have a lot of beers and weed and that we're just hanging out, no big deal. So he says he'll come by. And I guess I'm talking shit about Sully and we're all getting amped up, right until he shows up. When he gets here, he barely says hi. He grabs a beer from the fridge without even asking, downs it like he's in a hurry and asks where the weed is. So Papadopolis says 'It's right over here!' and pops him in the eye. Then Vietnam and me smack him. It would've been awkward if we didn't. So Sully goes down. And we're all kicking at him and he's fighting to get out. He gets up and he's running toward the door and I'm chasing him and I go in for a haymaker. But I slip on some blood and I just fucking nail the wall."

At this, Joe held out his hand, the top two knuckles of which were swollen to the point of deformity.

"What about the cop who lives next door?" I asked.

"He's in Rhode Island for the night. I'm walking his dog. So Sully makes it out the door and down the steps and we're all on the porch, all except for Burger. And I'm like, 'that's for disrespecting my house, you little bitch!' And he's like 'You just got yourselves fucking murdered,' and stuff like that. And he's bleeding and weaving and yelling at us and we're yelling back. That's when Burger comes running out of the house with a chair from the kitchen and chucks it off the porch and nails Sully in the face so the chair breaks apart and Sully falls down. Blood everywhere."

"That was my chair, too, by the way," Marissa offered, lighting a cigarette.

"For a minute, he's just laying there, and I'm afraid we killed him. But he finally gets up, bleeding and kind of wobbly, and runs off to his car. He revs the engine and runs it into my neighbor's van and peels out."

"Real fucking smart, Joe," Marissa said.

"Yeah, I hate to rain on your parade here, but what the hell were you thinking?"

"I don't think we were exactly *thinking*, in the sense that you mean it," Joe said, laughing the same laugh that had gotten us through our childhood.

"Okay. So what's the upshot? Sully and his friends—are they just fuckups, or are they honestly dangerous people?" I asked.

"Remember when Tim Duggan was blind for a week last summer?" Joe asked, with his ridiculous grin growing.

"Yeah."

"That was Sully's friends."

"Seriously. And this isn't just a drunk brawl at a party. You practically set up an ambush," Marissa added.

"It probably wouldn't have even been anything if he'd just acted decently when he showed up. But we were coked up and I guess it did get away from us."

"Got away from you?" Marissa repeated, growing visibly less amused. Joe shrugged, grinning.

The whole thing was senseless. And none of it surprised me. I'd seen dumber, crazier and even more violent from Joe and his friends over the years. This wasn't new. But, laughter aside, Joe was afraid now. And that was.

"So what are you going to do?" I asked.

"I'm trying to figure it out. I think I'm pretty safe here for now, what with my neighbor being a cop. It's just outside that I have to be careful. I'll stay away from the places Sully and his friends go, and not go out unless I have friends with me."

"What? Are you going to do that for, like, ever?" Marissa asked.

"I have two thoughts on that. The first is that this should blow over in time. Something else will happen to Sully. Also, he can't be that well liked by his friends. They'll get tired of looking for me."

"That's a pretty lame long-term plan," Marissa said.

"Maybe. But that's where Plan B comes in. Jim, do you think I could stay with you in New York?"

"Of course. God knows I'm paying enough to have the apartment sit empty."

"How much?" Marissa asked.

"I don't even want to think about how much."

"Really, I could stay there?"

"Yeah. I can give you the keys right now, if you think you're in real danger."

I said it without pause, despite my apartment's small size, despite Joe's habits and despite the close quarters when I got back. I said it without pause because Joe was the nearest I'd ever had to a brother. I said it without pause because I felt pretty sure he wouldn't take me up on it.

"I'm not sure yet. I want to get the temperature—ask around first. And New York is an expensive town. I want to get together a decent pile of money before I go. I think I can do that in a few weeks. I have an idea."

"Yeah?" I asked.

"Let's go get a drink and I'll tell you about it," Joe said.

11.

Joe had hidden his car, so I drove. We ended up at a place called Vincent's. It sat among weed-tangled lots and half-abandoned warehouses behind the highway, behind the train station, behind downtown, behind the showcase the city was trying to make of Shrewsbury Street. Vincent's felt hidden.

No one shouted out Joe's name when he opened the door. Animal heads and stuffed birds peered from the darkness above the bar. A five-item menu was drawn on a blackboard by the bar. It all bespoke a pleasant surreptitiousness. We ordered drinks and found a table at the back, by the bathroom and the cigarette machine. Joe took the seat facing the door. It was Sunday night and the crowd was sparse and sedate.

After a few sips of whiskey, Joe described his plan to me. He would quit his job, cash out his pension, buy a lot of cocaine wholesale, cut it and sell it carefully, only to friends, then do the same one or two more times. That way, he would move into my apartment in style.

"Now I wouldn't say anything. But you actually seem serious about this. So here goes. There are some holes in your plan," I said. "In fact, it sounds like a terrible idea from start to finish."

"Really? I think I've covered my bases here pretty well."

"Well, for starters, you will be selling drugs. There are still laws against that."

"But I'll only be doing it for a little while, and only to friends. That limits the chances of me getting caught to almost nothing. I've known a lot of people who have done it. Some have gotten caught and some haven't. It's all about keeping a low profile."

"But Joe, you're one of the least low-profile people I've ever met. And assuming that Sully and his friends are coming for you—wouldn't things be at their most dangerous now, when you're still at the top of their priorities? Wouldn't you be better off taking a vacation from work and getting out of town for a few weeks, and then coming back?"

"I can be careful for a little while. I can be low profile for a while, but not forever. I don't want to be looking over my shoulder all the time. This thing with Sully could take a long time to sort out."

Joe's phone rang. He puzzled over the number, then opened it. His eyes and mouth opened into a defiant smile as the phone call progressed.

"Hey dickbird, go ahead and try it. I have a state trooper living next door and a shotgun under my bed. You will not come out of it looking too pretty, I *promise* you! So bring it on!" Joe yelled into his phone and clacked it shut. "That was Sully. He said he and his friends were going by my house now with a can of gasoline."

"Jesus. Do you just want to skip town now? I could drive you down to New York if you need."

"Nah. They're just trying to scare me."

"You sure you want to risk it? You're not the only asshole in town who knows how to perpetrate an irrational act."

I wanted to argue with him for as long as it took. Failing that, I wanted to leave before I went down with him. I had done a great deal of both in our long friendship.

"Don't worry. These guys are tough in their own neighborhood, they're tough in a group at a party. But they don't travel much. And my apartment is in a totally different part of town," Joe said and took a gulp of more whiskey than could have been pleasant.

It was a heinous plan. But in a weird way, I trusted Joe to pull it off. His lunacy never put him in jail or the hospital for longer than a long weekend. And his lunacy certainly stood out against the grim monotony of the coming weeks.

"Well, it's one hell of a pickle you've gotten yourself into."

"A pickle indeed. I mean, I have a gang actively hunting me. How about them apples?" Joe said.

"You've come a long way from Venerini Academy. I forget, weren't you voted 'Most Likely To Be Actively Hunted By A Gang'?"

"I forget. It was either me or Anthony DiStephano," Joe said, cracking up.

We laughed and got more drinks, Sunday be damned. The middle-aged band started warming up at the front of the room. My driving instructor, a bald, acne-scarred man with a sad, hound-dog face, was playing bass.

"But seriously, you don't have a gun, do you?" I asked.

"No. That was a lie. But I'm getting one. I think Marissa's boyfriend knows somebody."

"Again, it seems like you're trying to put out a fire with gasoline. Say you get a gun, and say you do defend yourself with it, then what? You go to jail, at least until they can prove it was self-defense. And even then, they'll probably charge you for having the gun. Two stupids don't make a smart."

"I don't think I'll have to use it. But fuck it. Sully and them can fucking bring it on. I was born here and I have friends everywhere. I'm not going to just back down and run away. I'm a lot smarter than they are. So if I do go, it will be on my terms. I'm not going to New York with just a thousand dollars and starting from scratch."

"I'm just saying, it seems like you're putting yourself at risk for no good reason."

"Maybe it is foolhardy, but life is boring. I mean, I've gone to school, I've worked, I've travelled, I've done drugs, I've slept with beautiful women. And that's all great. But it's not *that* great. It's not *that* impressive. I've never had a job I wanted to keep, or met a woman I'd want to marry. It's all a big *so what*. I mean, tomorrow,

I'm back in the office, filing records and giving out parking permits. So let it get nuts. Let the dice fly high."

"That didn't work out so great for Caesar."

"Maybe not. But he had a good run, and I bet he wasn't bored. I honestly do not give a damn."

Not giving a damn was Joe's particular faith. It was his way out of a dead end. It protected him from the frightening moments that came with being at odds or in league with dangerous people. He had booze and drugs to keep from being bothered by the shallowness of dubious friendships and hookups. And he had not giving a damn to shelter him from the inevitable betrayals and disappointments of that life, from how the nights added up to very little over time.

The band started playing a Dire Straits tune. Joe got up to use the bathroom, and when he wasn't back after a song, I spun around, suddenly afraid. But he was at the end of the bar, hitting on a middle-aged Spanish woman who looked the worse for wear. I drank my drink and ordered another one, giving Joe room to operate. The band played a few more cover tunes and closed out their set with an original song about fast cars and child support. I looked back over at Joe. His mouth opened in big, crazy laughs, and the Spanish woman's eyes followed him, amused and hungry.

I went outside. The steps were icy, pocked with salt. The windows in the warehouses across the street were still lit, with no other signs of life inside. In New York, those warehouses would have been made into million-dollar loft condominiums ten years ago. But in Worcester, they just hung over the street, four stories of mostly dark windows. They were reassuring and ominous all at once. I dialed Emily's number, and beneath Vincent's blinking neon sign, told her voicemail that I was in town, and to call me. Emily was one of the handful of people I'd kept in touch with from Worcester. I knew she was living there, finishing a PhD in history at Clark after a long time out of town.

Back in the bar, Joe was chatting up the same woman and the band was still on its break. Joe caressed the woman's knee with his fingers. He wasn't exactly smooth, but methodical and practiced when approaching women. I walked over.

"Jim, this is Monique," Joe said, looking excited. I saw a quartet of empty shot glasses and chewed lime wedges before them.

"I told you, it's Moniqua," she said. *Mo-nee-kwa*.

"Nice to meet you."

"Oh honey, your friend is cute!" Moniqua said, her gap-toothed smile and lazy eye shining out over her cleavage.

Moniqua was probably very attractive around the time Joe and I started high school. And though her face told a chaotic tale and the perfume was a bit much, she was complemented by tight jeans, a push-up bra, copious makeup and a general lack of single women at the bar.

"You have a friend for him? Because I'm keeping you all to myself," Joe said and pinched her side. She giggled and gave him a deadly serious look. "He's a big New York executive, but he's in town for a few weeks."

As I waited for the cover band to deliver me from Joe's pick-up, Emily called.

14.

Out in the cold, I gave Emily my recap. It wasn't fun. The more you tell a story, the truer it becomes.

"Sounds like a perfect storm. You always wanted to get out of Worcester. Now you get shoved right back," she said.

"Apparently, all it takes is a crumbling economy, a divorce and an anomalous mass near my father's heart. Wicked are the ways of fucking fortune. What are you doing tonight?"

"Not much, just reading."

"I'm out with Joe right now. But it looks like he's got his hooks into a lady at the bar. And some street gang is hunting him and says they plan to burn down his apartment."

"Jesus, how long have you been back?" Emily chuckled.

"Five days."

"That's a lot of drama for five days."

"Never a dull moment, I guess. Can I come by in like an hour?"

"Sure. I'll go nuts if I have to read much more tonight. I'm at the same place."

In Vincent's, the band played an Elvis Costello number while Joe and Moniqua got sloppy at the bar. She clutched at his ponytail with her veiny hands and long, orange fingernails and he kissed her with the same overkill he applied to lighting a cigarette or eating a chicken wing. I settled up the tab and tapped Joe on the shoulder.

"Hey man, I'm going to head over to Emily's. Do you want me to drop you and Moniqua somewhere?"

"Emily? Emily Urbonas?"

"Yeah, from junior high."

Joe leaned his mouth near Moniqua's ear and said some words. She paused and did the same. They both came up smiling.

"Can you drive me and Monique back to my place first? We just have to finish these drinks," Joe said. Moniqua pursed her lips as Joe mispronounced her name one more time.

We left Vincent's and they climbed into the back of my rental car. I approached Joe's apartment and drove slowly past it, looking for the exhaust of idling cars, lit dome lights or other signs of people waiting in the parked cars that lined his street. I circled the block and pulled up to his house, checking my mirrors as I put the car in park. It sobered me up.

"We here?" Joe said, barely turning his head from Moniqua.

Looking back, I could see her jeans were at her knees. The orange streetlight shone off a patch of wet and dimpled upper thigh. She pulled up her pants, giving me a gap-toothed, drunk-eyed smile. I looked at Joe.

"Hey man, be careful and give me a call tomorrow. We should talk over your plan again."

I waited until they were in the house and the lights turned on, then drove back across town, down Highland Street, past the bridges and frozen pond of Elm Park and the monument to peace they'd put up across from the park that looked like a man and woman pushing a vacuum cleaner. Emily lived in a three-decker on Park Avenue, not too far from Clark. I parked on the street, climbed over a snow bank and rang her doorbell. She came down wearing sweatpants, a t-shirt and a pink bathrobe. She smiled big when she saw me.

"Hey Jim," she said. Even when excited, her voice never lost its flat, sarcastic tone.

Her apartment was a spacious half a floor, with a front and back staircase. Emily and her roommate had decorated it sparsely, but effectively. She motioned me over to a small couch and I sat down, surprised at how tired I was. She pulled up a footstool and sat across from me.

"I don't have much in the house, but I can re-heat some pizza for you if you want."

"Actually, yeah, I could go for a slice or two, if it's not too much trouble."

"Listen to mister New York City," she said playfully.

"What do you mean?"

"We're in Worcester. They're called *pieces* of pizza. I can't believe it. You've gone native down there."

"No. Not really."

"Okay, I want to know what you call the little candy bits that go on an ice cream cone?" she asked, crossing her arms in front of her.

"Sprinkles."

"What about *Jimmies*? I mean come on. It's practically your name. What about long sandwiches? You better not have forgotten this," she said, rolling her eyes.

"I know. I know. Grinders, *grindahs*. Now can I have a *slice* of pizza or what?"

Emily laughed, her green eyes sparkling and nose wrinkling. She was a small girl, and with her bathrobe and blonde hair, she looked more like she was blowing down the hall than walking. Sometimes we'd go a year without talking, but we always picked up where we left off. Emily put two slices into a toaster oven that looked like it had seen the Carter administration.

"So what's new? How was your Christmas?" she asked, leaning against the counter.

"Don't ask. It's only my second double-Christmas—one at Mom's and one at Dad's. But I think I'm getting better at it. At least I drank less this year. The worst part is the transition from one to the other. It's the holiday, and I'm leaving one of them alone. I mean, I'm up there, mostly for them, and failing even at that. It's no damn fun. They both tell me to relax, but that's not very likely."

"It's tough when it's right in your face like that. My dad moved out of state before the papers were even signed. I remember one Christmas, when I was little, I went to see him. I guess he was late driving me to the airport and I just remember running after my dad with my suitcase, knowing that if I didn't run fast enough I wouldn't be able to get home," she said, laughing as she told the last part.

The switch on the toaster oven popped up and a muffled bell went tink and the kettle started whistling. Back in the living room, I ate the pizza and Emily told me about her Christmas in Hubbardston.

"So Peggy, the aunt who tried to blame her DUI on hair extensions, she comes up to me after dinner and starts asking me about my hopes and dreams. Usually, she's drunk at this point and talking about her sisters' sex lives back when they were in high school. It's pretty gross. But she's almost sober and she's talking about life goals and looking me in the eyes and saying my name in every sentence. 'Emily, it's good to have dreams, like your PhD. But Emily, you need security in order to pursue those dreams, Emily.'"

Across from me, in her rocking chair and pink bathrobe, blowing on her tea between sips, Emily looked like she was dressed up like an old woman for Halloween. She leaned forward for her wide-eyed impersonation of Aunt Peggy.

"So I think—A—Peggy's going to start talking about Jesus, because that was sort of her thing in the eighties, or—B—she's going to ask to borrow money. I'm bracing myself for either. And she starts saying that people will lie about you, that they'll do anything just to keep you down, and that you just have to ignore them. So after like twenty minutes, she gets to the point—she wants me to sell sports drinks. It was a pyramid scheme."

"It would almost be better if it was Jesus," I said.

"I know. At least Jesus has some kind of track record. And then she got all mad when I called it a pyramid scheme. It's a 'vertical entrepreneurial paradigm,' she kept saying, and going on about the testimonials she had in her car."

"Did she get you the testimonials?"

"No, she got drunk and started telling me and my cousins about what sluts our mothers used to be, and how she always suspected our dead uncle was secretly gay."

We laughed some more and fleshed out our recaps. Finally, she asked me what I had planned for the next day.

"I have to drop off my rental car and get ready for Dad's surgery. But I'm going to be stuck in a hospital, then the rehab facility, and then in the apartment after that, so I'm up for something tomorrow."

"I can't believe you're back for so long."

"Well, someone has to help out. Mom's out of the picture and he doesn't have any other family."

"It's a good thing that you're doing."

"Yeah. When I made my plans, I was all pumped up on being the good guy and all that jazz. That was the story I'd told myself. The story made it easy."

"Well, it's true. It's not just a story."

"It feels like a story. In the story, everything was alright. I was alright. My childhood was alright. And Mom leaving Dad was just one more thing that had happened, distant, like the election or something. But I was in New York, with a girlfriend and job prospects, and so it had all worked out for the best. But now ... it's like ..."

"It's like you're stuck here."

"Yeah. And it's harder to tell myself that all's well that ends well. Now, I don't know. I'm just trying to keep my head above water."

"Then I don't know if you'll be up for going to see Jeff tomorrow."

Jeff was one of my best friends in high school, and he'd dated Emily. He was a funny, good-natured guy. But something happened to him in his first year of college, and he had to drop out. Back in high school, I'd taken my fair share of drugs with him, and at first I'd tried to calculate my share of the blame. But blame didn't matter as much as the diagnosis, which was that Jeff was schizophrenic. In the last few years, we'd fallen out of touch. Maybe that was just moving on. But it had a taint to it.

"Oh shit, I am such a prick. He called me at Thanksgiving and I never called him back," I said.

"Don't feel bad. I live here. I've been putting him off all semester. I mean, I love the guy ... But I'm also out of excuses."

"Is it that bad?"

"We talk on the phone every few weeks. He has his good days and bad days. They keep changing up his medication, so you never really know what you're going to get. Some days, he's mostly there. But more often, he's out of it. And those calls just suck. It would be a lot more fun for me if you went," Emily said, pursing her lips.

"Sure. I'll go. Can I have some tea?"

Back in the kitchen, Emily and I drank tea and talked more about Jeff—how it was hard to tell if the problem was the schizophrenia or the medication, how he wasn't really there a lot of the time, how he'd put on weight, and so on. It was an old conversation, a ceremony of frustration.

"So, Aileen is out of town. You can sleep in her bed if you want to crash here," Emily offered at the end of our liturgy.

Aileen's room was decorated with a few art prints and a big poster board collage of her friends. I pushed the pillows, stuffed animals and heavy comforter off the bed and pulled a cotton sheet over me. I listened for Emily's footsteps in the hall. But she wasn't coming. We weren't like that.

Just talking to her had taken some of the week's weight off my back. I closed my eyes and thought about old friends. First you're an infant, then you're a kid, and you get put in a town, then in a school. You pretty much have no say in it. But you find these friends who will always know you, no matter how far you wander. They become another family, the family of your heart, corny as it sounds.

15.
Monday, December 29

Out on Park Avenue that morning, Emily laughed at me while I dug a fresh shirt from the open trunk of my rental car and changed between the traffic and the dirty snow bank.

Emily directed me to Jeff's group home, at the foot of Vernon Hill. Jeff met us out on the porch, where he was smoking a cigarette. He'd put on more weight since the last time I'd seen him and had to be nearing two hundred fifty pounds. He was always tan, but the brown patches around his eyes had darkened and spread. He was wearing a Pink Floyd t-shirt and a red, beret-type hat I couldn't quite figure out. He wanted to show us around the group home and introduce us to his housemates. I said that instead, we should go for a drive. A lot of things in life are sad, and maybe you shouldn't turn away. But you don't have to dive in face first, either.

In the car, none of us could come up with a place to go. We drove around a while and wound up at a shopping center near the Millbury line. Its acres of parking lot sat above where they were widening Route 122 to better connect Worcester to the Mass Pike. Not knowing exactly what to do, we went into a big bookstore and got coffee. Jeff, as was his custom, had forgotten to bring his wallet, so I bought his elaborate, chocolate-raspberry-caramel coffee.

"So what's new, Jeff?" Emily asked.

"You know, just bopping around," Jeff said, then pursed his lips in an uneasy smile.

"Are you still working at that fake-flower place in White City?" I asked.

"Uh, what, *Michael's*? No I left there a few weeks ago."

"Oh, that's too bad. What happened?"

"They wanted me to take these big shards of glass and, like, climb a mound of broken glass and put them on the top of it. It really wasn't safe, so I stopped showing up."

Like most of Jeff's stories, it didn't make complete sense, but you could make out a germ of what must have happened.

"How's Janine doing?" I asked. Janine was Jeff's girlfriend, who he'd met in his last group home.

"She was doing good. But then she got into a fight with this Chinese girl at the club, and it got kind of out of hand and she started cutting herself. So she was in the hospital. Now she's with her mother until after New Years."

I gave Jeff my recap, omitting nothing from him. Jeff chimed in here and there with something strange, or just spacing out.

"It's funny how they call it 'open-heart surgery.' I wonder if it ever actually does open people's hearts, like in the other way, like open them to love," Jeff said.

That was probably as close as profound as he got that day. Unlike in the movies, where mentally ill characters exist mostly to indulge the screenwriter's poetic tendencies, schizophrenia had not made Jeff an oracle. A lot of what he said consisted of confused and confusing descriptions of interactions or situations that didn't completely exist. Nonetheless, we could piece together most of Jeff's recap. Most of his days revolved around going to the club, a day program for people with similar problems, and hanging out with Janine.

"There are some new girls at club. There are always new people in the winter. But by summer, we usually go back down to the normal number. Some of the new girls look good," Jeff said.

"Maybe you should trade up," Emily said, smirking.

"They just look good on the outside," Jeff said.

"That's why they keep the insides on the inside. I never heard of a sexy pair of lungs," I said.

"Or a sexy liver. Can you imagine? 'Barb has a real knockout pair of kidneys on her.' And 'I could watch her spleen all day,'" Jeff laughed, free for a moment from the discomfort and suspicion that always showed too clearly in his face. And for a moment, I had my friend back.

16.

I dropped off Jeff and Emily and called Dad. He said he'd meet me at the rental car place at the airport in an hour. At Logan, I dropped off the gold rental car and complained to the rental car clerk about the broken radio. She gave me a break on the price. I found Dad's SUV and we drove back to the Fountainhead.

Whizzing down the Mass Pike, I closed my eyes and resumed an old prayer that I'd develop some consuming obsession, learn a foreign language, become an expert on Buddhism or the War of 1812, just about anything that would fill the empty days of Dad's convalescence. Once we got to the apartment, Dad called and put me on his auto insurance.

"That was more painful than the surgery will probably be. If you crash this one, I'll revise my will and give it all to charity," he said after he put down the receiver.

"Dad, that's a hell of a way to talk to the guy who's going to be in charge of your meds."

He laughed. I laughed. After spending most of our first two decades together somewhere between suspicion and hostility, the present situation was funny. Nothing was forgotten, some of it was forgiven, and we were in this mess together.

"Seriously though, we let you wreck two cars. You're over your limit already."

"I admit, one I did crash. But the engine seized on the other one. That wasn't me."

"Because you did some crazy shit with it and tore open the oil pan."

"Mom might have done that, or the oil pan might have just been faulty. I'm just saying you can't prove that I did anything, and we will never know."

I knew. I ripped it open driving in the Shrewsbury gravel pits with Jeff.

From there, the night became less fun. Dad showed me where he kept his will, his long-term-care insurance papers, his living will, his prescriptions, his PIN numbers and the keys to his storage locker. A feeling of terrible acceleration—that it was all happening too fast—churned my insides. We sat on the couch and watched the news, then got a pay-per-view movie. The movie was a slight variation on the man-who-can-beat-up-all-other-men genre. A very slight variation. But the bad guys got theirs, and got it in a satisfying way. Dad got up and tossed me the remote.

"You tired? Why are you going to bed so early?"

"It's going to take me awhile to get to sleep. I figure I'd better start early."

"Are you scared?"

"I mean, Jesus, people die during facelifts and tummy tucks. This is open heart surgery. I'm not exactly afraid, but I can tell that my thoughts are going to go around and around for a while."

"But you said this place does this surgery all the time," I said, looking for some words to slow the acceleration.

"I know. It's routine. Just relax. It'll be fine. I'm going to get some sleep."

Dad looked me in the eyes, nodded and went to his bedroom. I was twenty-nine and old enough to know what he was doing just then. He was being the man in the situation. I don't know how he slept or if he slept. I only got two or three hours myself.

Part Two—The King Philip Memorial Wing

If Worcester folks from either 1848 or 1898—or 1948—could visit downtown Worcester today, their first question might be: Where is everybody?
—Albert B. Southwick
150 Years of Worcester: 1848 – 1998

17.
Tuesday, December 30

That morning was a bleary exercise. I drank half a pot of coffee and kept asking Dad if he needed me to do anything. Coffee and dread propelled me. I've had dreams where I'm being led to my execution, and this felt a little like that. On the car ride to Newton, Dad kept bringing up new concerns, new chores. His friends would call, and I should call them back to tell them how the surgery went. I should call the rehab center and the people who would be putting rails up in the bathroom and hallways in his apartment, and the nursing service and so on.

"After the divorce, first thing I did was to make sure I got long-term-care insurance through the Veterans Administration. They're going to lose a fortune on me," Dad said, trying to sound proud.

I nodded and drove. Words were just out of reach.

"And you better eat all that food you bought—I bought—at the supermarket. You got enough to last if we don't meet until judgment day," he said.

"Well, I'm not going to fucking starve while I play nursemaid."

"You better eat all of it. Even if I die," Dad said, coaxing a laugh.

The hospital was a big institutional beige brick sprawl. I parked and we walked through the early-morning dimness and chill of the parking lot. The lobby was all beige walls with dark blue upholstery and wood accents. It was the embodiment of reassuring normalcy. We checked in and a woman who described herself as a concierge and took us into the hospital itself. There, the fluorescent lights bounced off the linoleum in the glare of another routine emergency.

Leaving us in a curtained-in room with a bed, Dad changed into a hospital gown and sat on the bed. A nurse came in, followed by the anesthesiologist, cardiologist, oncologist and surgeon. The nurse, a plump Italian woman in her early forties, stayed the duration. The doctors each had something to say, mostly hello. I already knew the gist—a lump they couldn't identify—too close to the heart—cut through the sternum. I didn't really want to hear the rest of it. It's not like I was going to be called in to the operating room. I just gave them hard, clear looks as they spoke to Dad, to let them know they should take this surgery seriously, or else. It was all I could think to do.

The whole thing ran more quickly than I'd expected, partly because we were in an operation-only wing of the hospital, and December 30th isn't a popular day for that kind of thing.

After the last doctor left, the nurse gave Dad a sedative. The gown and the fluorescent lights made him look pale and his growing relaxation worried me, irrationally. We looked at each other while the nurse fussed with tubes and wires and the curtains. By the time he got to the pre-op room, Dad was pretty out of it.

"So do you live around here?" the nurse asked me, mostly to fill the silence.

Her face seemed too lively, too expressive, like she was used to talking to children or retards.

"No, I live in New York."

"New York City?"

"Yep."

"Oh my God, I love New York. I was watching *Flip This House*, you ever watch that?"

"No."

"The other night, this woman bought a little apartment in Manhattan for five hundred thousand dollars, then she re-did the kitchen, the bathroom, everything, repainted it, tore out the carpet, put in new floors. She sold it for over a million dollars. I couldn't believe it."

I tried to tell her with my eyes that what I wished for most in the world was to wipe her name from the book of life. After a few minutes of silence, she showed me to the waiting area and said it would be few hours, at least five, before I could see him. They'd made the waiting room big enough for the emotions that would, inevitably and despite their best efforts, erupt there. It had indestructible blue furniture and bright wood walls, under kinder lighting. I sat in one of the armchairs, dazed by dread. The TVs that angled down from the upper corners of the room showed a bitchy old lady adjudicating the legal fallout of a failed relationship between two sub-morons.

In the astonishingly uncomfortable blue arm chair, I discovered that I could not play along with the magazines and their cheery, advertiser-friendly, full-color neuroses. Maybe Africa is a mess, maybe I do have bad body language, maybe western economies are facing a great depression, maybe I do have ten to twenty pounds of waste trapped in my colon, maybe I don't know what she really wants, maybe the suits in my closet are a year out of date. But I had bigger fish to fry at the moment, and no way to fry them.

There was a big Irish family on the other side of the waiting room, whispering to each other about the court show on the TVs. After an hour, I got up and just started walking until I was outside.

18.

I found Dad's car, got in and started it. At the gate of the parking lot, it became clear that in the duress of the morning, I had lost the parking ticket. I explained my situation to the old whiskey-nosed Irish guy in the booth. Humorous and sports-related buttons covered his orange safety vest. When explaining my error didn't work, I asked politely to be given a break. Then I inquired how well he understood what a fucking prick he was. When that didn't work, I gave him twenty-five dollars. Injury loves insult, it seems.

Growing up in Worcester, I didn't really know much of Massachusetts east of Natick. So I followed the road I took to the hospital into Wellesley, a manicured suburb of Boston. I parked the SUV by the train stop and walked up to the main drag. Most of the shops catered to women in late middle age with too much time and money—expensive doodads to hang from your porch, set in your lawn or put on a coffee table, big hats, clothing for dogs, garish handbags and absurd jackets. I found a Starbucks and sipped my coffee among the soft music and pale wood walls until it occurred to me that it was more or less identical to the hospital waiting room I had fled.

Back out on Main Street, I was too surly to be around old ladies, Korean college girls or the Saabs and Volvos that dominated the strip. I was about to go back to the car when I saw a bookstore. I checked the shelves, then asked if they had the book I was reading about Hadrian. They didn't. I browsed the tables of cookbooks, TV-spinoff books, ghostwritten celebrity self-congratulations, and yes-you-can bullshit—all the blatant garbage that took the place of the book I wanted. I was about to exile myself back to Main Street, when, by the door, I saw a rack of books marked "Local Interest." I only looked to stoke my growing furor, wryly wondering what it was that human house pets in a town like Wellesley could possibly be interested in. But I found a book about the history of Worcester. I flipped through it and saw a long chapter on King Philip's War. There was a book about the war on the shelves as well. I bought both and left. The idea of having a few books to read in the hospital calmed my fury for the moment.

Fists clenched and muttering, I was clearly not someone who belonged among the boutique shops, church spires and smug Colonial charm of Wellesley. Back at the hospital, they would be better prepared for the distraught, with closets full of tranquilizers, if it came to that. I walked back to where I parked.

In the cold, pale sunlight, on the windshield of Dad's SUV, something waited. It couldn't be a ticket, because I remembered putting quarters in the meter, too many, actually. But there it was, a parking ticket. The text explained I had parked in the spot the wrong way. I looked left and right, then circled the car, to see if there was someone I could murder. Then I took a deep breath, tore up the ticket and gave the finger to anyone who might be spying from a nearby building, like a true Mass-hole. Maybe that's how they get that way.

19.

Boredom had soaked into the Irish family in the waiting room. The clean-cut, red-haired, mid-twenties son in a polo shirt, the punked-out teenage daughter with dyed-black hair and dark circles under her eyes both flipped listlessly through magazines. The younger, redheaded kid played indifferently with the action figures in his lap. And the overweight, watchful and stern mother just stared off. The older son talked to the mother about getting coffee, who asked the other kids, who gave him a consensus. My cell phone said I had several hours to go. My brain wasn't up for the trip to the 1600s that my new books required. I took deep a few breaths and closed my eyes. When I opened my eyes, I saw the punky Irish girl was looking at me.

With a smirk, I got up and charted a course for the hospital cafeteria. After getting lost more times than I'd like to admit, I found the half-empty cafeteria. I loaded up a tray with Swedish meatballs, fries and a donut and got a table by a window overlooking the whiskey-nosed parking lot attendant from earlier in the day. I watched him take tickets and give change from his booth. I wished him ill. I was down to a few fries and the donut when the punked-out teenager from the Irish family plopped down in the chair across from me.

"So what's your tragedy?" she asked, sipping her diet Coke provocatively through a straw.

"No tragedy. I'm just here for the magazines and the food."

"My father is having part of a pig heart sewn onto his own heart because he ate like a pig all his life. Nobody but me thinks that's ironic," she said, her eyes darting around in their deep brown circles. She had a thick Massachusetts accent. *Paht of a pig haht.*

"Huh. My dad's having an anomalous mass removed from near his heart. We'll see."

She smiled. It took the edge off my anger.

"Where's your mom?" she asked as if I was a child lost in the mall.

"Divorced."

"And his family?"

"His mother and father are dead. He has some half brothers and sisters that I never met. I don't know if he told most of his friends. He doesn't like to be a burden."

"What about to you?"

Regarding her more closely, she wasn't as young as she seemed at first, just skinny and dressed to dispute the claims of adulthood. Her black hair was tied back in a ponytail. She had a long, almost wolfish face. Compared to her ruddy, stocky brothers, she was definitely the mailman's kid.

"Just lucky. Any other unpleasant truths you think I'm overlooking? How about that my father could die in there? Oh wait, I already got that one."

"I'm just saying," she said. Then she looked at me and things went quiet for a moment. "How about this place?"

"It's okay as far as these things go. You live around here?"

"My parents and my little brother live in Sherborn. I live there too, sometimes. I'm going to Framingham State."

"Where's Sherborn?"

"It's near Natick. How about you? Wait, can I guess?" she said, pulling up her chair and getting excited. It felt like someone had chosen to visit me in the land of the dead. I didn't know what to say and I didn't want her to go.

"Shoot."

"I'm going to say Brookline. I have a cousin there and that seems like where you live."

"Why's that?"

"Because you dress like him, like a yuppie, but not. And you're wicked sarcastic. Well? I'm right, right?"

I paused for a minute and watched the long-coated doctors walk by behind her.

"Actually, I live in New York. But I'm from Worcester. And I'm staying in Westborough while my dad recovers. That about covers it."

"New York, heh? Well, I still think I did a good job of guessing. I was just thinking of around here. I didn't know I'd have to choose from the whole world," she said, putting one hand over the bracelets on her other forearm, leaning forward and smiling.

"No, you did alright. It's not like you guessed I was from Leominster or something. By the way, my name is Jim."

"I'm Olive. It's a pleasure," she said. *Uh pleashuh.* She held out her hand and I shook it.

She told me how her father's surgery ruined her winter break, how lucky I was not to have to deal with my family right now, how exasperated doctors could sweep into the waiting room at any moment with news of our fathers' deaths, how her mother kept losing her cool and making things worse, how the whole calm atmosphere of the hospital was a sick lie, and other impious things.

"Fuckin' Judge Judy and fuckin' soap operas, how the hell is that supposed to help? And you can't turn off the TVs if you want to. The nurses don't even *have* the remote," she said.

"I know, and the fucking magazines. It's like 'well, they're holding my dad's ribcage open and cutting around his heart at this very moment. But I sure would like to know what *Runners World* has to say about the new Reeboks with the extra fucking springs inside.'"

"Right, what the hell? God, why can't you smoke in here? And that fucking wop nurse, I know that's racist, I'm sorry, you're not Italian are you?" Olive said in what seemed like one breath.

"No, I think I had the same nurse, go ahead."

"My dad is already half unconscious. And my mom is barely holding it together. And the nurse starts talking about how her husband says that her plan to remodel the kitchen for the fourth time in six years is excessive and how she is trying to get him to *see the light*. No bullshit, those were the words she used."

"She talked to me about a TV show about remodeling."

Just then, Olive's little brother came up to the table and started pulling on Olive's black cardigan.

"Mom wants you to come back," he said, his eyes pinched half-shut between his bulbous cheeks and his bulbous forehead, all covered in freckles.

"Is the surgery done? Did the doctor come out?"

"No. She just wants you back."

I saw Olive pull a black ball point pen out of her sweater pocket and grab a napkin off the table. She started writing as she addressed her little brother.

"Tell her I'll be back in a minute."

"She said to come back *now*."

"Okay, I'm going. You are such a *pain*," Olive said, folding and pushing the napkin to me, then getting up and leaving.

I opened the napkin. It said probably more than it should have: "OLIVE FROM THE HOSPITAL" then a 508 phone number, then "SHHHH." I stayed and finished my donut and watched whiskeynose work the sparse traffic.

20.

Back in the waiting room, Olive and I passed the hours looking at each other and pretending not to. It was the sort of petty and ridiculous thing that living people do. My surgeon came back before theirs did. He was an Indian guy, just a couple years older than me. His eyes were sober and competent, like he could do three more of the same surgery that day. From what Dad told me, he might.

"The surgery went well. We removed the mass. And looking at it, I don't think it was malignant. But we'll know more after we run some tests," he said in the middle of a lot of words that disappeared.

"Can I see him?"

"I think the nurse will let you know when. We're moving him to the ICU. It should be another hour or so before you can go in."

After he left, Olive made a not-too-furtive gesture asking "What did he say?" I gave her a quiet thumbs-up. Between meeting her, and Dad's good news, the next hour passed faster than I probably deserved. In the surgical ICU, Dad could have passed for dead if not for all the machines and beeping screens to say otherwise. The room had glass walls and a huge sliding glass door. The patients on either side of it were ministered to in identical fashion in a long row of high-tech sarcophagi. I tried just to look at his face, which seemed neglectfully unshaven around the breathing tube. But he had too many tubes and wires going into and out of him.

"Hey, Dad. How are you doing?"

In a movie, this is where I would say my soliloquy. But I was too tired to even be pissed off, never mind philosophical. I watched him breathe and beep for a few minutes. I stepped outside at the same time as the nurse who was checking on the young black man in the glass sarcophagus next to him.

"How long is he going to be like this?"

"Which one? Monaghan?"

"Yes. My father. The man who is lying over there," I said, perhaps with too much pepper on it.

The nurse, a tall blonde with a cold manner to her, walked with me over to his bed and took his chart from the foot of it. She was wearing scrubs, which negated any sex appeal she might possess in the outside world. She spent a minute looking it over and probably an extra minute killing time just to let me know she was in charge.

"He'll be intubated for at least the next three days, and mostly unconscious. But you're free to stay with him as long as you want."

"So, would he be upset if I just came back tomorrow? I mean, he'll be pretty doped up between now and say, like, noon tomorrow. It won't mess up his recovery, will it?"

"He's pretty stable. We like to say that sitting and talking helps the patient. But he'll be out of it for the rest of the night," she said, looked me over and moved on.

My exhaustion had become a dark curtain lowering over everything. I did the math and decided the coming weeks scored me dutiful-son points out the ass, and left. I gave whiskeynose the ticket and four bucks and drove back to Dad's apartment building.

The dome lights and pale blue doors in the apartment hallways repeated into distances obscured by plain disinterest. I was so exhausted and out of my head that the Fountainhead actually felt like my natural habitat. In the apartment, I put an action movie on the TV, loud. I was all alone, and started looking for porn and pills, because I felt I was owed that much. I found some blood-pressure prescriptions and some old Tramadol, but nothing that would get me high or put me to sleep.

I pulled the blinds away from the sliding glass door that opened onto the narrow balcony. Beyond the parking lot and the street was a low hill that used to be a landfill. I remember driving by and seeing the bulldozers work a corkscrew up and down the pile of mottled dirt there. After a decade of letting it settle, they covered the mound with sod, parking lots, a Wal-Mart, a McDonald's and a Friendly's. Beyond the stores and restaurants, a wooded hill hung over the Route 9 traffic like a wave that would never crash.

On TV, the hero realized, with rage and horror, the terrible truth about the corporation that manufactured the robots in the movie's idea of the future. I was asleep on the couch before he could make things right.

21.

After a few hours, the phone in my pocket rang.

"Jim, what are you doing, like, right now?" Joe asked.

"Sleeping, why?"

"Because that plan we talked about—I did some asking around and I thought about what you said. I think I found a way to get out of here faster. But I need help. Could I borrow, like two or three hundred dollars tonight? An opportunity came up that I need to jump on like immediately."

I paused while I remembered Joe's plan. From my pause, Joe took as read whatever I was supposed to have said and continued.

"My brother, don't worry. Seriously. I have this so under control you wouldn't believe it. But I need your help to make it happen. I can even pay you back, say, four hundred next week, if you loan me a whole three hundred," Joe said.

I stood up to clear my head and took a deep breath. Walking over to the big glass door, I stared out into the night.

"I don't want interest. I just want you to be careful. It's one thing to be a drunken yahoo about town. What you're talking about is something different."

"Like I said, everyone involved is a friend. This is about as safe as this kind of thing gets. I just really need your help with the money part of it."

"Fine. But I do need this money back, and sooner rather than later."

Even against my better judgment, tired and disoriented, on an errand with no possible reward, on a pain-in-the-ass cold night, I was glad to go see Joe. When you saw him, he was always there, almost too there. He might run out on you to get high or laid, but he never ran out into the automatic conversation of the recap, the recited anecdote, or the well-manicured opinion. Unlike so many people, I never felt lonely talking to him.

The cold in the parking lot woke me. Crossing out of Westborough on Route 9, I passed a glorious set of bright white lights set atop high poles, as if a visiting platoon of gods had made camp at the foot of a massive rampart. But it was just a Honda dealership, new and pre-owned. I pulled into a bank branch in Shrewsbury and went to the ATM under a cloudless sky. The sand on the parking lot crunched under my sneakers. The concrete seemed especially hard from the cold. My neck itched because I hadn't shaved. Every detail of the walk to the ATM became especially vivid, the way things do when you suspect that you are making a sizable mistake.

At the ATM, I checked my balance. It still looked like a lot of money. But it had to last into an unforeseeable future. The severance from Bigelow was a good dose for six months. Not long after that, it would come time for hard decisions. I could afford the three hundred if it would help Joe. I took out a full five, to dilute the egregious fee the machine charged. I met Joe at the Bean Counter on Highland Street. He was engaged in a debate about the Iraq war with a hippie girl and a scruffy guy in a long, black overcoat, who had paused their chess game for the argument.

"What you refuse to see is that this is a war that goes back to the mid '70s in Tehran, when the Ayatollah took our people hostage …" Joe said. Then he caught sight of me and got up to let the couple discuss among themselves how much they disagreed with him.

"Jim, what's up? Let me buy you a coffee."

I demurred and we walked down Highland, past a cluster of businesses, restaurants, liquor, record and clothing stores, past the Store Twenty Four, toward Elm Park, where Highland Street is just three-deckers remodeled in a Victorian style. Once there, I handed Joe the fifteen twenties folded in half without breaking stride.

"Thanks. Where are we going?" Joe said.

"I don't know. Just out of the way."

"Nice tradecraft. But you could have just given it to me in the coffee place," Joe said and started laughing. I couldn't help but laugh too.

"I don't know. I was never good at this stuff. You remember when I sold off that half-sheet of acid? I had that poor kid follow me into a swamp in Holden to make the deal. How that reduced the suspiciousness, I'll never know."

"I remember that. It was Freddie Ostrowsky. You scared the crap out of him. He told me he thought you were going to rob him or something," Joe said, the momentum of the hilarity rolling over us, two maniacs laughing alone in the cold as the cars rolled by. We collected ourselves and walked back.

"What are you up to tonight?" he asked.

"I am still beat; I'm going back to Dad's to get some more sleep. How'd it go with that girl the other night?"

"Who, Monique? It was cool, I mean weird. I got her shirt off and she had all these scars on her stomach. I asked her what they were about and she just shrugged and said 'things happen,' then we started getting it on."

"Scars?"

"Like a lot of them, and not like surgery scars, well, maybe some of them."

"Jeez. She let you turn off the lights at least?"

"Nah. She actually insisted on keeping them on. It was almost kind of hot. Almost."

We made plans for New Year's Eve and I left. Back at the Fountainhead, Dad's bed was empty. But I opted for my inflatable bed. Call that what you will.

22.
Wednesday, December 31

I woke early and called back the people who had left messages on Dad's answering machine. The conversations with the people who picked up were pretty much the same as the voicemails I left. Some offered whatever help I might need. I said thanks. That was all there was to say. Only one guy, Gerry, kept me on the phone any longer than that. He had a thick New England accent. Dad had worked with him. Now they played golf together.

"Your dad told me you were staying up for his recovery."
"Yeah."
"You're doing the right thing. When my mother was dying, she was down in Cranston, Rhode Island. I let my sisters handle it. I just wrote the checks, paid for the hospital, the at-home nursing, everything. It wasn't even an hour away. I said I was busy. I got

down there a few times, but that was it. I said, 'she's a proud woman, she doesn't want me to see her like this.' You know how I found out she was dead?" Gerry asked and let the pause hang in the air. It was a dramatic pause I could imagine him using on a sales call. I didn't feel like playing along and let the silence go on a minute.

"I was on vacation in Hilton Head. I got a phone call from my sister's husband that she had passed. And I'll tell you something. There's not a day, not an hour, really, when I don't regret I wasn't there." *Theeya*.

"Well, I don't have any sisters and he's not dying. But if you want to stop by, I'll give you the number for the hospital," I said, not being in the market for a pep talk or a life lesson.

The hospital was emptier than the day before. Walking in, I wished for the hundredth time since the divorce that I had a brother or a sister. I asked directions to the ICU from the nurse at the front desk, which had a sparkly boa and party hats taped to it. It was New Year's Eve and some of the patients in the ICU were going to die that day. You could tell from the families. They clustered in the ICU waiting room, spoke in low voices and took turns visiting the glassed-in room. I saw Olive's red-haired mother, sitting alone, exhausted, but dry-eyed in the ICU waiting room, which was like the surgery waiting room, but bigger. I assumed Olive's father would live. At the ICU's front desk, a big nurse with an old-fashioned pill-box hat said I could see Dad. The door opened with a whoosh when I pushed a button. And there was Dad, his story now told by the unfurling of colored lines on eight different screens. The door whooshed shut behind me. A breathing tube was taped to his stubbly mouth. His face looked gray.

I tried to regard the situation as strange instead of horrible. I'd read once that bees, because only a fraction of them can actually procreate, shouldn't be considered organisms. Rather, the hive was the organism. I imagined Dad as being part of a larger organism, sustained by it. But it wasn't the happier thought I was looking for.

"Hey Dad, it's me, Jim. How are you doing?" I said, just to be polite, in case.

Neither the jagged lines on his unshaven face nor the jagged lines on the many little screens responded. I watched him for a moment, then opened my book about Worcester.

Cracking the spine, I hoped for a good creation myth for the city—something that placed Worcester in the flow of dramatic historical events, or a poetic early scene that would give an insight into the nature of the place. The world, especially in the ICU, could always stand to make more sense. But there was no sense to be found in the book. Worcester was born like a headache on the land.

The first colonists abandoned their homestead because of rattlesnakes. And after they found a new site, they only stuck around for about seven years. Then they fled back to Boston and other better-fortified towns when an Indian rebellion, called King Philip's War, swept the state. After that, Worcester was only sporadically and sparsely settled for the next forty years. It had nothing but enemies in those days—Indian attacks, a proxy war with France, rocky soil for farming and a long, hilly trek to the sea. Even Britain opposed Worcester's existence for a few years.

"It is not in His Majesty's interest you should thrive," read one official communiqué to settlers in Massachusetts at the time. Here in the 21st century, we don't have real kings and we barely even have a God left. But in the ICU that day, it appeared that whatever seat of Majesty still held sway was saying much the same thing. A mysterious and fickle hand inflates or depresses the stock market, assigns sicknesses, reroutes highways and changes the priorities of the masses. And it was not concerned that Dad or me should thrive.

I put down the book and flipped through the handful of TV channels they gave Dad's room.

"Can I get you something from downstairs—a magazine, a snack? Just let me know."

With no answer, I wandered past the dying and the on-the-fence to the cafeteria. It was all but deserted there. I got an egg sandwich and a coffee and took the same table as before, watching whiskeynose in the morning light. He was watching a tiny television in his booth. I wasn't hungry and Olive didn't come by. At the gift shop, I picked up a Sports Illustrated. The cover showed a young quarterback, mouth agape, in the middle of some fist-pumping celebration. I left it on the wheeled table by Dad's bed, where he did not stir. Nurses cycled in and out, some offering little quips that passed for friendliness. They asked what I was reading about and turned back to their work when I told them Worcester. Someone came by with flowers from Gerry. A doctor came in for a minute and told me Dad was recovering according to schedule, and that they'd have the mass biopsied by the 2nd or 3rd. Around seven, I decided I'd done enough for the day.

"See you later, Dad," I said, expecting and receiving no response.

On Route 9, the supermarkets and the liquor stores buzzed with last-minute shoppers. Even the mall was full, its parking lot a buzz with people gathering items against the coming year. My back and shoulders were so tight they stung as I drove. It felt like my body was pulling itself apart. I passed Mom's apartment building on the hill and wondered what she was doing for New Year's Eve. Turnpike Liquors shared its sign with the blue outline of the state of Massachusetts—elongated enough to hold all the letters of the word LOTTERY. The old clerk inside turned the sign to *closed* just as I got in the door.

"Looks like you got in under the wire," he said. *Wiyah*.

I picked up a bottle of whiskey and an eighteen-pack of Coors Light cans and put them in the back of the SUV, under a fleece Dad kept back there. I thought about grabbing a swig from the bottle to ease my shoulders for the drive to Worcester. But I imagined the jack-booted state troopers manning checkpoints in their effort to bring the whole state to heel, and refrained. I called Serena.

"Hey, hold on one second while I go in the other room," she answered, sounding a little tipsy.

"Getting started a little early over there, no?"

"You know us gals. We're just getting dolled up at my place, and having some drinks."

"Oh yeah, you have a whole pack over there?"

"Just me, my cousin Jessica, my friend Jessica, Amanda and Davida."

"And where are you going tonight, looking so good?"

I passed the huge, blinking radio towers in front of the state police barracks. I checked my speed and tightened my grip on the wheel.

"Davida's cousin is deejaying at a club in midtown—Bubble or Shampoo or something like that, so we get in for free. How about you?"

In the background, I could hear the busy laughing and yelling of her friends. Picturing her apartment on the upper west side, with its wood floors and low ceilings, I remembered how it felt going home with her to it that first night. It was a single girl's apartment disheveled with all the busy-ness and distraction of her life, but homey still. I wondered what it might look like to the next guy she took there.

"Well, I'm on the road right now. I just left the hospital. And I figure I could get down there to see you by midnight, if I put the pedal to the metal in Dad's old car."

"But what about your dad?"

"I could go down, see you for a bit, crash for an hour or three, then drive back."

"You're such a romantic. But my cousin Jessica is staying over at my place, and I don't know what the deal is with bringing more guests to the club. Plus, it's impossible to get to it in a car because it's near Times Square. Maybe tonight isn't the best night."

"Okay, just thinking out loud."

"Anyway, you always say New Year's Eve is just a hype."

"Yeah, you're right. I guess I'll just hang out with Joe and them in Worcester. Don't you go kissing some scummy club dude at midnight. They have the internet now. I'll find out."

"Never. And don't you go native with one of those Worcester ladies you talk about."

"If you listened when I talked about them, you'd know it wasn't bloody likely."

I passed the Fountainhead and decided I was dressed well enough for the night to come. I started to get excited about the whiskey and whatever would ensue.

"Well, it better not be," Serena said, after a pause, not just hers, but also in the high-pitched background chatter.

"Sounds like we have a deal," I said.

"Absolutely, Senator."

She called me that sometimes. I liked it.

"Well, I'm going to get off the phone before I wreck my dad's car and add to his woes."

"Okay, call tomorrow."

"I will."

In Shrewsbury, I turned off Route 9. We had moved there when I started high school. Dad had gotten a big sales job, and Shrewsbury was the Beverly Hills of Worcester County, if you can imagine such a thing. It had changed since then, with the woods made into subdivisions that bespoke post-Reagan affluence rather than old New England charm. But the old Shrewsbury was a small and provincial place. On the street we moved to, there were a handful of families who were not just third-generation Shrewsbury, but third-generation *that street*. They seemed to be in some of competition to see who could be the least friendly to us. And after a few scuffles, I resigned myself to the friends I had in Worcester.

But the place still gave me the shivers. Wherever you grow up is sacred ground, consecrated by hatred or by nostalgia. The shiver was enough to rebuke the appearance that I was nowhere of any consequence.

I called Joe as I drove past my old street, cursing it quietly as I did. Joe picked up and said to come over whenever, said he'd be able to pay me back by the end of the night, and said that the password was *Total Recall*.

The road drifted down the hill we had to run for football practice at St. Johns, past a Colonial schoolhouse. The SUV rode smoothly over the dry streets along Lake Quinsigamond. I tried to stretch out my shoulders. But it just moved the pain around.

23.

"What's the password?" asked the tall skinny guy who shoved his weight against the door, rattling it in its frame. Wire-rim glasses and a flop of brown hair framed the part of his face visible through the little window by the door.

"*Total Recall*, now open the fucking door, it's two degrees out here," I replied.

The skinny guy opened the door and stepped back a few feet. He had a revolver in his hand. It was too big and too shiny and made him seem even skinnier. I froze in the doorway just the same.

"Are you a friend of Joe's?" he asked, stepping back a few feet.

"Yeah. If you want, you can tell him Jim Monaghan is here."

The skinny guy blinked. He seemed embarrassed. He didn't seem like the guy who would be holding the gun in any situation.

"Oh, you're Jim. I'm sorry. I'm Russ. Man, it's nice to meet you. You're the guy who lives in New York. Joe's told me about you."

"Hey. It's nice to meet you. Let's get inside. It's miserable out there."

In the apartment, Marissa was doing bong hits with a guy in hospital scrubs and a guy I played football with in high school, Tom—Mullaney or Maloney or Muraney or Maroney—a big Irish guy. I told him *what I'd been up to* for the last twelve years since we

71

last spoke. I hurried through it, as his attention wandered far and wide from moment to moment. His own recap was just a stoned outburst.

"I'm just, you know, chillin'," Tom said, laughing.

I nodded, saying the beer needed the fridge, and wandered into the kitchen.

"I'm saying it would have failed in Germany, too. I mean, look what sprang up there instead of Communism," I overheard someone say, as I walked into the kitchen.

Joe was sitting at the kitchen table, arguing with Russ and a girl who looked like Russ with a wig. A Spanish girl with a deep furrow of exposed cleavage sat next to Joe at the table, drinking, smoking and watching him with eyes that seemed too awake, until she smiled them half-shut. The silver revolver sat by the cereal bowl she used as an ashtray.

"I'm just saying that if they had tried it in an educated, industrialized …" Russ started.

"Jim!" Joe yelled, popping out of his chair.

Joe was ready for New Year's Eve. He was wearing one of his favorite shirts, a black silk button down with a tiger that started on the stomach and reached around to the back. His hair was tied back into a tight ponytail. He got up and crushed my sore back with an enthusiastic hug and introduced the Spanish girl as his girlfriend, Escalita.

I showed him the bottle and Joe rinsed out two mugs. He put some ice and a healthy dose of whiskey in them and raised his glass to toast.

"To good friends and guns on the kitchen table," I said.

Joe started laughing. But I kept a straight face to discourage him, being impatient for the drink. He stopped laughing and the whole table toasted. I took a healthy sip, but Joe downed his like a shot.

"I have to watch it. I'm trying not to get too fucked up tonight," he said, blinking.

"Yeah, sure. What's going on with the gun?" I asked, dropping my eyes to the gun on the table.

"Oh I'm sorry, I didn't introduce you to Russ."

"We met in the hallway."

"Russ has a license to carry the gun. He's actually a marksman. He's been in competitions. His dad was a deputy …?"

"A major in the staties," Russ said, sitting up a little straighter.

"Anyway, I wanted to have some people over tonight. But Marissa was worried about word getting out and the wrong people showing up."

"Yeah. You were the worried one," Russ said. "Joe calls me up and says he'll get me dinner, drinks, drugs, anything I want if I'll come to his party with a gun. And I'm like 'that's a great idea. Let's invite a guy with a gun, then fill him with liquor and drugs. That would really add something to the party,'" Russ said.

"Like a reverse piñata," Joe said.

The table laughed and I poured myself another drink.

"Thanks again, man," Joe said through his laughter.

"For you, Joe, it's no problem," Russ said, sipping from his bottle of root beer.

"Man, this is good—tonight's going to be great. I have some of my favorite people here. And we have drinks, everything we need, for an all-night rager. And there are some real hotties coming over too, probably after midnight."

At this last bit, Escalita stomped on Joe's foot with her overflowing high-heeled shoe.

"I mean for Jim. Those girls are nice enough, but nowhere near as hot as Escalita here. I mean, Jim, is my girlfriend hot or what?" Joe announced, making Escalita blush and smile all at once. Then Joe's cell phone rang. He puzzled at the number, then rose and walked away to take the call.

"… I might know what you're talking about, but I might not … Who told you that? … Well, you should have them call me … No, then they can pick it up … I'm just saying they shouldn't have told you anything … It doesn't work that way … Okay, okay, if you're a friend of Jeffy, I guess you can come by … But have Jeffy call me first … It's just that I have a bunch of people here … call him and have him let me know …" Joe said into the phone, annoyed.

It was the first of several such calls throughout the night. He turned his attention back to the table.

"I'm just saying that there will be more ladies here soon. So sit tight, relax. Ladies and drinks and friends, and I'll be able to pay you back before the night is out *no problem*," Joe said to me.

"There's no hurry on that. Really," I said.

Joe drank his Budweisers, Russ his root beers, and me my whiskey. The radio was the loudest thing coming from the living room. The party wasn't exactly a rager. But I liked it better that way.

"Then the other night, Sully called again. And he actually said he was going to take my eyes out and show them to me, so I'm like 'okay you fucking moron, how are you going to show me my own eyes?' Then the line goes quiet for a full minute. Literally, an entire minute. And I can hear him breathing. Finally, after an eternity of thinking, Sully says 'I'm gonna do them one at a time,'" Joe said, and laughed his hyena-like laugh.

There was a knock on the door. Russ put a businesslike look on his face and picked up the gun. I followed him down the hall, partly for the sordid spectacle of it, partly because Joe and Escalita had started to make out. The big black guy at the door didn't even have to give the password. He gave Russ a big hug.

"Careful Corey, I have a gun."

An even bigger white guy with small eyes and an all-green Boston Red Sox hat followed him. After Corey introduced himself, the bigger guy introduced himself as Gino. Then there were three pale, small girls overwhelmed by their winter coats. They waved pale hellos to me, a stranger. In the living room, I noticed that the TV and cable box were gone. Joe and Marissa had made the apartment party-proof, putting everything in one of the bedrooms.

Back in the kitchen, Joe, Corey, Russ and one of the pale girls had found something to argue about. One of the girls, Tara, took off her winter coat. Her shirt half-revealed a graceful pair of breasts. Joe took Corey into his room and both returned ready to argue against and for pacifism, respectively, with renewed vigor.

"Christianity is probably the single biggest transformation in recorded history. And Jesus was totally a pacifist. The early church was mostly pacifist. And they sure won," Corey said. He slugged down a Miller Lite with a bend of his massive arm and cleared his sinuses with vigor. I was glad to see him staunchly on the side of pacifism.

"Yeah, it really worked. Tell that to the fucking martyrs," Joe said.

"In the long run, it was the martyrs' side that won," Corey offered.

"True. True," Joe said, nodding his head and leaning his kitchen chair back.

Joe aimed a huge, devilish grin at me.

"Jim, do you want to get truly fucked up tonight?" he asked, his look defying the gravity of responsibility, legality and even the most obvious safety concerns.

"Yeah. I have to go to the hospital tomorrow. But whatever."

Then Joe's phone rang, and I watched him have more or less the same obstinate negotiation as before. I guess he was being cautious, like he said.

"Oh shit, get in here, it's almost New Years!" Marissa yelled out from the previously dormant living room. We all piled in from the kitchen.

My cell phone said the year had ten minutes left. Joe started making out with Escalita. Tara, with her graceful neck and low-cut shirt distracting all of creation from the faint acne scars that poked through the grainy Technicolor of her makeup, looked around, but not at me, to see where to go.

"We should get out the TV," Marissa said. But she had settled back onto the couch.

"I'll just find it on the radio," Joe said.

"Find the New Year on the radio? That's fucked up," Gino offered from the folding chair he dominated. He wore a Celtics basketball jersey over a t-shirt. The bong sat at his feet.

"I know, right, like it's a time machine or something," big Irish Tom said.

Joe started turning the knob through the FM stations until he found the shouting, the crowd noise, the local accents, the higher octave to which the Massachusetts cold will raise the voice, all of the right signs. It was a classic rock station, broadcasting live from Copley Square. The radio blared the forced excitement of the pre-countdown. Joe and Escalita made out next to the bloody hole in the sheetrock.

"Get a room, you two," Tara said with a peevishness in her voice, and slid into the seat on the other side of the couch from me.

Joe held out his middle finger and kept kissing until Escalita finally became embarrassed. I leaned back and then forward to see what or who Tara was looking at. Finally, the radio started counting down at sixty. Marissa started counting down with them, then lost interest. We all counted down from ten. At zero, we all yelled. Corey and one of the small, pale girls kissed. Russ and Joe made out with their girlfriends. Tara looked around, but not at me. Marissa gave me a big, comical kiss on the cheek. Tom and the guy in hospital scrubs stood around dazed.

After the hullaballoo, I went into the kitchen get another drink. Joe followed, with his phone on one ear and his finger in the other. I looked at him quizzically and he swiveled away from me.

"… Is he okay? … I mean, what does 'stable' mean? … What hospital … And you're sure it was Sully and them? … They're not still hanging out on Green Street, are they? …You don't know anyone who knows where he lives, do you?" I heard Joe say into the phone, before he walked into his room and shut the door.

After a few minutes, Joe threw open his door, walked past me into the living room and told Tom, Corey, Russ and Gino to come into the kitchen.

"You guys know about the thing that happened with Sully a few weeks back? Now Sully and some of his friends just put Smitty in the hospital. They tried to curb him, but I guess he crawled off and they broke both his collar bones. He's so fucked up that he's in intensive care," Joe said.

Marissa came in, then Tara, and the story re-circulated, with Smitty doing this and Sully doing that, and Smitty going here and Sully calling these guys and Smitty talking to these other guys. My head spun from the murky complexity of the story, the parking lots, nicknames, street names, suspects and so on.

"Fuck. We should call the cops," Corey said.

"And tell them what? That me and Smitty and some other guys brutally fucked up Sully without much good reason and this was his revenge? That's a case they'll really want to make. Anyway, I can't call the cops right now," Joe said, nodding to Corey, who nodded back.

"Joe, I know what you're thinking, but really, what are you going to do tonight?" Corey asked.

"I'm going to find them."

"You can't go after these guys. I used to know some of the guys that Sully's with now, and they don't give a fuck," Corey said.

"*I* don't give a fuck," Joe interrupted.

"I'll drive you over to the hospital. You're just drunk and pissed off right now," Russ offered.

The argument continued at some length, with Joe determined to drive around until he found Sully. Corey, Russ, Gino and I told him to let it go, at least for tonight. The bottom line was that Joe was a big guy, and a brawler, but not the one-man vengeance machine he imagined himself to be at that moment. Corey wouldn't go with Joe to Main South, where Sully's friends lived. Russ wouldn't lend him his gun, even just to wave around and maybe hit someone with—and just for the night, as Joe put it. Gino said we should all just get high and chill out until tomorrow, and the rest of the living room agreed.

24.
Thursday, January 1

"Fuck you all. I'm going out to find these motherfuckers," Joe concluded and grabbed his coat.

I followed. To try and calm him down, I said. Truth is, I didn't have all that much to say to the other people at the party by that point. The cold, the action, the dim possibility of danger all sobered me. The stars showed through the bare branches of the trees clear and bright. Joe's white Buick started on the third try. He revved the engine, then squealed out of his parking spot.

"Go easy. The cops are out in force and you're over the legal limit."

"Fuck that, man."

"Hey asshole, I'd rather not go to jail tonight, not for some bullshit DUI. Get your head together. Take a fucking breath. You want to do this thing you're talking about? Then be smart," I said. *Smaht*.

Joe stared off. The car bumped its way down his potholed mess of a street. He applied the brake more judiciously and seemed collected by the time we reached Lincoln Street.

"You're right. I'm going to be rational. I am going to find these fucks, one by one and get them."

"Do you even know who they are?"

"Not off the top of my head. I think I could recognize one or two of them. But I have some idea of where they hang out," Joe said.

Another reason I agreed to join him was that I didn't think we would find the people he was looking for. We skirted downtown and drove down Green Street, which was busy with people going from bar to bar, getting in and out of double-parked cars. Joe jammed his car into a tight spot by an abandoned auto-repair garage, like one more crooked tooth in an overcrowded mouth. I followed Joe into The Dive

Bar, where a tall, fat guy with long blonde hair found Joe immediately.

"You heard about Smitty?" he said.

"Yeah, what happened?"

"I guess one of Sully's friends saw Smitty here and called Sully. Well, I guess he got a bunch of guys together and they got Smitty when he went out to his car."

"Do you know where Sully went? Where his friends went?" Joe asked.

"No. I don't really know those guys."

"I'm getting some people together to fuck these guys up big time. You in?"

"Naw man. I'm pretty tanked. I'm just going to chill out tonight. But hang out a minute. Let me buy you a drink."

"No thanks. I've got to go."

When we got outside, I remembered that we were almost thirty years old. That was why no one wanted a part of his feud. Back when we were nineteen, twenty, I had seen some really violent things happen, and had even been marginally involved a few times. I wasn't a badass, but I was there. But the real crazies from those days were gone. Luke was in jail now, gone away for carjacking, then after a month of freedom, for attempted murder. Mike Fahey was dead. Malachi, famous for having bitten off someone's ear in a fight, had joined a carnival, I heard. Another old friend, Tony Howard, was in Worcester after a stint in jail, but was now too angry and violent to have around. They were the guys Joe was looking for that night. But the guys who were still around had mostly grown content with the bars, and their rage didn't go too far past maintaining a goatee or keeping a fully loaded bong at home.

Joe walked us past the cover charge at the Lucky Dog Music Hall, where the band had finished for the night. Tired of following him, I saddled up to the bar and ordered a drink. He went around the room, doing more telling than listening from the look of it. But his call to arms had no takers there either.

"Have a drink," I said when he had circled back from a far corner of the room.

"We have to go. I think I know where to find these guys."

"Okay then, have a shot," I said, hoping to induce him back to the less dangerous pleasures of civilization.

We did a shot of well whiskey, then went back outside. Joe nodded to the cops parked on Green Street. We pulled out of the parking lot in a choppy eleven-point turn. We crossed under the railroad and highway bridges, around the vast failed downtown mall, and then downtown, past the big high-rise apartment that looked like it had been flown in from Houston.

Past Chandler Street, the storefronts and apartment houses were run down. The lights flickered unevenly behind the convenience-store signage. We were in Main South, a rough part of town. The cold that night was unyielding. But people were out, walking down the street or just standing around, looking furtively over their shoulders or just eyeing the traffic. Joe turned off Main Street, and down a narrow street lined with three-deckers in disrepair.

"Where are we going?"

"I'm looking for Sully's car."

"That's it? That's what we're doing—looking for a car?"

"Yep. It's a black Toyota," Joe said.

"Toyota what?"

"I don't know. It's one of the smaller ones. But it has silver rims, the spinning ones on it."

"Okay, I'll look out for it on my side."

We cruised the narrow streets between Chandler Street and Webster Square and saw a lot of cars. At one point, I did see a small black car with garish, shiny wheels parked on my side of the street. I stiffened in my seat and waited until we were a few streets away before I said anything at all.

"So what's up with Escalita?" I asked.

"She's been my girlfriend for about two months. She's pretty sexy, isn't she?"

"Yeah, not too shabby. What's her story?"

"She goes to Worcester State at night and cleans houses during the day," Joe said.

Slowing down by a black Honda, I saw Joe hoping that it was Sully's car and then relieved that it wasn't.

"How long have you been with her?"

"Since October about."

"I didn't get much of a chance to talk to her. She seemed to have your tongue in her mouth all night. So what's the story? Is there a future there?" I asked, trying to nudge the conversation away from the savagery we supposedly sought.

"It's tough. I mean, I really like her and she turns me on. But she can be really annoying sometimes. And when I confront her about it or lose my temper, she just says I wouldn't understand because I grew up white and lived in a house."

"Why? What's her story?"

"To be fair, her story sucks more than most. She's her own aunt."

Joe let that one hang in the stale Buick air. When something so awful is so close at hand, you'd better be able to laugh, or it might get hard to breathe. We laughed. We felt bad about it. But we laughed, and picked the bones of that tragedy for every shred of laughter it had on it.

"I don't care what you're arguing about. That's a hell of a trump card," I said.

"I know. It even works when we're arguing about what to watch on TV. She just has to hint at it."

"That's a hell of a hint."

"I think I'd need to get cancer, or survive a concentration camp, just to step up to the same card game," Joe said.

We laughed some more. It deflated our sense of mission. Joe didn't eye the cars lined up against the snow banks on the narrow, crummy streets so closely. We passed a few big apartment buildings and hung a right past the Pickle Barrel.

"You think you're ever going to settle down?" I asked.

"I don't know. But I don't think I've ever been with a girl who didn't get annoying after a few weeks. I mean, they only have so much to say. Even the smart ones start repeating themselves after a few weeks. And then there are just so many of them, always a new one to make you look past the one you're with. I can't imagine a girl I'd want to be with for life. She may be out there, but I haven't met her. As long as I'm getting laid, it doesn't really matter."

"What about Theresa? You were with her for a few years."

"She was probably the closest I ever came. But I didn't really know about women back then. She didn't talk much, so I always imagined that she had all these great thoughts, so I didn't get bored as fast. But I still cheated, so there's that."

Joe lit a cigarette with his still-swollen hand. I rolled down the window partway and the cold picked at my face.

"How about you—you going to marry Serena?"

"I don't know. If I ever get back to New York I might."

"What?"
"You hungry?" I asked.
"Yeah. I guess this can wait."

25.

The Lincoln Street Denny's was packed. The cop assigned, Officer Dowd, was the son of the Officer Dowd who'd stood by the Denny's register late into the night when we were teenagers. I'd seen his brother take Joe off to jail once. The sons both had their father's drooping, weak jaw and blank blue-eyed stare.

Joe knew the hostess, an energetic Italian girl with boils the size of a rat's eyes on her cheeks. She yelled out his name as soon as she saw him and hugged him close. Dowd seemed to wince, as if he nursed a crush on the hostess. She took us straight to a table. The crowd waiting on the concrete bench by the Grab-A-Prize game murmured, uncertain if they were the proper ones to be outraged by us cutting the line. We sat down at a corner booth in the far part of the restaurant.

"Man, it's weird, I never thought I'd be glad to see a Dowd," Joe said.

"I don't get it. Is Denny's like some medieval fiefdom, passed down through the male line of the Dowd clan? After a few generations in the department, you'd think they'd want something higher up, more glamorous."

"I guess it's good overtime," Joe said.

Joe examined the color photos of the many options the night still offered, combinations of meat, eggs and cheese. Joe sat up and looked to his left, right, then twisted around to see if there was a window behind him.

"Oh, before I forget. Even with all this bullshit tonight, I can pay you back."

The wad of bills was disorderly in every way. But it was all there.

"Thanks," I said, putting the money into my pocket.

We gave our order to a harried looking waitress and talked about old times at Denny's.

"Remember that? The cop said 'I don't care what you do, just don't shoot me.' And then Dowd told Smitty he'd put a boot so far up his ass that he'd be tasting shoe leather for a week. That was a little too vivid for me at the time," Joe said.

"Was it just because we were tripping, or were the cops acting weird that night?"

"I don't know. But they definitely should have arrested me and Nick. I remember Nick running and knowing I had to run too. The cops were chasing us around the parking lot in a van. And we were running in figure eights to get away.

"But they were like, very cool after they caught you. It was so laid back, like we were just some guys on acid, hanging out with our friends, the police."

The food came, and then, the trouble. There were only a handful of places to get food after closing time, and Denny's was one of the most popular. Joe perked up in his seat, then ducked down and looked me in the eye.

"Shit. It's Ki. Don't turn around. And, yeah, shit, he saw me. We have to get out of here."

"Ki?"

"I know him. He's tight with Sully and them. And he definitely saw me. He's going outside now, probably to call them up."

"What should we do?"

"We could grab him and beat the shit out of him until he tells us where Sully is."

"I think you've seen too many movies. How about we just get out of here?"

"Let's."

Joe started eating his food in cartoonishly huge bites, chewing as little as possible. The vein in his forehead bulged from the effort and the lack of oxygen. I calculated the cost of the meal, and how much worse it is to be punched in a full stomach than an empty one. I left my food alone. Getting up, I put down thirty-five dollars, just to be safe. We got our stuff and headed out. The hostess was too busy to stop us with a good-bye.

But Dowd was not too busy for us. I won't recount the whole exchange. The problem, it seems, is that we left the money on the table rather than paying at the register. The acne-scarred hostess came by to say it was alright and the waitress even chimed in, saying we'd left a generous tip. But the Dowd insisted that we'd violated the way things were done. It was the kind of pointless exercise in petty authority I'd seen ten million times growing up—from daycare overseers, school teachers, crossing guards, little league umpires, nuns, state troopers, especially state troopers, convenience store clerks standing sweaty and nervous in front of the rack of porno mags, toll booth collectors, nuns, people whose lawn you walked across, liquor store clerks—the whole damned breed who take as their purpose in life the transformation of every moment into a prison. They are not a breed exclusive to Massachusetts, but the Bay State sure has a talent for producing them.

Like savages forced to adhere to the rites of the Catholic Mass, we paid at the register. Dowd could not understand our hurry, nor could we explain it. We left Denny's watching Lincoln Street for cars driving too fast, turning too hard up the slope into the parking lot. But it was quiet. The streetlights shone down cheap orange light on the parking lot. The wind whipped from the interstate, just beyond Lincoln Plaza shopping center. We walked around the corner, and there was Ki. He was a pale black guy with a thin mustache, in a big winter coat and baggy jeans. His face was screwed up like he smelled something foul. He was about an inch shorter than Joe.

"Joe Rooooossoe. What's up, *Joe*," he said, pronouncing *Joe* like it was a vicious slur.

Joe said nothing, just watched Ki and walked toward his car. I saw Joe's hands clench. Ki got in his way and then jumped back as Joe approached. I stayed on Joe's elbow. From how he was moving, it didn't seem like Ki would try anything on his own, but you could never tell. With another fifty feet of insults between us and the car, we walked past the fenced-in area where Denny's kept its dumpsters. The cheap orange light was twice as bright in there, reflecting off the frozen garbage-water puddles. It seemed exactly the kind of place where you might get beaten into some state it wouldn't be easy to return from. I quickened my pace at Joe's elbow, coming up even with him.

"What's this *Joe*? Your *boyfriend*? You Joe's boyfriend?" Ki said, jumping back and away from me.

"Fuck you, bitch," I said, my mind blank with fear and anger and offering no better words.

I stepped past Joe. Ki skipped back several steps until he was at the bumper of the car next to the Buick.

"Ki, kid, what are you going to do?" Joe said, emboldened, spreading out his arms.

"You made a bad mistake, Joe. You're going to have to pay and pay big time. Smitty wasn't nothing compared to what's going to happen to you," Ki said, jumping farther from us after he said Smitty's name.

Joe stared at him with big eyes and a shit-eating grin on his face. Ki kept his distance. Joe took a few quick steps at Ki, raising his hands. Ki skipped away. Joe unlocked the car and we climbed inside. That's when Ki ran at the car, hoping to hit Joe before he got the door shut. But Joe closed the door too quickly. We started driving off. Then Ki started really yelling, calling us all sorts of things, safe in the parking lot.

"Let's get the hell out of here," I said.

"I feel sick," Joe said. "I shouldn't have eaten that stuff so fast".

Sloppily cruising down Lincoln Street, I imagined a night of poor sleep on Joe's couch, of listening for footsteps at the door, or for tires on the street as a hangover glazed my eyes and crowded my head. But that was still better than what I'd imagined in the fenced-in area by the Denny's dumpsters. I decided to be grateful for it.

"Well, this year is off to one hell of a start."

"Happy New Years, Jim."

26.

I know it was unmarked, but I should have seen the cop car parked by Joe's house. I blame the whiskey, the adrenalin and the moons over my hammy that I never got to eat. They met us at Joe's porch and took out their badges. The taller one of them looked familiar, but I couldn't quite place him in the dark.

"Joe Rousseau?" said the shorter one, who had a thick head of white hair and deeply squinted eyes.

"Who's asking?" Joe said. He always gave cops a hard time, and they usually returned the favor.

"I'm Detective Johansson, and this is Detective Volpe."

"Ira Volpe?" I asked.

He paused a moment, then recognized me. Ira and I played high school football together at St. Johns. He was a stocky Greek-Italian kid, a natural defensive tackle, who got a scholarship to BU. We'd been friends on the team, but otherwise ran in different circles.

"Jim Monaghan?" he said. "What the hell are you doing here? I'd heard you were in New York."

"Can we come inside?" Johansson interrupted.

"I don't think so," Joe said.

"Well, would you like to come to headquarters?" Johansson said.

"Am I under arrest?"

"Not yet."

"Then we can talk right here," Joe said, as if it wasn't one degree outside. It was weather that made the snow banks granite-hard.

"Jim, let's talk in the car," Volpe said to me, gesturing.

Volpe gestured. I followed. Joe pursed his lips, seeing that this would take longer than a simple brush-off. The unmarked car was warm inside. Volpe started it up and turned on the heat. It was a big American car and the heat smelled faintly of warm plastic.

"Jesus, Jim, it's been forever, what are you up to?"

I gave him the recap—sick dad, between jobs in New York, knew Joe from grammar school, just got dinner at Denny's. I looked out the window and saw Joe smoking on the porch, talking to Johansson, giving his big, defiant smile while the cold stung them both. Ira gave his recap—finished BU, sold mutual funds for a few years, hated working in an office, took a pay cut and moved home to join the WPD and got promoted to detective last year.

"So, to get to the point, why the hell are we sitting here at three in the morning, having this conversation?"

"Like I said, I've known Joe forever. I just wanted to get out of the hospital and my dad's apartment for the night."

"Jim, you've never been a good bullshitter. Don't start now. What were you guys out doing just now?"

I guess I shame easily. It's one reason I was never much of a criminal. I couldn't find a lie, so I told the truth.

"Some guys from down in Main South attacked one of Joe's friends and I guess they really did a number on him. Joe wanted to find them. I went along mostly to try to keep him from getting hurt."

The radio blurted numbers, comments, beeps and static.

"Okay. That's more or less what we heard."

"Jesus. You guys really have your ear to the streets. It all just happened."

"Let's just say that you're not the only friend of Joe's who was looking out for him tonight."

Outside, Joe was leaning against the banister on the porch, smoking a cigarette with the same taunting grin he gave Ki.

Johansson was patting him down. But the cuffs weren't on. Joe was smiling and I could see his mouth forming wisecracks.

"Did Joe say how all this started? Drugs? A girl? I'm really just looking to get this thing squashed before it gets serious."

"I think it just started over nothing, really. From what I heard, Joe just thought that Sully was 'disrespecting his house,'" he said."

"This kind of shit usually starts over nothing. I got a sixteen-year-old kid with serious brain injuries, probably stupid for life, all because some girl in his math class told her boyfriend she had a *dream* about him. Some of it is enough to make you think mankind is just a fucking joke." Ira paused and looked out the windshield. His eyes were vacant for a moment. He collected himself quickly and continued: "Do you have a full name for Sully?"

"No, do you?"

"We're narrowing it down," Volpe said.

From the window, I could see Johansson making his way with hurried, precise steps down the walkway back to the car. Joe was standing on the porch as if he had just won a fight, smoking a cigarette and smiling big. Johansson knocked on Volpe's window. Volpe opened it a crack.

"You done with him?" he asked Volpe.

"Yeah. Jim, it was good to see you again. I want you to steer clear of this whole business. Spend time with your dad. And if you hear anything, just call me."

He handed me the card I realized he'd had in his hand for the last five minutes. Johansson put his hand on my shoulder and grunted. I got out of the car and went back to the house. Joe was still on the porch.

"Jesus, let's get inside," I said.

"One second," Joe said.

He took off his coat and stood in his short-sleeved, button-down tiger shirt. He smoked his cigarette defiantly, waiting for them to pull away. I went inside. It sounded like a sizable group had moved from the living room to behind Marissa's closed bedroom door. They had grown raucous, from the sound of it. Russ and some people I didn't recognize were playing a sleepy game of cards in the kitchen. The gun was still on the table and Russ had gotten himself a beer. The clock on the oven said it was three. I was sober and my eyes hurt.

"How'd it go?" Russ asked.

"We just drove around for a while. What's up with the cops?" I asked.

"How should I know?" Russ said, too quickly, and looked back down at his hand of cards as if they demanded intense concentration.

"Were they here before?"

"Yeah, they came by, looking for Joe. Marissa wouldn't let them in. Were they still out there?" Russ said, trying to sound disinterested.

I said yeah and noted that the party wasn't going to die anytime soon. I started to wave everyone good night. Joe finally came in from the cold. He went straight for the kitchen counter and downed two fingers of bourbon.

"Even when those motherfuckers don't have anything to say, they take forever to say it," Joe said, coming up for air after he'd grimaced down the drink.

"What's going on?" Russ asked.

"Just cops following up on what happened to Smitty. God, that one cop was a prick."

"Who was it?" Russ asked."

"Johnson, Johansson, something like that."

"I've met him before. He's not that bad. What did he have to say?" Russ asked.

"Just the usual shit. Just to 'leave it to the cops before anyone else gets hurt.' Blah blah blah."

"Maybe he has a point," Russ said, studying his hand.

"Jim, can I talk to you for a minute?" Joe said.

Joe closed the door to his room behind me, crossed the room quickly and pulled the shade, even though his room only looked out onto the building next door. I leaned back on Joe's mattress. He checked two drawers in his gray-metal desk, leaning over them so I couldn't exactly see what it was that he counted in each, twice.

A massive Bob Marley poster hung behind him. Bob was staring off with a joint the size of his thumb having just left his lips, smiling with the promise of stoned freedom. That was one more trap they had waiting for you when you hit fifteen or sixteen. I thought of the misery of those years, of Joe telling me that he wanted his friends to smoke his ashes when he was dead.

Joe stopped counting and raised is head suddenly. He went over to the old wood door, locked it, then went back to the drawer and started counting again. Content, he shut the drawers and pulled a chair around.

"What did your old football buddy want to know?" Joe asked.

Joe alternately thought it admirable and stupid that I'd played high school football.

"Just what we were up to. I told him we were driving around looking for Sully, that he and his friends had put Smitty in the hospital and that it started over a dumb, pointless fight."

"Why did you do that, Jim?"

"He asked. And we hadn't done anything illegal."

"But now, if I *do* do something to Sully, or even if something just happens to him, I'll be the first one they look for."

"I didn't think of that. But hey, that's just one more reason to leave it alone, get out of town like you were saying. I'll even give you your three hundred back if it will help."

"Getting out was the old plan. Now I have to stick around to settle this."

"Jesus Christ! Settle what? Sully got beaten down, then Smitty got beaten down—sounds even to me. I mean just drop it, just get out."

"Like I'm afraid? I don't think so. This is where I'm from. I'm not leaving."

"Not like you're afraid, like you don't want to look over your shoulder at Denny's. Like your life and your freedom is worth more than teaching a lesson to some jackass."

"Like you? Like your life?"

"Listen, I'm just trying to help here. But I'm going to take off. I'm beat."

"You're leaving? I thought we were going to get fucked up together," Joe said.

"Maybe this weekend. It's three in the morning, I already sobered up and I have to be at the hospital tomorrow."

On Route 9, tired and unsatisfied, I checked my phone and saw that Serena had called, but I'd missed it. The whole road back to the Fountainhead was just one big, nondescript obstacle, devoid of reward, devoid of life, devoid devoid devoid.

27.

After a bad night's sleep, I spent a minute trying to remind myself where I was, and a minute to convince myself I was somewhere else. My room was a drywall box, with a table for Dad's laptop, a few half-unpacked cardboard boxes and a disorganized bookshelf next to my inflatable bed. I showered and pulled on some fairly clean business casual clothes for the hospital. Come Monday, I'd call my contacts again, follow up on resumes … Out in the frigid apartment parking lot, I caught myself talking out loud, laying out my plans. I remembered that Dad used to do that when he was getting into his suit in the morning.

The hospital was quiet and I went to Dad's room without saying hello to anyone. I was glad to hear the door whoosh shut and close out the scraps of small talk and shoe squeaks in the hall. I looked at Dad, breathing and beeping. My book told the story of how the Revolutionary War passed mostly around Worcester. I put it down and opened my book about King Philip's War.

From Sturbridge Village to the Freedom Trail, there was always too much history in Massachusetts, always some fresh bit of dusty dullness for school field trips. But I'd never even heard of King Philip's War. Philip was the son of Massasoit, the chief who'd helped the Pilgrims survive those first few winters. I read for hours about the unlikely past of the places I'd grown up—the Praying Indian towns of Natick and Grafton, the razed settlements at Marlborough and Deerfield.

The book on King Philip's War spent a lot of time on two Indians who'd converted to Christianity and learned to read and write. They played both sides of the fence in the war, and had even acted as Philip's translators at different points. Philip had the first one, John Sassamon, killed after he warned the Colonists about his war plans. The second one was named James Printer because he worked as a printer in Cambridge. After the war was done and Philip was dead, the Colonial authorities required that Printer bring them the heads of two Indians before they'd let him off the hook and give him back his job in Cambridge. The book wondered at the wavering condition of the two men, belonging to their respective tribes by birth and race, but also to the world of the settlers by their efforts to learn to read and write.

Dad remained still. I closed the book. I thought of Joe and then I thought of Farragut Ward.

A nurse came and went. On the news channel, the TV told me that Christmas retail sales had disappointed. And a girl was kidnapped in Montana.

The cafeteria was a crappy refuge from Dad's ominous presence. Chicken sandwich and a soda on a tray, I found my table by the window. New Year's Day was quiet throughout the hospital. Half the cafeteria's heat-lamped shelves sat empty and more than half the tables were free. Whiskeynose was still in his booth, though, button-covered reflective vest over his heavy coat, handing out change to exiting cars and watching his portable TV. It did me some dark kind of good to see him working the holiday. Vindictive and hungover, I watched, hoping that the cold would grow colder, his boredom deeper, his sense of a wasted life more keen. I picked at my dry chicken sandwich.

"Hey," Olive said.

I didn't see her walk right up to me. She had put her black hair up in little pigtails, and her sweater and torn t-shirt showed the edges of a red bra fringing her pale cleavage.

"Oh, hey, Olive. What's going on?"

She sat down across from me, smiled perfunctorily, then took a deep breath and commenced.

"Well, my dad's not going to die, but that won't stop my mom from acting like he will. And we took one car here so I can't get away from her except to get some shitty food. And it looks especially shitty today. Other than that, not much, things are peachy."

"Happy New Year," I said, thinking of kissing Olive.

"Are you going to be here for a while?"

I looked down at the chicken sandwich that I was ready to abandon. I paused.

"Yeah. Just let me get some more coffee."

"I'll get it for you. How do you take it?"

I watched her narrow ass shift left and right under its plaid skirt as she walked to the empty cafeteria line. She came back with an order of fries and two coffees. She sat down and drowned the fries in ketchup.

"So he pulled through okay. That's good," I said.

"Looks like yours did too."

"Yeah, how'd you know?"

"The ICU is a small town. How's he doing?"

"The doctor says he's okay, but he's still out of it, with the tube and everything. It's going to be a long recovery, even if they don't have to go back in for more surgery. We'll find that out Monday, I think."

"This might suck less if it wasn't the holidays. There's like, nothing to do to distract you from all of it. My father's opening his eyes every six hours and pulling at the tube they put down his throat and my mother's crying, saying rosaries or yelling at us. I actually asked for more hours where I work. And I work at a freaking *Ruby Tuesday's*. My mom would kill me if she knew."

"Tell me about it. There's nothing on TV, and no one's at work. It's dead and probably will be for another week. It's like time hardly moves," I said, excited to share this misery.

"And it's not like either of our fathers are even dying."

"Exactly. It's just like dress rehearsal for it."

"And that's almost worse. I know. I'm sorry. It sucks for me to say that. I'm sorry. That's not true," she looked down at the wood grain pattern on the table's plastic surface. The dripping french fry in her painted and chewed fingernails hung in transit between the cardboard tray and her purple lips for a moment.

"Don't worry. I know what you mean."

"Right? It's not even like anything will change after this. Someone dies—you get sympathy, you get to act out. Something ends, some other things change."

"But with this, everything goes back to normal, except a little worse," I said.

"Exactly. Jim, you're not the yuppie you look like."

"Nor are you the freak you make yourself out to be, Olive."

She blushed. She took another french fry. I took a gulp of the burnt coffee. We agreed without discussion to go back to the ICU separately. My hangover had turned giddy at having found some respite from the loneliness of the hospital.

Gerry was in Dad's room when I got there. He had taken the comfortable chair by the bed and put his flowers and his coat on the smaller, less comfortable extra chair.

"Jim, I was wondering if I'd get to meet you," Gerry said, offering me his hand, covered with hair and heavy with a broad watch and a pair of rings.

Gerry wasn't too different from how he sounded on the phone. He was short and hairy. It looked like he'd had his hair cut and styled on the way to the hospital. His dark eyes and quick smile looked sincere enough. He wore a green golf shirt with a logo on the breast that said it was expensive. Despite the accusation buried in his hello, I was glad to see him. It beat being alone in that room. Gerry seemed at ease there, which I didn't think anyone could be.

"Yeah. I was just getting some lunch and I got caught up, I had to make a few phone calls," I lied.

"How's he doing?" Gerry said, looking down at Dad with a little frown.

"They say he's stable and that he's recovering by the book. But I wish he'd say so himself. I thought the breathing tube would be out by now. But they're saying it'll be there until Saturday or Sunday."

"I can imagine this is tough. Were you here last night?"

"No. He's pretty out of it. So there's nothing I can do here. I saw some friends out in Worcester."

Gerry asked about my night with the eagerness older men have for hearing the exploits of younger men. And I gave him a sanitized version, and there was a lot to sanitize. From there, we did our recaps—where Gerry had worked with Dad, what Dad had said about me—small talk, daily concerns. I could feel the muscles in my shoulders knotting up again. Gerry stayed another hour and we picked the bones of the Patriots, Red Sox, Celtics, Bruins, stocks, politicians, cities and suburbs, career, home, golf and occasional drunkenness that comprised the horizon of Gerry's life, as it was supposed to do for me. After he left, I hung around for another few hours, watching what the news network itself would call 'filler.' I thought about the long weekend ahead and I thought of Olive. I called Serena once I'd found Route 9.

"Hey you," I said, trying to be fun.

"Hey," she said, flatly.

Someone cut me off on the road and I got distracted. It made the flatness of her hello sound even flatter and made me forget to keep the banter afloat, to joke through the gloom imposed by the day in the hospital.

"You okay?" I asked.

"Yeah, just hungover. Listen, I'm just hanging out with Hannah and Aria right now. Can I call you back?" she said, sounding more distracted than me.

"Sure. I'll talk to you later."

Back at the Fountainhead, I divided my clothes into piles of clean, dirty and maybe. I stacked some of Dad's half-unpacked boxes in the corner. I couldn't seem to speed through the TV's hundreds of channels fast enough, so I went to the Fountainhead's health club and climbed onto the elliptical machine. I needed the exercise, even if just for my back. Twenty-nine and a chronic back problem. Mortality is too weak a word. I commenced fake running over imaginary distances under the fluorescent lights for a long time.

But after that, a shower and a frozen pizza, I was still racing through the channels. In the TV's glare, I imagined the bars in all the chain restaurants in the Metro-West suburbs at nine-thirty on a Friday night, the single women leaning forward from their stools, pushing their breasts forward and their asses back, hoisting fruity drinks in elaborate glasses, picking at popcorn and tortilla chips in the restaurant's engineered gaiety. I imagined the local bars, tucked into the town centers of Westborough, Marlborough, Framingham, with patrons who'd known each other their whole lives. I thought of taking a few Tylenol PMs from Dad's bathroom and calling it a night.

I really would like to say I called Serena first. I would like to say I was drunk or profoundly anguished. I would like to say I had a damn good reason when I called Olive. I would like to say we commiserated until our frustration, anxiety and grief forced us together. I would like to say she made the first move. I would like to say I didn't know what I was doing. I would like to say I didn't know what would happen. I would like to say it was necessary. But I can't.

Olive was dressed the same as she was in the hospital that afternoon, and that decided it. Our first kiss occurred at the opening of the heavy apartment door. There was no trepidation or hesitation. Her small breast with its red knot of nipple heaved warm under my hand. From the knock on the door, through the threshold of the apartment, out of our clothes, onto the couch, into her to the last bucking spasm, the whole thing had the quality of a rubber band snapping, forceful and inevitable. The first time was like that, anyway.

It was around two when she left. I flipped through the channels slowly and fell asleep on the couch to a Robert Redford movie about skiing.

28.
Friday, January 2

Regret and shame from the night before did pursue me down Route 9 to the hospital. But there was something about it I couldn't leave alone. It was the spot of life that I needed more than I regretted.

The inside of Dad's car smelled like years of spilled Diet Coke. I cranked up the heat and cracked the window. Led Zeppelin was screaming on the radio, like they always did on car radios in Massachusetts. I passed the interchange with I-495, where Raytheon used to make the Patriot Missiles that lit up the skies of the first Gulf War.

I had spent a long morning sending in resumes and writing e-mails, and I felt appropriately helpless. I planned again how I would explain myself, ambitious and enterprising but reasonable and obedient, in an interview. I hoped that would be enough, because, for all my white-collar credentials, my own survival is largely a mystery to me. I'd made research reports—not shoes or missiles or loaves of bread. I'd traded the reports for money my employer made by deeply arcane means. I could trace it all back to the creation of paper currency and banking in the 12th century, I guess.

But how would I trace this—being unemployed and trapped by in a place I hated? Now some smartass could say well, you're trapped by your bourgeois morality. But I say that bourgeois morality is the only thing that ever paid my bills or afforded me the quiet hours I count as freedom. It all made me sick with an unanswerable uneasiness.

I passed the Sheraton done up like a huge Medieval castle. Nondescript concrete and glass office buildings perched on the shoulders of farther hills. After Natick, the towns started to take on that intentional New England shine, like they were trying out for PBS. Not even the snow banks, blackened by road salt and exhaust fumes could diminish the *upscale* feeling of things there.

Parking outside the hospital, I took some breaths and walked to the hospital without my coat. I walked slowly, deliberately looking away from whiskeynose's booth as I did. Dad was still intubated and dormant in his glass cubicle. The lines on the screens looked a little perkier, but what do I know?

I kept reading about King Philip's War. During the war, the Colonists emptied out the Praying Indian towns and sent them off to Deer Island, in Boston Harbor. Half of the Praying Indians died when the Colonists got too busy to send regular supplies over to Deer Island. A hell of a way to treat your friends. I thought of the senior vice president asking me if I was loyal. I wondered what loyalty had ever gotten anyone.

After a few hours, Dad's oncologist came in carrying a leather folder overstuffed with paper. He was a little old Jewish guy with white hair and eyes that seemed too big and too alert for his face. He introduced himself and then stared down at the pages in his folder, then at the clipboard on the end of Dad's bed. He checked and rechecked some things, his eyes blinking with careful curiosity.

"I have good news for you and for your father. The mass the surgeons removed was completely benign."

"Really, what was it then?" I asked.

"I was surprised. It was actually a non-toxic goiter—a swelling of the thyroid gland. It will usually swell up in the throat. But this one went south. So that's good news. It's completely benign and your father won't need any more surgery."

I nodded and swallowed. The fear that entered the room with the word oncologist had passed.

"So is he the first one to ever have this condition?" I asked.

"No. But it is uncommon."

The hair on top of my head prickled with rage.

"Could a more qualified doctor have seen this for what it was, I mean, instead of going through the … ordeal … of open heart surgery?"

Dad beeped and breathed behind us. The nurse waited outside to monitor and adjust the machines.

"I understand how you must feel. But the condition is so rare that it's not even something we test for when we find a mass like your father had," the doctor said, looking up at me with big wounded eyes. He was in earnest. I felt like an asshole.

"Okay. I was just curious why we were here."

The doctor said some more things about how anomalous the mass was, about how dangerous its position was and something more about tests, but I had withdrawn. We shook hands and he left.

"Well, that's good news," I said to Dad.

The TV said that somewhere in the Middle East, a group of grown men were burning the American flag and jumping around with automatic weapons. It said that someone from Washington would fly over and talk to them about that.

"I'm going to get some lunch, you want anything?" I said to Dad, whose eyelids twitched. I took that as a good sign.

I skipped the cafeteria and went out to the parking lot. The sky was clear and pale, the sun was bright, if not warm. The trees and buildings were brown and gray, the snow banks white and brown, the ground just gray. It wasn't much for the eyes, but warm and vivid after the fluorescent lights of the hospital. Instead of Whiskeynose, a surprisingly friendly guy from Africa took my ticket and my money with a please, a thank you and glad tidings for the rest of my day. I drove through Wellesley and got back onto Route 9, where I found a D'Angelo's sub shop. A young kid with sloppily dyed hair coming out of his D'Angelo's baseball hat took my order and struggled with the cash register. The manager came over. He was a pale guy, so skinny that his eyes seemed like they were on opposite sides of his head, like a fish.

"I got this, Sean, you go to the chopping station," the fish-eyed manager said. "And remember what I said: It's like a zone defense. So if Tanya needs help at the grill, give her an assist."

The manager looked past me as he finished the transaction with perfunctory courtesy. Then he was back on the long-haired kid, who apparently wasn't cutting the peppers right. The long-haired kid let his reluctance be his protest and watched the manager cut the peppers correctly. The kid was learning what can only be learned the hard way—that you have to work. It made me glad not to be young anymore.

Back at the hospital, Gerry and another guy, around the same age with a combed shelf of dyed brown hair, were sitting with Dad.

"Hey, did you go *out* to lunch?" Gerry asked, as if he was building a case.

"Yeah. There's only so much cafeteria food I can take."

I introduced myself to the new guy, who said his name was Robert and said we'd spoken on the phone. We sat and made small talk.

"IBM finally caught on that these guys were basically just buying the hardware from them, installing their own software and reselling them for twice the price. So IBM decides that it can just do the same thing, so it doubles the price of the hardware and starts going after their clients," Gerry said. *Hahdwaya.* He was wearing a suit with a shiny gray tie and big cufflinks, obviously on a break from work.

"And so, another one is going to bite the dust," Robert volunteered, pressing his lips together.

"So, how do you know my dad?" I asked Robert.

"We worked together at Rebus Tech when it was a billion-dollar company."

"They were all billion-dollar companies in 1999," Gerry added.

"Don't remind me. That was four jobs and two houses ago. How about you? Your dad says you're in finance," Robert said.

"I was an equities analyst. I'm between things now," I said, surprised to be fitting in at the grown-up table.

"I've been between things for three years now," Robert said.

He nodded and his shelf of dyed hair shook slightly. Gerry shifted in his seat and looked at a blank portion of the hospital wall.

"I've never seen it so tough out there. Your dad got lucky when he got his job at Aerovan. But Robert, Dan Wong, Fred Landon, all these guys who were on top of the world just can't get a second interview ever since the bubble burst," Gerry said.

"I heard from Freddie. I think he's going to take that job down in Atlanta," Robert said.

"What's his wife have to say about that?" Gerry said.

"Plenty, I'm sure. But someone has to pay the mortgage."

"How long was Freddie out of work?" Gerry asked, chasing away the fundamental concerns Dad presented with powerful trivia.

Robert and Gerry took turns recounting the reasons for their personal woes. When the tech bubble burst in 2000, half the businesses in the Route 128 and I-495 corridors were suddenly driven to their knees. And no one wants to hire a sixty-year-old salesman with three decades of experience, not when they can hire some thirty-year-old guy for half the money. Gerry and Dad had taken pay cuts to land on their feet. But Robert was looking at a forced early retirement, doing twenty hours a week at Barnes & Noble, mostly to keep from going crazy.

Then Gerry said he had to get back to the office, holding eye contact with each of us for a long second, which was his version of warmth and sincerity for the unemployed and sick he was leaving behind him. Then Robert and I struggled sporadically to fill the air for a half hour, while the nurse checked in and out. The hospital room began to feel like the inside of a submarine, with every beep and intercom quip only deepening the sense of dread and bad luck.

"So, this is a nice hospital. How much is it?"

"Uh, I have no idea. His insurance covers it."

"Yeah. I'm surprised to see so much of Gerry. He said he was coming by tomorrow, too. I wouldn't have guessed. You can never really tell who's going to step up with things like this," Robert said.

Before long, Robert found a reason to leave. On the news, some actor angry about the environment was holding a fashion show where the models all wore gorilla masks. A middle-aged man said he was not impressed. I went around the channels a few times and then left.

29.

It was already dark when I pulled out of the parking lot, trying to return the honest goodwill that the African guy at the toll booth seemed to radiate. At a stoplight over Route 128, I saw I had missed a call from Serena, and called her back. She was taking the bus home from work when she answered. The conversation started nice enough, with her saying she missed me and me trying to cover my guilt with affection.

"When do you think you can come back, maybe just for a weekend?"

"I don't know. Maybe the week after next. I have to see how much help Dad needs after he gets out of the hospital. He's got the rehab facility after this. Then there's a nurse. But I think he's going to have a hard time with really basic stuff at first."

"It's really good that you're doing this," she said, because that was what you were supposed to say, especially when you're about to start complaining.

"Yeah."

"I miss you," Serena said in a voice full of childish, pouty emotion. It pissed me off.

"I miss you too."

"I wish you were here."

"Well. Me too."

Then there was a long pause, which was her gathering the courage to say something unpleasant, or just withholding speech in the hopes that I'd make some kind of gesture. It pissed me off.

"Listen, if I could be down there with you, I would, believe me. I don't like being up here, if that means anything. It just sucks, going to and from the hospital every day. I don't know. Some of Dad's friends were there today. Maybe they can look in for a day or two and

I can come down next week. But I don't really know right now. My dad is still fucking unconscious."

The outburst pacified her enough that we could get back to mundane chatter—her hangover from New Years, her friend Davida who was cheating on her boyfriend, drama at her office and some guy in the office I'd never heard of, who she went out of her way to say was annoying her. I said the yeahs and the ohs.

"You going out tonight?"

"I'm still hungover, but I think Davida wants to get a drink. She's trying to figure out what to do."

"If it helps, I vote that she go to a convent."

"She can't do that, she's Jewish."

"That's even better. They're always looking for converts, especially from the Chosen People."

"I'll tell her. How about you? It's a Friday night after all—even in Massachusetts."

"I don't know. I think I might just work out and watch some TV."

"Well, don't get into a serious depression up there."

"Okay."

On Route 9, a cluster of apartment buildings gave way to a terraced hill full of Toyotas, which gave way to an empty showroom. The faded rags of a *Halloween Outlet* banner flapped by its big windows. By the Sheraton castle, Route 9 filled with traffic from the Mass Pike. We all drove west together, a headless snake of red taillights. I was two red lights from the Fountainhead when Joe called.

"Jim, hey man, what are you up to?"

"Just driving back from the hospital. What's up?"

"Do you want to hang out tonight?"

"I don't know. I'm pretty beat."

"Tell me about it. I kept going after you left. I woke up in the back of Irish Times yesterday. Then I started all over again. I was all kinds of fucked up when I rolled into work today. But I figure a little hair of the dog should fix me up. You down?"

"I don't know. What's going on tonight?"

"There's a party up on Burncoat. I was just going to have some beers and then head over there. It's a small party, but I'm sure I can bring a few people. You down?"

"I guess so," I said, imagining the darkened apartment ahead.

99

"Oh, and Jim, do you think I could re-borrow that three hundred? It'll just be like I took longer than planned to pay it back. Sorry."

"It's okay. Let's get some dinner first though."

"How about Coney Island Hot Dogs?"

30.

A glowing pink fist clutches a ten-foot hot dog tight enough that yellow neon mustard drips in steady, sequential drops down one whole story of the building. In the winter night, the sixty-foot neon sign shone like a revelation. The sign flashed old America—the burst of money and optimism grimed by decades of disregard—elevator buttons burned by cigarettes, the steel bar and padlock improvised across a vending machine, futuristic cars from ten years ago with their paint jobs faded, curse words etched into the plastic of a pay-TV in a bus station, grandiose pride losing out to weariness.

Coney Island Hot Dogs was just past downtown, by a railroad bridge and a car rental place that used to be the Greyhound station. The place was dark and spacious inside. Joe waved from a wooden booth in the back. I ordered a few hotdogs and a soda. The dogs came on steamed soft buns, with onions, mustard, relish and chili.

"Jim, what's up?" Joe said, enthused in a way that seemed plain impossible after eight hours hungover in the security office of a state college.

"Just hospitals and helplessness—not a ton to report, really."

"I don't envy you one bit. Should I come by the hospital and say hi?"

"I don't think so. He'll be out of it for a while longer."

"Well, he never liked me."

"I think he blamed you for me fucking up in high school. And then there was that fight with your mother, when she called him a fascist."

"To be fair, I think she called his opinions fascistic. It was the first Gulf War—they were times that tried men's souls."

We laughed into our hotdogs. The seat in the booth was hard and smooth as a pew. The table had been haphazardly carved with initials joined by plus signs, old rock bands and stray obscenities.

"I still get chills thinking of it, the green skies on CNN, and the baggy pants," Joe blurted between guffaws.

"It truly was *Hammer Time* for a whole generation."

The vein bulged in Joe's forehead as he struggled to laugh around the bite of hot dog. He swallowed it peaceably and then broke into his machine-gun laugh, drawing a look from the old men at the counter.

"What was it that started the fight?" I asked, once the laughter had subsided.

"My mom drove me downtown to break the window on the army recruiting center after the war started. But it was already broken when we got there."

"My dad wouldn't just overhear that without saying something."

Then we talked about Dad, how he was doing, how he was misdiagnosed and how the incredibly invasive and destructive surgery had proven unnecessary, how the recovery would likely progress, what Joe hoped the visiting nurse would look like (Spanish with big cans). I told him about Olive.

"No fucking way. Well, I'm going to buy candles and watch the skies. Because if you're cheating on your girlfriend, then forty days of darkness and a rain of frogs can't be far behind."

"It just happened, well, I mean, that's not it. It's like each thing that's happened in the last few months took one more option off the table. I saw an option, an opportunity, a choice and I took it."

"Man, I'm the last person in the known world who's going to give you a hard time about cheating. I'm just surprised."

"Me too. I'm trying not to think too much about it. It doesn't have to be anything other than what it was, a blip on the radar, an anomaly. I'm surprised I did it. It's just that everything seemed to be going so well. That's what I kept telling myself. But …"

Joe opened his mouth as if to say more, then looked down at his empty paper plate, then at me. He nodded and we got up for another round of dogs. The Greek guy at the counter was talking to the oldsters there about the virtues of salt versus sand for snow removal. On the other side of the wall was a darker room, housing the Coney Island Hot Dogs bar in which rustled the even older men, sipping away the long night.

"So, before I forget, here's the three hundred," I said back at the booth. I took the money out of my wallet, holding it close. "But, what happened to the money you were supposed to make?"

"So New Year's Eve, I covered most of my costs in like the first two hours. I made your part of the money back before you even got there. And I'm doing like I planned, only selling to good friends. The whole thing is going like gangbusters. And I'm hardly even touching the stuff myself."

"So far so good."

"I actually blame you a little."

"Oh yeah, of course. After that shit I pulled, any self-respecting, small-time drug-dealing operation would have to go right off the rails."

"Yeah, be a smartass. I mean that you left that bottle of whiskey at my house. So there I am, the party is still going on in Marissa's room. I'm still jacked up from Smitty and the thing with Ki, and then the cops, so I have a few drinks to mellow out. Perfectly reasonable plan, time-tested and everything. But the other half of the bottle later, I'm Santa Claus on shore leave and I start cutting people deals on the coke I have. Then I start letting people have it on credit. And I'm like, 'don't worry, I'll remember,' so I don't write down who I'm giving it to or how much they owe me. So instead of making a profit, I actually lost fifty bucks on the package that I bought."

"You remember any of it?"

"I mostly kind of remember who was there. So I called around and asked for the money they owed me. Only Gino even admitted to owing the money, and he said he'd get it to me next week. I know I sold some to Kyle on credit. But he says it was a trade, and he probably paid for whatever he did, in spades, actually."

"Kyle?"

"Yeah, Kyle McGinn."

"Oh quiet Kyle, from way back."

"Yeah, him. Anyway, he's a great guy. I think he's coming by in a bit. He seems mild mannered, but he's an utter madman. He snuck us into the back of Irish Times at like five in the morning. All I remember is what he told me later. He said we drank until about seven. Then I just said 'that's it,' and curled up under the bar. He's a part owner, so he told the morning crew just to clean around me."

"Sounds like a good guy."

"It gets even better. The note he leaves for the bartender says I can drink free all day. So they wake me up at noon, and the bartender has two shots waiting for me. What the fuck—it's a day off, so I drink them and start flirting with the bartender who is hot with a capital *ot* and she finds me a toothbrush and some toothpaste, so I don't have to go home."

"Or because of your breath."

"True. True. So the place is quiet until about seven. By that time, Joe Rousseau International Man of Barbarism is in full effect. And I'm talking to everyone, drinking and playing pool. I win a few games and I'm feeling pretty invincible. It must have been around nine and I get into a discussion about the Olympics with these total losers who go to WPI. And they say I can't jump over the pool table. Now, you have to realize that at this point in the evening, I am God's own action figure. We decide to bet ten dollars on it."

"Sounds reasonable enough, for you, for that blood-alcohol level."

"I guess Kyle is back at the bar at this point, but I don't see him. So anyway, I go for it, not taking into my calculations the lamp hanging just above the pool table. I get a running start, leap, slam my head into the lamp and hit the pool table hard. That's when the powers that govern Irish Times decided I'd had enough and sent me on my merry way. But Kyle made my exit more ceremonious than it otherwise might have been."

"He sounds like a good guy so far."

"That's not even a third of it. So I pull out of the parking lot and stop at the first intersection. Now, this is right in the middle of downtown Worcester. At the red light, I apparently I decide that a nap is in order. Luckily, Kyle comes out of the bar for some unknown reason and finds me there passed out at the wheel. Next thing I know, I'm on my couch, and it's time to go to work."

We laughed and ate the hot dogs. An old guy got up from the counter and put some coins into the jukebox, which began playing Frank Sinatra's *Very Good Year*.

"What's going on with Smitty?"

"He's okay, conscious and all that. His jaw is wired up and they broke his collarbone and a few ribs. He lost a lot of blood. I feel like shit that I didn't visit. I guess it's too late tonight. I'll go by tomorrow."

From there, our conversation drifted to Joe's quote-unquote plan to get Sully back for Smitty, with the help of some people I'd never met, including a guy named Fitzie.

The names took me back—names systematically mangled through laziness and misplaced enthusiasm. I remember those times more in images—cigarette ends dancing in the darkness of a keg party in the woods, drunk girls, their lips leering and their pants wet from a fall or worse, awkward teenagers high on stolen cigarettes and afternoons AWOL from high school, walking down train tracks to where kids from another part of town waited under a highway bridge for a fight. There were stories galore—drugs taken, punches thrown, insults and jokes traded, arrests made. But it's the images that stuck.

"… but Vietnam says that the bouncer said he will definitely call him when Sully comes by," Joe concluded.

As he spoke, it became clear that his plan for revenge was pretty vague. It depended on luck more than anything. Worcester is a small city, but not so small as to make a reckoning inevitable. The whole thing would blow over, if not for the anger that defined so many in that town. Gypped by the seasons, trapped by the long memories of neighbors, teased by the productions of television, stuck and cut off by only half-articulable obstacles, the anger animates screaming hardcore bands and sneering cashiers the same. It is as set and jagged as the granite curbstones. It doesn't have anything better to do. It is just waiting for an excuse. It sits above everything like smog and bends the sunlight. It makes the people in Worcester funnier and more intense than any I had met elsewhere. And it makes them dangerous.

And Joe, telling me why he wouldn't leave town, wouldn't avoid Sully, was just as angry and just as obstinate.

I wish I could say I talked him out of it—the part-time drug dealing, the vendetta. I wish I could say I talked him into skipping town. I wish I could say I found it all more worrisome than amusing.

"I'm only saying it in case nobody else is. Just be careful," I said.

I remembered that I had Joe's $300 curled up in my hand. I noticed his eyes drop to it.

"So what's the three hundred for?"

"It's in case things get really crazy and I do have to get out of town, I want to have some money on hand. The holidays are over, so sales might be slower. But I also won't be as likely to get drunk and just give it all away."

I wish I could say his insistent foolishness wasn't the only sign of life in my day. I wish I could say I withheld the $300. But I can't.

I gave him the money and Kyle showed up. He was a tiny guy, maybe a hundred forty pounds soaking wet, covered with freckles, as though camouflaged. He said hi and went to get a tray of hot dogs. He came back with about eight of them.

"I'll never figure out how you eat so much and stay so small," Joe said.

"I work a lot, I screw a lot and I shit a lot. I can't figure out how you two ever got so big," Kyle said between bites.

I gave Kyle my recap and he gave his in between bites.

"Roofing. I have a crew of about twelve guys. We work year-round, though it slows down in the winter. And I own part of the Irish Times, and part of Rehab, the club upstairs."

"No shit. I wouldn't have guessed it"

"Right? When we all used to hang out, I was wild, robbing gas stations and stuff."

"I didn't know you were up to so much shit back then. You were always so quiet."

Kyle shrugged with his mouth full and his eyes down, as if to say 'how do you think I got away with it?'

"So what's up with this party tonight?" Kyle asked.

"It's Chris and Rory and them. They're getting a keg. It should be alright. They don't want a lot of people. They don't want their place getting fucked up. But they shouldn't mind you showing up. And Jim should be fine. He's upstanding as hell. They said there'll be a lot of girls. Rory said it would be 'a stocked pond.'"

Joe nodded at the prospect of a night of drinking and Kyle made short work of his hot dogs. We drove over to the Burncoat neighborhood, finally finding a house at the foot of the hill, near the Norton plant. The party was in an apartment on the bottom floor of a subdivided house.

31.

Things didn't feel right from the get-go. It took Rory a while, and some audible hassle to get to the door, and too long to open it for us. When he let us in, Rory didn't look too good, raw around the eyes and nostrils, his skin too pale even for the short winter days. We walked through a small hallway to the living room, where he gestured us toward a couch. In the living room there was a keg, but it wasn't set up. When I saw that Rory was wearing sweatpants, I turned to Joe to say something.

"You guys just sit down, get comfortable. I have to get the tap for the keg," Rory yelled, walking quickly down the hall.

Only Joe went to sit on the couch. He was comfortable and settled when Kyle looked at him and shook his head, quickly. Joe sat up, but then sat back. I noticed the same Bob Marley poster that Joe owned hanging above the couch. We heard the murmur of voices, then a louder murmur and footsteps. Kyle looked at Joe with alarm, but Joe just shrugged.

Sully was not much to look at. He was medium height, medium build, with medium-brown hair. He looked more Italian than Irish. But he was more than medium angry. I figured out it was him from the cast on his arm, the lopsidedness of his bruised face and the insuperable rage in his eyes. In his good hand, he carried an old-fashioned billy club, made of pale wood, with a strap at the bottom. Behind him was a three-man Rainbow Coalition of revenge. One was Ki, the pale black guy we'd met outside Denny's, one was a fat Asian kid with a scraggly goatee and the last one down the hall was a tall redhead with nearly translucent skin. Kyle charged straight at Sully, who raised his billy club just in time to have his nose re-broken by the tiny, flying man.

That was the highlight of the fight, which was over in a few minutes. We retreated quickly while throwing and taking punches from Sully's friends. Terror moved my limbs through paces I thought I'd forgotten. I know I landed a good one somewhere on Ki's face because he fell down and my hand hurt like hell afterwards. My head rattled as the tall Irish guy landed a few on me around the door. The shock of the attack, the sneering faces of our enemies and their clear intent to do us harm were more upsetting than the pain of the punches they landed.

By the time they stopped chasing us and started calling us names, I had a black eye and Joe a bloodied nose. Our triumph was that we made it back to our cars. I was breathing heavy, and was rattled as hell as I followed Joe's Buick away from Burncoat Street. The streets were empty. The placidly changing streetlights and the quiet houses behind their darkened yards mocked us.

Joe's apartment was empty when we got there. I took my time rinsing my face and hands and checking the swelling in the bathroom mirror. I could hear Joe and Kyle arguing. I took my time, contemplating my fresh black eye. In the living room, Joe argued with people on the phone, trying and failing to recruit them for his feud.

"What do you say, Jim? I say we go back to Rory's and settle this thing once and for all," Joe said as soon as I walked out of the bathroom. His voice had been rendered utterly ridiculous by the bloody tissues jammed into his nostrils. He was holding a shovel. I started to laugh, but checked myself.

"Man, you know what I think about all this Hatfields-and-McCoys shit. I am decidedly out."

Kyle was in the living room, quietly watching a TV show about the Patriots. He had a ziplock bag of ice against one side of his face.

"Any ice left?"

"You could go grab some snow from outside," he said, shrugging.

The well-scrubbed men on the TV discussed the game in thick New England accents. The Pats were playing the Colts Sunday at Foxborough. Dad had tickets, but gave them to Gerry.

"What do you think?" I asked the air.

"The Pats should kill them. The Colts are all dinged up, and the coach doesn't have his head in the game. Not only that, but they're fuckin' chokers," Kyle offered, engrossed in the show.

Joe was in the next room, on the phone, telling his story and trying to cajole someone else into action. I could hear the parrying action of it, the counterarguments, the feigned disappointment, the invocation of Smitty, the challenges to their innate masculinity and their purported loyalty.

"You're not going back there, are you?"

"No fucking way. Joe's got to let it go. And he has to be more careful. He can't just go off to parties like he's used to doing," Kyle said.

"What the fuck, right? That was a bona fide ambush."

"No shit it was. But man, this isn't like back in the day. We had a lot of pissed-off, nothing-to-lose type guys. Shit, I guess we were those guys. But they're gone and we've grown the fuck up. You can't settle most of the scores you'd like to settle. You and me, even Joe, we have too much to lose. You just have to walk away and try to make something better where you go."

"He doesn't want to hear that."

"I know. And that's part of why I love the guy. When he says something, he means it. Even if it isn't practical, even if it doesn't even make any sense."

Joe came out of the kitchen to where we were sitting on the couch.

"Are you guys serious that you don't want to go back there with some baseball bats and tire irons and get some *justice*?"

"Very serious," I said.

"Me too. You started this bullshit. I have a liquor license in my name. This is the last thing I need."

"Fine. Then I'm going to bed, bitches," Joe said. The bruising from the smack to his nose was starting to spread out to his eyes, like a raccoon's mask.

Outside, the cold soothed my bruised eye and swollen hand. I was jumpy from the fight, and had a pit in my stomach like I could cry. Last thing I wanted was go back to the Fountainhead.

I drove around Worcester, down to Lincoln Street, then past Institute Park and the Armenian church, to the Worcester Historical Society, around the WPI hills back to Main Street, where people were driving back and forth. I passed Irish Times, the nightclubs, Mechanics Hall, City Hall and a mirrored high-rise bank building. I drifted by the shuttered Paris Cinema, which had shown pornography to a furtive generation of New Englanders, down the downtown common, past the library and the oxidized bronze statue of a man having intercourse with a turtle. The common culminated in the old Galleria, a mall that had sucked the life out of the once-bustling downtown stores. It had gone out of business twice and sat empty, waiting to be plowed into condos.

Beyond that were signs of the future—the Centrum now named after a local credit union, the glass convention center and the sparkling medical complex straddling the train tracks. The last spasms of the Massachusetts Miracle were finally reaching downtown, pushed by the staggering real estate prices of Metro-West, all the way to *Wistah*. Passing from downtown to the foot of Shrewsbury Street, you could most clearly see the fresh overlay of faux-Colonial elegance and the stunted glamour of Boston onto an industrial city a half-century past its prime.

Stopped at a red light, I checked my face in the rear view mirror. The redness under my eye was darkening. The skin was hot and taut from the swelling. I tried to laugh at the black eye like I'd laughed at minor misfortunes before. But it didn't feel right. Helplessness loomed large behind every building, and winked from the mirror.

Maybe it was the long hours in the hospital, seeing how long it would take to get back from a simple bit of bad luck. But all I could see around me was the 10,000 varieties of death—surgery, fist fights, boredom, a dwindling bank account, depression, social disgrace and spiritual neglect. It wasn't a joke or some distant entertainment. It was a very slow variety of mortal combat. Squinting and shaking my head, I drove back to the Fountainhead, determined that something must be done. I would help Joe whether he wanted it or not.

Part Three—The 10,000 Varieties of Death

Thus on July 3 the Massachusetts Council had instructed Goodkin to order Printer, who had likely expressed an interest in securing amnesty for himself, to demonstrate his fidelity "by bringing som of the enemies heads." (Here, "heads" may mean "scalps.") Apparently, Printer succeeded in securing the necessary badges of fidelity and returned to English society; he soon returned to his work at Cambridge Press.
—Jill Lepore
The Name of War: King Philip's War and the Origins of American Identity

32.
Saturday, January 3

I woke early to the hot throb in my face. A deep anxiety in my gut made the apartment feel like a cage. I numbly hamstered on the elliptical machine in the apartment complex fitness room until sweat washed through the swollen, painful slit next to my eye. The pain spurred me on, into the day. Shaving, the mirror said I was a criminal or, at best, a hockey player. I strained my left eye open to a medium-sized slit.

The previous night's determination remained—I would help Joe. But first, I had to save myself. I dug around until I found a legal pad in one of Dad's boxes. Dad had covered the first ten or so pages on the pad with lists in the squashed loops of his cursive. I turned to a blank page, and in the pale light of the room's window, I plotted my escape. If I got a job, I would *have* to go back to New York. The list was a dreary dredging of trivia, a raking over of coals. I filled two pages with fragile plans and slender reeds of hope. I got to work on the computer.

Serena had sent me an e-mail, saying she'd sensed my frustration over the phone the day before. She offered to come up the next weekend. So the question was no longer if she was falling out of love with me, it was if I deserved her love. I thought of Olive and cringed. But it's hard to forgive or really condemn yourself for something you're thinking of doing again. I started to write back, but abandoned it and headed for the door.

I drove slow. I had dubious depth perception and little peripheral vision on my left side. That day, Route 9's series of anonymous lakes and inscrutable corporate headquarters were so familiar that they hardly existed. In the hospital, Dad's breathing tube was gone. His unfocused eyes settled just beyond me. I went up and took his hand, gently. It was dry and limp.

"Hey Dad, you made it. It's good to see you awake."

He looked at me and struggled to choke out the word 'hey.'

"When did you come out of it?"

After struggling to choke out a word, he just shook his head to indicate he didn't know or couldn't say.

"Well, you didn't miss too much. The doctor said that the mass isn't cancer, so you don't need any more surgery. And your friends Robert and Gerry came by the other day."

More with his face than his head, Dad nodded.

"And look, you're up and about in time for the playoffs."

Dad nodded again, as if resigned, and closed his eyes. I sat in the inflexible wood and polyester chair, book in lap and watched the men on TV argue about how the weather would affect the San Diego offense. Dad woke a half hour before kickoff, surprised to see me there. He blinked a few times. He grunted thinly and looked at me, then blinked again, and after a moment of puzzlement croaked 'your eye.'

"Yeah. I was at a party in Worcester and a brawl started. And I got caught up in it. It's no big deal."

"Joe?" he croaked after some effort. Even in his state, Dad sure could ask a loaded question.

"Joe was there. But there were also some guys I knew from St. Johns," was my loaded response. "I don't know who started the fight. I just got caught up in it."

Dad made a face of disappointment.

"It was just a fistfight. I'll be more careful."

With his mouth ajar, Dad surveyed the bruise again and croaked 'doctor?'

"Come on. It's just a black eye."

Dad started to shrug, then winced, and settled for pursing his lips.

"We have Tennessee at San Diego for the early game. Then it's the Seahawks at the Giants."

Football had always been a blessing for us. It meant spending time together without talking, especially with Dad struggling to speak and the left side of my face a purple reminder of so much he disliked. The nurses came in for their sometimes baffling and sometimes awful errands. They made a point of ignoring me. The black eye had changed me from the devoted and dutiful son to the violent and unemployed son. The black eye was one of those things that created a subtle but real exile from the middle class. Dad's friend Robert showed up a half hour after the game ended. Another friend, Dan Wong, showed up just before the kickoff of the second game, with three big foil bags of chicken wings. Dan was half-Chinese and the other half must have been a bear. He was just over six feet tall and he had arms like legs and legs like torsos.

"So Jim, I have to ask, what the hell happened to your face?" Dan asked at halftime.

"I was at a party with some old friends and a fight broke out."

"No kidding, where was it?"

"It was in Worcester."

"Ohh, *Wistah*. You gotta watch out in *Wistah*," Dan said, exaggerating his own accent.

"How about you Dan, where do you live?" I asked.

"I just moved from Newton to Natick—South Natick, actually."

"Is that the part by the mall?"

"You mean the Natick Collection? No, it's actually the old part of town, by the Charles River."

"Oh, that sounds nice," I said, wondering to myself how the hell I had gotten into a pissing match with this guy.

The second game was less fun than the first. Dad slept through it and Dan Wong stuck around. I left before it was done.

33.

The guard was watching the playoff game on a little TV at Mom's apartment complex when I pulled up. He let me through without asking any questions.

"Oh my God, what happened?" Mom asked fast upon the hello.

"I was at a party in Worcester and there was a fight. It's no big deal. Just a bruise."

"It looks bad. Did you go to the hospital?"

"No. It's nothing, just a bruise. It just happens to be on my face. I got plenty of these growing up."

"Can you see out of it?"

"Yeah. It's fine," I said, booming my voice a little.

"Do you want some ice?"

"It's too late for ice. Don't worry about it."

Her low-ceilinged apartment was bright, like there were one too many lamps on. She was wearing a baggy red-and-green sweater with a pattern of abstract wreaths. It had been more than a week since Christmas and I felt guilty. But then I thought of all the shit I had to do because she left Dad. That balanced out my guilt. It was a great feeling, just take my word for it.

"Well, what do you feel like doing?" I asked.

"I'm okay with anything, we could eat in, eat out. Whatever you want."

We went back and forth like this some more. She and Dad used to do it too. It's supposed to be a polite, pliant, generous gesture. But it seemed more like they had both just run out of appealing options. Indifference is a type of politeness, but not the best one. I finally said we should stay in, that I was beat. More than I wanted to admit, I just wanted to sit down in front of the television. I wanted nothing more than to be obliterated by its boundless reservoir of dinosaurs, convicted murderers and others worse off than me. It was the thing I'd hated most when I hated the suburbs—the way my parents and so many other people I'd needed in some way would get lost in self-abnegation before the flickering box. But, can of Diet Coke in hand, I succumbed just the same. No one gets converted to this way of living, I thought, they just get tired. And I was that. Someone on the TV swabbed a belt buckle and it turned bright blue in the dark. That was important to finding the killer, the TV said.

The TV was loud as hell. I turned it down. But Mom reminded me her hearing was bad and I turned it back up, just a hair past what the TV's speakers could gracefully deliver.

"We can get whatever you want. I'm going to have one of my diet meals I think," Mom said.

She had been on a diet since about nine months before she left Dad.

"Okay, maybe just some Chinese."

Mom lit a cigarette, then got up for a fresh soda. A heavyset, grayish man on TV talked about the DNA content of saliva. Mom sat down and watched with me. A ruddy man in sun glasses enumerated the difficulties of surrounding a house like the one the killer lived in. Mom tried to make conversation while I focused on the TV, playing the role of Dad's ghost.

"So when was this party?"

"Last night."

"Was Joe there?"

"Yep."

"Did he get in the fight too?"

"Yep."

"He didn't get hurt, did he?"

"Just bruises."

I don't know why, but it was like a Chinese finger trap—the more questions she asked, the less I wanted to answer them. I couldn't make my answers much more curt, so I just took longer to deliver them—who else was there? why did the fight start? was anyone else hurt? was the place where the party was held damaged? did the hosts own or rent? and so on. Finally the show started up again. It isn't walls that separate us, but TVs.

"Did Joe know the ones who started the fight?"

"Can we wait for the next commercial for the rest of it?" I asked. I should be more even-handed about all that comes with being an adult of divorce, but it doesn't come easy. The killer almost escaped, was caught and arraigned. A commercial came on.

"So, did he know them?" Mom asked, not missing a beat.

"I don't think so ..."

After more parrying, Mom left to pick up the Chinese food. I ate it, and she picked at something from a rounded cardboard tray that approximated food. By then, we'd changed the subject.

"I swear, he's got to be the only dumb Jew I've ever met," she said about a man she worked with, and we laughed a bit.

Mom paused as if to say something important. I held my breath and hoped it wasn't a boyfriend. I wondered what it would be like to punch a man twice my age. But it was a false alarm.

"How is your father?"

"He's recovering. He woke up today. He'll be fine."

Then Mom looked at me as if to invite me to say more. But I just shrugged, looked down and ate. There could be no possible benefit in passing information from one of them to the other.

"How are you doing?" Mom asked, indicating the whole situation by how she said the words.

Mom had her bouts with depression. The latest one directly preceded her leaving Dad, and she was attuned to it. I appreciated her asking, though she might not have known it.

"I'm fine. Just doing what I have to."

After dinner, I could have stayed at Mom's. But I said I had to do laundry back in Westborough.

"So are you going to have time this week? Maybe we could get dinner," Mom said.

It sort of drove a knife into my heart. I said yeah, said I'd have to see what was happening at the hospital and so on.

It's hard to love your parents enough. It's just how they sit in you. No gesture or gift ever seems to communicate or exhaust it.

But, driving past the reservoir and the apartment complex that faced it, a terrible feeling, even beyond that, a sense of immense waste hit me. Traffic snagged while a pair of drivers sorted out a fender bender by the stop light. I idled with everyone else by the eastern shore of the reservoir, looking at the old dam and its granite church-like building, wondering, what did I waste? What was I wasting? Bright, white lights shone down from the apartment complex above me. Past that glared a black and yellow sign for a sushi restaurant. The landscape gave no indication anywhere of exactly what had gone wrong, only that something had.

Back at the Fountainhead, I called Serena and got her voicemail, which was a relief. I tried to sound sweet on the message. The effort counts almost as much as the real thing. It wasn't even eleven, but I was exhausted.

On the inflatable bed, I closed my eyes and adjusted the too-small blanket. I thought of how scary it must have been for Mom to leave Dad after thirty-seven years, of how unhappy she must have been to leave. It was her overmatched fight against the 10,000 varieties of death. It made getting to sleep hard. Lying there, I was pursued by the feeling that something irreplaceable was being wasted. It vibrated in my gut.

I got out of bed and found my wallet with Ira Volpe's card in it. I figured there's no bad time to call a police station, and called his office line. His line rang a half-dozen times before I was transferred to an old woman with a reedy voice and little patience. She told me Detective Volpe wasn't in and I should talk to one of the detectives who was. Before she could transfer me, I asked when he would be in. She said he'd be in at five, five-thirty that evening, then clicked me over to a sleepy sounding man who I hung up on.

By then, my gut had calmed to a basic sort of dread. I could sleep on that.

34.
Sunday, January 4

They'd moved Dad from the ICU to a regular room in another wing of the hospital. It was bigger and less futuristic, with curtains and fewer machines. Dad even had a roommate on the other side of a curtain. It was an older man in worse shape than him. The guy's wife was holding his hand. They whispered occasionally—a real, live ghost at the feast. I'd brought a bag full of boneless chicken parts for the game. I tried to find a place for my coat and reached for a chair that was actually a toilet with a removable bottom. The days ahead flashed, coming toward me as unstoppably as kickoff.

"You want some chicken?" I asked.

Dad scrunched up his face to indicate no, and we watched the game. It was competitive and physical from the get go. Dad was nervous and engrossed, struggling through his pain and lingering chemical torpor to harrumph at the TV. It wasn't until halftime, with the Patriots holding the lead, that we talked.

"You barely made it. I was getting worried."

"I overslept. I was up late."

"Were you out in Worcester?"

"No, I was just watching TV."

"Did you see your mother?"

"Yeah."

"How's she?"

"Fine."

It still hurt him to speak. So I kept my own questions to ones with yes and no answers. You could guess everything going on with Dad just by looking at him—the pain, the drugs and so on. The people on the other side of the curtain whispered some more.

The Pats held the Colts to a field goal in the second half and had the game wrapped up with five minutes left. The win was an irrational glimmer of optimism for us. We'd hacked the ice off the aluminum bleachers at the old stadium with our drivers' licenses. We'd watched when fans carrying off a goalpost were half-electrocuted by a power line outside the stadium. We'd had football to talk about and watch together during that first rapprochement after a bitterly contentious adolescence. And the Patriots started winning when things began changing with us. That's what it meant, coincidence or no. After the game, I gave Dad a hug, gently. His own hands were light and trembling to reach my shoulders. The hug was awkward for me and painful for him. I sat back down to bask in the triumph reflected in the tiny hospital TV's recap.

"These chicken things are good. I'm going to get some soda. You want anything?"

Dad said no, looking more alert and less pained than I'd seen him since the surgery. In the long, windowless corridors of the hospital, I wondered if it was dark yet. The hospital was neither day nor night. I had a Diet Coke can in each hand and was leaving the cafeteria when I ran into Olive.

"Well, if it isn't the invisible man. Do you have a minute?" she asked.

Her voice showed aggravation, but she looked good. Olive was wearing a tight black and white dress from a thrift shop with an even tighter black sweater over it that opened to offer up her pale cleavage. She had on dark red lipstick, a lot of eye makeup and smelled of cigarettes. It all turned me on. I could tell she had something rehearsed, a speech that started with how I said I'd call, carried on into an ultimatum, and concluded with a proclamation that she didn't care what I did. But my black eye turned the tide. It hurt less, but a dark purple and yellowish outline was setting in, making it look worse.

"My God, what happened to your face?"

"I was out with some friends in Worcester and I got into a fight. It's no big deal."

"Does it hurt?"

I shrugged to indicate that though it did hurt, I certainly wasn't about to say so. It was a cheap ploy, but I wasn't above it. We went back to my usual table, where I could watch Whiskeynose locked in his booth with his tiny television.

"So what's new with you? How's your Dad?" I asked.

"Dad's going to have to do this again, it turns out. Maybe next year, but they're talking about doing it while he's still here. They don't like the look of another one of his valves. So the whole clan is going to get to do another stint in the hospital—hooray."

"Sorry to hear that."

"Do you want to just, like, run off to San Francisco with me? Maybe we can change our names."

She said it like a joke that required only that I not laugh for it to come true. In that moment, she wasn't my regret.

"It's the best idea I've heard today. But I can't," I said, gesturing all around me to explain it.

"Yeah, that's right. I forgot. You can't even call me."

"I'm sorry about that. I have Dad, then Mom, then my friends back in Worcester. And things are crazy there. I want to tell you about what happened to my face, about all of it. I really do. And I do think of you. You're the bright spot for me here. There. I said it."

"Said what?"

"What you wanted me to say when you came on all sour a few minutes ago."

"I just wanted to know why you didn't call."

"What are you doing tomorrow night?"

"I'm not just coming over. That was just that time."

"Okay, we'll go someplace. You know your way around. You pick."

"I'll think about it," she said.

He dark lips pressed against each other to stifle a smile. I touched her hand and it opened to the touch.

"I'll call this time."

Exhilarated and wondering what the hell I was doing, I made it back to Dad's room.

"Jesus, you go to Atlanta for the sodas? You missed the kickoff. Dallas is about to score," Dad rasped, his impatience trumping the pain.

"Sorry, I got turned around in the other wing. Then I got a phone call."

"It's okay. I had the nurse help me to the bathroom when you were gone."

"Oh shit, and I missed all the excitement."

I opened Dad a soda and we settled down to watch the game. There was a lot of scoring for a playoff game. Between the first and second quarter was a plug for the late night news. Below the eager weather man, the time flashed—after five thirty. I took a breath and excused myself. I went outside to make the call. It was warming up, almost to the freezing point. Snow was on the way.

"Ira Volpe," he answered, and the background noise filled in behind him.

"Ira, it's Jim, Jim Monaghan. We talked the other day."

"Yeah, Jim, what's up?"

"Well, it's just that this situation—the one from the other night—it has me a little worried. I wanted to sit down and talk to you about it, get your take, see what I can do. Do you have time?"

"I could do later tonight. I'm on until one tonight, unless someone gets shot. But uh, it's cold out and the Pats won, so I should be free."

"How's nine sound?"

"Sure, you know where headquarters is, right?"

Worcester police headquarters was an impregnable cement block with no windows until the fifth story. In the middle of downtown, it stood as a monument of hostility towards the city's residents.

"Can we meet somewhere else?"

"Where?"

"How about the Boulevard Diner, on Shrewsbury Street?"

"The old dining car?"

"Yeah. Eggs and coffee are on me."

"See you at nine."

Back in Dad's room, the elderly roommate slept. His wife watched. Dad stared at his dinner—a covered plastic bowl of broth with a big spoon.

"What took you so long? I even farted while you were gone."

"Farting, hospital food—why do I always miss the good parts?"

Dad started to laugh, but that invited a near cataclysm of pain. He smiled instead.

"I guess you just have shit luck."

Halftime was ending. The game carried on, one heroic sack, one heroic long bomb at a time until heroism lost all meaning. It was 42–38 by the time Dad fell asleep with five minutes left. I pulled up his blanket as a way of saying good-bye. It was snowing when I gave Whiskeynose my ticket and my money.

35.

The snow fell through the streetlights, renewing the landscape. I drove slowly after Dad's SUV lost its grip on the road by a half-built, Tyvek-skinned car dealership. I got to the diner early, and ordered sausage, eggs and a coffee. The place was a onetime dining car parked for good on Shrewsbury Street, down the hill from the tracks of the Worcester-Boston railroad. The place was so small that everyone had to make a solid effort to ignore each other. A woman and her daughter bickering in and out of whispers, assassinating each others' characters between the clatter of plates, were the main event that we ignored. Ira was also early, showing up before the food. He pointed to his left eye and shook his head as he made his way over to the booth I was in.

"I told you to stay out of it," he said, seeming disappointed. Somehow he seemed a lot older than me.

"It's just a black eye."

"I know. But it could have been worse. There's one thing I learned it's that there's really no limit to how bad these things can get."

"What things?"

"The fights that break out over nothing. They usually end worse than the ones we can make sense of. Really Jim, you should know better. You're not one of them. And you're what? Thirty almost? I mean, you're too old for this nonsense."

In high school, Ira had been a big kid, big because fat and then big after years in the weight room. He'd slimmed down and gotten old in the intervening years. Lines radiated from the corners of his eyes and creases connected his broad nose and the sides of his mouth. He had an old man's slow-moving eyes.

"You're right. I didn't know what I was dealing with. I went with Joe to a party. He said it was a friend of his invited him. But it was a set up. They were waiting for him. Things could have gone very badly."

"That how you got the shiner?"

"Yeah."

"Anyone else hurt?"

"Just bruises. We got out fast."

"Sully was there?"

"Yeah, him and some of his friends. Sully had a billy club. It was set up by this guy Rory, who was supposed to be Joe's friend. He looked pretty strung out."

"Now where does this Rory guy live?"

"In the Burncoat neighborhood, off West Boylston Street."

Ira continued with the cop questions—do you know his last name, were you drinking, had you met these people previously, how do you spell Ki, where exactly on West Boylston Street? He wrote parts of it down, but not the parts I would have written down. By the time he'd exhausted his questions, I'd finished a coffee and most of the eggs and sausage.

"So what can you do with all that?" I asked as he paused to write the last of it down.

"Not much. It's thin—maybe assault, if you wanted to press charges. But it's a stretch even then. With the billy club, maybe we could try for aggravated assault, but I'd need Joe and this other guy to give statements.

"I don't think they would go for that," I said. "Is there any way you can get Sully to back off Joe? I think Sully is involved in some shady dealings—drugs and whatnot."

"Who told you that?"

"Joe."

"How does he know?"

I was going to say something vague, something about how people talk. But I hesitated for a second or so, and that was all Ira needed.

"Exactly," he said, before I could say anything.

I suppose he saved me the trouble of lying. I put a yolk-covered piece of sausage in my mouth and tried to act unruffled.

"I don't even know why you're trying to go to bat for this guy. I mean, you're college educated, you live in New York City, and you look like you're doing pretty well. So why get your face messed up for this guy who obviously can't be bothered to look out for himself?" he asked.

"Ira, I've known the guy since I was ten. In high school, we went our own ways. But he's a real friend. You don't get too many of those. So, to lay it out there, I guess I'm asking for a favor. I'll keep trying to get Joe to drop this stupid feud of his. But I need you do something to squash this on Sully's end, lay pressure on him and his friends. It'll be one less thing to investigate."

"I'll look into it. But I don't know how much I can do. Other than that, there's only one other way I can think of to put a stop to this thing, if you are really worried about your friend getting hurt."

"What do you mean?" I asked.

"You can tell us what Joe is into. Get him off the streets for a little while. Give the dickheads who are after him some time to screw themselves up. It'll happen sooner than later."

My face may have gone pale, but I was careful not to hesitate again. You can't see nausea.

"The guy may be a rowdy drunk. And okay, he may get high now and then, but that's all I have on him. And that's a lot thinner than the freaking set-up we walked into the other night. If he was alone, he could have been killed."

"So you're telling me that he's not selling coke, not buying guns?" Ira said, seriously.

It took a second for me to realize that to Ira, these things were what they sounded like. It struck me that by knowing Joe and the guys around him so long, one gun or a few eight balls of cocaine just didn't add up to the kind of seriousness that they did to the law. They seemed like the instruments of great underground revolt against a depression the size of the world. But here they were, laid bare by my new ally, as the felonies that they were.

"I never heard of any of that. That's not what this is about. It's just a nasty brawl."

"Maybe you should talk to your friend Joe about that other stuff before you defend him."

"I really don't know what you're talking about, or what you might have heard. I just want to help my friend."

"And I just told you how you can."

"Okay," I said, nodding.

"Are you really getting this?" Ira asked, gesturing down to his empty cup of coffee, looking at me coldly.

"Yeah."

Ira shook my hand and left. I felt like a fool, and even more helpless than before. I gestured to the old Italian guy behind the counter for the check and he gestured me to the register. Ira's coffee cost $1.05. Breathing heavy, I walked through the snow to Dad's SUV. I watched the snow in the pale orange street light. The flakes fell like notes in some perfect, infinite piece of music. But they'd become dirty, icy piles that lingered into mid-March. It was all fucked, but fucked in a pretty sort of way.

Going down Belmont Street, with the whole valley of Lake Quinsigamond and all the parking and shopping of Shrewsbury opening up before me like a drunk ex-wife. At White City, I pulled off the road to think.

In its first life, White City was an amusement park on the edge of the lake. They turned it into a shopping plaza before I was born. Since high school, it had shed its record store, its improbably gorgeous neon sign, and its movie theater. I parked by what had been a toy store so vast that I once peed my pants at its overwhelming promise. I turned off the car, and watched the windshield fill with snow, blotting out the back-lit, cursive sign of a dried-flower superstore for the thousands of households kept just so by the dour repression of their children. In the silence, I cursed the future, and cursed the caution of expensive lives. I was halfway into reconsidering the curse when my cell phone rang. It was Joe. We talked a few minutes before he got to the point.

"Jim, I hate to even ask. I mean, I'm sorry, but I need to borrow another three hundred. I'm really sorry. But I need it."

"What for?"

"Well, can we meet up to talk about it?"

"Joe, I'm still unemployed. I didn't get a new job over the weekend, you know? I'm not sure if I can swing it. Let me call you back tomorrow about it."

"Okay, because I need it soon. Where are you?"

"I'm in Westborough. I'm in for the night," I lied.

We agreed to talk the next day. I turned the car on and drove back to the Fountainhead. Out of respect for its power over me, I left the TV off and went to bed, thinking about Joe and Volpe, back and forth.

Finally, a long fantasy of Olive in the land of forgetfulness put me to sleep.

36.
Monday, January 5

Something urgent and persistent woke me. I fumbled around the apartment until I found the source—a speaker with buttons in the living room. The voice on the other end said the medical supply company was downstairs in the cold and the fresh foot and half of snow. Pulling on pants and rinsing out my mouth, I looked in the mirror. I had slept on my left side, so the eye was almost swollen shut, its purple turning brown. A fresh wound looks menacing, but a stale wound looks squalid.

I welcomed the two West Indian men with a hand truck full of aluminum railings and a toolbox into the apartment. The living room and the hall were a mess. I had a bad habit of leaving my pants where I took them off. I cleared the debris from their path and got out of their way. I looked over my list of things to do and sat down at the computer. The two men measured the hallway and the bathrooms for railings and the like. I was tweaking a cover letter for a job that I didn't want when they knocked on the door and gave me a form to fill out for the insurance company. Then they left.

Yellow sunlight streamed off the still-white snow outside, through the big glass door in the living room. Quiet and alone, the world could be anything. I could be the narrator and the interpreter of my own story. These moments of solitude are the closest I've found to freedom or to being awake. I did a little dance in the living room to underline this point to myself, removing my pants and swinging them over my head like a lasso. Then I went into the kitchen to make coffee.

On a roll, I e-mailed some friends in New York, e-mailed Emily in Worcester, wrote Serena back, writing the things I ought to say. It was a workday and I was working, typing and checking things off my list. I watched the financial news for a few hours. The news had gone from troubling to bad to ominous in the last few months. Red arrows tracked the Dow Jones, as the investing public lost its illusions about what our prized enterprises were worth. The yelling white men on the TV almost had me believing that the world we'd built would soon resort to barbarism or mysticism.

But what did I know? Despite my close attention to the trembling of the global financial markets on the TV, I was just a guy in his underwear on the couch, waiting for the cable guy.

The cable guy showed and I made up some work to do to get out of his way, hunting through more job descriptions. The adjectives— "passionate," entrepreneurial," "committed," "dazzling"—didn't seem like me. I couldn't fight the sensation that I was digging my own cavernous grave with each cover letter and resume.

It took the cable guy a little less than an hour to get the TV and cable all set up, after which he gave me the special moron's tour of the remote control until I gave him a tenner and said thanks a lot. The nurse called to say she would be by the day after tomorrow to look at the apartment to make sure everything was in place. She sure didn't sound like a Spanish broad with big cans. She sounded cold; I don't want to say clinical, but I suppose I just did. With that done, I looked at the computer, and recited the eight percent unemployment rate and assured myself that I was better qualified than at least nine percent of the population. I looked out the glass patio doors at the landfill flattened and rehabilitated for family dining establishments. The daylight was failing, but hadn't failed yet.

I called Olive. She was getting off her lunch shift at Ruby Tuesday's and said she was surprised I called. We made plans to meet at a place she picked, a sushi place on Route 9. She said it was all yupped out, but she knew the bartender. Then I called Joe.

"Jim, I can't talk now, I'm at work."

"Just calling to see what's up."

"Nothing, just tired as hell. Listen, can I call you back tonight? Do you think you'll be able to help me out with that thing we talked about?"

"I don't think so. It's not life and death, is it?"

"I don't think so, but I'm not sure. Listen, I just got spoken to about too many personal calls. I have to go. But I'll call you back later."

I raced outside to get some daylight. By the time I made it to the cold parking lot, the sun was just an orange glow on the hill behind the Target megastore. I raced to the hospital. In the room, a nurse tended to Dad's roommate. The roommate's wife watched, leaning forward like she was just about to say something. I nodded and smiled and hurried to Dad. Dad napped before the TV, a bowl of broth and saucer of Jell-o. After a minute, he woke up with an infant's look of disoriented curiosity.

"Hey Dad."

He nodded, and tried to shake himself more awake. The shake didn't wake him, but the pain it brought on did. He looked at me a minute, drawing breath through his mouth.

"Hey. How are you doing?" I asked.

"Okay. I had a dream about cars, cars crashing, cars driving along, parked cars, a lot of parked cars. Then tow trucks in the night," he said, his rasp no longer the obstacle it had been.

"Was it a good dream or a bad dream?"

He took a minute to answer. He looked around, calm except for his eyes, which still seemed desperate for orientation.

"It was both."

Then he was quiet. I filled the silence telling him about the railings in the bathroom and the cable TV by his bed.

"It's a lot of TVs for one apartment, for just one guy. When I'm better, you can have the old one," he croaked.

"Thanks. I'm sorry I couldn't make it until now."

"And you probably have to go soon."

"No, uh, not exactly."

"You're not all cleaned up and dressed up for me. Do you have a girl in Worcester?"

"Something like that. But it's no big deal. I can stick around as long as you want."

"Jim, I'm on so many drugs right now. I mostly sleep. And when I wake up, I can hardly tell. I have the pain in my dreams too, except it's a big leach on my chest, or a face trying to break through the skin, or a mine cave-in."

"Jesus. It sounds like they're giving you the strong stuff."

"It's not strong enough," Dad said, then closed his eyes and drifted off into something that looked like sleep, but worse.

I forgot my books in the car so I watched the news channel. I couldn't focus—it was all images, people loitering in malls, vast parking lots, ships loading or unloading, men in suits talking or sitting and watching the one who talked, the floor of a stock exchange, bar graphs and missiles. The TV was adamant about all of it. I reached for the remote in its spot between Dad's forearm and belly. He flinched, grabbed the remote and woke up.

"What are you doing?" he demanded.

"Just changing the channel."

"I'm watching that."

"You looked like you were sleeping."

"I wasn't. I was watching that," he said, pissed off.

It was good to have him back.

"Okay, okay. Take it easy. You want some food, or a magazine or anything?"

"I'm fine. I still haven't read the magazine you left here the other day. I can't hold it up for very long."

"Oh, well, I guess I could read it to you if you want."

Dad made a face like I'd recommended that we slow dance. I shrugged. A few minutes later, he fell back asleep, or what passed for sleep. I got up to leave.

"See you tomorrow, Dad," I said, hoping he wouldn't hear me and wake. He didn't at first.

But he opened his eyes, startled, when I took my coat from the chair. I cringed at having to stay much longer, but reminded myself of the hundred reasons I came to Massachusetts in the first place.

"You're still here?"

"Yeah. I was just about to head out."

"Just you and me, huh?"

"Yeah. I'll stick around longer if you want."

"No, no go ahead."

"You sure?"

"Yeah."

"Okay. Have a good night, Dad."

"Okay," he said, closing his mouth as if there was a bad taste in it.

Whiskeynose seemed to sneer when he saw how little of my day I'd spent with Dad and how little money I owed his booth. But I think he was just the sneering type. I hit the road and made it to the restaurant, *Sushi Samba*, early.

37.

The place was just too big. From passing cars, I'd seen it fail as a Bistro, Steakhouse, Barbecue and Italian seafood restaurant before its current incarnation. The place had tableside grills and a sushi bar on the sprawling floor below, anchored by a huge golden Buddha. I wondered if the Italian place had a huge golden Crucifix in that spot, imagined Christ in Golden agony watching over the waiter as he pushed the veal special. I ordered a beer in a bottle and waited. The bartendress smiled through her suspicion. A man with a black eye, no matter how preppy his polo shirt, would always be suspect in an upscale place.

The TVs behind the bar, above the bar and behind me showed all that could be shown about the Patriots, Celtics and Bruins. Olive came through the door looking good. She wore black, like she mostly did. Her skirt was short and her top made her even more inviting. She kissed me hello, then said hello to the blonde.

"I go to school with Jemma," she explained as Jemma brought her a tall glass filled with a bright red liquid. "So what's going on, brawler?"

"Oh right, the eye. I had the cable guy and the nursing people over at the house today, setting things up. They probably thought I was one of those criminals who kills old people and cashes their Social Security checks."

"House? I thought you said he was in an apartment?"

"He is. I guess old habits die hard. I'm used to him being in a house. It's going to be close quarters once he moves back in."

"Don't tell me about close quarters. I never thought being at work would be such a relief. Between my mother and my dweeb brothers and the fucking hospital, this holiday is pure hell. The nurses in that place—if you aren't dressed in Ann Taylor yuppie wear, no offense, then they look at you like you have some *disease*."

"At least with the black eye, they back off."

She finished her drink quickly. Jemma brought us another round without saying anything. We talked about Framingham, Natick and Sherborn, and the Metro-West suburban cloud. We finished our drinks and Jemma delivered more, her smile intensifying to the point where it almost wasn't a smile anymore.

"I'm surprised they didn't stop you at the door to this place."

"Well, they have a lot of seats to fill," I said, making eyes at the quarter-full restaurant.

"Still, these places are all uptight. It's all yuppies out here in the Metro-West, except for the old men. I have this one old man who comes into Ruby Tuesdays and drinks his coffee at the bar. He lives across Route 9 in one of those little apartment buildings and walks over. He mostly just talks about the Red Sox and about back when Framingham was orchards and factories. But sometimes he'll talk about World War Two."

"He sounds interesting."

"You would think that. But he's really not. I like him just because he'll come out and say he doesn't like what's going on. He calls them the 'get-rich-quick crowd.' But mostly he's mad because he doesn't understand what's going on. He doesn't understand why he's the only old man sitting in a chain restaurant at noon, when it opens, talking to people. I guess I don't understand it either."

"I can relate. The whole thing drives me nuts. You drive someplace, unbuckle your seatbelt, turn off the car, get out of your car, lock it, buy whatever you need, unlock your car, get in, buckle your seatbelt, start the engine, drive home, open the door, get what you bought, close the door, make sure the lights are off if it's night time, lock the car, go inside and so on. It's just grating. In New York, in any city where you can live without a car, it's like you can hide from the twenty-first century for just a little while longer. It's more of a holdout than a triumph. But I'll take it."

"Okay, Broadway Joe, enough societal commentary, so what did you do to your face?"

She smiled and listened. And I was already a yuppie to her. So I told her the whole story, from Sully's beat down to my meeting with Volpe.

"Jesus. That makes my mom's uncomfortable flirtation with the cardiologist almost look dull. What are you going to do?"

"I don't know. I keep trying to talk Joe down. I'm still trying to figure out what I can do."

Jemma brought us another round and said cheers.

"To bizarre dramas," Olive said, the words almost rhyming.

"Yeah. May they only kill strangers."

We toasted, drank and then kissed, then kissed some more. We looked at each other affectionately. I think it made us both uncomfortable. We looked away, back to our drinks.

"So, you got the railings all set up?" Olive asked flatly, changing the subject.

"Yeah. It wasn't too much of a hassle."

"My mom's taking care of all that. When's your dad going back home?"

"You mean, to the apartment?"

"No, to heaven," she said.

"You must be a joy to have around the ICU."

"Just answer the question."

"It depends on what the doctors say. He has to go to a rehab facility first. How about yours?"

"They don't know yet. His scar didn't heal right and they had to reopen it and drain it and all kinds of other terrifically arousing things that you should talk about while you're on a date."

"You're funny, you know that?" I said, a little drunk.

I kissed her again. She pulled back and looked at me with her eyes wide. Her cheeks flushed through their usual pallor. She licked her lips a little.

"What about that thing you were going to show me in your car?" she asked.

"What thing?"

"The thing in your car," she said through her teeth, rolling her eyes.

The bartender said we owed her nothing. I left a five just to be decent. The snow banks by Route 9 still looked like snow. The cold pressed us to follow through. In Dad's SUV, I turned the heat up high. Before the heat could fill the space, we were mostly nude in the far back seat, humping strenuously among Dad's golf balls, brochures, Diet Coke cans and other detritus left back there. She was an aggressive girl, and I needed her more than I thought. When my eyes met themselves in the rearview, they liked what they saw. After, we lay back there, covered haphazardly by our own clothes

"Finger in the butt, huh?" Olive said.

"I don't know, it seemed like the thing to do. Was it too much?"

"No. It was just a surprise. It must be a New York thing."

"Must be."

Then we got quiet. We both refrained from more talk of our futures or our fathers or the terrible dread that inhabited our daily lives. So we had nothing to talk about. We lay there, waiting for the other one to prove that premise wrong. Finally, I kissed her and started putting my pants on.

"So what do you want to do?" she asked, while we dressed in the back seat.

"We can cruise around and get drinks somewhere else. Whatever you want to do. I do need to get up early tomorrow. The nurse is coming by to look at the apartment in the morning."

"Yeah. I have to get up early to see my dad before work. My mom is pissed that I didn't go today."

"Call it a night?"

"Sure. If you want to," Olive said.

Her face was a darkened mystery, only half illuminated by the cheap orange parking lot lights through the tinted back windows of Dad's SUV. Too much grief, too much anxiety and too much sex. We were separated by what had joined us. The sensation of distance and waste stirred in my abdomen.

"Yeah."

We made plans to talk and to meet and so on. She went to her heavily bumper-stickered old Volvo and drove off. I waited in the parking lot for her to drive away. It seemed like the proper thing to do. I sat a little longer and called Joe, but got his voicemail. I tossed the condom in the snow and pulled out of the parking lot.

Circling back onto Route 9, I headed west once more, past Mom's apartment complex, past the shut down trolley tracks, past the Clean Machine car wash, past Walter Dyer is Leather, past the Ford dealership between the Ford dealership and the Ford dealership, past all the car dealerships like bone marrow cleaning the highway's blood, past the McDonald's playground that promises a home in the trees, past the office park with its hundred small-time employers, past the Super Discount Liquors that rises up from the dissonant grid of an older town plan, past the motorist in the shabby car and the cop who pulled him over, past hills restrained by concrete walls, past Temple Plaza with its learning center and Chinese restaurant, past the Stop N Shops and Super Stop N Shops, past two dozen businesses hanging on by a thread, past the lakes with names and the lakes without names, past the Friendly's and the unfriendly people on the road, past the interchanges with state and interstate highways, past streetlights strung up like the highway was a party, past all of it.

38.
Tuesday, January 6

"Glad you decided to stop by," Dad said, muting the TV, which showed a mug shot of bedraggled man in half a Santa costume. Dad's voice was full of hiss and gravel, but obviously not so painful to use anymore.

"It's only noon. I was waiting for the nurse to come by. But I got the day wrong."

"What time did you figure that out?"

"You're pretty feisty today. How do you feel?"

"A lot of pain. At least I have some of my wits back," Dad said.

I could see him fight back a wince. He'd pronounced that final *k* a little too hard for his own comfort.

"They're still giving you medication for the pain, right?"

Dad showed a button in his hand that was hooked up to his drip of painkiller. He took a slow breath and started talking more calmly. If he wanted to start an argument, he'd have to wait until his stitches and his throat were less raw. That much was a relief.

"I'm trying to go easy on the meds. It's just one more thing I have to deal with later. You hear of these people who go in for surgery, what have you, and they come out with full-blown drug problems."

"That's good. But go easy on yourself. Anyway, when did you wake up?"

"Early. It was still dark. I never really noticed how bad TV is in the morning."

"Well, at least they opened the curtains."

"It's great. I can see the fucking clouds. It's riveting stuff."

"What do you want me to say? You do know you just got your chest ripped open the other day. You can either be patient or go crazy. I'm hoping for patient, but if it's crazy, then that's fine. But remember, I get power of attorney."

Dad laughed gently as he could manage. It still hurt, but he still laughed.

"Dear God no," he sputtered.

"That's right. I'll give you a little allowance."

He laughed a little more, restraining himself because of the pain. I laughed too.

"Trust me, I'll be holding onto my sanity with my fingernails."

Dad and I swapped conversation, watched TV and flipped through the magazines. Even when he drifted into a nap, it was good to know he was lucid and alive. How much his surgery weighed on me only became clear when the weight began to lift.

"Listen, don't get defensive, but I want to talk to you about that fight you got in," he said, apropos of nothing.

"Like I said, it was just a scuffle at a party."

"Still, you have to be careful with bar fights, anything like that. You never know who you're dealing with. You never know what they are capable of. When I was in the army, we were training down in Biloxi. Well, we had the night off, so we went to this honky-tonk not too far from the base. And this friend of mine, I'll never forget, this guy Reed starts chatting up this little Southern Belle. Well, one of the rednecks at the bar comes over and they get into it, and the redneck gets thrown out. So we leave a few hours later and this redneck is waiting in his truck with a shotgun. He doesn't say anything, just shoots Reid with a shotgun full of birdshot, which would usually just hurt like hell. But he hit him in the neck, and Reed bled to death in the parking lot."

Dad had a way of underlining his points boldly, especially when he drew examples from his own youth.

"I know. I'm careful."

"Well, be more careful. You really don't know who you're getting involved with. They could be friends of Joe, but that doesn't mean they're your friends too. It's better to just walk away. You have nothing to gain."

"I know."

The nurse came by to check on Dad, who announced to her that he had farted again. She seemed pleased and amused by this.

"They say to tell them. They're not supposed to feed you unless your bowels are moving," he said.

"You actually don't need to keep telling me," the nurse said, and left.

Dad's roommate stirred. His wife whispered something. Then he half-groaned something back. We paused to give their thin, sibilant exchange room to pass.

"So how are things with Serena?" Dad asked when the whispering stopped.

"They're okay. I mean, I haven't seen her in almost two weeks, so it's all over the phone, which I dislike. But it's one of those things. She gets a little pouty and I get annoyed and then we make up."

"Over the phone."

"Exactly. You see what I'm saying. She might come up next weekend."

"To the apartment?"

"No, I said I'd get her a hotel."

"I'm sorry. It's just there isn't any room. I think I'll be at the rehab place next weekend. But the apartment is probably a mess."

"I know. It's no big deal."

Then Dad, who had been awake for around five hours, started squeezing the button that released the painkiller into his veins. He had held the pain at bay as long as he could, for me, or just for some of the trappings of the thing called being alive. He got drowsy quickly and didn't hear me when I said good night. I paid Whiskeynose for the parking and hit the road, eager to go anywhere except Dad's apartment.

39.

Once on the road, I called Joe and we agreed to meet at the Wonder Bar, an Italian restaurant on Shrewsbury Street.

The Wonder Bar in Worcester was mercifully old and dark. The wood of the booths was darkened with the cigarette smoke and fingerprints of two generations. Brown soundproof tiles made the room feel dark and close. A silent old jukebox glowed by the bar like a neon hearth. Joe already had the gunfighter's seat in the back, facing the door. He raised his Budweiser when I entered. Our booth had a tableside jukebox. But it was out of order, with a wine list taped over where the songs would have displayed themselves.

Joe was wearing khakis and a plaid button-down shirt and his hair was back in a tight pony tail. The bruises under his eyes from the fight were clearing up more quickly than my black eye.

"Good call on this place. The beers are only two bucks," he said.

"So what's going on?"

"Just work. It's supposed to be pretty mellow until school starts. But my supervisor came up with all these new, useless jobs for me to do. And he's going to give me and some of the other guys in the office a new bullshit 'code of conduct' that we have to sign. How about you?"

"Dad's doing better. He's talking. We hung out today. So what's this about needing money?"

"Well, I ran into some problems. I need to pay off the guy I bought the coke from to get more so I can pay you back and some other stuff. I sort of screwed up."

"This whole thing is a screw up. If you're worried about paying me back, don't worry. If you cut your losses at this, you can pay me back in ten years."

"I still think I have a good idea with this. I just need to iron out some parts. And I am going to need cash on hand if this thing with Sully keeps escalating. But thanks for the offer."

"So what the hell happened?"

"This last part was pretty ridiculous, actually. I was out with Vietnam. He said he knew some guys in Leominster who wanted coke, and who would trade me a gun for some coke."

"Of course. What could go wrong?" I said.

A heavyset Italian woman came by and took our orders for beers and a pizza.

"Right? So, we have guys in Leominster, who also want to buy coke, who I've never met, and who trade guns. It sounds like the best idea since the Marshall Plan," Joe said, laughing at himself.

"Flawlessly conceived, as always."

"So, Vee and I drive out to Leominster and meet these guys at a bar. They have us follow them to this boarded-up shopping center. Now I'm scared because there's no one around, and we also look suspicious as hell. And the guys we're dealing with are these huge Irish guys with neck tattoos. What is up with neck tattoos, by the way?"

"It's a way of saying you never want to work indoors, I think."

"Right? So they sample some coke, and then they say they want to take the coke with them when they go to get the gun. I say no and they say, okay, forget about it then. So we go back and forth and I let them take half of what I was going to give them, which is like a little more than an eight ball."

"Which they just got from a stranger for free."

The waitress came back with my beer.

135

"See, I thought that. But I'm counting on Vietnam being good friends with these guys. But then I noticed that he reintroduced himself when we met them. So I asked, before I gave them the coke, and Vee said again that he was tight with them. So after twenty minutes sitting in this abandoned parking lot in God-forsaken Leominster, he says he actually only partied with them a few times, but they seemed like good guys. A half hour in, he says he actually only got drunk with them once, but they stayed out all night. After almost an hour, he says that there were a bunch of people out that night too, and that he might not know these guys that well."

"So many things don't make sense. But let's start with the gun. Why do you want a gun?"

"It was partially Vietnam's idea. Someone slashed his tires last week and he thinks it has to do with Sully. It's just for protection, like for the other night. If I was alone walking into that house, I would have been fucked. But there's a reason they call it an equalizer."

"Do they?"

"I think. Wasn't there a show called The Equalizer? Didn't he have a gun?"

"I think that the guy was The Equalizer. I'm sure there was more to it than just him having a gun."

"True. A guy with a gun isn't a great premise for a show. Not on its own."

"Anyway, what the hell happened to just laying low?"

"I'm trying to lay low. But look what happened. I mean, I really didn't expect that Rory would pull that kind of bullshit. I've known him for a long time. I guess, in hindsight, that he was a little scummy."

"Did he hang out at the YMCA back when we were in junior high?"

"Sometimes."

"I thought he looked familiar. He was a little prick back then. I remember giving him a bite of my candy bar once. So he licked the whole thing and then asked if I wanted it back."

"He always used to do things like that. Whatever. He'll get his."

The waitress came back with our pizza and we ordered more beer.

"So you want to borrow another three hundred to get a gun?"

"Well, first I want to get you your six hundred back, then I want to make some extra, then I may get a gun."

"By selling ... by doing what you were doing?" I asked. Again, my awkward impulse toward clandestine discussion made Joe smile.

"I know. It sounds like when we used to get a football caught in a tree, so we'd throw a baseball bat at it until that got caught in the tree too, so we'd throw a shoe and so on. But it's not. I just have to be cautious and disciplined and not try to make all my money back at once."

"What happened to getting out of town?"

"Well, now I owe money on the last batch I bought to sell. And the guy I bought it from is a friend who I don't want to let down. And except for a few places and a few incidents, I feel pretty safe."

"I don't know. I'm all for Joe Rousseau jumping Snake River Canyon on a head full of acid. But it seems like you're in a situation with Sully and them where it's just a matter of time before you get hurt."

"Maybe it's just a matter of time until Sully and his crowd gets hurt," Joe said and chugged at his beer.

"Well, by a certain way of thinking, it's just a matter of time before the mountains and the sea get theirs. That's not what I mean. By staying here, you risk being caught unaware or outnumbered. By getting a gun, you risk doing something you really don't want to do, no matter what you say. By keeping on like you're keeping on, you risk going to jail."

"Okay, here's where you're wrong. One, I think the Rory thing taught me to be careful and always go to non-public places with a group of people. Two, the gun would probably just be for protection. Three, I know what I'm doing and the cops won't be a problem."

Ira Volpe flashed in my mind so vividly that it took an effort not to speak his name. Joe and I argued until the pizza was half gone. The argument persisted for a while, without covering any new ground. I finally gave up, wondering whether I was trying to convince Joe to let up or to convince myself I had done all I could.

"So, can I borrow the three hundred?"

"I don't know," I said.

Joe started in again, his voice full of incredulity that I hadn't been completely swayed by his earlier arguments.

"I mean, I don't know if I have the money. I should get my last severance check this week and I have to see how much it is after taxes and COBRA. I may have to borrow money from you," I said.

It was a lie, and Joe seemed to know that. But he left it alone.

We finished our pizza and headed over to his apartment. The place was tidier than usual, and too hot. Marissa was watching TV in the living room. We said hello and went into Joe's room. I sat in his old desk chair and leaned so far back it seemed dangerous. Joe dug out a book he'd just read about Rommel and handed it to me. Then he got a phone call. Like any neglected friend in the cellular age, I took to picking through his stuff. He had a big, army-style footlocker. The lock was off, so I opened it and found a mess of fishing supplies, magazines, photos, action figures and, occupying one end, a stack of pictures of naked women printed off the internet. They were all Spanish with big cans—more-perfect copies of Escalita. On the phone, Joe went on and on into his cell phone about who was who, where they were, who they knew, what kind of people they were, how long they would be there.

"What's up with all the computer printouts?" I asked as soon as he got off the phone.

"Oh. I print them up at work."

"You go find the pictures on the internet and then print them up and take them home?"

"Yeah. It's incredible, I mean," he said, walking over to the footlocker. "Here, check out this woman."

The grayscale toner on the office paper couldn't diminish the smoky beauty of her Latin face, nor the enormity and spherical perfection of her breasts.

"I mean, Jim, someone somewhere on this same planet gets to fuck her. Just try to get your brain around that!"

"I'm sure that there's also someone who's totally sick of her. Imagine that."

"He must have already fucked her."

"Who was that on the phone?"

"It was a friend who wants me to meet someone down at the Dive Bar. They want some stuff."

"So you know this person?"

"No, but a good, good friend is vouching for them. Do you want to come down with me?"

"All I'm hearing is Leominster Part Two. I mean, it's a Tuesday for God's sake. Let this one go. I don't think you can keep counting on people's good will the way you're used to."

"I think it's cool. If you don't think it's cool, then you should definitely come and get my back."

Joe squatted and unlocked a desk drawer. From it, he took one of three little tied-up wads of cellophane.

"You're locking it up now?" I asked idly.

"I'm not altogether sure what's up. But some people complained about light bags. I didn't think that Marissa would take any of it for herself. But I'm not sure. I'd rather lock a drawer than be wrong and lose a friend."

Marissa gave us a little wave from the couch as we left. The nighttime had clenched the air into a deep freeze that would crust the snow to ice.

Following Joe's Skylark, we crossed all of Worcester's asymmetry to Green Street. The ebb crowd of a Tuesday night filled the Dive Bar. I scanned the crowd for a face I'd recognize, looking for Sully or one of the guys from Rory's apartment. I spotted Kyle. Like Joe, he had taken a hit to the nose, and wore a bruise that spread to both his eyes. He was chatting up a Chinese girl with tattoos on her arms and a graceful beer belly. Joe went the length of the bar to find the person he was looking for. I stopped to talk to Kyle.

"Jim, I'm glad I'm not the only one who got marked up in that scuffle. I told the guys who work for me that I got hit with a football outside my house."

Kyle gave proper rhetorical time to *guys who work for me* and *my house* for the benefit of the Chinese girl. It seemed he had won her over enough for him to talk with me for a minute.

"Scuffle? It was more like a freaking ambush. What the hell was that?"

"That was the ass-whupping Joe had coming to him. We just got in the way, and got paid for our trouble," Kyle said.

"Well, fuck it. I'm glad we were there. One of them had a billy club. It didn't look like they were just looking for equal justice."

Kyle had a way of retreating into himself before he spoke. Maybe it's because he'd grown up a small guy and had to rely on his wits to get what he wanted. He retreated then.

"Don't get me wrong, I love the guy like a brother. And I know he's smarter than most people. But sometimes the dude is just an idiot. Did he tell you about Saturday night with Willie Brown?"

Kyle proceeded to tell me about how Joe and he were at Denny's after a night at the bars. Joe went out for a smoke and met a black guy in a big white winter coat.

"So Joe's like 'do you know who this is? This is Willie Brown.' And Joe says the guy is a legend in Great Brook Valley, and that he can get Joe a gun. But, the guy needs a ride back to the Valley, because his girlfriend took his car to go to the hospital or something. He had some story. Joe's my ride, so we go to the Valley, and Willie Brown says he knows a place to get Joe a gun—all because we gave him a ride."

"That sounds like a fair trade," I said, and paid for my beer.

"So anyway, we give Willie Brown stops into this building and then that one. And the Valley, you know, it just sucks. It's five degrees out and there's all these crack heads standing around trying to sell us their jeans. There's a fucking dumpster on fire. After a few stops, Joe says 'I don't think he's going to get us a gun.' Willie Brown is just making deliveries and we're driving him around. But Joe won't let me just ditch the guy. Finally, we get to this one building that no one is even *parked* near, with most of the lights on."

"What the hell?"

"Right? And Joe's my ride so, I'm stuck. And it's gotta be at least four. So Willie says that he wants us to come in to this last place with him. I park where the other cars are parked, far a-fucking-way, and we walk over. Inside, it's like a horror movie, like night of the living dead. And Joe whispers to me 'this is an actual *crack house*,' and starts cracking up laughing."

"So what happened?"

"Joe had this thing, like it was important to be polite to Willie Brown. So after the crack house, he said to forget about the gun and then made up an excuse and we dropped Willie off at one more place. Speak of the devil."

"Kyle, Shona, what's up?" Joe said, reinvigorated. "Let me buy you all a round and a shot."

"Someone tell Tarzan that it's Tuesday," Shona said and smiled.

Joe bought a round and few more shots. Drunk, we drank until too late for a Tuesday. It was a good time, laughing about old times and people we knew or didn't know, laughing at Joe, and telling stories. It gave me a break from the growing sense that I had a terrible choice to make.

I drove mindful of the vigilant suburban cops of Shrewsbury and Westborough. A Walgreens and a CVS were still open, reassuring the traffic that with cough syrup and potato chips, Route 9 cared like a mediocre mother might. Eventually, I pulled into the Fountainhead.

That night, I dreamed of boarding a ship and leaving too many things behind, leaving my pants behind and leaving my name behind.

39.
Wednesday, January 7

The buzzer was a surprise for all of a second. I buzzed the nurse up and mouthwashed away what I could. The housekeeper had been in the day before, but I was a less presentable sight, my face unshaved, my eye blackened, my clothes slept in, and my repartee off by a too-detectable half second from the hangover.

Sometimes people just don't like you and there's nothing you can do about it. Joyce, Dad's nurse, was a good example. In her early middle age, Joyce was neither attractive nor unattractive. Attractiveness was irrelevant for her right off the bat, like it might be for a fire truck. I took her around the apartment, pointing out the bathroom railings like I was showing a report card. But the black eye had decided it for her. She told me what she would and would not do and looked at everything in the apartment except me. Joyce was clearly a vital second income somewhere, and I was one more obstacle in her day. I took her disdain to mean that she would do her job. She left before I had the chance to wake up much. I was glad to see her go.

I turned on the TV and slept until around noon. Still hungover and at a loss, I wandered the internet. Aside from the naked ladies, there was no encouragement there. The responses to my resumes and follow-ups all promised to keep me on file, and precious little else. Each form letter to my inbox was a tiny little kick in the balls. The e-mails from friends were no better—recaps demanding recaps in return, or jokes requiring jokey responses. Serena's e-mail was within the same parameters of automata seeking reassurance. I reassured.

Eventually, I left the apartment. The day was one of those dreams where I couldn't run, despite myself. My shirt took seven months to put on and my time with the toothbrush lasted longer than World War Two. It was two by the time I parked at the hospital.

"Hey, what happened? Did the cable guy come by again?" Dad said when I showed up. It came out lacking humor, despite his effort. He smiled up the corner of his mouth so it looked like a sweater caught on a nail.

"Sorry I'm late. I had the nurse come by and then I sent off some more resumes."

It was, overall, a bad day at the hospital. Dad was taciturn and in pain. We sat most of the day in the hateful silence that descends on two people watching TV with too much or too little to say to each other. I knew that silence well. It had crept in and destroyed my parents' marriage. Watching it, you wouldn't guess anything was wrong. It's so unexplosive, like the rain that seeps into cracks in the road and expands with the cold. It's the least dramatic thing in the world, but it tears the road to shreds after a decade or so. I begged out around six-thirty and followed the traffic back to the Fountainhead, stopping at an ATM on the way.

Once in the apartment, I took off my pants and looked out the window at the flattened landfill and the lit plastic signs on and around it. I tried to imagine the woods full of Indians that burned Marlborough in King Philip's War. But the cheap aurora borealis blasting out from the Wal-Mart parking lot lights rebuked me.

"Hey," I said into my cell phone.

"Oh hey, what's going on?" said Serena.

"I just got back from the hospital and wanted to talk to you," I said, trying to inflect some charm into my voice.

"I just got back from work, actually. It's so cold outside. Some people from the office wanted to go out for drinks. But I cancelled. I think I'm getting the flu. Actually, I was about to call you, it's about the weekend after next."

"Yeah, you're coming up, right?"

"Well, I just heard from my mom. I guess my cousin Andrea is coming into town to visit NYU, and she wants to stay with me. So, can we reschedule for the weekend after?"

"I guess so. I haven't booked the hotel yet. Let's figure out a date."

"Can I call you about that next week? I have to ..."

Through her voice, I could hear her roommate, or someone, moving around in the same room, then a clatter of dishes. I poked the bruise under my eye to feel at least that. We talked some more about our daily lives, giving our recaps. The automata was reassuring, a dubious bridge over an unfathomable uncertainty. I told her about Worcester and Joe, saying only he was in trouble with some rough customers. She listened, but didn't have much to say beyond that being *too bad*. She had lived in New York almost as long as me. *Too*

142

bad was our response to a beggar on the sidewalk, or a drug addict holding up his pants as he limped quickly down the street. It was sympathetic, but terse. I didn't bother getting into my dilemma and said I'd call later in the week to figure out a weekend for her to come up.

I dialed Joe, but hung up before it rang. Then I did the same to Volpe. I called Olive, but she didn't answer. I sat down and stood up.

40.

I drove the short distance to Shrewsbury, down familiar streets with neat houses and yards full of child-trampled snow. I pulled up to the house we had moved to when I was in high school. An older couple had bought it. The walkway was shoveled, but the snow in the yard was untouched. The house across the street was unlit, so I idled in the street by it for a few minutes and eyed my onetime home.

With Dad's SUV suspiciously idling on the silent suburban lane, I recited my dilemma, hoping it would become clearer to me. First off, Joe's always-dubious plan had gone off the rails. And in the absence of a plan, blind forces take over. Coincidence, accidents, mistakes, forgetfulness, recklessness, alcohol and unconscious urges wind up deciding how things turn out.

What I could do was give Joe the money, and then tell Volpe about his stash of cocaine. That would get Joe off the streets for a stretch, keep him from buying a gun and give the feud with Sully time to cool off. Or, I could give Joe no money, tell Volpe nothing and hope it all worked out. I saw the curtains move in my old home and drove off.

In the end, I suppose I couldn't bear the thought of one more thing being out of my hands. Pulling into the parking lot of Hickey's Liquors, I called Joe.

"Hey, I checked and I got that last payment from work. I can lend you the money."

"That's awesome. Thanks a million."

"Yeah, no sweat. I'm in Shrewsbury, where are you?"

"I'm home, come over. I swear, I'll get you the whole thing back as soon as I can."

I passed St. Johns High School and slowed down on my way to do its bidding in the worst possible way. I fortified myself with the memory of Sully's ambush at the party, with the news of Smitty beaten into the hospital, with the image Joe waiting in an empty Leominster parking lot for a gun. The danger seemed real, but what did I know? Joe had tangled with dangerous people and put himself in dangerous situations before. And he'd always found his way out, if not smiling, then only damaged in temporary ways. The snow on the St. Johns athletic fields was pure and undisturbed.

Joe greeted me at the door. His hair hung loose and he was wearing a bright yellow t-shirt. We went into the kitchen. He was eating pasta with crushed tomatoes out of a Tupperware container. He offered me a plate of it. I said I already ate and asked what was going on.

"Just hurting. Man, work was no fun today. You ever have one of those hangovers where it feels like your bones are broken? That and my boss told me he needed me to, what was it? Yeah, he wants me to 'take ownership' of this whole bunch of bullshit busywork scanning old parking violations. I never even wanted to do it and now I have to 'take ownership,' whatever that means. It's not like I'll ever benefit from it. But I was so zoned out I just nodded. What's up with you?"

I told him about Serena cancelling, Dad being surly and the live-in nurse being the antithesis of a Spanish girl with big cans. Then I said I had the money for him.

"Just tell me you're not going to buy a gun with it," I said.

"I'm most likely not going to. We'll see what happens. By the way, did you hear about Matt O'Brien?"

"Who?"

"The guy who held horses mouths open for a living and beat me with a chair that one time at Tortilla Sam's, with the crazy tattoo on his lower back."

"Yeah, the nut job you kept taunting on the phone."

"Him, well he killed two guys and almost killed another guy over at the Palladium. I heard he was trying to rob the place, but he shot the manager before the guy could get the safe open. It was after a show and he wanted the gate receipts. So he shot the three guys, couldn't get into the safe and then couldn't get out of the club. The cops had him at the door," Joe said, satisfied and vindicated.

"Jesus Christ. That's no joke. But, please man, promise me that you won't buy a gun with this money."

Joe took me up on this offer to be serious for a moment.

"I promise."

I gave him the money.

"I promise not to use this money to buy a gun," he said, holding up the folded bunch of twenties I'd given him. He smiled his devilish grin.

"Just be careful," I said.

"Careful's my middle name."

"It's more like your fucking antonym."

It was funny that something as abstract and bookish as an antonym could exist in same lives we were living. We chuckled. For a moment I could forget what I was doing there. I started telling him about my job hunt and the frustration of pleading for so many jobs I didn't want.

"Well, that's what it was always seemed like they were pushing us towards. The nuns, St. John's were all getting you ready to efficiently do things you'd rather not do," Joe said.

"I guess so. But what else are you going to do?"

"There's hanging out. There's getting drunk. There's getting laid."

"There's all that. But it doesn't add up to much."

"What's it all supposed to add up to?" Joe asked. The tone in his voice said he was gearing up for an argument.

"Some sort of purpose or accomplishment, some sense of moving forward."

"Forward to what?"

"To more responsibility, more authority, more money, to things getting more interesting."

"And so it's authority, responsibility and money that make things more interesting?"

"They can," I said, making a really poor case for how I'd spent the last decade or so, and having a hard time of it. I thought of what it was like for a Praying Indian, just before King Philip's War, questioned in the woods by an old friend.

"That's not my idea of interesting," Joe said, shrugging, putting on the imperturbable smile that was his argument-face.

"Well, I have no choice but to work. And it kills the time," I joked.

"It kills more than just the time."

"Well, it's just civilization. It may not be much, but it seems to have beaten out the competition for now."

"True, true. I guess that makes us its discontents."

"Pretty much. They didn't mention that one at career day."

"The discontent bit is more like a hobby than a career. I'm too tired after work to do it more than an hour a night, unless I'm drinking."

This was the Joe I loved—sober, focused and funny. It was one who I had seen less and less of since high school.

Escalita showed up. She had a way of passing through a room, a grace I hadn't noticed before. She radiated a strange sense that everything, even the things she had no way of knowing about, were as natural as the rain. I rose and she kissed my cheek hello, leaving a wake of sweet perfume behind her. Joe gave her a plate of pasta and poured his own portion on a plate as well. I said I should go, that I needed some sleep. I walked out into the cold and over to my car, feeling terrible, and relieved at the same time.

41.

Parked outside Joe's house, I called Volpe. He sounded busy and irritated and said he could meet me either in three hours, just after midnight, or on Saturday. I said midnight at the same diner and he agreed.

I drove to Vincent's and drank at the end of the bar. The whiskey made my face unclench and my mind wander. I followed that impulse until I was more than a little drunk. The patrons were a mix and there was no single answer as to what was going on in that place. In the car, I practiced my sober voice, and then drove to the Boulevard Diner. I ordered some eggs and coffee to mask the whiskey on my breath. Ira Volpe showed up just after the eggs. He looked bone tired and pale, almost yellow. He hung up his coat on the hook over the booth and gestured for a coffee.

"What's up?" he said.

"Listen, I've been thinking about what you said. And I've heard some things that I don't like. If I were to tell you something about Joe, maybe enough to get a search warrant, could you try to keep the charges down to a misdemeanor?"

"You been drinking?"

"A little. Is that a problem?"

"No. If I wasn't on duty, I'd have one with you. This week fuckin' sucks. You hear about that psycho killed three innocent people at the Palladium?"

"I did. Three?"

"Well, it's three now, another one just died. My boss is on all of our asses to do something, but he doesn't seem to know what."

"I heard about that. It's a shame. Joe knew that guy, the killer, he used to prank call him."

"That sounds about right. Your buddy sure knows how to choose his enemies. So tell me, is Joe in enough trouble that it's worth him getting a record and maybe going to jail for a few months to get him out of harm's way?"

"It might be. But is there any way he could just get like, a house arrest? Maybe just for a few months. Can you rig that if you were ... Well, before I say anything, can we talk off the record?"

"What does that mean, like we say things and then pretend that we didn't say them?"

"Yeah."

"It depends on what you say."

I drank my coffee and decided that being in this far, I might as well continue.

"So say there's a guy who had about three hundred dollars worth of cocaine. If you knew where it was enough to get a search warrant, could you still look all over the apartment for it before you found it, so he wouldn't know who told you?"

"I guess so. But if the person who told us was just fucking around and warned his friend, that person *and* his friend would lose *all* of my goodwill. Is that off the record enough?" Ira asked, more tired than angry.

"Okay. Now, do you know a judge you could talk to who could recommend house arrest?"

"It's not unthinkable, if the guy didn't have a record, or if he wanted to give some people up. After this O'Brien nightmare, we all just need to make some arrests out there."

We negotiated from there. Ira acted more confident about his promise of house arrest with every detail I gave him. So I kept on telling him details, including the locked desk drawer in Joe's apartment. Ira went out to his car to get some forms for me to sign. I hadn't occurred to me that I'd have to sign anything. I picked at my eggs for what seemed like a long time before he came back into the dining car. He had the carbon-paper forms mostly filled out. I started reading the carbon paper pages, but almost got sick about three quarters of the way down the first page I was supposed to initial. I knew the phrase "Confidential Informant" from cop shows, so that wasn't what hit me. I flinched when I saw that Volpe had checked a box pertaining to my payment. It said "$30." After that, I stopped reading and just initialed, initialed, initialed, signed and signed. After that, he gave me a voucher for my payment. Then he got up and put out his hand and we shook.

"You're doing the right thing here."

"I hope so. Just hold up your end, please."

Volpe said he'd try and left. I pushed my plate away and wondered why you can't ever take back anything you do in this life. I wished I was drunker. I paid and drove through downtown, up Highland Street, then down Park Avenue to an Irish bar. I went in and knocked back a few drinks among the solitary men watching *Cheers* reruns on TV. I watched the bottles until they cleared the place at quarter to two. From there, I drove down the road to Emily's apartment. When you have problems, make yourself someone else's problem—it's an old trick.

I buzzed until her roommate, Aileen, came downstairs. I told her through the door to tell Emily that Jim was there and needed to talk to her. Emily came down, dressed in pajamas and a bathrobe and let me in. On the ground floor, I started to apologize and explain myself, but she disarmed me with a sideways cock of her head and told me to come upstairs. In her apartment, she sat me down on the couch, then went into Aileen's room to explain things to her. Emily finally sat down next to me on the couch.

"So Jim, what's wrong?"

I told her everything, starting with my meeting with Volpe, then about Sully, the ambush, Leominster, Willie Brown. I was drunk and full of doubt and rambled on about Olive, about the terrible sense of waste and helplessness that I couldn't shake. I told her about Serena cancelling, and about all the sounds in the background of her phone calls. She listened patiently.

"I know that waste feeling," she said. "It's like there's something or someone in front of you that you can't touch. And the more you look at them, the farther you get. I don't really know what it means."

For a moment, I felt understood. My nerves, which had been flapping in the breeze all week, grew still. I leaned in and kissed Emily. It felt right. She waited a second or two before laying one of her small hands on my collarbone and gently pushing me away.

"Listen Jim, I'm glad you're here. And I'm glad you told me all that. But you know us. You know that this isn't that."

I nodded and sat back on the couch, by turns befuddled, embarrassed and relieved. Emily left the room for a minute and came back with blankets and pillows and made up the couch for me. She gave me a long hug and said good night.

On the couch, I looked at the window-shaped patches of light on the ceiling and wondered if the world wasn't a makeshift hospital where the doctors and patients kept changing places.

Part Four—War Town and Worm Town

But a small part of the dominion of my ancestors remains. I am determined not to live until I have no country.
—Metacomet, also known as King Philip

42.
Thursday, January 8

I fought waking until a square of light fell directly on my face. Emily was reading a thick book about Alexander Hamilton at the kitchen table when I sat up from the couch. My whole body vibrated with the ache of hangover. Pretty, in jeans and a big sweatshirt, she looked up from her book without moving. Her roommate wasn't around and the apartment was very still around her. The dust danced in the sunlight. I got up slow.

"I thought I should let you sleep. You seemed pretty wasted last night."

"Yeah. Sorry about that, and sorry about the other thing," I said and hoped I wouldn't have to say more.

"It's okay. After all these years, you get a pass."

"And tell your roommate I'm sorry I woke her up. Am I covered for apologies?"

"For now," she said and smiled.

"What time is it?"

"Ten," she said, which by her inflection was late, but by my reckoning too early. I burped up a little whiskey and grimaced.

"So what do you have planned for today?"

"I promised my advisor I'd read all these books over break and I am way behind. So I have devoted my day to Alexander Hamilton's early plans for industrializing America. You want some breakfast?"

"I don't know. Yes?"

"I have eggs and oatmeal."

"Maybe some oatmeal. My stomach is a little jumpy."

She started making the oatmeal at the stove. I blinked, at home for the first time since I had come to Massachusetts. I opened the book on Hamilton for a look, saw the word *tariff* three times in a paragraph and closed it. The wood grain of the old kitchen table was more my speed.

"So I was thinking about what you told me about Joe. Did you really talk to that cop, Ira, last night?" she said, stirring the pot and then turning around.

"Yeah, I even filled out some forms, so he could get a warrant. I did all of that."

"I think it's a good thing you did."

"If it works out. Otherwise, it might be the worst thing I could have done."

"Regardless, you did something. You're looking out for the guy."

Pulling up the sleeves of her sweatshirt, she poured the oatmeal into a bowl, then retrieved a box of brown sugar from a cupboard she could barely reach and sprinkled it over the oatmeal. The dust in the sunlight swirled when she walked over with the bowl.

"This is a situation where good intentions may not matter. I just hope I'm not being misled here."

"Obviously. But still, it's a good thing. I think it had to be done, and done by one of his friends."

"Well, the only thing I can do now is warn Joe. But I can't even do that. Fuck."

"Back when I was at Smith, a group of my friends hung out with this kid from town. His real name was Jaime, but he called himself Brando. He was a few years older than us and always knew where to find drugs and parties. We met him when we were freshmen and he was a funny, self-deprecating guy. He might have been gay, but he wasn't out. He'd get us coke and X and we'd have a lot fun. But by the end of my sophomore year, he started getting bitter, even violent sometimes, and we just stopped returning his calls. Sometime in my senior year, he hung himself. I only heard about it a few weeks later. But I always wonder what I, or anyone, could have done, if someone, anyone, had been looking out for him. I mean, where were the people who cared, who could have stopped him from getting to that point, from doing what he did?"

"It's the million-dollar question: How do you get between someone and their self-destruction?" I asked, eating again.

"It's one of those things. I don't think you can. But I think you have to try. Do you ever go to church anymore?"

"Hardly at all, maybe once every few years. Catholic school cured me of it. Why, do you think I should get the diocese involved?"

"No, it's just the idea of trying to help people, to change people. It reminds me of church, of all that steadfast effort for impossible things, like turning the other cheek, or just having faith. I started going to Sunday Mass again last year, almost every week. I don't think it gives me much peace, but it gives me a proper place to be honestly uneasy about all the impossible things, all the things that are out of my control."

I finished my oatmeal. We looked at each other and both knew it was time for me to go. Outside, the sky was a clear merciless shade of pale blue over the dirty snow and sandy streets. Back on Route 9, I considered going to a Mass, then thought of the pale wood and bad art of the modern churches. It made the whiskey churn in my belly. Passing a shuttered mini-golf course, I smelled myself and decided not to stop into the Fountainhead for a change of clothes. Coffee and gas later, I was in Dad's room. There seemed to be fewer tubes and wires going into his gown. He was napping in front of the repeating stream of cable news. He woke suddenly when I went for the TV remote cradled in his forearm. It took him a minute to get his bearings. We talked in sputters and spurts.

"I like that shirt," Dad said.

It was a polo shirt with brown and blue stripes.

"Thanks."

"Did you have that on yesterday?"

"Yeah. I guess I did. I had a late night."

"You've been having a lot of them lately. That's a good thing. You should have some fun. I didn't mean to sound like I was giving you a hard time the other day. This place probably makes you want to blow off some steam. So who's this girl?"

"Who?"

"The one you've been going out with?"

"Oh, I don't know what's going on there. I just met her a week or so ago. It's funny. I met her here."

"In the hospital?"

"Yeah, you can store that one away for when you start dating again. The food sucks, but the ICU is full of vulnerable chicks."

"When I was your age, I could go out any night of the week and take a girl home. They weren't always gorgeous. But any night of the week."

"When was that, 1970? Everyone tells me that was a good year."

The little hospital TV filled up with a computer-animated mushroom cloud full of bullet-pointed factoids over the Manhattan skyline.

"You really need to get a job," Dad said when the commercial came.

"Really? I had no clue. I was just sitting around, twiddling my thumbs and waiting on the salary fairy. Thanks, really. Thanks for the fucking tip."

"Hey, hey. Take it easy."

"Me? I am taking it easy. But why don't you tell me to eat? Why don't you tell me to breathe? That's not exactly advice."

"Fine. Forget it," Dad said, lowering the corners of his mouth so his eyes widened, the implication being that I overreacted.

In my experience, overreacting is sometimes the correct thing to do. I looked across the room and noticed that Dad's roommate was gone. The curtain was pushed round to the wall, and the bed awaited a new customer.

"What happened to the old guy in the next bed?" I asked.

"His cancer spread. They moved him to a hospice."

"That's one of those places they put you to die?"

"Pretty much. I'm stuck here until Tuesday, the doctor said. I don't want another depressing roommate."

"He wasn't so bad, except for the dying. He didn't talk anyway."

"Yeah, he was fine. But his wife, Jim, you didn't hear it—she would start saying the rosary when you left. I mean, not even whispering. And I'm here, trying to sleep, so I clear my throat, but she keeps at it. So I ask her to stop it. She ignores me again. So finally, after twenty minutes, I buzz the nurse and I tell her. The nurse tells her to pray more quietly."

"I guess she was distraught."

"Oh, that's not the half of it. When the nurse leaves, the woman starts praying out loud again, so I yell at her to shut up and buzz for the nurse. So the wife comes over and pulls the curtain away and points at her eye and her neck and then at me and makes a hissing noise. It was the strangest damn thing. Here I am and I can't even wipe my own ass, and now I have this crazy woman putting a goddamn gypsy curse on me."

"I thought she was a Catholic."

"Catholicism is different for women, it's all about hexes and candles and bribing the saints."

"Fucking witchery," I said. We both started laughing at the perverse tableau of Dad harassing the soon-to-be widow, and me accusing her of witchcraft.

"I'm just saying, why can't I catch a break? I know it's a hospital, but can't I get a less-depressing roommate? Why can't I get some nineteen-year-old sorority girl after her boob job?"

"I don't think they give those to guys who just had open-heart surgery. Insurance and whatnot."

"I'm just saying."

"How's the pain?"

"It's okay. It's just in one section in my chest, well, the upper half of my torso, well, most of my torso, shoulders and arms, and neck. The point is that if I just don't think about it, it's pretty manageable. But it wears me out. I think I sleep about fifteen hours a day."

Dad shook his head. He looked old, but somehow identical to how I remembered him from when I was a kid. His hair wasn't gray and he had a mustache then. His cheeks were less baggy back then, and not so full of red capillaries. His eyes weren't as crowded by folds of skin and his eyebrows weren't as wild and overgrown. But I had to work to recognize the differences. Something was so much the same that it mooted everything else.

"Hey, if you're going to the cafeteria, I could go for a Diet Coke," Dad said, smiling at his failed attempt at subtlety.

I said okay and got up. The hyperbolic voices of the news anchors exploded into life before I was two steps away. I ran into Dad's friend Robert in the hallway, waved and said I'd be back in a few minutes. The cafeteria was crowded, so I wandered like a kid in a new high school looking for a place to eat lunch, with my tray of chicken nuggets, soft pretzel and Diet Cokes. I spotted Olive at a table by the cash register.

"Oh, hey," Olive said, looking at me flatly.

She was wearing jeans along with a black top that had too many straps to make sense at first glance.

"Nice to see you too, sunshine."

"I guess that was supposed to be you being charming."

"I'm sorry, did I shoot Morrissey while I was sleeping?"

"Hardy har," she said, and smiled despite herself. But she flattened her mouth and deadened her eyes almost immediately.

"Hey, really, what's going on?"

"You should have called."

"I thought I did."

"No, you should have called before that. I was going to call to tell you. But I figured you'd probably take a few days to call me back if I did."

"Okay. Well, I didn't say I was going to call and you didn't ask me to," I said, sensing where this was headed and hating myself for adding to the momentum.

"Never mind. I didn't think you'd understand."

"Well, I've had a lot on my mind. Believe me. I am trying to keep so many balls in the air right now that I can hardly think. I have a best friend who is going to get himself killed in a blood feud, a resume that's not getting read, a mom I keep meaning visit, a girlfriend who's forgetting my name day by day, a bank account that's eroding with every fucking pretzel and hospital parking ticket. Basically everything is swirling down a big toilet bowl. It's all spinning away and so if you want, fine, I am fucking sorry if I didn't fucking call."

In the midst of my outburst, I had shoved my soft pretzel across the table and onto the floor. Olive leaned over and picked it up. She put it back on my tray and made a gesture as if to dust it off. She looked at me. She bit her lip, and her eyes looked like they were getting dewy.

"So what is it? Is it your dad? Did he get worse?" I asked, softly.

She shook her head. Emboldened by my rage and her vulnerability, I did what I had learned many times before not to do.

"Is it your period?" I asked.

She nodded and laughed a little, a tear shooting across the mascara barricade and down her face.

"I was going to tell you to go fuck yourself," she said, laughing a little through the tears.

"I'll bet you were."

We got up and embraced. It was a hospital, and emotion wasn't out of place—just Catharsis Day in Cafeteria B. She watched me eat my chicken nuggets and the dusted-off soft pretzel. We made plans for her to come over later and then left. We kissed good-bye before parting for our respective dads' wards.

Robert and Dad were talking when I got there. Dad was wearing his brave face. I remembered it from an office Christmas party when I was nineteen, a big event held at a hall in the Boston Ballet. As we entered the already-full party, Dad turned to me and said "Watch me work the room." He had that face on. It was happy and ready for everything, except maybe honesty. I pulled up one of the chairs and gave Dad his Diet Coke.

Dad and Robert talked on about old co-workers—who was where, who lost a spouse and who gained one, who went back to school and who went back overseas. By the time Robert left, I was as tired as Dad. I could tell by how he squeezed the handle in his hand that Dad was doing his late day run on the pain medication, calling down the curtain on the day.

43.

I drove back down Route 9 like an idle child scribbling the same line over and over again in hopes of tearing the paper or destroying his crayon.

At the Fountainhead, I showered, shaved and dozed in front of the TV. The buzzer gave me enough time to rinse my sleepy mouth out with Diet Coke before Olive came up. She was dressed sexier than she'd been at the hospital. We gave an honorable amount of lip service to the notion of going out for dinner and drinks before we made love on Dad's bed. We ordered Chinese food and did it quickly on the floor of the living room before the delivery guy showed. Each screw shut out the day before and the day to come a little more.

We ate spareribs and made fun of the unfortunate coeds being slaughtered on the pay-per-view horror movie.

"You'd think a boob job that retarded would at least protect her from a lawn dart," Olive commented on the film.

"Well, thank God they outlawed lawn darts. Now you can only find them at the most diabolic of yard sales."

"Really? We always had lawn darts," she said, stripping a string of meat off the rib. Her face shone in the flickering blue light of the darkened living room.

"They must be old. When I was a kid, someone chucked one over a fence and killed their neighbor's child. So there was a campaign and they outlawed them."

"People are such pussies. It's like when I get in my mom's car, the fucking thing starts beeping like crazy just because I didn't put my seatbelt on. It's like all the whiny pussies won some war."

"Keep talking and I'm liable to fall in love."

"I didn't think they told you about love in your little cubby hole in New York City. I thought it was all fuck-and-run and onto the next hip thing."

"I guess. But I did hear about romance during one long, cold winter I called my childhood. And I almost killed someone with a lawn dart when I was a kid. So I'm not going to fight the Trilateral Commission of Pussies on that one."

"Really?" she said, putting an egg roll into her mouth in a way that excited me.

"I was at a birthday party, in the third grade. This kid, Tony something, was up in a tree and he called me an asshole. I looked down at my hand and it had a lawn dart in it, so I threw it at him. It missed his face by an inch or two."

"You're a dangerous man, with your grammar school attempted murder and your yuppie brawls."

"Oh am I?"

I paused the movie and we were at it again, this time over the inflatable bed. Then more Chinese food and more gore, a little slice of pig heaven.

"So what is this?" Olive asked at last.

"I don't know."

"We fuck, trade snarky comments, and commiserate over our damaged fathers. That's all?"

"Sounds like three out of three to me."

"But what about your *girlfriend*? And by the way, nice job sneaking that into your little tirade this afternoon. And what about you not calling?"

"I mean, we met in the ICU. So when that's over, will just we decide we don't need each other? I don't know, and it's not because I haven't thought about it. I really don't know how anything in my life is going to work out at this point."

Olive didn't say anything. She just looked down for a minute, and pushed herself closer to me on the couch. We ate more Chinese food in the flickering blue TV light that means safety and relaxation to most of the industrialized world. And sometime between the heroine's last stand against the undead madman and the movie's credits, I surprised myself, if not Olive, with a fourth time on the rug. I remember thrusting inside her and stopping, as far inside of her as my honest Irish penis would go.

"Come *on*," she said.

"I just want to be inside you, to stay there a minute."

"That's not what this is," she said, bucking her legs and arching her body against me.

44.
Friday, January 9—Sunday, January 12

I woke with fried rice in my navel to the sounds of Olive rooting around the apartment. I wondered whether to act awake or not. It sounded like she was having trouble finding one sock in particular. She leaned down to give me a kiss good-bye. I heard the heavy wooden front door of the apartment swing shut with a squeak and a slam, and then heard no more. When I really woke, two hours later, it was because I couldn't breathe. My nose was clogged and my throat was tight. A long hot shower left me not much better. I moved through the apartment as if it was full of water, and was winded by the time I cleaned up the Chinese food. I had a wicked cold, as they say.

Sniffling sick, the next three days passed without vivid sensations. The sounds grated, the conversations dragged. I saw Dad at the hospital, saw Mom at her apartment and fended off her attempts to cure the incurable common cold. I drove like an old man, too subdued for all the machinery rushing around me. I watched football and football highlights until I hated football. I piled blankets over myself and watched the people on TV do their asinine thing for a grateful nation. In an exhausted and sleepless twilight, my eyes unfocused themselves for hours on end, lost in the eyeball noise of the TV. Each sniffle and cough affirmed my withdrawal from e-mail, from the gym, from the phone.

I called Olive to say I was sick and that's why I might not answer her calls. She asked if she should come over. Then I gave Serena the same call. She said to get some Echinacea and drink a lot of fluids. I withdrew again to my bubble of fever and flickering. It seemed like something more than a cold, more than a mild flu, was at work. A huge wave of exhaustion had crashed on me. It was an excuse to not be altogether there in the hospital, or with Mom, or with the TV.

After a few days drifted by like a dream of nonexistence and sweatpants, I wished the sickness would continue. Sunday, the Patriots won their way to the AFC Championship. I watched it in the hospital with Dad and Gerry. I was sweating and so feverish that I actually thought their victory might benefit me in some way.

Sunday night, after a nap, I woke more normal than I'd prefer. I watched highlights from the Patriots game on a half dozen channels and couldn't figure out why I had thought myself so blessed a few hours earlier. Stinking with sedentary sweat, I pulled up the blankets and tried to unfocus my eyes, but the TV was telling me very definite things—things that reminded me I shouldn't watch so much TV. It meant I was getting better. I stayed under the blankets until it was uncomfortable. Then I picked up my book on Worcester and read for a few hours.

They don't write too many histories of middling cities. A lifetime Worcester local wrote the book, trying to loosen the grip that cold, plain irrelevance had on the city. I flipped forward to the slim section on post-war Worcester. The city's population fell by thirty thousand people between 1950 and the end of the century. The histories of middling cities tell the story of how fortune can take you halfway and leave you there.

Take Route 9, take Worcester—the hand of God touched neither, nor does either place have much you can't find elsewhere. It's not the home of the lost tribe, nor the site of Olympian grandeur. So why care? They are defeating questions to ask about any place or about any person. I couldn't answer it, and that was my answer—I too was irrelevant. Maybe that was the reason for the rage of the New Englander.

With such thoughts gathering, my phone rang.

45.
Monday, January 12

I didn't recognize the number, but saw it was from the 508 area code. And 508 is where it all started. This thing that encompasses everything I know, everything I can imagine. This thing that I'm told is common enough to pass without remark. This thing called my life began in the 508 area code.

"Jim, where are you?" Joe asked immediately.

I could hear a car engine and muzak behind him.

"The fucking Vatican. Where do you think? It's like three in the morning."

"It's four. Can I come over?"

"To the house, my dad's place? In Westborough?"

"Yeah. I'll explain later. I'm in trouble and I need to figure out what to do. Can I come there for the night?"

I gave him the apartment number and hung up. I looked out the window. Route 9 was empty and the sky clear, with a half moon hanging over it all. I thought of the distance to Worcester. The problem was distance, always distance. The distance was too much to make its stone-strewn farmland worth the trouble, then too far off to bring troops in time to chase out the Indians, too far to bother fighting the British over. My phone rang again. I didn't recognize the number.

"Is he with you? Don't lie to me," Ira Volpe said over the phone. I could hear a smattering of voices behind him.

"What are you talking about? I'm fucking sleeping. I have the flu."

"Joe Rousseau. We waited and waited for your boy to come home and he never did. We finally executed the warrant. Did you warn him off?"

"No. I've been comatose with the flu the last two days. I haven't spoken to anyone but my dad and his friends at the hospital," I said *hauspital* like it was a magic spell. The phlegm lodged in the back of my throat had forced the proper Massachusetts pronunciation on me.

"You better not be jerking me around, or our deal is off and I will make sure your boy goes into the darkest, deepest hole in all of MCI. If he calls, tell him to turn himself in. Then call me."

"I will. What did you find in his apartment?" I asked him.

Ira paused for a moment, taking a breath as if to speak, then hung up on me. My hiatus was over and I was back. Joe showed up wild-eyed with a plastic bag full of beers. His hair was out of its ponytail and hung almost to his shoulders. I was still in Dad's sweatshirt and sweatpants, unshaven and pale. I guess I looked like even more hell than that.

"Jesus, you having a nervous breakdown?" Joe said as he edged into the apartment.

"Just the flu. What's going on? I'm not an accessory after the fact, am I?"

"Only if I tell you what I did."

"Cute."

"What's the matter, man? Is this a bad time? I can go somewhere else. Actually no, I can't," Joe said, cackling.

"Sorry man, I'm just sick. I'm glad you came out."

We sat down on the couch and Joe opened a beer. The can was big and had a picture of a cartoon alligator on it. He offered me one and I passed. He asked me what I thought of our president elect. He was a man that a quarter of adults liked, a quarter didn't, and half couldn't be bothered to vote for or against. There was more to it than that, enough to debate, and we did. It was normal talk, a tea ceremony in a besieged town. Joe finished his alligator beer, took a deep breath and looked at me plainly.

"So, the story is that I may be going to jail. The cops busted into my apartment with a warrant and found my stash. It's not a lot, because I sold most of it over the weekend. But it's enough for distribution charges, probably. Marissa called when I was at Escalita's and told me. I'm trying to figure out what to do."

"Jesus. Well, what are your options?"

"I was thinking them over on my way here. I have about six hundred dollars on me. Is it okay if I wait to pay you back?"

"Sure. That's fine. So what are you thinking of doing?"

"That's the question. Running doesn't make much sense. My money will run out and they'll find me if I try to get another job."

"You could stay at my place in New York, figure things out there. But I don't know if the picture will be much different. You should call a lawyer, see what you're up against, and then figure things out from there."

Joe opened another can and looked around the apartment. He leaned back on the couch and nodded his head.

"This place is nice. It seems well built, well maintained. You can smell the paint and the carpet glue in the hallway."

"Is that what that is? I just thought it smelled like warm plastic."

"Man, why can't you just like things?" Joe asked me.

I opened my mouth to answer, but had no answer for my mouth to make.

"My bad attitude toward Dad's apartment is not the most pressing issue right now," I protested, and we returned to the age-old question of fight or flight. Neither prospect looked good.

"It's all connected now. With the internet and just the kind of checks they do when you apply for a job, open a bank account, rent an apartment or even buy a stereo, they would find you."

"There's got to be another option. I'm just not thinking this through," Joe said, rubbing his face.

"It's almost six, let's get some sleep. You can stay here for a day or two. I don't know how hard they're looking for you."

Getting up, my head spun. The flu still had a hand in me, and I steadied myself on the arm of the couch. I went to the room I occupied and dragged my inflatable bed out into the living room. Joe was already spread out on the couch when I got back. I turned off the lights. It was a sleepover, like when we were kids.

"I hope I don't get put in a cell with Matt O'Brien," Joe said.

"You won't."

"Remember that girl Barbara?"

"Maybe. When were you with her?"

"When I was a bouncer at the Lucky Dog. The Dominican girl with an ass like a shelf, and super nice. Remember we e-mailed about her? You told me to tell her about the genital warts."

"Oh yeah. You really liked her," I said.

A car pulled out of the Fountainhead parking lot below, and a rectangle of light collapsed as it crossed the ceiling of our shared darkness.

"When she went back to D.R., she wanted me to go with her. I wish I had. None of this would have happened. I am a fucking moron."

"Well, you probably had your reasons for not going."

"Yeah, I guess. She was getting jealous and generally not letting me have any fun by that point. I think she went back as part of an ultimatum. But maybe she saw this coming in her own weird way. She was a smart girl. She would know what I was thinking before I did sometimes."

"It's not that hard to figure out what you're thinking most of the time."

"True, true. Still, I wonder what might have happened if I'd gone with her."

"Don't beat yourself up. You probably would've found a way to get yourself into trouble down there."

"Thanks, buddy. You're a ray of sunshine over there."

"I'm just saying. Being some other place doesn't change who you are, or the type of things you do."

"True. True. Character is destiny, as the Greek said. But do they have an extradition treaty?"

"The Greeks?"

"No, the Dominican Republic."

"You can look it up tomorrow," I said, with sleep beginning to slur my words.

46.

Joe snored like a hippopotamus sauntering through a wood chipper. But I still managed to sleep until noon. Through his guttural rumbling, I shaved and showered the last of the sickness off of me. Well if not strong, wary if not anxious, I drove off into the cold, bright Monday. Volpe called, sounding tired and beaten as I drove past the Cineplex wedged into the joint of Routes 9 and 135.

"Did our boy call?" he asked.

"He did, but he didn't leave a message."

Volpe just hung up. I had a sense there was something I wasn't seeing, wasn't considering. The feeling lingered like an uncleaned room. Other state highways merged with Route 9 and vanished, each listing towns with English and Indian names, every name a tale of age-old misapprehension.

In the hospital, Dad had a new roommate, an obese guy not much older than me. His thick legs were wrapped tight with gauze and elevated. He watched everyone who passed the room with bulging eyes, uncomfortably aware. I pulled the curtain behind me and sat down by Dad.

"The new guy makes me nervous," Dad whispered.

"Me too. And I talked to the plastic surgeons. They said they couldn't get you a fresh bimbo until tomorrow. The weekend is slow for boob jobs."

"As long as you checked," Dad chuckled.

Then the new roommate got a visitor. She was just a little bigger than him. They started whispering about something, probably us. There was no other news in the hospital. Dad thought one of the night nurses had a crush on him, and that the TV networks totally misunderstood the reasons for the latest crash in the markets.

"Is everything okay with you?"

"Yeah. I'm just getting over this flu. Why?"

"Because one of the nurses said a detective called and asked if I was staying here."

The walls tightened, making me again a child trying to hide his misdeeds from his father. I reminded myself to keep my face slack until my mouth could find words.

"Oh. I think I know who it is. Joe said a detective was trying to get in touch with me because the cops wanted to talk to one of the guys from the night we got into that fight. It's nothing. I'll ask the nurse for his name and call him back."

I stopped myself, knowing how a lie tends to ramble.

"I just want you to know that if you're in trouble, and you need help, just ask. You aren't alone. Divorced or not, there's nothing your mother and I wouldn't do to help you."

Shame is the word for it. I felt like I was breathing a rainstorm.

"I'm not in trouble. I'm just, just doing the best I can here," I said, unable to mask myself.

From there, we talked about the Patriots, about his transfer to the rehab facility, about his friends, before finally letting the TV say our nothing for us. I only stayed a couple hours with him that day. I said I needed some rest, and left. Back at the Fountainhead, the apartment was a mess. I put a bag of take-out Chinese food by the inflatable bed in the living room. Joe was in his boxers by the computer.

"Hey, what's up?"

"Just looking up state sentencing guidelines. You know there's not a single source for finding out online. Someone should put up a website," Joe said.

"A website with criminal state statutes probably doesn't cater to the most lucrative market in the world."

"True, true."

I told him about the take-out and went into Dad's room. Without bothering to shut the door, I flopped face down, half on the mattress. I opened my eyes and saw a brown stain the shape of an hourglass. Smelling the stain, I figured it was Olive's. I imagined the cost of new sheets and cursed the indefinable thing that made things happen like they did, then drifted off to sleep. When I woke an hour later, Joe was yelling into his cell phone. I couldn't make out what he was saying, only that he was talking to his mother.

"I know ... But listen ... I don't think they can fire me unless I'm convicted ... Whatever, I'll get another job ... After that, I mean ... Okay, you don't know what you're saying ... there's a *huge* difference between two years and a suspended sentence."

I grabbed a cold egg roll and waited for him to get off the phone. I watched some muted TV, while Joe debated around the edges of the only choice he seemed to have. He promised his mother he'd call her back and hung up.

"Shit. Shitty shit chunks on shit bread with shit sauce and a side order of shit-fried shits. Shit," Joe said, sitting down next to me, somehow smiling at his predicament.

"Good news?"

"I have to turn myself in."

"Tonight?"

"Nah. It's late. I'll do it tomorrow. That way I can get in, get processed, get bail and be out that night. I just have to look at it that way. It's like going to the DMV."

"Except that instead of renewing your drivers' license, they're plotting to take away your freedom," I said.

"That's the kind of difference I'm trying not to think about. I'm focusing more on the DMV-like aspects," Joe said and laughed.

"So tomorrow?"

"Yeah. I have to. The cops keep calling my mom."

The fried rice was open on the TV table. I took it and leaned back, kicking my feet up on the inflatable bed. It was still early, but dark and cold and devoid of any promise outside. For the next few hours, we traded fantasy escape scenarios and speculated about what ignoble snitch had told the cops about Joe's very recent, very small, and mostly unprofitable side business, and wondered why they would do such a foul thing to such a decent and beloved guy as him. Maybe I could have been honest with him that night. Maybe.

"Man, I keep thinking about when I got suspended, back at Venerini. I still remember Sister Maria telling me to stay behind after she gave you your detentions. She said it all businesslike, like it had nothing to do with her—that I was just no damn good," Joe said.

"She was the worst. I think it was a setup. Why did they let us sit next to each other at Mass? It reeks of entrapment by that calculating, ice-in-her-linty-cunt Sister Maria," I said.

"True. I remember Sister Maria telling my mom about all the stuff I had done, and suddenly I just relaxed. It was like, well, I am a bad kid and my punishment has arrived and there's no use fighting it anymore. I could just sort of go with it after that. I feel a little like that now, like it's just out of my hands."

We talked until it was late, then turned the lights out and talked like in old sleepover days, him back on the couch, me on the inflated bed. It was mostly old-timey stuff, about girls in junior high, about St. John's, and then finally about jail.

"There was Mike Marsh, he went away for carjacking, remember him?"

"Yeah. I almost got roped into a gang fight with him and some other guys once."

"He got out and he was never the same. The first week he was out, me, Mike and Kyle were at a party and he starts saying how we all thought we could beat him up. We were all telling him to chill, that we were just hanging out. Then he punched me behind the ear and kicked Kyle in the stomach and ran out."

"Didn't he try to kill someone after that?"

"Two people, a guy and his fiancé. He stabbed them each forty times. Just fucking nuts. But the knife was too small and I guess they both lived. They picked him up for having an open container at Hampton Beach a week later. He's gone for a long time."

The apartment had thick concrete walls and nothing broke the long silence that followed. I thought of the dead ends so many of those kids had run into, and thought of the bluster and enthusiasm with which they'd run into those dead ends. We can all spot a dead end—a rat in a maze can do it. But we do not all agree on which ends are dead. I thought of Joe, of my exit interview at Bigelow.

"Well, get a lawyer and play ball," I said. "Stay out of jail. If they offer you a deal, take it. I don't care what bridges you burn. You can skip town, stay with me in New York, go to the D.R., whatever. It doesn't matter as long as it's not jail."

"Man, I can't snitch. The guy is a friend. You remember Walshie?"

"The guy who had his hand shot off?"

"Yeah, he's an old friend. He gave me the coke at cost because we go back so long. He's only dealing in the first place to get the money together to go back to school."

"You know, it's great that he's your friend and it's great that he wants to go back to school. But in the final equation, I don't care about him. Your mother doesn't care about him. Your future cell mate and your future employer doesn't care about him."

"I don't know. Loyalty has to count for something. And I always felt bad that I got so wasted that night and had leave when he got his hand shot off. I always thought I could have done something if I'd been there," Joe said, trailing off at the vague and impossible idea of *doing something*, which sounded, at that point, like something between a fantasy and a flat-out lie.

"You shouldn't have gotten involved with this stuff. They make things like loyalty and decency impossible. Look at Rory. He traded you in, maybe even to be killed, for a few nosefuls of that shit. And look at the guy who turned you in, he was probably facing the same trouble you're looking at. This isn't *The Godfather*, and the only reason people talk about honor among thieves is that there isn't any such thing. You can disagree, but look at the fix you're in."

Joe said nothing. And I had no more to say. Sleep found a foothold, took over and plumbed the depths. I had a dream about a long conversation with the devil. But I can't remember what we said. There was pale girl sitting next to me who became paler and paler the more we spoke, and there were souls flying over the houses of Worcester to somewhere in Africa, looking down at us.

47.
Tuesday, January 13

Joe was gone when I woke. He had folded the sheet and blanket and rearranged the pillows on the couch. In the apartment and the hospital parking lots, the air smelled like smoke, like it always does before a snowstorm. The sky was heavy and gray with a dull shine, like a wall made of pearl.

In Dad's hospital room, the fat guy with elevated legs was there, but Dad was gone. Imagining death, escape, or emergency surgery, I rushed over to a nurse. She reminded my father's half-negligent son with the still-visible black eye that Dad had been moved to the rehab center. I asked where the rehab center was and she rifled through a file, then a drawer and came up with a Xeroxed page of directions from the hospital to the rehab center.

The rehab center was off a quiet street in Marlborough that I passed twice before spotting the street sign. It was a brand new building that looked like a massive suburban home. The old woman at the front desk had me sign in and then told me that Dad had gotten in four hours ago and I was the first visitor.

"Just please take me to his room," I said.

After making a show of just how long it could take her to straighten the papers on her desk, the old lady and I walked a series of hallways to Dad's room. Whoever ran the place had laid the décor on thick. Paintings of duck ponds and old white churches, of sailboats and Cape Cod sand dunes covered the wallpapered walls. Every few feet, the hallways had alcoves with telephones to call for help and little baskets of dried flowers. The homey touches ended at Dad's room, which differed from his hospital room only slightly. It had the same rolling TV-trays, the uncomfortable, uninviting chairs and the little TV suspended by an adjustable arm from the ceiling. Dad seemed upset when I got in. After a distracted hello, I realized that it wasn't me he was mad at.

"Fucking TV."

"What's the matter with it?"

"It's like a hotel TV. They only give you like twenty channels and then they charge you like twelve bucks to see a movie on pay-per-view."

"Doesn't insurance cover it?"

"Maybe in your dreams or in Sweden. It's just a fucking rip-off."

"Well, the room is nice. There are some woods outside the window. You can watch the snow fall."

"I'm going to complain to the management."

"You okay today?"

"Yeah, it's just that they changed my medication the other day. I'm constipated and I'm having trouble sleeping."

"Sorry I was late. I got turned around on my way here. Then I couldn't find the street this place was on."

"That's fine. They made me do the physical therapy for an hour today. It was *embarrassing*. I couldn't hold my hands above my shoulders without help. It hurt like hell."

I repeated all the things the doctors had said about patience, about healing, all the things you say when it isn't your body that has broken down in ways you can't believe or accept. Out the window, the first flakes of the coming storm scouted out the backyard and the gray trees beyond it.

"Maybe I can get you a DVD player, they're only like twenty bucks. Or maybe some paperbacks and magazines. Maybe you can focus better with the new medication."

"Yeah, maybe. Pick up some magazines tomorrow," Dad said, flipping through the stations faster and faster. "I don't even think I get ESPN on this fucking thing."

I watched the network news with Dad. Countries signed agreements, fighter jets destroyed a series of buildings, billions of dollars sloshed here and there. The news anchors sang their songs for people who had just gotten in from work, to help them understand the small part they had played, and where the next knock might come from. It smoothed over the chaos and uncertainty that lay ahead in Joe's bail hearing, my unsent resumes and Dad's convalescence.

Sometime after the news, Dad's dinner came. It didn't look much different than the hospital food, except that the portions were bigger.

Dad faded and I said good night. I drove through the dream that the snow made of the roads. The flakes fell like notes in a fugue under the streetlights, and slapped the windshield with the irregular and too-fast rhythm of misfortune itself.

I opened one of Joe's alligator beers left in the fridge. The pale light of the kitchen made the chaos of the living room sadder. Kicking the inflatable bed out of my way, I sat on the couch and called Joe. My call went straight to a recording that said his voicemail was full. Squinting, I recalled the number and dialed his mother, Justine. I always liked her, but hadn't seen her in a few years. We exchanged pleasantries and recaps, then I asked about Joe.

"Well, I drove him to the police station early this morning. Never mind the shame of it, I had to take a day off work for his bullshit. So I have my book to read, and I'm waiting around and waiting around and finally, I see that everyone is leaving the courtroom where they're holding Joe's bail hearing. So I find a bailiff and I ask him 'what's going on?' and he says that the judge has cancelled the rest of the hearings for the day because of the storm. And I say it's not even snowing outside yet and I point to the window. And I know this judge, he's an old man who lives out in Barre and always shuts down early so he can drive home before the roads get bad. So Joe is going to have to stay overnight."

"Jesus, that sucks."

"Well, he should have turned himself in right away. Not only would he be out by now, but his bail would be lower. He already owes me five hundred bucks for car repairs."

"You must be able to talk to someone in the court to get his bail lowered, you must know someone."

"Sure, I know everyone. But after twenty years as a parole officer, I don't want to go around and advertise the fact that my son was arrested for selling cocaine. I'm actually glad he's doing a night in jail. He won't listen to sense. Don't get me wrong, Jim, I'm going to do everything in the world to keep him out of prison. But he deserves a night in jail," Justine said.

On her end, I could hear her pour out a bowl of kibble for her dog. She was a tough lady, free-spirited and bombastic, a break from the constant caution and concern that defined so many of my friends' mothers growing up.

"I don't know. You're probably right."

"Jim, I know you're his friend. But I see this every day. I know how it works. The innocent don't wind up behind bars too often or for very long. Usually by the time someone is arrested, it's the tenth or the twentieth time they've done the thing they were arrested for. I just hope this will get Joe to grow up. I used to tell him all the time—that it looks like fun, just hanging out and getting high, but he'll leave himself without any options. Of the people I deal with at work—the ones who aren't morons or sociopaths or totally screwed up by the people who passed for their parents—most just woke up one morning after years of hanging out and didn't think they had any choice but to do the dumb thing that got them locked up."

"I guess so. But what do you do after you get locked up?"

"Some people can turn it around. I don't know why some do and some don't. I see some of the dumb ones make smart changes and some of the smart ones just get dumber," she said and paused. I couldn't figure out what to say. "Oh, God, how did this happen?"

I couldn't answer. I tried a mixture of repeating what she had said and something I didn't believe.

The snow filled up the edge of the balcony outside. On the TV, the network stations scrolled weather warnings across the bottoms of their shows. I put a can of soup in a pot and turned on the stove. I called Volpe, but he didn't answer. I passed the rest of the snowy night eating soup and watching TV. I slept on the inflatable bed, which lay where I'd kicked it.

48.
Wednesday. January 14

Too lazy to shovel, I spent five minutes getting the SUV into four-wheel-drive to drive over the low snow bank that had trapped it in its spot. I drove to Tatnuck Bookseller.

The old Tatnuck in Worcester had been a mainstay of my teenage years. It occupied a massive former factory. Its bookshelves shared the old rough-hewn wood floor with saurian industrial machines too big to be worth removing. But it had closed down a few years ago, and then moved into a shopping plaza in Westborough. It's always a little painful when someplace you've grown attached to closes down. But it's almost a personal insult when people try to pretend that it's part of a larger improvement. I jumped the snow

171

bank and went inside the new Tatnuck. I winced under the fluorescent lights and walked past the section full of wind chimes, candles and doodads, grabbed five or six sports magazines, along with a couple news magazines and went straight to the cash register.

At the rehab place, Dad and I passed the hours until his physical therapy. I didn't want to be there for it and I didn't think he particularly wanted me to watch. It was a short visit.

The snow had made the landscape as bright and hopeful as Christmas. Caught at a red light, I watched children sled from a hilltop apartment complex down into the parking lot of a bowling alley in Shrewsbury. The fresh snow made Route 9 into something more than just its petty cadging for a buck. It rose and fell, over foothills for a mountain that never came.

In Worcester, I found the streets that would take me up the hill to Bancroft Tower. The tower was an eighth of a medieval castle, built from the large rough stones that made Massachusetts such a foul place to be a farmer. One of Worcester's old time aristocrats, a Salisbury, built it for another, a Bancroft. The low tower was square and the high one narrow and round, both ridged with toothed battlements at their tops. I parked by it and looked out. The hills of Worcester concealed the city from itself, obscuring a full view of downtown from most angles. I pushed my hands into my jacket pockets and walked over to the towers that were not useful or beautiful. The cold insisted I move at a half-jog to inspect it.

Beneath its jagged arch, I looked in the locked gates at the low mat of old leaves, a solid padlock kept from the public. The tower was one of those anomalous parts of Worcester like the statue of a boy screwing a turtle in downtown, the Coney Island Hot Dogs sign, the huge Polar Cola polar bear overlooking the highway, Spider Gates cemetery by the airport, the six-way free-for-all intersection at Kelley Square, the Gothic clock tower of the abandoned mental hospital on top of Belmont hill, the Blackstone canal buried beneath downtown, the old neon 'White City' sign, the Hebert Candy Mansion, the street signs proclaiming Gold Star Boulevard by the armpit of two Interstate highways, East Park with its granite winged lions in front and the huge cliff rising behind it. They made the city, usually so prosaic, seem like a dream on the verge of revealing an impossible meaning.

The cold made me jog back to the car, stopping only to read the inscription again. "This memorial was built by his friend and admirer Stephen Salisbury, III." Back in the car I wondered at friendship. I wondered how it could matter, how anyone could matter to anyone else in a world ruled by the blind forces of power, money, fear, hunger, horniness and boredom. I turned up the heat in the car and looked at the city, all white below the unruly branches of trees and the plowed-brown roads. The life below fought through the frost with snow plows and mail trucks. I considered my day and my reasons for driving back to Worcester. And it seemed that friendship was one of the only things that did indeed matter. I called Joe, but got the same recording. I sat in the SUV and wondered what to do with myself. I called Marissa.

"Jimbo Monaghan, did you hear about Joe?"

"Hear what?"

"My God, it was crazy. Like ten cops came busting in the other night and tore our apartment apart. It was nuts. I guess someone told the cops what Joe was doing and they got a search warrant. It's totally crazy. They said they were going to come back and arrest me. But then Joe turned himself in."

"Has he gotten out?"

"I think he's getting out later today. I talked with his mom. She says she shouldn't bail him out. But she totally will."

"How much trouble is Joe in?"

"I don't know. The cops seemed pretty serious. But I don't think they found that much stuff. I'm hanging out at the apartment if you want to meet up."

Marissa opened the door for me at the apartment and cleared some papers, clothes and pieces of broken furniture off the couch so I could sit. She said she had rum and tap water if I was thirsty and I opted for the water. The place was every bit the wreck Marissa said it was. She had cleared a path through the debris between her room and the bathroom, but not much else. I said silent little thank you to Volpe for making it look like he didn't know exactly where to search.

"The place is such a friggin' wreck that I've been staying at my mom's place the last few days. I am going to clean. But anything that's not mine or that I don't use, I'm just going to throw in Joe's room. I mean, this is totally his fault," she said, turning a chair upright.

I shrugged my assent and she picked through the mess. I tried the remote, but the TV wouldn't turn on. Marissa made little piles from the clutter and cursed to herself. She returned a bookcase so it was flush against the wall and started replacing the books, pausing to take out a photo book. She sat next to me with it. It beat cleaning.

"This totally sucks. He was hardly even doing anything. Why the hell did someone drop a dime? It's such a shit thing to do," she said.

I nodded. Above the clutter, next to the TV was the old bloody hole in the wall from the struggle with Sully. You could just see the outlines of the blood stain and a pink cloud from some half-assed scrubbing. From where I sat, the stain looked as old as the Constitution. In her picture book, Marissa came to one of Joe shirtless, standing gut out in a big grass field full of cars and people dressed in bright-colored clothes. Joe was smiling with his eyes half-lidded and his mouth agape.

"That's from Reggaefest, a few years back. If we ever should have gotten arrested, it was then. Me, Joe and Rich Papadopolis went in on two hundred ecstasy tabs that we were going to sell there. We hid them in a hollowed-out loaf of bread. We thought we were slick. But our ride, this guy Keith, totally flaked and left without us. And I forget why, but all we could rent was a U-Haul. So we drive the U-Haul up to Vermont. I think we were about a hundred miles away from Reggaefest when the U-Haul broke down, and it like, really broke down. There was smoke coming out of the hood and everything. We ended up getting a ride to a service station from a state cop. We must've driven like fifty miles in that cop car with just this loaf of bread. The cop probably thought we were crazy."

"Jesus. You brought the loaf with you? How did it work out?"

"We made it to the festival, sold all the pills and got high as balls. Then when we got back, Rich complained and got his money back from U-Haul. He's good at that stuff."

Marissa jumped up from the couch and went back to cleaning and cursing. I thought of leaving, but couldn't come up with a good reason or a decent place to go. I leaned my head back and willed the time to pass. Finally, Joe and his mother came in the door. Justine's shoulders were coiled, as if ready to punch someone—likely Joe. The left side of Joe's mouth was bruised badly and his lip cut. His hair was wild, barely restrained by a rubber band.

"Jim, what's up?" he said, smiling.

"Nothing. Just thought I'd swing by. What happened to your face?"

"I'll tell you in a minute. I have to shit like you wouldn't believe."

"Well, that's a great way to greet your guest, Joseph," his mother said, while Joe walked off.

Justine shook her head and picked up a chair to sit on. She wore blue jeans and a thick wool sweater, knowing the futility of dressing up for a bail hearing. She said it was good to see me and then went full-bore into the drawn-out debacle that the day had been. Her eyes bulged with exasperation as she talked about the cruel indifference of the criminal justice system and what she did to bend its ear. She squinted as she laid bare the specifics of Joe's bail.

"So finally, they give Joe his belt and his wallet. And we can go. But I want to talk to someone to file a complaint. I mean, you saw his face. I think we have legal grounds, even if another prisoner did it. They have to monitor those cells."

"So did you?" Marissa asked.

"Well, Joe starts telling me to just forget it, that he has to go home and shit. He's practically yelling it. I tell him to just shit in the police station, but you know how he is. I tell him to wait anyway, but he goes around me and asks the desk sergeant to call him a cab, then he asks me for *cab fare*. The whole thing was just squalid."

"So what's the story? Is Joe going to jail?"

"We have another court date in two weeks. They gave Joe a lawyer. But he doesn't seem that sharp. I know some lawyers and I'll start calling around to see if I can get some kind of deal. I'd really like it if Joe could stay out of jail without bankrupting me."

Then Justine and Marissa, two of the people who loved Joe most in the world, started in, verse for verse and chapter for chapter, about his selfish, disrespectful and pig-headed ways. With some practice and a great deal of effort, I might have been able to get in a word edgewise.

After a half hour of, we all paused at the sound of the toilet flushing down the hall, then they resumed. The toilet flushed again a few minutes later. Then the shower started. Joe walked out another half-hour later in a towel. His mother, then Marissa, yelled at him to put on some clothes. He retreated to his room, and took his sweet time before returning dressed in a pair of slacks, a red t-shirt and a pair of boots.

"Joe, you're going to help me clean up, *right*?" Marissa said, her voice more bombastic than plaintive.

"Really Joe, Marissa shouldn't have to clean up any of it. It's not her fault that this place was torn apart," Justine added with all the momentum of the last hour's bitch session.

"I'm going to take care of it. I just got out of *jail*, so just give me a minute. Just leave it, really," Joe said and smiled, just to make sure they were riled.

"No. This mess is your fault and you should clean it up now," Marissa said.

"She's right."

Maybe they were right. But I had the gnawing sense that I'd wind up cleaning too, unless Joe stuck to his guns. I raised my eyebrows in solidarity with him. Joe looked around, nodded and went into his room, returning with his car keys and coat.

49.

"What are you doing?" Joe's mother asked.

"Jim and I have to go out for a minute. We'll be right back."

"Where are you going?" Marissa asked.

"Just out, for a second. We'll be right back."

Joe nodded at me and I nodded back. I had no idea what he had in mind.

"Joseph, where are you going?" Justine asked.

"Just out. Jesus. Take it easy. I'll be back in a minute."

"Two cars?" I asked as we crossed the deeply dug pathway across the shallow front yard.

"No, I'll drive," Joe said.

We hopped into his Buick Skylark and started driving. Down Main Street, past the nightclub where Joe's old nemesis had killed three people just about a week ago, past City Hall, and into Main South. Joe stopped at a light, switched on his turn signal, paused, and then decided to keep going straight.

"Where are we heading?" I asked.

"Lincoln County Road or Armageddon," Joe said, but didn't laugh. He just stared through the windshield at the sparse city traffic as we neared Webster Square.

"I don't care. You just gave me a scare with that blinker in Main South."

"I guess I gave myself a scare too. I know where Sully lives now. I found out the other night. I keep thinking it was him who called the cops."

"Sully?"

"Yeah. But it doesn't seem right. It just doesn't add up."

After Webster Square, we hung a right onto Route 9 and went west, toward Amherst and New York State. I didn't think we were making a run for it. If we were, we would have gotten on the Mass Pike. And anyway, we weren't in a road movie. We weren't in California. No matter how much we raged or how what we might try, we were in Massachusetts and Massachusetts was in us. And Massachusetts is not wide open. Trees and hills tightly circumscribe its sky. Massachusetts doesn't say you can be new again. It's historic like a haunted house. Even the Pilgrims just kept on with their old willful miseries, in a glacier-scraped land where farming was hard and the winters worse than home. The snow banks turn brown and the cold shuts down five out of six things you'd like to do on a given night. In Leicester, the high snow banks crowded its two westbound lanes into one.

"Up ahead is the dead man's curve. It's famous," Joe said.

"Well, then be sure to speed up. I'd hate for us to be the guys famous for making it crippled man's curve."

And there it was—Joe's magnificent, inappropriate, unstoppable, and for the moment, life-threatening, laugh. It took him over like a fit of glossolalia. The laugh always came with an invitation to join him in its weird ecstasy. I joined, but watched the road, for fear that he didn't.

"If you have to do that, pull over, or at least slow down."

That just made it worse. He could barely keep his forehead off the steering wheel, he was laughing so hard. But he did slow down. The rest of that night, we saw a hundred dead man's curves and crippled man's curves, and laughed at every one.

"So I have to ask. What happened to your face? Was that the cops?"

"No. The cops were pretty nice, for the most part. They were mostly just annoyed I took so long to turn myself in. This," Joe said, gesturing to his face "was all in jail. Jail was a nightmare."

"What happened?"

"It wasn't anything like you've heard."

"Not all rapey?"

177

Joe wanted to laugh at that one, but didn't.

"Actually, it almost was a little rapey. After the judge cancelled court for the day, they shipped me and a bunch of other guys out to the county jail in West Boylston. I was in a four-man cell with two other guys. One was an older guy who kept combing his hair with his fingers, then patting it down. I saw him rub a loogie into his hair to keep it in place. He said he was in for his political beliefs. But that obviously wasn't the case, which I'll get to. The other guy was this black kid, who I got along with at first."

"At least you had one friend."

"Well, that's what I thought. So me and this black kid, whose name is Kane, we get to talking. We're getting along really well, talking about the places we hung out and stuff like that. But then we start talking about people we both know and I figure out that he's Ki's older brother and he figures out that I'm *that* Joe, Joe Rousseau. For a minute, I thought we were going to get in a fight. But we agreed to leave our differences outside the cell for the night. Jail was bad enough. They gave us baloney sandwiches for dinner and I tried to get some sleep."

"So far so good."

"Yeah, good, right until I wake up with the hair-comber guy's hands rubbing on my package."

"Oh shit."

"That's right, it got rapey. And this was just jail. They say that jail is nothing compared to prison."

"It's not a great introduction to penalized life."

"Well, I hope it's the entirety of my penalized life, except for those other times. Anyway, I feel his hands, so I wake up in a flash and punch the hair-comber on the side of the head. He runs off to his bunk and starts howling like a monkey. Then Kane is awake and he's pissed and asks why I beat up the hair-comber. I try to tell him what happened and he's not buying it. Now, Kane isn't a big guy, but he surprises me by punching me in the stomach, so I'm already sucking wind. I grab his neck and he starts hitting me in the face. Then I get him on the ground and I'm banging his head into the concrete floor and the hair-comber is going absolutely berserk. He's making sounds that aren't even human. So there I am, throttling Kane to death and looking over my shoulder like '*what is that sound*?' Then the guards come and ask me nicely to stop attempting to murder Kane, and I do.

He didn't have to go to the hospital, so they didn't have to fill out any forms, so I just got put in a cell by myself."

"Sounds like a posh arrangement."

"Compared to being locked in with a weird pervy dude and my worst enemy's friend's older brother, it was the fucking Holiday Inn. But even in the new cell, there were guys across from me, snoring and talking and moving around, so I couldn't take a shit there. You hungry?"

"Yeah, let's stop at the next place."

There were a lot of trees, stone walls, town squares, cemeteries and a lot of silent, snow-crammed lanes branching off into the darkness, but not a lot of places to eat. Occasionally the road would open up straight for a moment and we'd be surprised by a windshield full of stars. The shadow and the orange glow of the streetlights played off Joe's face. I think it was in the middle of Spencer, some town that's ninety-nine percent darkness and snow, that we passed a big, granite World War One memorial obelisk by a stop sign.

"Look at that," I said.

"What?"

"The World War One memorial there—just imagine all those goobers from Spencer who signed up, who left the trees and wood-frame houses of their safe irrelevancy to be slaughtered in Flanders."

"I can relate. I'd risk a lot to get the fuck out of Spencer," Joe said.

"I think about war sometimes, how it makes sense for the kids who fight it. It's just being pissed off and wanting a place in the world. The army gives you something to tide over both of those impulses."

"After nine-eleven, my friend Paul Girardi joined up. He was a pissed-off guy before that. He also said that it was like he wanted to either exist or not exist. But he didn't want it to be up to him. I guess he thought that war would decide it for him in a way that regular life couldn't."

"Never heard that one before. So war lets you know whether or not you're supposed to exist."

"Like I said, Paul was an intense kid," Joe said, watching the road. "But the last laugh was on him. The army has him counting boxes down in Mississippi, last I heard."

In one of the Brookfields, we stopped at a pub by a graveyard. The old regulars at the bar seemed at odds with the management's efforts to give it a Berkshires-rustic feel. As a result, the place wavered between being twig-and-wreath illusion and video-keno reality. The grizzled locals eyed us with suspicion. We ignored them and ordered dinner and beers.

"So where are we going?" I asked after the beers arrived.

"Just down the road. I don't feel like being around right now. I just want some freedom, just a long drive to nowhere."

"Well, whatever, I'm down. It's nice, just hanging out, with no drama."

"Yeah. I miss you, man. Do you ever think you'd move back to Worcester?"

"I don't know, probably not. My life is down in New York. And I was never really all that at home in Worcester."

"Unless I move to D.R. or maybe South America—someplace with lots of hot Latin women—I don't think I'll ever leave. I mean, as long as I can be with hot women and good friends whenever I want, why go anywhere else?"

Though nearly every adult choice I'd made argued against him, I said nothing and ate. We finished drinking when we finished eating and hit the road. Route 9 out west was just another rural highway, broken by the occasional blinking traffic light and dotted with occasional wooden houses built too close to the road.

"So what is going to happen with you and this case?"

"I'm going to talk to my lawyer on Friday and see what the deal is. I can always sell out Walshie if I have to. I mean, Walshie's a good guy, but that and three bucks will buy you a latte. After that night in jail, I think I care more about my freedom than I do about my good name among Worcester's criminal community. I mean, like you said, this isn't *Godfather Two*."

We only had about three beers apiece, and caution wasn't comfortable on him. But Joe drove slower after dinner. Northampton was closed down, though brightly lit, in the freezing quiet of winter break. Past town, the darkness was more absolute, the cold more extreme, the snows deeper and more exotic.

"We're getting into King Philip country," Joe said.

"I was just reading about him."

The dark hills suddenly seemed alive with the violent obstinacy that's born into all men. The snow seemed opportune for stringing out a foreign enemy, and the hills ideal for ambush. But the well-plowed streets, new street signs and modern houses revealed by the streetlights all indicated vacation houses.

"No shit? Is the book any good?"

"It's alright."

"Can I borrow it when you're done? I've been looking for a good book about that war."

"Sure. It's funny that they never taught us about it in school, even with it happening all around where we grew up."

"After like two hundred field trips to Sturbridge Village, maybe they could have brought it up."

"Every year, Sturbridge fucking Village."

"That fucking place. It's like, great, they made everything by hand and wore uncomfortable clothes. Yeah, I get it, the past sucked," Joe said, getting excited.

"Meanwhile, we were going to school near half a dozen battlefields."

"To be fair, I don't know if King Philip's War was the most teachable moment. I'm not sure how far you are in the book. But I don't know how they would explain it to kids. I mean, it was more of an outburst by a dying people than a war. King Philip even knew he didn't have a chance. He had a famous quote about it. The quote doesn't exactly make sense …"

"It was '*I am determined not to live until I have no country.*' I re-read it a few times in the hospital the other day. It makes less sense the more you read it. But you do get his point."

"Okay, so we have a ballooning horde of Colonists, the despair on the part of a dwindling native population, then add in that it was a gruesome war of attrition."

"The bloodiest, per-capita, in US history."

"And in the end, the Pilgrims, whose grandchildren would sign the Declaration of Independence, killed off thousands of Indians and sent the remainder into slavery. I guess I could see why they skipped it in the textbook."

"It's definitely harder to explain than the sawmill and the chicken coop at Sturbridge Village. But it's a hell of a story."

"Fucking Philip, he was doomed, just flat-out fucked. But he gave it a shot. And he was even winning for a few months."

Joe made a left onto a farm road that twisted between rough snow banks up a hill. From there, we made lefts and rights at random, climbing hills in the Buick, just following what looked interesting in the mostly empty land. Here and there, the stars would taunt us, or the half moon would escape the tree branches. The night was hilarious. Dead man's curves, my continued unemployment, Joe's future in prison, the farms under three feet of snow, my Gothic mistress, the old Colonial barns with Saabs inside, and the fact that Joe had told his boss he'd be at work the next day. We just laughed and laughed. Lost in Western Mass, the sun began lighting up the sky unignorably behind us.

"Well, it looks like we broke the night," Joe said.

"That's no mean feat for the middle of January."

"I should start heading back if I'm going to get to work by nine."

Atop the hill we'd been climbing was a long, straight road lined with trees in perfect rows, planted at regular intervals. Joe slowed the car as we approached it. The trees' million black, arthritic fingers reached over the Buick. We said nothing as we contemplated the gentle and patient mind that must have planted them, trusting in the soil, the road and a future populated by people upon whom his care would not be wasted. It was a long silence, one so pungent you could breathe it in.

"Jim, we're still going to take acid with our grandchildren, aren't we?"

"Yeah, we are."

"Promise?"

"Yeah. You promise?"

"Yeah."

We had made the plans when we were nineteen—we'd send our children away for the day and take acid with our grandchildren. They'd hear some wild talk out of their grandfathers. And we'd experience the hallucinogenically enhanced satisfaction of fathering a line of offspring, and of a life mostly lived. We liked our absurd plan enough to bring it up every year or so, just to make sure the other wasn't losing his nerve.

We passed a sign saying we had entered Peru, Massachusetts, which seemed altogether impossible. We looked at each other with our mouths agape and then laughed uncontrollably for having found such an unlikely place. We found the Mass Pike a half hour later. The sun was up and in our eyes the whole way back to Worcester. In Auburn, we stopped for some Egg McMuffins and coffee to dull the pain of our unlikely place in the day.

At Joe's house, we embraced and parted. I drove with the early rush hour traffic to Westborough. My fellow travelers passionately multitasked their ways to the countless office parks from Shrewsbury to Boston. I dragged my satisfied, unemployed carcass to an inflatable bed.

50.
Thursday, January 15

Three hours of sleep left my skin hot and my brain sluggish. I made it to the rehab place in the early afternoon. Dad had finished his physical therapy for the day. For the first time since the surgery, Dad felt better than me. He was sitting in the armchair by his bed, flipping through a magazine with the TV on.
"Hey Dad, you're looking good today."
"Don't let it fool you. I just can't take any more time in bed."
"That's a good sign. It means you're getting your energy back."
"Either that or they're only giving me half my dose of pain pills and selling the other half out the back door. This one nurse, she's a sneaky little thing, always on her cell phone, with these long nails ..."
"You want me to look into it? You sound crazy. But I'll look into it."
"Nah. You're probably right. I just have too much time on my hands. I'm just fired up because I wiped my own ass today."
"I like that, Dad—how you didn't just keep that to yourself. That was good."
"I thought you'd be concerned. I mean, I didn't want you going without sleep, wondering how your father's ass was being wiped," he said.
Then, with little alterations, we pushed the joke until we were both laughing, he was clutching at his chest and I was nearly dizzy. It was reassuring. With a series of small, practiced maneuvers, Dad got himself out of the chair. Using his walker, we walked down a long wallpapered hallway to a sunroom, where an old lady in a wheelchair listened to headphones and stared at the snow and a young man fiddled with his laptop. They paid us no mind as Dad worked his way into a wicker chair across from me.
"You look like hell. Did your flu come back?" Dad said serenely. He wore his listening face, which he debuted sometime in the last decade.

I mumbled something about Joe having some trouble and me staying up late with him. Perhaps knowing how little he liked answering questions, Dad didn't ask too many. I appreciated the courtesy. The silence broke when the young man began pounding on his computer's 'enter' key and cursing Microsoft Vista under his breath. He reached for the computer as if to throw it, then calmed himself and just stared off. We sat and talked in the sunroom about politics and sports, about everything except our seventeen years living in the same house, largely at odds. By the time we walked back to his room, Dad was as ready to sleep as I was.

The late afternoon sunset shone through the gaps in the bare trees like a jack-o'-lantern at the end of Route 9. It was my second drive into the sun that day. As I passed her apartment building, I called Mom and told her my flu was back and I'd have to cancel our plans for that night. She sounded a little hurt and I felt a little bad. I said I should feel better tomorrow.

Back in my inflatable bed at the Fountainhead, the sheets and the simple sensation of lying down made me almost too excited to sleep. The scattered sounds coming from the hallway—people coming home from work, school, daycare—detached themselves, like the audio in a movie falling out of sync. I was most of the way gone into the gentle reveries that precede dreams. My phone rang. I answered before it occurred to me not to. It was Serena.

"Hello stranger," Serena said.

"Oh, hello. I was just napping."

"Oh," she said, disappointment weighing her voice. "Should I call back later or something?"

"No. No, I'm fine. Just resting my eyes."

"Are you still sick? I was going to send you some herbs my mother recommended. But I figured you'd be better by the time they got to you. Did you get my e-mail?"

"No. I've been off the computer lately. Things've been hectic. They moved Dad to a rehab place and, Joe who I told you about, was arrested," I said.

It took me a second to realize I was telling the truth, and to stop. From there on, I sanitized my story, toning Joe's arrest down to some marijuana and omitting things like Dad wiping his own ass, and my nights with Olive. Serena's recap sprawled reassuringly into arcane issues of office courtesy, minor dilemmas and problems that belonged to people I'd never met. But a lot of her stories did seem to take place in bars after work, with her friends, of whom I would always be a little suspicious.

"Sounds like you've been going out a lot."

"Yeah, I know. Davida just broke up with her boyfriend. So she wants to go out like every night. And, do you remember Eric?"

"No."

"Well, I used to work with him. He was a graphic designer. But he got laid off about a month ago and now he's a bartender at this lounge on the Upper East Side and he gives us drinks for free. So we've been going out there a lot. It's a really cool place. We'll have to go when you get back."

"Sure. Just behave yourself up there."

"You know I'm being good. I miss you."

"It's only a few more weeks. What's the story with next weekend? Dad will be back, but I'll get us a hotel room."

"I'm not so sure about next weekend now. At work, we have a big project due that Tuesday and my boss said we might have to work over the weekend. I'll let you know next week, after ..."

My ears filled with the sounds of rushing blood. I could feel that I had lost focus and she was slipping away. Maybe not that week or the next, but sometime before March grew warm, she would want to have a talk that ended with us as the strangers we'd started out at as. As we said our syrupy, overlong good-byes, it seemed that we said them not because we meant them, but because we didn't.

I tried to put off my sense of foreboding to sleep deprivation. And I had almost reached the replenishing waters of oblivion when my cell phone, by then my goddamned cell phone, rang again. It was Olive and I answered.

"Hey, I can only talk for a second because I'm at work. But do you want to get a drink later tonight?"

"I would absolutely love to do nothing more, well almost nothing. But I'm operating on three hours of sleep. There's been some crazy shit happening lately that I'll tell you about later. But now, I can't hold my eyes open another minute. How about Saturday?"

"I think I can do that. Did your Dad go to rehab?"

"Yeah, yours?"

"They're taking him to some place in Newton next week. What is your Dad's place like?"

"It's nice, a lot of dried flowers and oil paintings and not so many dying people. Can I call you tomorrow?"

"Okay."

"Okay."

"Good night."

"Bye," Olive said and waited, like I waited for the sound of the phone on the other end clicking off. I clicked first, but not immediately.

With that, I had gone three for three on disappointing phone calls with the three women who mattered most in my life. That's hardly a good sign, I thought. I silenced my phone, for fear of what else it held. Making my final saunter into the deep caves and rushing waves of sleep, I wondered what was wrong with me.

51.
Friday, January 16

I woke just after dawn, with nothing but morning before me. The morning was a hateful kingdom. Its pale yellow sunlight stung like the taste of orange juice two days too old. Its TV shows were psychotic show trials of forced enthusiasm for things that no sane person could love. Its roads and corridors were crowded with muttering zombies hurrying off to joyless obligations. Its silence wasn't pregnant with inspiration or mystery, but with nameless recriminations. Its promise was a long, healthy life that smells like a new car and tastes like Styrofoam.

So I did what people do in the morning. I did what I was supposed to. I checked my e-mail, replied to friends and Serena. I planned my responses to the few e-mails back from possible employers. I checked my calendar and checked the news, soaking it all in as though the consumer price index, the new president's cabinet, the success of a Midwestern bank robber, the progress of the war, each needed my close attention. With nine a.m. safely past, I went to the Fountainhead fitness center and climbed onto the elliptical machine. After a week of sickness and so forth, the first five minutes hurt. But I kept at it almost an hour, pushing and pulling like the hamster of the month, trying to sweat some of the hateful confusion out of my system. Showering and shaving, I felt like a full-fledged, qualified adult for the first time in more than a week.

At the rehab center, I waited for Dad to finish his physical therapy and watched Dad's little TV. I eyed the stock ticker and the disaster ticker stream below the manicured faces of the anchors, watching for a clue, an opening in the double-dutch where I could jump back in. After an hour and a half, an orderly walked with Dad back to his room. I freed up the armchair, but Dad went straight for the bed. He said it was his first day of a new stage of physical therapy. His hand shook as he gestured for the remote. I tried commenting on the cable news, but he had zoned out. We watched TV until he fell asleep.

Still high from my encounter with competence, I drove back to the Fountainhead and sent off a few dozen more resumes for jobs I was only remotely capable of tolerating or performing. I dug through scattered piles of clothes for a clean shirt and killed the two hours before I met Mom. It took a little driving around to find the restaurant—a homey, little Italian place in downtown Natick, just off of the main drag. Mom was early. She was always early. It was one more way she was polite, one more thing she could pull out in an argument, I thought. That's where my head was at.

I sat across from her and ordered a glass of wine. The place was like a thousand other middling Italian places up and down the East Coast. It was dark, with rustic touches like old paintings of gondolas and villages on the walls, and straw-wrapped Chianti bottles on the tables. Its menu was a succession of piccattas, marsalas and parmigianas. Mom talked about my cousins, then mothered, suggesting jobs I could apply to, asking me about my cover letters. The food was good, solid food. Mom asked about Serena, and I said I guessed she was fine.

"Do you think things would be going better if you were still in New York?"

"Probably. Sitting there with a staticky piece of plastic jammed up against my ear isn't my favorite thing to do. Then I get aggravated on the phone and I think that aggravation shows up as aggravation with her."

"Your father was the same way. He never liked being on the phone."

"I remember. Anyway, I don't mean to say that Serena isn't a good conversationalist because she is. It's just that being out of touch makes it easy to forget about things like that. And then it's just natural. You respond to what's in front of you. Your eye starts to wander."

"Do you think she's seeing someone?"

"I don't think so. She's just out drinking with her friends. But neither of us is living in Medieval Europe."

"What does that mean?"

"I mean that there aren't great, heartrending romances any more, with noble sacrifices and long love letters. Being with someone has a lot to do with convenience—with intersecting situations. But what happens when the situations stop intersecting is anyone's guess."

We each looked down at our plates after my near miss of that particular nerve. Mom was eating neatly, and I could see the strategy playing out on her plate. It would leave a whole meatball and a neat tangle of spaghetti for her doggy bag, which she would give me whether I wanted it or not. It was almost enough to make me cry. But the beat goes on.

"So, how about Joe? How is he?"

"Yeah, he got arrested. I went out with him to blow off some steam and talk over his options the other night. We were up late."

"What was he arrested for?"

"The police broke into his house and found some drugs."

Mom's eyes widened in shock and curiosity.

"What kind of drugs?"

"Marijuana," I lied.

"Was it serious, is he going to jail?"

"That's what everyone is trying to figure out. I'm going to make some calls either tonight or tomorrow to get a better idea."

"You and your friends. Even in preschool, if there was an impulsive, troublemaking kid—you'd be his best friend by the end of the day."

"I think the crazy ones are your only chance. Most people are so boring that they're barely even there. You're never going to get anywhere with them," I said, knowing how Mom loved when I said terrible things she not-so-secretly agreed with. She smiled.

"It's true," she seconded. "And the more boring they are, the more they want your attention. There's one woman at work who comes up to my desk every day to complain about her boss. She tells me her boss said this, tells me what time her boss showed up, what her boss was wearing and when she wore it last. Then she tells me that she has one foot out the door. She says it twice a day, at least …"

Mom went on telling her tale of the boring woman, which despite her flourishes and outrage, became a boring story in the process. I drank my wine. The tired woman who'd been staring off from the back table came over and took our plates. We left the restaurant around eight. There was no decent movie to go see, no café to go have dessert at. I walked Mom back to her car and said good night. I was on the road when Joe called.

"Those fuckers are making me take sick days for when I was in jail. It's total bullshit. I asked them: 'What if I'm acquitted, do I get the days back? Do I get reimbursed?'"

"At least they didn't fire you. Aren't they all cops?"

"Fuck them. I almost lost it in the office. I was a total mess yesterday. What the hell were we thinking? Who drives around until eight in the morning? Sober?"

"I guess we do. But we did at least discover the lost city of the Incas."

"Fucking Peru, Mass. That was the capper. Man, I left work at five oh one that day and went to my mom's house and slept for about fifteen hours straight. I still have to clean up my place."

"Jesus. I hope you don't run into Marissa."

"Whatever. I'll clean it. But tonight, I'm getting fucked *up*. My friend John Crowder is getting kicked out of his place in off Highland Street so he's throwing a complete and utter rager tonight. He says he's got six *cases* of booze and someone's supposed to bring a whole tank of nitrous."

The image of a night at a Worcester party with Joe flashed before me. A night of cursory introductions and forced conversations with strangers, and of interminable remember-whens with the people I did know. A night of insisting that I was just in town for a few weeks, met by doubting nods. A night of not getting fucked up enough to feel at ease, but still getting too fucked up to drive home without risk.

"Man, I'm going to pass. I'm still a little wiped out and my only clean shirt just got splattered with tomato sauce. But maybe tomorrow. Call me when you get up?"

"Okay, will do."

"And Joe, please, when you go to this thing, go there with a lot of friends. Be careful out there. You don't want another ambush and you don't want them to revoke your bail."

Joe said that he knew, and that it would be cool, and we signed off as I descended the hill by the I-495 off-ramp. At the Fountainhead, someone must have been having a party because I had to park at the far corner of the parking lot. I walked the cold and starry hundred car lengths to the halogen-lit doorway. Dad's apartment seemed like a barely tolerated house of exile to me when I arrived. But the mess I'd made had made it almost a home. Inside, I watched people sing and build and kill each other on the TV. I picked up my phone and called Jeff. This time he picked up directly, without his group home roommate handing the receiver off to uncertainty itself.

"Hey man, it's Jim, how are you?"

"Oh, hey, Jim, man, what's up?" Jeff said, sounding out of it.

We each gave our recaps. Mine was short because I didn't feel like going into detail. His was short simply because he wasn't doing very much. We talked around our recaps and played at sounding normal. He did it because he thought I required it. And I did it because I thought I had to set the bar for sanity.

"Well, maybe you should go back to school," I said somewhere in our masquerade of banality.

"I know. I will go back to school and receive training for the profession of my choosing," Jeff said in a robot voice that made us both laugh like fools.

The old Jeff reached out and told the truth—that his damaged mind was now unable to become the machine that we, his peers, demand it become. He told the truth funny. And our laughter forgave his infirmity as well as my pretensions of health. Our laughter reminded me that a thread would always connect us, despite the failings of mind, body or character that would invariably occur.

From there, our conversation drifted more freely across old times, sneaking out, driving around with other escapees from their homes, mild things that seemed momentous after lifetimes as children in our parents' homes. We talked until it got too late, like animals feeding excessively before another long and certain famine.

52.
Saturday, January 17

The next day was so routine that my memory of it is pale as the tale of a tale of a tale. The weather was cloudy and cold, as it should have been. Route 9 was commercial and drab as it should have been. Dad was surly and exhausted as he should have been. I didn't care about the day-old tomato sauce stain on my last supposedly clean shirt, as it made no sense to dress up for the rehab place.

The only blip of life came when I was talking with Dad at the rehab center. We were talking about the time right after Mom left him. He said it was ironic that I had become his best friend. We both knew what he meant and said no more.

Driving back from the rehab facility, Olive called and delayed our date until later that night, as she should have, given my own half-assed efforts for her affections. And I failed to insist or charm, as fit my own record of ambivalence. Automata ruled the day, as it often does.

Joe called and invited me to the second day of the raging party he'd called me about a day before, as he should have. And I declined, as made sense. Then Olive canceled on me. I was in Dad's apartment, reading my book about Worcester, when she called.

I can find the day on a calendar. It was Saturday, January seventeenth, the day before the AFC and NFC Championship games, three days before Dad was supposed to return to his apartment from the rehab facility. I remember, because it mattered later, that my blue polo shirt stank and suffered from a central tomato sauce stain.

I rummaged through Dad's t-shirts and put on one with a modern Patriots logo, known as the Flying Elvis. But the logo looked wrong—too modern, slick and forward moving. So I grabbed an older white t-shirt with a rip in its side-seam, bearing the older team logo on it. The old logo was Pat Patriot bent poised toward the viewer, archaic and pissed off—an honest face from the decades before the Massachusetts Miracle. That logo had only made it to one Super Bowl in thirty years, and then lost spectacularly. You could see Pat Patriot's weather-beaten face and his physical normalcy, his frailty as he leaned toward you and growled. The shirt was thin from wear and fit well. I put it on and watched TV, where the bright achievements of the world floated up and vanished like cinders from the raging inferno of a vast frustration.

I called Joe and he gave me the address of the party. I grabbed my coat and hit the road, stopping for gas in Shrewsbury next to the abandoned gas station and across from Trippi's Big & Tall and The Gun Room. Despite having been to a few hundred iterations of the party ahead, I was excited. It looked like a good night to get drunk and let the chips fall where they may, I told myself as my savings filled up Dad's SUV.

The pink sky over the farther hills shone unprecedented and pregnant with possibility, despite the cold, despite being nearly thirty years old, despite the dull track record of Massachusetts, the grim track record of reality as a whole.

The party was in an apartment just off Highland Street. It was somewhere between dying and being born when I arrived. There was still a lot of liquor, a foamy-but-live keg and a tank of nitrous oxide, which was the star attraction, in the quietest corner of the room. People emerged from stupors long enough to inflate another balloon from the tank, inhale it and find a place to lay themselves, lost in the chemical narcissism that wonders "Am I high enough?"

Joe was the hot center of all sound at the party. He was arguing with a lanky blonde guy about whether Matt O'Brien should get first-degree or second-degree murder. He gave me a half-drunk hug hello and admitted to getting some sleep in the kitchen that afternoon. Joe found me a fresh bottle of scotch, said the host of the party had left and took me to an evacuated bedroom. We sat on a pair of the milk crates that furnished it.

"So I wanted to run this by you: The more I think of it, the more I think I may have to snitch on Walshie. But I want to warn him ahead of time. How would that work—if they went into his place and didn't find anything?" Joe said, drinking clear liquor out of a commemorative Celtics glass.

"I guess it's one of those things you have to negotiate with the cops or the DA or what have you. Is cooperation enough, or will the deal depend on the results of what you tell them?"

"The new lawyer said I would probably have to cooperate in some way. But he didn't get into specifics. I have a list of guys I would hand over on a silver platter. Hopefully, I won't have to snitch on Walshie."

"You're sure this is what you want to do?"

"Jim, don't tell anyone this, but I can't sleep and I've been having nightmares when I do get to sleep—all about just that one night in jail. That's why I stayed at my mom's, and why I slept here this morning. I can't even imagine spending another day in jail. I'll basically do whatever I have to, so long as it keeps me out of jail."

"I think that makes sense," I offered, thinking of James Printer, the Praying Indian, with a decapitated head in each hand.

By ten o'clock, the nitrous-oxide zombies in the next room were a flat-out downer. So we left in Joe's car. He said to bring the scotch bottle and I did. We took swigs of it in a public parking lot off Green Street.

"This is where Sully and his goons got Smitty," Joe said.

"You sure we should be here?"

"Yeah, don't sweat it. We're going to the Lucky Dog. They all know me there. Want to finish this bottle?"

"Man, let's make a night of it, not a four hours."

"You're no fun anymore," Joe said, taking a long swig of the scotch and giving me the finger while he did.

I met him halfway with a swig of my own that sent up a throaty prayer to the vomit gods. It felt good. That night, I agreed with the whiskey that daily life is a poison that needs to be yakked up.

At the Lucky Dog, Joe got us in for free. The band playing that night was a variation on the chubby guy screaming incoherently over a wall of angry guitars. This one had two chubby guys screaming, one bald and the other with a goatee. They sort of took turns unwinding their vocal chords for the sporadically enthused audience. It was loud as hell.

Joe knew everyone, shaking hands, yelling down the bar and waving to a half dozen people on our way to two seats at the bar. He bought us some shots. They went poorly with the scotch. I tasted licorice, cherries and lighter fluid. The noise from the band was so extreme that our conversation consisted of what we could shout or gesticulate. Between songs, Joe made introductions to people he knew, comments about the women at the bar, and an offer of cocaine. I declined the coke and Joe vanished with someone whose name I didn't quite get.

I ordered a beer to settle my stomach and Kyle showed up, wearing a clean white windbreaker, new white sneakers and a white baseball hat. It looked like his Saturday night wear. He asked about Joe and I pointed to the bathroom. He made a face and turned to get the bartender's attention. The first band finished and the next one was setting up when Joe came out of the bathroom, looking excited. The drugs, noise and people all gave him what he wanted. And what Joe wanted not to do was lower his voice or his eyes.

Walking over to us, Joe worked the crowd at the bar, shaking people's hands, embracing them, waving and yelling to the people he saw and hugging a cheerful fat girl, then kissing her until she pushed and someone pulled him off in a friendly sort of way. He laughed in the face of the guy who pulled him off. He did all this in the twenty feet between the bathroom door and where Kyle and I were standing.

Nothing seemed wrong with any of it. It was the kind of craziness that moved the time along, carried Saturday night further from the weekly realities. Everyone was glad to have Joe there, fucked up as he was. Joe gave Kyle a big hug and let rip with a wild, coke-and-booze-soaked oath of fealty and friendship. Between bands, you could talk.

"Feeling good, Mr. Rousseau?" I asked.

"I was just thinking about that. I mean, yes, I am high as the Sputnik puppy's kibble bowl, but do I feel good? I mean, I'm so excited my heart is trying to crash through my ribs and I want to chew my own teeth. But is this feeling good? I don't know. Hey, Jim, are you almost done with that book about King Philip's War?"

"Not yet, man. I'll give it to you when I'm done."

"Did you read the account of the Mohegans torturing the Narragansett that they captured? You would remember it if you did."

Joe was breathing heavy and talking in bursts. He paused to say a quick, emotionally exuberant hello to a guy and two girls who were heading toward the door.

"I don't think so."

"It was written by an English guy who was hanging out with the Mohegans just before the war started. Anyway, the Mohegans took a Narragansett warrior as a captive. Then they took him back to their camp and stood around him in a circle. And the Narragansett started singing. Then the Mohegans took him apart, bit by bit, over the course of, like, twenty-four hours. They broke his fingers, then skinned his arms—all kinds of awful shit. But the Narragansett, he just kept singing. He'd pass out from the pain or the blood loss periodically. Then they'd wake him back up. And he'd start singing again."

"That's crazy. Was it a ritual thing?"

"I've been thinking about it. I think he sang just to say *fuck you* to his torturers," Joe said, his eyes big and his face wild, with the vein bulging in his forehead, making it look as though his ponytail was all that kept his head from exploding. He gave two middle fingers to imaginary torturers to underline his point. "The guy, the Narragansett, sang because he knew he was flat-out fucked, and all he had left of himself was defiance."

"Do you want another drink?"

"Yeah, totally. But, what was I saying? I was saying something. You asked me something."

"A drink?"

"No. But yes. But before that."

"Uh, I asked if you were feeling good."

"Oh yeah. Well, that's exactly the question. I guess that in my own spoiled, white-guy-on-drugs way, I feel like that Narragansett. The bastards may get to me, but they'll never know it. And I may be fucked, even the lawyer my mom is paying will concede that point. But I'm still singing."

"Yeah, about that …"

"Let's do two more shots. Rum this time?"

"Whiskey. I'll get this one."

Then the band began. They introduced themselves in a nervous, self-effacing sort of way, making bad jokes. Then the guitars emitted a loud, menacing thrum and impenetrable high-pitched thrashing. The once-nervous lead singer—a tall and obese white guy with a shaved head, baggy t-shirt and a braided, dyed goatee—let out a shrill and throaty roar. Conversation again vanished from the room. After a couple songs, Joe went to the other end of the bar and started talk-yelling with a group of girls down there. Kyle was over by the stage, nodding his head enthusiastically to the roar and screech of the music. I stayed where I was, trying to enjoy my light beer, thinking of Worcester in the 1600s, left abandoned over long decades, freelance and French-sponsored Indians marauding its hills. I thought of Worcester since World War Two, losing jobs and people, grasping at straws, building a mall downtown. I thought of the screamer on stage and the Narragansett, defiant, fucked and singing.

The next few songs passed wordlessly because of the deafening noise. I saw Joe coming out of the bathroom, looking like he was being carried on the shoulders of a grateful nation, his mouth wide and his eyes roaming. He bumped into Kyle and they started toward the door. He yelled into my ear that they were going outside for a smoke. I yelled I'd go out to meet them as soon as I got the drink I'd ordered. The bartender was a thin, pale girl who looked enough like Olive that her coldness surprised me. She took her time getting my drink and then even longer giving me change.

I was sorting my change from her tip when Kyle poked his head through the door looking alarmed, mouthing words I couldn't hear. I followed him outside and around the corner, toward the yelling and a small crowd.

"What the fuck is your problem, buddy?" I heard someone yell as we rounded the corner. The sidewalk on the side street was dark. A small crowd stood back and watched the scene. No one spoke. The orange streetlights cast shadows on their faces.

A short, clean-cut white guy in a new, brown leather jacket pointed a gun at Joe. And Joe, in a black t-shirt, walked toward him, his arms outstretched and a wild, open-mouthed smile on his face.

"What are you going to do now?" the guy yelled at Joe.

"What are you going to do? Shoot me?"

The guy fired into the narrow, cracked sidewalk, and most of the crowd took off. The TV show had become real, and they wanted no part of it. Kyle and I started yelling at Joe—something about chilling out, letting it go, going home, shutting the fuck up, forgetting about it. Something like that. But Joe was transfixed on the guy with the gun and he didn't acknowledge anything else. His eyes and smile were wide, taunting. We yelled, but something kept us from stepping between them. Maybe we should have been, but neither of us was ready for this situation.

"Go ahead. Shoot me, then. You don't have the balls," Joe said.

The guy shot twice. The second shot hit him in the stomach. Joe dropped his arms and deflated. He staggered to the sidewalk to lean against the building. The sound of the gun and Joe's sodden loss of levity made the situation real in a way nothing had ever been real before.

Kyle and I ran to Joe, who leaned against the brick wall, and sank, doubled over to the sidewalk. I looked up at the guy who had shot him, who just stood there, awkwardly. The shooter's face numb and slack, as disarmed as us by what he'd done. He looked around, took a few steps back and a few steps forward, his eyes big with shock, lost in the question of whether or not to flee. It was enough to tell me he was done shooting for the night.

Kyle took off his white windbreaker and put it over Joe. The white windbreaker was drenched in blood in seconds. Joe trembled more with each breath. His face was pulled tight and serious with the effort of it. We crouched over him, adjusting Kyle's windbreaker over the wound, not sure what else to do. The shooter started to shrug his shoulders. He looked familiar, with buggy eyes I had seen before.

"Ambulance!" I shouted at the shooter. "Call an ambulance now! Ambulance! Now!"

The shooter dialed his cell phone with his gun hand. Joe wasn't speaking, just taking small shuddering breaths in the shadow created by Kyle and me. His blood had soaked through the white windbreaker and started to pool on the sidewalk.

"Officer needs assistance ... ambulance ..." I heard coming from behind us.

Joe's face was losing its taut seriousness. His eyes wandered, only occasionally pausing on our faces. He shivered. The shooter paced behind us. He stopped now and then to try and fail to light a cigarette with his gun hand. He kept muttering ohmygod or okayokayokay or don'tdiedon'tdiedon'tdie, while keeping his distance. Kyle and I repeated to Joe to stay with us, and that he was going to be fine, and all the other crap we'd seen on cop shows and in action movies over the years. But we registered less and less with him as the minutes passed. Joe's eyes wheeled around the world above him, but did not focus. He shivered and coughed up a little blood. I have no clear idea of how long it was before the ambulance and cops showed up, shouldered us out of the way, and took Joe.

Once Joe was tied to a stretcher and loaded into the ambulance, Kyle pointed at the shooter. The police took the shooter aside, but not like a murderer, more like a neighbor who'd borrowed a lawnmower. One cop took his weapon, another took him over by a cruiser. But no handcuffs. The whole scene was bathed in siren lights. I followed the shooter to where a pair of cops put their hands on my shoulders and told me to stand back.

A big crowd had gathered from all the bars on Green Street, and Kyle was yelling with tears in his eyes that the cop in the leather jacket was the one who shot Joe. From the crowd, someone threw a shard of ice at the cruiser where the shooter stood. Kyle stood at the front of the crowd, pointing and yelling in a polo shirt.

"It was him that shot Joe," someone yelled.

"That's that fucking Dowd," someone else yelled.

The cops saw a mob, and put Dowd the shooter in the back of a car, which drove off. I wandered back and forth through the crowd, between the cops and the Lucky Dog. I was in some kind of shock. I was looking for someone. But I couldn't figure out whom.

The mob focused on the cops who remained, throwing insults, ice and bottles. Before long, a whole phalanx of cop cars came rolling to the defense of the officers on Green Street. They waded into the disorganized crowd, which was torn between an inchoate thirst for revenge, and a desire to get out of the cold. They arrested Kyle and this Spanish guy who was just looking for any fight he could find. Then the mob scaled back its ambitions from revolution to just making snide remarks about pigs, and started filtering back into the bars.

I noticed that my hands and arms were getting cold. That made sense, as I had no coat on. Looking at them, I saw that they were covered in Joe's blood. And the blood was getting cold. I realized I had to go. Grabbing my coat off the bar stool in the Lucky Dog, I noticed the blood on most of Dad's Patriots t-shirt.

My whole physical and mental existence seemed as precarious as a spinning top. I focused on the task at hand, repeating to myself to put on my coat and go get my car. Outside, the cops were dealing with the stragglers and the curious, but the mob had vanished. I shoved my hands into my coat pockets and asked one cop where they had taken Joe Rousseau. He said he didn't know and told me to move away from the front of the building. I started walking back to Highland Street, repeating a mantra of things I had to do. I carried my body under the railroad bridge, past the Galleria, across the Common, down Main Street. There were few cars and no people out on foot.

On the long walk, I entertained myself with daydreams of getting to the hospital and seeing Joe, sitting up in bed with his wild grin and another crazy story to tell. I thought of us as old men, taking LSD with our grandchildren, and Joe breaking out his bullet-wound scar for them to marvel at. It made me laugh out loud, a lone madman in downtown Worcester on a frigid night. My cell phone rang.

"Jim, did you hear? Joe was shot. Kyle's in jail," Marissa said by way of hello. *Shewat*.

"Yeah, I was there. I'm going to get my car now."

"What happened?"

"I'll tell you when I see you. I need you to call the police and the hospitals and whoever else and find out what hospital they took Joe to, then call me. I'll tell you when I get there."

"Okay. But just tell me this. Did Joe really get shot? Was he okay?"

"He got shot. I don't know if he's okay. Find out the hospital and call me back as soon as you can."

Cell phone still in my hand, I trudged up Highland Street, past the monumental WPA Auditorium. I wanted to call someone, to tell someone. But the thought of talking made me dizzy and sick on the inside. I couldn't think of who to call or what to say. I focused on moving my legs. I passed Tortilla Sam's, a few closed stores, then took a narrow side street and found Dad's SUV. I sat inside and focused on waiting for my phone to ring. To think of anything made me nauseous. I sat like that for about ten minutes.

"They took him to UMass. I'm already on my way," Marissa said, and hung up.

The ride between Highland Street and UMass didn't exist. It was a meaningless and unnecessary aggravation. Everything—driving, parking, walking the labyrinth to the Emergency Room—didn't register. Nothing would register until I found out what happened.

I focused on making my mouth form the words of the questions I needed to ask. Otherwise, I would slip into the image of Joe grinning from a hospital bed, or the image of Joe's eyes growing less responsive in the sidewalk shadows. And each made me feel like I was flying apart.

I saw Marissa a moment before she saw me. She was already crying. She ran up to me and threw her arms around my neck and squeezed. She squeezed too hard for it to be relief. I knew then and my whole body froze. Numbness all but removed me from my body, blotting out sight and sound for a moment.

"Oh God, Joe is dead."

"Already?" was all I could say.

Part Five: What a Good Time Would Cost

Those noble traits that marked the wild man's course lie buried in the shades of night.
—William Apess
Eulogy on King Philip (1836)

53.
Sunday, January 18

The rest of the night came in fast waves of crushing reality alternated with numbness. The flickering fluorescent hospital lights went from being unbearable to nonexistent and back to unbearable again. The police, seeing the blood on my hands, took a statement. They asked innumerable questions, hammering away about whether or not the shooter identified himself as a police officer. I answered in yeses, nos and don't knows—nods, head shakes and shrugs.

When the cops were done, I saw Marissa sitting with Joe's mother, Justine. They were crumpled onto each other. I took a few steps toward them. But, self-conscious of all the blood on me, I walked away, and focused on getting out of the hospital.

The hospital signs, the parking lot lights, the letter-number codes denoting different parking levels, the lock-unlock buttons on the keychain were the only respite I had from the growing certainty that everything from my eyes to my guts was about to topple irretrievably. I had no answers, no solid idea of what had happened, only a whispered memory of how to start the car, obey traffic laws and get back to the Fountainhead. Passing out of Shrewsbury, I started to cry. I wondered if I should pull over and really have at it. But even that small bit of thinking frustrated the urge to sob. I focused on driving, then parking, focusing on the tangible otherness of the world. It was the only safety.

Inside the apartment, I fell on the inflatable bed. To ask what I wanted at that moment was a thought that travelled straight into a nauseous chaos that I could not bear. But my body needed to collapse as badly as the rest of me. I slept a few hours, waking to piss. And before I reached the bathroom, the night's events hit me with physical shudder, and kept me up.

The sun was rising on the other side of the apartment building, lighting the distant hills. Rawboned and out of control, I called Marissa, but got her voicemail. Looking around the apartment for clues about what to do with myself, I showered and shaved. That was something people did, after all. The blood had faded and was starting to crack on my skin. It took a lot of scrubbing to get it out of the hair on my forearms. In Dad's bathrobe, I walked into the dark and silent living room. I should cry, I thought. And though something was moving in my stomach, I didn't. I got up to pour myself a drink, because that's something people do. But I forgot what I was doing on my way to Dad's scotch bottle, with the paper tax stamp over its top. I reached for the bottle, then changed my mind, then wondered if I should have changed my mind. It wasn't too different from having a concussion. The only clean shirt immediately evident was Dad's Patriots t-shirt, the one with the Flying Elvis. I put it on.

All the automata, all the habits and preferences that once swooped me through my days had now taken on an awful echo of uncertainty. On the couch, I moved my mouth around the words *car keys* until I could muster the will to gather my car keys, wallet and phone and leave the apartment. The sky above the Fountainhead parking lot was muffled by pale clouds. Out past Boston, dawn was establishing itself by half-measures. I looked at the sky and contemplated the afterlife, because that is something people do at times like these. But the image of Joe slumping to the pavement put all my thinking to halt.

I was halfway to Worcester when I realized I hadn't turned my headlights on. Downtown, the traffic consisted of police cruisers, and beat-up cars furtively driving home in the late, late Saturday night. The occasional bakery or newspaper trucks shouldered through the cold of their early Sunday morning. Passing the old Showcase Cinema, I realized that I had no clue where I was going. I turned up Chandler Street. The streets were so empty, and I had so few places to go that I wondered if I wasn't the one who had died.

Here and there, driving down Park Avenue and then down Highland Street, it seemed the tears were finally about to come. It was like trying to puke up a cinderblock. I pulled into the gas station across from Tortilla Sam's and idled there. I wanted to be with Marissa and Kyle and Joe's mother. I wanted to be as close as possible to the ground zero of this thing that had so completely disarmed me. I thought of calling Justine, but something about it frightened me. I called Marissa again and she picked up.

54.

"Jim, oh my God, oh my God," she said, saying what I didn't dare say in my solitude.

"Yeah. I know. I can't believe it," I said.

It was the best we could do. No combination of words could yet carry weight against the unfixable event.

"I'm at the Honey Farms on Highland. I've just been driving around. Where are you right now?"

"I'm with Justine. But her brother and her sister are here and her sister has been hinting that I should leave. I don't want to, but I'll probably go. You want to meet me back at our apartment in like, twenty minutes?"

"Yeah."

I went into the Honey Farms. Its fluorescent lights blinded me. In a daze, I nodded to the obese, mustachioed man who controlled access to the cigarettes and dirty magazines behind him. I poured myself a Styrofoam cupful of coffee. He took my money, looking at everything in the store except me. Outside, I took a painfully hot sip, cursed, and threw it in the garbage. In the white noise of the waking city, of the cleanup crew unlocking Tortilla Sam's, I started to cry.

Leaning on Dad's forest-green SUV, and bawling into my hand, with my face a leaky mess, I thought, well, this should kill twenty minutes. I laughed at my prevailing instinct for time management, with the same convulsive desperation. I laughed until I almost puked, going down on a knee on the gas station concrete. A cop car rolling down Highland Street slowed, then slowed some more, then decided not to bother with me.

In the car, I wiped my cheeks and laugh-cried at myself some more. Laughing and crying both got at that cinderblock in my guts, one handful of sand at a time. I drove to Marissa and Joe's apartment. On Highland and Lincoln Streets, the churches were starting to come alive. At the apartment, the lights were on, but nobody answered my knock. I tried the door and it was unlocked. Inside, it looked like someone had robbed the place. But I remembered it was in the same disarray the other day. I sat on the couch and fired up the TV, because that's what people do. Marissa opened her bedroom door, then jumped back and spilled her purse on the floor.

"Jesus Jim, you scared the shit out of me. How did you get in here?"

"The door was open."

I got up and we hugged hard, her crying and me just holding on. Then I helped her pick up the contents of her purse.

"What the hell happened?" she asked.

I told her what I saw outside the Lucky Dog.

"So you didn't see how it started?" she asked.

"No. I got there at the end. Did you hear anything?"

"Stefanie told me what she heard from Kyle."

"Kyle's out already?"

"I guess so. I guess that they didn't charge him with anything. They just took a statement and drove him home. I think like half of those guys work for his roofing business in the summer."

"Kyle was out there when Joe and the other guy started arguing. But I never heard what happened."

"I guess that Joe and Kyle were outside smoking, talking to one of Escalita's friends. Then this crackhead guy grabbed her purse and ran. So Joe, who Kyle says was out-of-his-head fucked up, went after him, along with this other guy. I guess the other guy caught the crackhead first. But Joe showed up and pulled the other guy off the crackhead, head-butted the crackhead, and then yelled at the crackhead not to mess with his people, or something. The crackhead dropped the bag and ran away."

"Joe and his fucking head butts."

"I know. So the crackhead ran off and the other guy started yelling at Joe. The yelling turned into shoving, and that's when the guy pulled out a gun. At some point, the guy may have said he was a cop. But what kind of fucking maniac cop goes out to a bar with a gun? I mean, this guy should go away for a long time ..."

"I can't believe it. I really can't."

"I was hanging out with my boyfriend when I found out. I got like ten calls in a row. Then my fucking moron boyfriend told me to shut off the phone because he wanted to fuck. I started yelling at him and he left. He's such a friggin' moron. God, this sucks so much."

Marissa leaned into me and I put my arm around her and she started sobbing. We sat that way for a long time. She cried and then stopped and then started again. I mostly stared off, trying to look at anything but the hole in the wall with the partially washed away blood stain.

I imagined stepping between Joe and the shooter. I imagined myself never calling Volpe back, and imagined a less desperate Joe Rousseau, who wouldn't walk into a bullet for largely inchoate reasons. I imagined a dozen ways I could have been a better friend. I wondered if this was my fault, because that's something people do in these situations.

"I think I want to leave the place this way, as a tribute. What do you think?"

We laughed at the state of the apartment. Instead of cleaning after the police searched the place, Joe and Marissa had each picked what they needed from the disarray, in a long poker game to see who would blink first and clean the apartment. It made me miss him.

"It might be a fitting tribute. But I don't think it's what you'd call a great decorating idea."

"I have to call like a million people," Marissa said, getting up from the couch.

"It's barely seven in the morning."

"I know. But it's a death. You call people at odd hours when there's a death."

"It's what people do," I volunteered.

Motion and talking—they helped. Sitting alone with the cinderblock in my gut didn't. Marissa started calling people, her voice loud on the hello-sorry-to-call-so-early, then dropping as she delivered the news, followed by shared sobs. I heard two or three calls and then went into Joe's room. It was a worse mess than the living room, with all the dresser drawers pulled out and the bookcase flipped and leaning on its side against a wall. I cleared off the bed and tried to remember why I had gone in there. I decided to lie down and think it over.

I was still tired when I woke. Again, the memory of the previous night hit like an electric shock. Morning sunlight oozed through the window. I checked the clock and congratulated myself on having picked up two more hours of sleep. Marissa was asleep with her open cell phone still in hand in the next room. I brushed my teeth with my finger and left.

Driving out to Dad's rehab facility, I had my wits about me a bit more. I stopped for coffee and food at a Dunkin' Donuts in Westborough.

"Go Pats," the little Irish girl behind the counter said to me as she gave me my change.

"What?"

"Go Pats."

"Who?"

"The Patriots. Your shirt. The game today."

"Oh, right. Yeah. Thanks. Go Pats."

Taking my orange tray of food from that nearly shattering experience, I ate an egg sandwich and stared out the window, past the parking lot, at the traffic. I considered the playoff game that day. It would decide whether or not the Patriots went to the Super Bowl. It seemed like the sort of science fiction that strains credulity. But I would watch it, because that's what people do.

55.

I parked at the far corner of the rehab center parking lot, left my coat in the car, and walked to the wrong entrance. Little things kept escaping me. It was early, barely in range of the lengthiest pregame shows. But Dad was awake and alert, watching people talk football on TV, when I got to his room.

"Whoa! You're here early. You must be excited. And you got your shirt on. Don't worry, they're going to put the game on the big screen in the rec room. I was thinking we'd get a pizza and some wings. Are you okay?"

"Joe was killed last night. He was shot to death."

Dad's face dropped. His cheeks hollowed, his eyes widened and his jaw went slack. It was a face I realized I'd been making all day. He asked what happened and I told him. He said I could go back to Worcester or do whatever I wanted—I didn't have to stick around the rehab center if I didn't want to.

"No, I mean, what can I do? He's dead. I can't go do something to make it better. I'll watch the game with you and then maybe head over to see his mother."

"Okay. I'd like to watch the game with you. But do whatever you have to. Is there anything you need?"

I said no and we talked a little. But conversation didn't come easily. Dad rarely talked about death. It wasn't until the surgery that he'd made arrangements for his own funeral, and he wasn't comfortable talking about it.

"I know I was never the biggest Joe Rousseau fan. But he was always a good friend to you. I mean, when you started at Venerini, he already knew a lot of people and still, he made room for you."

"Yeah," I said, biting my lip, wanting to cry, but not wanting to cry in front of Dad.

"It's funny. I had a feeling that something was going to happen, not like I could tell exactly. I used to get the feeling in Vietnam, before we'd run into some shit, just this feeling."

"Really, that doesn't sound like you."

"I know, I'm the last guy to buy into all of that. But it was a feeling I had all last week. I thought it had to do with the surgery."

Watching the ex-athletes on TV laugh at each others' jokes, I searched my memory of the last few weeks for some inkling, intuition, dream or psychic clue I'd had of what was coming. But the cupboard was bare.

Dad maneuvered his walker down the serene and clean hallways to the rec room, where an old woman waited. She was watching an old man tell an old woman what her old teapot was worth on the big TV.

"I have this reserved in ten minutes for the game," Dad told her. The woman was old and frail and her eyes darted around in a wholly unsettling way.

"I didn't see your name on the list."

"It's there. Go check."

The woman, with great effort, got out of her armchair and onto her own walker and shuffled to check the TV reservation sheet, which was on a clipboard with its own little table, next to yet another small basket of dried twigs and flowers. The trip required an absurd amount of effort and discomfort on her part. But the woman's age-old instinct for spite demanded she do it nonetheless.

"You blocked out the whole day," she said.

"There are two games. So I filled in seven hours."

"You can only reserve two hours maximum. It says so on the sheet."

"Well, I'll get someone else to reserve the next two hours."

The woman grumbled and murmured and Dad ignored her as she thumped back with her walker. She retrieved some wadded up tissues from her armchair and left the room with a grumbling sigh.

"I can't wait to go home," Dad said.

I ordered a pizza and some chicken wings, after a lengthy hassle from the massive woman at the front desk that resulted in me promising that Dad wouldn't eat any of the food I ordered.

The game started and it was more intense than I expected. Dad was emotional, at once serious and not—like he was watching a movie that he only intermittently knew was not real. I tried to play along, but my habits continued to fail me. The players were serious, yelling, gesturing and sucking wind. To them as well, the AFC Championship Game seemed like a movie that they only intermittently knew was not real.

Five minutes into the game, the room was full of patients and staff. I gave up my seat to a guy on crutches. Nurses and orderlies, and even the massive, surly cow from the front desk came over to watch the game and cheer on the Pats with honest fervor. She ate some of our chicken wings. The Pats won handily enough to be slapping each other on the back for the game's last five minutes. Dad's arms and shoulders weren't strong enough to give him a high five. I hugged him and left.

56.

Driving back to Worcester, the people on the road were wild with victory. Passengers leaned out of windows to wave their fingers and yell about the Pats. Cars honked and flashed their lights in exultation. I kept my windows closed and the radio off and honked only when drivers spent too much time congratulating each other at traffic lights. For the first time since I'd quit the team at St. John's, I hated the game of football.

The sinking in my stomach wasn't just from so many people cheering on the day that Joe died. I'd also forgotten to eat. I stopped into a D'Angelo's for a grinder. The fluorescent lights in the restaurant blasted my pegged-open my eyes. It tinted the tan skin of lithe Spanish girl behind the register a pale green.

"Anything else?" she asked. "A drink?"

"Yeah. Sure."

"What kind?"

"Diet Coke."

"What size?"

"My best friend from childhood was just shot to death."

"Oh. Uh ..."

"Medium."

Stopped in her tracks, she murmured something like sorry as she took my money. I took the sandwich to a booth and watched the honking traffic pass through the darkness. The sun was almost completely down. I called Justine from the Formica booth. Her sister Claire, who I'd met a few times, picked up the phone.

"Hi, it's Jim. Uh, I'd like to stop by sometime today or tonight to talk to Justine. I just thought I'd call first."

"Jim, first off, thank you for calling. Justine's really in no condition for visitors to just drop by. Please pass that around. Let people know. She's sleeping right now. But if you want to come by for ten or fifteen minutes around eight o'clock, that would be okay. But it should just be you, do we understand each other?"

Claire was always the toughest member of the Rousseau clan. She was famous for beating Joe with a frozen pork chop. It was right after Joe's grandmother died, and he stumbled drunk into his grandparents' house demanding food. Claire, then as now, took matters into her own hands.

I got into Dad's SUV, called Mom and told her about Joe. It was all I could think to do. I had a hard time listening to what she was saying. It was too much to hear, too many questions, too many words. Then Marissa called and I said good-bye to Mom.

"Jim, what's up? You should have woken me up when you left," Marissa said.

"You probably needed the sleep. I know I did. Anyway, I had to go see my dad out in Marlborough. I'm going over to see Justine in a little bit. Do you want to hang out until then?"

"Sure. Come on over. I'll go over there with you."

"Well, I just talked to Claire and she asked, well, she told me to go over just by myself."

"That's so fucked up. My mom went by with a whole Tupperware of ziti earlier, and Joe's uncle Mark just took it from her at the door, and didn't even let her in. I don't understand why you'd want to keep someone's *friends* away from them at a time like this."

"I'm not going to get into a fight about it. You know how you feel—imagine what it's like for Justine. They're just trying to take care of her."

Marissa argued that they were handling the whole thing wrong. I argued less and less as she went on. I was in Shrewsbury and Marissa's diatribe had drifted to the many legal, professional, personal and physical indignities she hoped would visit the cop who killed Joe. She conjured a future of protest marches, stern judges, and general horrors she imagined would face a former cop in a maximum-security prison. Her rant was a shelter from my own thoughts. It's something people do. She said we should avenge Joe's death.

"Yeah, I guess. But you can't shoot someone back to life," I said.

No rage, no complaint, no wise saying would bring him back. This was a beating that neither of us had much choice but to sit still for. But Marissa kept on, listing friends who knew judges or local political figures, and what they would do, imagining the terrible, mobilizing outrage that would race through Joe's hundreds of friends. I also wanted Joe's death to mean something, but right then I couldn't fathom how it would. We were still on the phone when I pulled up to the granite curbstone jutting like a new tooth from the snow bank's icy gums. Marissa told me that someone was knocking on her door.

She answered the door with a cigarette in her drinking hand and started laughing like crazy when she saw me, the phone still to my ear. From the look on her face, I could tell that, like me, she'd been walking into walls all day. We hugged for a minute. Then her phone rang. I wandered over to the window to see that I had left my headlights on. Going back to the car to turn them off, I saw I'd left the keys in the ignition.

Marissa's efforts to clean the living room had degenerated to just putting everything in a pile against the wall. She was drinking rum and Cokes and smoking.

"You think leaving your keys in the ignition is bad. I almost got put in jail. I've been driving on an expired license. I keep meaning to get a new one, but I also keep getting away with it. So I ran a red light on Park Ave this afternoon, and a cop pulls me over. He asks for my license and registration and I just start bawling and telling him 'My best friend was shot by a cop,' and all that. So he gives me a warning and tells me to drive straight home."

"No ticket?"

"Nope. Even the warning was just a verbal warning. Hey, did you get a call from the guy at the *Telegram*?"

"No, what's he writing about all this?"

"I hope so. He called me and Kyle and a few other people. I told him that the cops were fascist thugs who were bound to kill someone sooner or later and that the Dowd family was the most retarded of the bunch. Then I said that everyone loved Joe and no one would ever want to hurt him. I gave the reporter your number."

The *Worcester Telegram & Gazette* was the daily paper in Worcester. Like most news outlets, it liked to find mourners at their disheveled best. Marissa started in again about her grand plans for justice, or at least vengeance. But I couldn't help thinking that most of the plans would fall apart the moment any real effort was required. She said that a bunch of people would be at Ralph's later that night, and I should meet them there.

I left Marissa early and stopped at a gas station for coffee. In Dad's SUV, I watched traffic negotiate the six-way intersection at Kelley Square without the guidance of a traffic light. The many roads originally met at the banks of the Blackstone Canal, which ran under the intersection, and on to Providence from there. The canal had made Worcester a city and the city made the canal a sewer, and then buried it. It was one more ghost in my haunted afternoon.

I finished my coffee and drove to Joe's childhood home. For the second-largest city in New England, Worcester has a surprising number of unpaved roads. They weren't all in ramshackle neighborhoods, either. The streets were just never paved. Joe had grown up on such a street, and Justine still lived there, in a little house which she'd made cozy. It was crowded that day. His aunt Claire was there with her two adopted Vietnamese girls, who were silently playing in what had once been Joe's bedroom. Claire, Mark and a blonde woman who must have been Mark's wife sat in the kitchen, flanked around Justine. I gave Justine a hug and said I was so sorry. I pulled the last chair up to the table and the kitchen seemed crowded. We exchanged condolences and numb attempts to understand what had happened.

"What did Faye say, Claire?" Justine said.

"When?"

"When you told her about Joe."

"The heaven thing?" Claire asked, and Justine nodded. "My little girl, Gloria, when she heard what happened to Joe, she said 'Justine shouldn't be sad. Joe gets to go to heaven and not have to wait a whole year for Christmas.'"

Justine nodded sweetly, her face contorted into a difficult smile. I didn't know what to say about that. It made me want to weep. I made the face—the eyes bulging and the lips pressed together too hard. It kept the tears at bay.

"And the awful part is that Joe still owes me five hundred dollars," Justine said after a long silence, rising to take a piece of notebook paper off the fridge. Joe had signed it at the bottom. "It was for car repairs."

Justine zigged and zagged between tortured inconsolability and glib impertinence that night.

"Jim, can I talk to you in the next room for a minute?" Claire asked.

We went into the living room, its floor crammed with bags and its surfaces jammed with dishes of food. Claire sat across from me. She had short hair, rectangular glasses and a demeanor that held the world before her to very strict standards. She told me the wake would be Tuesday and the funeral Wednesday and then eyed me carefully.

"So Jim, how are you holding up with all of this?" she asked me.

"I'm okay. I mean, it's taking some effort, but I'm putting one foot in front of the other. I don't know."

"Well, we've gotten some calls from the *T&G* and the *Globe* about Joe. I just want you to know that the family doesn't want to make a statement just now. And we'd rather that Joe's friends not speak to the press, either. There may come a time to make a statement, and we may take legal action. But until we get more facts, we'd just rather just keep this a family matter. So, as Joe's reasonable, grown-up friend, we'd like you to try to pass that on. Nobody's expecting miracles, but do pass it on, capiche?"

"Okay."

"Me and Mark and his wife Cynthia were talking about Joe. Cynthia's first husband, Jerry, died of an overdose in an apartment off Vernon Street when he was Joe's age. So we tend to see what happened to Joe in those terms—alcoholism, drug abuse and so forth. Do you think Joe was an alcoholic?"

I stumbled and equivocated. I felt a cold dread that this would be the story—the unfortunate alcoholic—told about the man who I'd loved like a brother, who had been essential to many of the good things I had experienced and become. After verbalizing my confusion for too long to be convincing, I found an opinion.

"No. I don't think Joe was an alcoholic," I said.

As I'd find out, nothing belongs to you anymore when you die, especially not your own death. Your death becomes a way for people to explain or justify themselves. It becomes a cautionary tale or a legend, depending on the teller's agenda. And the living will always have their agendas. It's a curse that comes with having everything else.

Claire and I went back into the kitchen. Justine stared at each of us with soft, searching eyes and we stared at her more or less the same way. She looked away and I looked out the kitchen window, into the darkness. Words continued to fail all of us. But being together made that failure, and all the other failures of the day, easier to bear.

"Well, I'm sure you have somewhere to be," Claire said to me, bulging her eyes to make it clear that this was her version of being polite.

I embraced Justine and Claire and shook Mark and Cynthia's hands. I looked back at the house before I opened the SUV door. The tears started coming as I recalled the street in the summer time.

When Joe and I were about twelve, Joe had learned how bats use echolocation to catch bugs. So he'd gotten out his fishing pole to catch bats. In the dirt street, he'd cast straight up into the sky, and then run away from the weighted hook that fell back down. He must have tried for an hour, casting and fleeing. Another time, around that same age, we'd gotten into an argument and thrown each other's shoes onto the roof of the house. It took all of Joe's arguing, cajoling and pleading to talk his mom out of driving me home early.

I climbed into the car to cry in private. My gut buckled with the sobs that finally seized it. Gasping for breath, it didn't feel good. But it felt necessary.

57.

Ralph's blinking sign broke the darkness. I parked around back and wandered the crumbled lot to the door. The bouncer and the first five people I saw inside, seeing my Patriots' t-shirt, offered high fives, and I played along. At the back bar, by the pool table, I spotted Fin, an old friend from a long time ago. His full name was Shawn Finley, but everyone called him Fin. He had the same slack-jawed, hollow-cheeked look I did. He spotted me. I waved and ordered a pair of bourbons. Fin sat alone at the glossy wood table, drinking a beer. After a confused handshake-hug, I sat down and passed him one of the bourbons. Through the jukebox, the nearby chatter and the ceiling, a hardcore band thudded.

Fin had a goofy haircut, too big on top and too close on the sides. He looked at me a moment with wide eyes, then smiled and shook his head. Among all the yahoos from when we ran wild, I always liked Fin. He wasn't stupid and he genuinely meant well. But mental illness had hit him in his early twenties, and precluded a great many things.

"Jim Fucking Monaghan. I thought I'd never see you again. Man, how about this shit?" he said, his eyes widening further, as if to physically take in Joe's death.

We repeated that it was unbelievable, back and forth, like criminals getting their story straight.

"I know. I mean, I always thought it was like Joe had this weird assurance on high that this wouldn't happen. That's why he was always so fearless, so …"

"So fucking stupid," I offered, surprising myself.

"Yeah. It's just like you got used to him being a nut and getting away with it."

"It's like some kind of law was broken. Slanche," I said, raising my glass.

We threw back our glasses of bourbon too fast, and took a second to unscrew our faces.

"Man. That is strong. I'm not supposed to drink with the medication I'm on. But I've been doing good lately. Or I was," Fin said. Once a ladies' man, he had put on a lot of weight.

"Yeah, how are you doing with all of that?"

"It's fuckin' manic depression. So it's unbelievably great then it's a fuckin' endless nightmare. Either that, or I'm on the pills and I'm a zombie who can't get a boner. I've been seeing a lot of your buddy Jeff, lately. We go to the same club."

"Yeah, I just talked to him the other day. Well, I guess I'm not supposed to offer. But I'm having another."

"What else can you do at times like these?"

I gave the goateed Irish guy my credit card and told him to keep a tab open. Over fresh bourbons, Fin gave his recap. He was living with Tony Howard, a guy I knew from a long time back. Tony was fresh out of prison and crazy. He woke Fin up the day before by putting a revolver against his forehead. It didn't take much wisdom or much love for me to advise Fin to move out. But he acted as if it did.

After a few more drinks, Marissa and Kyle showed up. And our part of the bar filled with people who knew Joe, everyone drinking into the shock, because that's what people do.

"So what was going on when you got out there? When did the guy pull out his gun?" asked a tall black guy with glasses. He also had the sunken cheeks and slack jaw.

"Well, after the crackhead guy ran off with the girl's purse, Joe and the other guy ran after him …" Kyle said, and told the story right up to the part where he was arrested. His voice dropped at the end. He wagged his head and came up with a drink.

"Did the guy say he was a cop?" Marissa asked.

"I'm not sure. There was a lot of yelling back and forth before I got back. He might have," Kyle said.

"Well, what was it? You either heard him say it or you didn't."

"I don't remember. I just saw the gun and thought I should get some help. I only remember what they said after Jim and I got back to them."

"Kyle, he either said it and you heard it, or he didn't say it and you didn't hear it. Which is it?"

"I don't know. I don't think he said it," Kyle said.

Marissa looked at me for more information. But I wasn't ready to mine that memory. I shrugged and drank. It took about three hours to learn that drinking doesn't help much with grief. The sensation that something was careening between my Adam's apple and navel kept me sober in the worst way. So I defied my Irish heritage and said good night before I was honest-to-God drunk. I walked through the darkened lot to Dad's SUV, feeling very alone. I did what anyone would do in that situation. I called my mom. I could tell from the sound of her voice that I woke her.

"Mom, it's me, Jim. Can I stay over tonight?"

Worcester to Framingham is a forty-five-minute drive on Route 9. I drove like I do when I'm half drunk—as if my personal freedom is on the line. The effort saved me from thinking. All around me, the woods and shopping plazas teemed with threats far worse than a sobriety checkpoint. The roads seemed wobbly, the lakes looked hungry, the parking lots rippled like quicksand and the sky threatened to suck up everything. I breathed and breathed again, because that's what people do. Making it past a suspicious guard at the apartment's front gate, I found parking a quarter mile from the door to Mom's yellow-brick building. She buzzed me in and I walked the hallway to the elevator.

Fumbling with my car keys, I dropped them on the high-traffic carpet in the hallway. On the door by my keys, someone had taped up their kid's artwork. It was a crude drawing of little people, big people, unidentifiable animals and scattered shapes. Above it all was scrawled "I AM SPECIUL." The door was one of about a dozen in the low-ceilinged, red-brick hallway. It struck me that this nondescript apartment building would be impossibly special to that kid. It would be his entire world for what seemed like forever. And one day, after years away, he would wonder what exactly that all-encompassing time and place in his life had been about. And he would return and see how peculiar and specific his world had been.

Bent, drunk and lost in thought, I almost fell over. I picked up my keys and found the elevator. Mom was bleary and disheveled when she let me in. Her age showed in her thick gray nightgown and her uncombed, thinning hair. She gave me a long hug befitting my fucked-up state, informed me of the meager options in the fridge. She had questions, and offered to listen. But I said I just wanted to sleep.

58.
Monday, January 19

Mom was surprised to see me up so early. We talked for a minute before I realized I wasn't up for talking. I cleaned up, put the Patriots shirt back on and folded up the bed. Mom offered to make breakfast, but I said we should go out, and said I'd drive. Just past the mall, she asked how I was doing.

"I'm okay. Sleeping is hard. This—it's not like being depressed. It's a physical thing, nausea, then exhaustion, then laughing for a second and then crying. You probably remember it from when Grandpa died."

He'd died before I was born. But she'd told me about it more than once. I was starting to understand why.

"After your grandfather died, I remember feeling like I'd been skinned. It was like I had no protection against anything, even the little things. I remember being glad when the weekends were over, because I could go back to work. And that meant I could stop crying. Oh Jim, I'm so sorry you have to go through this."

"How long did it last?" I asked.

"The mourning?"

"Yeah."

"Well, I don't think I was really myself until after a year, a year and a half."

"What changed?"

"I think it was time. Time changes all of this. But there was something. I had a dream not too long after he died where your grandfather told me to go to Montreal. I didn't know what he meant, but I remembered my mother had talked about a shrine in Montreal. So, well, your father was a lot more understanding in those days, and we flew up there, just for the day. We got off the plane, and we didn't speak French and didn't know where to go. But we eventually found the church. It was on a big hill. When I went inside, I felt the most overwhelming sensation of peace, like everything was okay."

Mom directed me through downtown Natick. It was quiet and safe. I had no memories of Joe there. We found a little diner near Town Line Liquors, where all the denizens of dry Wellesley went for booze. The diner was plain, essentially a room with tables inside. But the menu described twenty ways to make eggs. Mom ordered the French toast and I ordered coffee and the house omelet, which incorporated every ingredient the place had. The waitress was middle-aged, with a bird's nest of curly blonde-gray hair and a face rosy with winter-broken capillaries.

"I know you're upset. But this will pass. Don't do anything risky."

"Like what?"

"Get in a fight, or drink too much. I'm just worried."

I shrugged and sipped my coffee.

"Are they going to bury him?" Mom asked, sitting down across from me.

"I don't know. I guess so. I remember Justine saying she liked cremation, though."

"I always liked the idea of a grave. I just think for the first generation or two after, it's good to have somewhere to go, somewhere to visit."

"I guess so. Like I said, I don't know what they're going to do with him."

"It's strange, how death affects you. I remember, when I was young, going to a wake for the father of a friend of mine. This was back when they held the wake in the family's house. They had an open casket. That night, I had a dream where her father sat up in his coffin and pointed at me and asked 'Have you seen Gomorrah?' I was a nervous wreck for the next week."

Mom seemed as if she was still wounded by the man's death and unnerved by his question. Like everyone else, she was helpless before what was happening. But at least she was awake to it. She made me feel less alone.

My omelet tasted like everything. But my appetite wasn't working. After breakfast, Mom and I went to a big bookstore in one of the massive shopping plazas on Route 9. We walked the aisles, lost and then found each other by the register. She'd found two books and

I'd found none. That appetite was dead as well. We went into the attached cafe. Mom bought me a coffee and herself a chai-tea milkshake. I slumped at an earth-toned table. The café's music selection coated the room in middle-class agreeability. It was also safe from memories. I looked out the window and supposed that all the wrong people had survived.

"This place is crowded for a Monday. Doesn't anybody work anymore?" I scowled.

"It's Martin Luther King Day."

"Oh."

Mom asked how Joe died. I told her the story as I knew it, adding the details I'd heard from Kyle the night before.

"How terrible," she said.

"It's terrible. It's a lot of things. It's a fucking waste is what it is. I keep trying not to feel this way, but I'm fucking pissed off. I mean, people fucking cared about the guy. People loved him. And he just pissed it away. He just spat in our eyes. He just *told* that fucking moron to shoot him."

"Anger is part of it," Mom said, looking around at the people I had roused by raising my voice in rage and obscenity. She stared away their stares.

I drank my boiling coffee and hung my head. I never wanted to say any of that. I never wanted to believe that we don't belong to just ourselves. I never wanted to acknowledge that we belong to everyone who loves us, and should take better care. I'd always hated that point of view—its worry, and its inhibition on personal freedom. But the truth of it was sticking into me like a spear.

We finished our drinks and I drove Mom home. We hugged an awkward good-bye in the car. Alone in the car, my thoughts broke into half-coherent fragments. I raced back to the Fountainhead and was asleep as soon as I hit the inflatable mattress. When wakefulness returned, it rattled me. I wandered the apartment. I plugged in my cell phone and saw that I had about a dozen messages. I called a few people back, Olive, Serena, Jeff and Emily. Those phone calls all run together in my mind. I gave out the facts and they responded with numb apologies, requests for details, rote platitudes and vague offers that I should ask them for *anything they can do to help*. Not that I'd have much else to offer in their shoes.

Serena said she'd come up if I needed her to, even though work was crazy that week. And I said I'd be okay. She apologized, and offered anything else she could do to help. I hung up, feeling bitter and hurt. It's infantile as hell, but I wanted her to insist. It's something worse than infantile, but that phone call ultimately decided things between us.

I hung up, and without thinking, called Volpe's cell phone. In some part of my mind, I imagined that he had the power, as a member of the Worcester Police Department, to recall the bullet that had killed Joe. I recognized how irrational the idea was just as his voicemail picked up, and didn't bother leaving a message. There isn't much you can say after your rescue fantasy has disintegrated.

Marissa called with the address of the wake—a funeral parlor over by Institute Park in Worcester. She said that her, Fin and Kyle were considering an encore to the last night's binge. I said maybe, and called Dad to let him know I wasn't coming by. Outside the window, the sun was sliding down, past Springfield and Amherst. I watched it, but watching, even staring, didn't stop it.

"Yeah, of course. Do whatever you have to do tonight. Just remember tomorrow."

"What about tomorrow?"

"It's when I'm coming home from this place. You have to pick me up."

"What time?"

"I think around noon."

"Oh shit. Joe's wake starts at eleven. Can I pick you up early—like eight or nine?"

"I don't know. I'll ask."

"Okay. Try to be insistent, though."

Hanging up, I cursed the fresh difficulty. I started putting on my shoes to go see Marissa, Kyle and Fin. Near the hot center of the pain, if not with Justine, then with Joe's friends, in his old, trashed apartment seemed like the only place to go. But I lost my way looking for my jacket and decided that I was in no state to go anywhere. The two hours of phone calls had drained me. I called Marissa.

"Monaghan, you coming over?"

"Nah, I have to get Dad out of his physical therapy place at the break of dawn if I'm going to make it to the wake on time. And I'm beat, anyway."

"Yeah, we've all been going in and out of naps. We were out all night. It was madness."

"Sounds like a good time."

"It was alright for a while. Then Fin almost got us into a fight with the whole bar when he yelled out that the Patriots were dog shit. So they threw us out of Ralph's. Fucking Fin, what a nut. It was probably smart—you leaving early. I'm starting to think that drinking doesn't help with this at all."

"It didn't seem to be helping when I left."

"Then Claire called this morning to bitch me out because of what I said to the guy from the *Telegram*."

"Oh yeah, that reminds me, she told me to tell you and everyone not to talk to reporters."

"Fuck that. She isn't the boss over all of this. I gave the reporter your number. Did he call you?"

"Maybe. My phone ran out of juice. I still have a bunch of messages I didn't listen to."

We made plans to meet for coffee before the wake and hung up. Taking a breath, I took off my shoes, smiled and shook my head. I was glad to have tomorrow's packed schedule to distract me. I was glad for the wake, for the chance to be at the hot center of the pain.

I grabbed some Tylenol PM from the bathroom. Lying back on the air-mattress, I hoped for more than five hours of sleep.

Lying there, I remembered a night in our sophomore year of high school, when I got high with Joe for the first time. He was excited to show me off his gravity bong, a carved up two-liter soda bottle. The drugs worked for him back then, when almost nothing did. He was still young enough to have a Wade Boggs poster in his room, but old enough to have moved down to his mom's basement. I remembered Joe's excitement, remembered stealing Doritos from under his stoned nose. I remembered waking up that morning on the mildew-smelling floor of his room, with nothing still working, and full of dread at having to tell Dad that I was quitting the football team.

And with all else failing me on the inflatable mattress, the drugs did work. They put me down, pushed me deep and kept me there for a long time.

59.
Tuesday, January 20

The thoughts came in before the sunlight. Facing the prospect of hours to kill, I cleaned the apartment. Any task was welcome, compared to wandering the unmapped regions of grief. I moved my bed inflatable back into the spare room. Two hours later, the place looked more or less like it did when I showed up four weeks ago.

Parking at the rehab center in the still-early morning, I thought: "Look at me, doing the things I'm supposed to do, as if nothing was wrong." That poke at the dragon sleeping in my guts was enough to conjure a crying jag that kept me in the car for five minutes. With my puffy, red face wiped and serious, I went inside and told the orderly at the front desk that I was there to check Dad out. He said that checkout didn't start until eleven. I informed him that circumstances required that I get him today. He said that wasn't the facility's procedure. He argued his case out of laziness, and I argued with wild fervor. He tried to keep me calm. I tried to break his will. He went to get his supervisor. It took ten minutes of fury on my part before the supervisor, a sleepy-looking man with white hair, started the process of springing Dad. He refused to look at me as Dad filled out the paperwork in his wheelchair. Then he hurried us out, as if he was ejecting us from a bar.

On the drive back to the Fountainhead, the home nurse called to say that she was standing outside the apartment in the freezing cold and would leave if no one let her in. I told her I was on the way. The nurse was just about as pleasant when we met her at the entrance to the apartment building. She picked up too keenly on my having forgotten her name when I introduced them.

"It's *Joyce*," she said, arching an eyebrow in disappointment.

With Dad working his four-footed cane on the icy ground, it took forever to get out of the cold.

"I see you've cleaned since I was here," Joyce offered, once we got to the apartment. "Or at least picked up."

"Joyce, I would love to talk more with you today about cleaning and so on. But I have to go to the wake of my best friend from childhood. So please just do your job today," I replied.

With all the focus I could manage, I helped settle Dad into bed with his two new remote controls. He was thrilled to have so many channels again. From the kitchen, Joyce bitched about the refrigerator being empty, which it shouldn't be, since she had explicitly told me she wasn't going to do the shopping or the cleaning. I gave her a twenty and told her to order delivery for the day.

My suits, shirts and ties were all dry cleaned and hanging in my apartment in New York, waiting for a shot at employment. So Dad muted the TV and described from bed which suits he thought would fit me. I picked through the closet and finally hit on a dark blue double-breasted suit with a chalk stripe. I picked a dark tie, which Dad argued was too expensive for me to wear. But he relented. I hugged him and left. Joyce was puttering around the living room, with that TV tuned to a cooking show.

Route 9 was crushingly vivid with memory. It was like my whole life was happening all at once just to keep what had happened from being true. I tried to breathe evenly, tried not to squeeze the steering wheel too hard. Crossing Lake Quinsigamond into Worcester, I drove past UMass hospital. Then past Bell Pond where Dad said he'd found a duffel bag full of guns when he was a kid. Then down the rougher end of Belmont Hill where one house flew an oversized POW-MIA flag for my whole childhood. When I was ten, I found out what it meant, and imagined the mother and father inside, waiting and hoping that their flag would somehow help their lost son. Then the foot of the hill where a teacher at St. Johns said you could see all three kinds of columns—Doric, Ionic and Corinthian—embodied in the Auditorium, Vocational High School and Courthouse. The whole drive was fringed with digressions. They grew more intense until I parked off Highland Street, across from Tortilla Sam's.

Outside the Bean Counter, I saw Fin. He was in a shirt, tie, khakis that were several sizes too big, and sneakers. He was pacing the sidewalk, smoking a cigarette. I waved and he walked up to me. He'd been crying. He gave me a big hug. We repeated our only article of faith—that we couldn't believe it, then Fin let go. He forgot his wallet, so I bought him a coffee and we sat down. Wild-eyed, he started talking.

"After you left, we kept on drinking and talking about Joe until late. Then some guys started chanting that the Patriots were going to the Super Bowl, and I just found out that's true. But it seemed disrespectful, and I was so drunk that I thought they were talking about something else altogether. Don't even get me started on what I thought. But I told them that they were dog shit and their Patriots were dog shit and next thing you know I'm about to fight the whole bar."

"Marissa told me."

"I don't care if the Pats are going to the Super Bowl, those guys were fuckin' dicks."

"It's a little hard to get excited about professional sports right now. So was that the end of the night?"

"Well, we had to leave Ralph's. So we went to a few more bars, then Kyle drove me and Marissa and some other people back to Marissa and Joe's place, and we drank what was left there. It was this nasty rum, but we finished it. I think Kyle and Marissa hooked up."

The door rang open, but it was no one we knew. Fin leaned in close and sought out my eyes with his.

"Jim, can I tell you something, something weird?"

"Sure."

"I fucked a girl who only had one leg last night. I did it on Joe's bed."

"I wouldn't worry about it. I'm sure that somewhere, Joe gets a huge kick out of that. No pun intended."

"It was weird. We were at the Dive Bar. I didn't even mean to hook up. I was just so fucking sad. And I started talking to this girl I kind of know. I felt like I was missing a leg, metaphorically, you know? And this girl Sharon—the one with a missing leg—it just seemed like she could relate, like me and her were on the same page."

"Sure."

"Other than the leg, she was pretty hot. Except that she was kind of heavy and had kind of bad skin. I don't know. She just seemed like she understood," Fin said.

"Man, there's nothing wrong with a one-legged woman. Could you, like, do more positions?"

"That's what I always thought! But then the stump rubs up against you and that sort of ruins it."

"Oh. I can imagine that. Ooh," I said and we laughed.

Fin and I talked about the wake and the funeral until Marissa showed up with Kyle and the father of her child. The father, Mike, was a solid guy I'd only met once or twice before. I had another coffee and Fin cried on other shoulders. Marissa sat down across from me with a cupcake. She was in a tight, black, almost-shiny dress. It was distracting.

"Do you think it's wrong to have a cupcake for breakfast? I think it's fine. A cupcake is just a muffin with frosting, if you think about it," Marissa said.

"I'm no expert, but I think a muffin is made from different stuff."

"Whatever, fuck it. Hey Jim, don't look, but is Kyle looking at me?" she asked in a low voice.

"I don't know."

"Shit. He's been all over me ever since we hooked up. That was just a mourning thing. I mean, should I tell him that? Just to make it clear?"

"I don't know. Kyle seems like he can take a hint."

"It's just that I have Mike here, and my boyfriend is going to be at the wake later. I don't want him all over me."

"If he does more than look, then say something."

"I'm fucking pissed at him. So he was there when Joe got shot. You were too, but only for part of it. And I asked him like a hundred times whether or not the cop identified himself before he fired. And he was all like 'Oh, I'm not sure. I don't think so.' And that's like *the most important* fucking point when this goes to court. So after we hook up, he tells me that he thinks the guy might have said something about being a cop before he shot Joe. But he waited until after we already hooked up to tell me the truth. It's just fucking scummy behavior."

Marissa's phone rang. She raised it to her ear, but missed her head. The phone flew over her shoulder and broke into three pieces on the floor. She looked at the pieces, then at me and we both laughed until our faces were red. The laughter scooped out some of the cinderblock in my stomach.

Out on Highland Street, Marissa stepped into traffic without looking. A car stopped short and honked. Marissa gave it the finger.

"Hey, take it easy. Watch where you're going," Mike said calmly.

"Fuck that. What are they going to do, hit me? They don't have the balls," Marissa said to both Mike and the traffic.

Upon saying it, her jaw dropped. She knew she'd just parroted Joe's last words. Then she looked at me and sputtered. The two of us broke into desperate laughter all the way to our cars.

60.

The funeral directors were two clean, white-haired Irish men, who reluctantly let us in early. Inside, Justine was talking with her brother and sister. Her brother's wife was keeping a respectful distance along with the two adopted kids on the other side of the room. Grief can be radioactive like that.

Grief pressed me against the windshield of my eyes, unable to consider my own speedometer, odometer or radio station. There was only what was in front of me—two rooms, both sober, clean and understated with white walls, beige carpet and wood trim. Joe's family received people in one room. Joe's closed casket was in the other. After embracing Justine and Claire, I went into the room with Joe's body and stayed there for most of the next few hours. It was less crowded, for one thing. For hours, a line of people stretched out the door, waiting to give Justine their kind, futile words

A parade from the past came by. Old friends, ex-girlfriends, classmates, acquaintances with whom I'd lost touch and would likely never see again. Jeff and Emily came by. The nerves around our upbringing sang as we embraced and talked in the benches in the back of the coffin room. In and out of tears, I visited the body again and again, kneeling by it to pray, as people do. I wanted to feel acceptance or catharsis. But no amount of staring or praying or crying would relieve what careened in me. I knelt by his box and groped for an honest thing to say.

Bon voyage was too glib and too French. *You dumbfucking prick* seemed too harsh for a guy who'd already been shot to death that week. *See you soon* seemed too maudlin and speculative. *I love you* felt right, but embarrassing. *How could you do this?* was the question I wanted, in all my rage, to ask. But it wasn't the kind of thing I'd ever asked him in all our time as friends. *I'll remember* I swore. That was the closest I could come to anything honest to say to the body in the box before me. But it wasn't all that satisfying.

I couldn't cry enough or talk enough or not talk enough. It was all in vain. There was a break after the first three hours and Justine came into the room to look at the casket with Claire. She just stood over the body. I went over to the pair of them. We just looked at each other, each looking for the other to say something.

"Oh Jim," was all she said, then the crying took over.

"It's going to be a long time before we really know what we lost. I don't know when," I said.

Then she and Claire left and I was alone with Joe again, with something new and terrible to say.

You said we'd take LSD with our grandchildren. Who the fuck am I going to do that with now?

It was enough to force my head down into my hands. Marissa came up behind me and put her arm over my shoulders.

"I know, I know. Hey, Mike went out to McDonald's to get some food. You want some?"

I nodded and, for the hundredth time that day, collected myself. Mike was in the back of the room with a bag of cheeseburgers and french fries.

Marissa and I, Kyle, Fin and two or three others stayed through the second half, along with Joe's family. I went back and forth, talking to people I hadn't seen in years on the benches at the back of the coffin room and then, on my knees, trying to talk to Joe. Claire and Justine went back to the coffin whenever the line of people thinned out. I was by the body with Fin when Claire opened the lid of the coffin. It was something no one else had thought to do. I held my breath and looked at his inanimate face—nostrils dry, skin alternately like powder and like wax. He was in a suit, and his big Iroquois-looking face was impossibly at rest. I stared, as if that would help it sink in.

"Claire, it would be an honor if I could be a pallbearer at the funeral," Fin offered.

"Joe's going to be cremated after the wake."

"Where is that going to be?" Fin asked.

"It's going to be a small gathering, private, just for family," Claire said firmly.

61.

Marissa said a bunch of people were going back to Ralph's that night, but I passed on it. I went to go see Dad and Joyce. But when I got there, Dad was asleep and Joyce was gone, leaving a long note in perfect cursive that listed the many things I needed to buy and do before tomorrow. The only item that seemed truly urgent was Dad's prescriptions. I checked my phone to see if I could make the pharmacy by seven and saw that I had another dozen voicemail messages, and that it was too late. I checked on Dad, whose bedroom door was ajar. He was snoring.

Still in a daze, I logged onto my e-mail account in the spare room. I had a lot of them, from Worcester and New York, a mix of ancient friends offering condolences and new acquaintances I was hoping would help me find a job. Reading through them, my entire life in New York seemed like a story someone told me when they were in a hurry. But I discounted that feeling of strangeness, as I knew I'd have to discount so many feelings. I got back to work for the person I would be when the feelings stopped. I scheduled and rescheduled a pair of interviews for the week after next. I spell-checked each e-mail twice, and I needed to. I walked into the living room and called Olive.

"Hey mister, I didn't expect to hear from you."

"Yeah, well, I was at a wake all day. Also, Dad came home from the rehab place this morning. So ... what are you doing?"

"Just chatting online with some friends, and watching some TV. You were at a wake?"

"Yeah. I'll tell you all about it. Come meet me. I want to see you, now."

"I don't know. I was going to ... okay."

We agreed to meet in the parking lot by the Newbury Comics, in the shopping plaza across from the *Natick Collection*. On the drive, the winds still blew hard inside of me, but I couldn't cry. I waited in the empty parking lot and turned up the heat in the SUV. I was hungry for something that would feel like life. Olive pulled up in her old Volvo plastered with bumper stickers. I walked out to meet her.

"How are you?" she said, offering me a kiss.

"I'm here. I'm breathing. I guess I'm doing pretty well."

We walked back to Dad's SUV and got in. Then things got quiet, even standoffish for a long minute. Not knowing what to do, I leaned over to kiss her. She kissed back for a moment, but I pulled away. It seemed that another appetite had failed me.

"So what happened? Whose wake were you at?"

And I told her all of it. There was no way to make the story pretty, to pretend there were any heroes or hope in it. At the end, she took my hand and we sat there.

"You hungry?" she asked after a long time in the quiet.

"I am. I'm starving actually. I didn't even notice until now."

"You want to get some Kentucky Fried Chicken and look at the lake?" Olive asked.

We got the chicken and drove to a spot she knew by downtown Natick where you could park and look at the lake. The snow on the frozen lake was untouched, pure and white. The moon shone down so the lake was like a movie screen playing a film about nothing. Every so often, a freight or commuter train would race along the opposite shore, howling like a mythical beast. We ate the chicken and used the bones like spoons to eat the mashed potatoes and gravy. When I cried, Olive didn't ask why or try to soothe me.

"My father got a new doctor. He wants him to go back into surgery next month," Olive said into the silence.

I looked at her, then took her greasy hand in my greasy hand and squeezed. The silence came back, better than the consolation either of us could offer. We kissed again, and this time it kept on. We crawled over the seat to the back of the SUV and I tore open her black stockings. We made love among the golf balls, Dunkin Donuts wrappers, old receipts and paper towels. I was aroused in a dire sort of way, defending my beachhead in the world of the living with each thrust, each toothy kiss. It worked a little better than my other attempts at catharsis, which is to say it failed. Afterward, we drove back to the shopping plaza, still quiet, as if the cold night was a church. The sick fathers, the chance meeting, the excitement of touching, the dead friend, the vast uncertainties all did add up to something. And when we kissed good night, it all seemed charged with an unguessable meaning.

But my sense of mystery didn't make it out of Northborough intact. When I got back, I could hear Dad's TV, which meant he could hear the door. I walked down the hallway and he looked up at me. The nurse had put a chair by the bed, which made his bedroom feel like a hospital room.

"Hey, how are you?" he asked, muting the TV.

I was getting sick of the question. But I gave it one more hedging, okay-but-not-okay go. I sat down in the chair. He asked about the wake and I told him.

"It's good that you're going to the whole thing. I don't know if it was the war or what it was, but I have a really hard time with that stuff. I'll go to pay my respects, but I'll leave as soon as I can. I hate going to those things. When's the funeral?" he asked.

"Tomorrow. I don't know if it helps—the funeral, the wake. But it makes more sense than anything else right now."

"Probably. What do you think of Joyce?"

"She seems a little bitchy, but professional at least. I don't know. How about you?"

"She keeps the heat up too high. And if you think she's a bitch, then you should hear her on the phone with her husband. It's nice to know that someone has it worse than me," Dad joked.

"Maybe she'll loosen up after a few days."

"I hope so. At least she's a worker. She saw a stain on the sheets and changed them right away. She said it looked like blood. Was that you?"

"No, I've been staying on the inflatable bed."

"I probably just washed it with colors or something. I'm still getting the hang of laundry. Hey, do you think you'll have time to pick up my prescriptions tomorrow?"

I said I would, said I was tired, said I was glad he was back and said good night. I shut the door behind me so I wouldn't have to hear too much of his TV and he wouldn't have to hear too much of mine. On TV, they swore in the new president again and again. Some people were ecstatic. Others weren't so sure. The Tylenol PM didn't work so well and it was late by the time the TV stopped registering.

62.
Wednesday, January 21

On burying day, I was up with the sun. Sitting up in bed, I started crying right away, then laughed at myself—old Wake-and-Weep Monaghan. Dad was still sleeping, so I hit the road for some coffee and his pills. The CVS wasn't far from the McDonald's, so I stopped for breakfast. I ate a McMuffin and stared at the space where the playground used to be. Now it was just tables bolted to the concrete through the Astroturf. Beyond it, I watched Route 9 through the crotch of a golden arch. The memories were thick and I was anything but alone.

When I was four or five, Mom worked Saturday afternoons at a travel agency in the Filenes at the Worcester Galleria. And Dad would drive me out to that same McDonald's in Westborough, then to his old friend's butcher shop across from the WPI football field. We did it every weekend. Dad scared me when I was a kid—being huge and short-tempered. But those afternoons were a window into his mystery. In Worcester, Dad always ran into people who I'd never seen or heard of before. But I could feel the history hidden in their handshakes.

The CVS had just opened when I arrived. Exhaustion and a fundamental reluctance showed on the face of the pharmacist when I showed him the prescriptions, Dad's insurance card and my driver's license. He hesitated and went to the back. The place was big. I strolled the aisles and picked up magazines and snacks for Dad. The pharmacist had the pills ready when I got back to the counter.

Back at the apartment, I looked at Joyce's long, coldly polite letter and decided the rest of the stuff on her list could wait a day. I dressed in the same clothes I'd worn the day before and flipped through the TV's many bad choices until I heard Joyce's keys in the door. She was in jeans and a green fleece with a hospital logo on it. She looked raw, freckly and stippled, as if she'd applied the opposite of makeup to come over. She was unpleasantly surprised to see me. Apartments always become smaller as the winter goes on, but Dad's would always be too small for three adults. I told her Dad was sleeping and that I'd gotten his pills from the pharmacy. She reminded me that I had failed to go grocery shopping. I said I had to go to a funeral. She asked what Dad was going to eat. I slapped a twenty on the kitchen counter and said to get delivery. She said I couldn't keep doing that. I said I'd be at a funeral all day and walked out, dramatically, without my coat. I hurried across the frozen puddles and crunching scree of the parking lot to Dad's SUV.

The sky over Route 9 was clear but not bright. The sun was still low behind me. I past the Econo Lodge and the sports bar, always under new management, perched at the intersection of Route 20. It was too early for the funeral. But a sense—that something was almost over—propelled me. I was nearing the end of this first, blistering and unhinging portion of grief. I pressed the gas pedal.

I malingered in the late rush-hour traffic on Shrewsbury Street, pausing at the traffic light by the Wonder Bar. I thought of how Joe laughed at the predicament he'd put himself in. I could still hear his loud, machine-gun laugh and thought of his peculiar, intense optimism. The optimism was for small things—that the night ahead wouldn't be boring, that he could find some excitement and satisfaction in what seemed to everyone else to be just passing the time.

Something was coming loose. Joe's laugh was doing it. And he had laughed in every dour face, every shabby fate that wagged at him from the steel desks, the fake-velvet seats of Oldsmobiles, the bolted down Dunkin Donuts' tables and the dirty plastic cash registers. I limped to the next red light, by the Boulevard Diner. I stared it down as if it could be intimidated. I stared until my eyes became blurry with tears and a Toyota behind me honked. Driving under I-290 and around the rotary by the train station, something did come loose. The staccato bellow of Joe's peculiar and belligerent joy rang in my ears and I had to pull over. That laugh. It was Joe winning his momentary victories over boredom, and then over the embarrassing and dangerous means at his disposal to fight boredom.

Circling past the refurbished train station, I found a place to stop. It was the parking lot of a vacuum cleaner repair shop that had been gutted and refurbished to sell wine and gourmet foods. In low, subdued spasms, I puked up a prominent piece of the cinderblock. Leaning over the steering wheel, with the traffic jostling past me, I remembered meeting Joe in the fifth grade. We were paler and hairless, our fingers always sweaty. We had both discerned that the world, though huge and mysterious, was largely unfriendly, and wanted us mainly to go where it sent us, and to be quiet about it. I remember by the lockers, Joe sold me a truly awful Atari game, called Haunted House. Later that week, I told him it was a crappy game and I wanted my money back. He said I just wasn't playing it right. That was the beginning of it. We got older and figured out more of the little mysteries. The world got smaller and sometimes seemed, in fits of hubris, to be downright small. But we shared the same basic suspicion of it, and made our very separate peaces. Well, cease-fires only last so long. And now Joe was dead.

Wiping the spit from my mouth and the tears off my cheeks with the back of my hand, I took some deep breaths. The wave receded. I made it to the funeral home in time to join the procession to the church on June Street. We drove slowly, with our headlights on, across the city. The funeral was across town, in a modern Catholic church, a triangle done in that yellow-brown institutional brick, with a simple cross on top. The parking lot was mostly full when we arrived. I shook hands, hugged, and shared my head-shaking, clueless grief with the people crowded in front of the church. The sense—that something was nearly over—made me a loiterer on the cold church steps. Joe's family made their way past in a protective formation around Justine, who was wearing sunglasses. I nodded to her but she didn't notice. Then Emily and Jeff showed up. Jeff was wearing a black trench coat with a black sweatshirt and black jeans. His eyes were wide and jumpy. Emily was wearing a dark-gray pantsuit.

"Hey guys. Thanks for coming."

Emily pursed her lips as though I'd said something absurd.

"No problem, man" Jeff said, lowering his head and looking solemnly at me.

"Hey, are you going to the cemetery after?"

"I didn't know if we should or not," Emily said.

"I'd like it if you did. You can ride with me if you want."

"Okay, sure," Emily said, looking at Jeff, who was nodding in a rhythm that had escaped the cadence of the conversation.

"Oh, I got you a present, do you want it now?" Jeff asked, jumping into the conversation from left field.

"Maybe after the Mass."

"Okay."

"What are you guys doing afterwards?" I asked, surprised by the high pitch of my voice.

Marissa passed me with Kyle, Fin, her enormous Italian boyfriend and Mike. She said she'd hold me a seat close to the front as she passed. I made plans with Emily and Jeff to go to the cemetery and then to get something to eat. Marissa waved to me from the fourth row when I entered the church. I kneeled and crossed myself, then walked down the aisle. In front of me was Joe's extended family, distant uncles and aunts, adopted and natural cousins, along with family friends who felt they were entitled or needed enough to sit up close. I wasn't the only one who wanted to be at the white hot center of the pain. A strange competition was afoot.

The church filled up. Except for his sworn enemies, almost everyone who knew Joe loved him. His ashes sat on a cart on the crimson high-traffic carpet at the head of the aisle, in front of the marble stairs that led to the altar. His urn was green marble, just larger than a shoebox. I imagined Joe—all six foot two of him, condensed to be buried. I thought of who he was—now condensed into anecdotes, to be buried in memory. It was all happening too fast. The priest began to say the Mass. Marissa periodically clutched my hand and I clutched back. I looked around at all the people, crying or staring dumbly into the front of the room. The Crucifix above the altar was one of those sterile, modern jobs—all pale wood and clean lines. The face of Christ was drawn and tranquil.

The priest obviously didn't know Joe and repeated what he'd heard from the family with full attribution. Claire gave a eulogy that praised Joe the precocious child, and condemned Joe the alcoholic. After Communion, I prayed without aim, mouthing the words *Oh God* over and over, with no other praise or pleas for Him. The Mass resumed with the Ave Maria, whose opening notes rose like the sun cracking the line of the horizon. A massive sob rose with it and seized my chest and throat. When it passed, I realized the Mass was nearing its end. For the first time in my life, I wished that a Mass would be longer. Even in remembering, I find myself reaching out for some remembered detail to slow down the narrative. But I mostly remember looking down at my hands, my lap and my shoes.

Too soon, too fast, the priest told us to go in peace.

Emily and Jeff and I got into Dad's SUV and followed in the procession out the west side of Worcester, up Airport Hill, and out of town, into the woods, into Paxton, whose town common was anchored by an obelisk to its war dead. We didn't talk much on the drive over there. The Veterans cemetery was where they were going to bury Joe. It was a humble place. Its large monuments commemorated the wars and the branches of the armed forces. The men and women and their families received small brass plaques in the lawn. Whoever ran the place had cleared the snow off the ground around the grave and dug a hole. A backhoe was parked behind a massive granite star that honored the men and women who served in the Navy during World War Two, including Joe's grandfather. We packed into the semicircle carved into the snow. Sobs erupted around the circle.

The priest, a gentle if ineffectual old Irish man, said the words *In the midst of life we are in death.* It sounded so baffling that I almost had to believe it. It was a shard of mystery thrown into the cooling tumult of my guts.

After his words, most fled the cold. I lingered, along with some others for no good reason. I spotted an old friend, John Bedill, who had been a friend of Joe's and an all-around good guy—until he robbed a sporting-goods store with a shotgun and, if memory serves, received a fairly stern sentence for it. I was surprised to see him out and about. We saw each other and embraced, released each other, nodded and went our separate ways, probably forever.

I paced and stared at the green marble box until it became clear that I wasn't going to out-linger the other lingerers without a coat. I walked down the snowy, trampled grass back to Dad's SUV.

63.

Jeff turned off the radio when I got in the SUV.
"The radio's fine. You can turn it back on."

Jeff didn't turn it back on, so I did, but quieter, so the Aerosmith song coming through the speakers was a tinny hiss. We pulled away from the grave and then stopped by the cemetery office so Jeff could use the bathroom.

"So are you okay?" Emily asked, climbing into Jeff's seat up front.

"You probably know better than me. I mean, I'm talking and walking and I want to get a sandwich or something. So I guess that I am okay. I'm not feeling the urge to drink my own weight or drive a hundred miles an hour. I guess that's what okay is, right?"

"I guess it's the best you can hope for."

"I just wish there was something to do. To name a street after Joe, or pass a law, or to make it so that cop goes to jail. I wish there was some clear lesson in all this, besides don't taunt a man with a gun. Or I wish it had changed something in me, that I could take all of this and use it to become a saint or a millionaire. And there's none of that, no lesson, no meaning, no purpose. I mean, is he just another guy who threw away his life because he couldn't figure out what he was so mad at?"

"You have to give it time."

"It's like, your whole life you try to think positive, to make the best of bad situations, to fix problems and so on. But there's no way to fix this, no way to deal with it, no good to be gleaned from it. He's just dead. There's nothing to do and practically nothing to say."

"I don't think there is anything to do. Things will change in their own time."

Jeff came out of the bathroom, walking with a stumble back to the car. Circling out of the graveyard, we saw the funeral directors, along with a guy in coveralls, converging on Joe's grave. Through the woods, we found Worcester again. There was a reception in the church basement, but I skipped it. We drove around aimlessly, finally stopping for some sandwiches at Elsa's Bushel and Peck, then crossed the tail end of Lake Quinsigamond, passed St. John's and climbed into Shrewsbury.

"Can I have my sandwich?" Jeff asked.

"One minute," I said. "We're almost there."

There's a park connected to the lab in Shrewsbury where they invented the birth control pill. On a service road between the lab and the park is a gap cut about two hundred feet deep into the trees and brush to give it a view of Worcester. It's a lovers' lane that no lovers ever seemed to visit. Driving the SUV right into the snow bank, I parked there. It wasn't late, but the sun was already lowering itself onto Worcester.

"You know, you shouldn't miss Joe too much. You're going to see him again, in another life," Jeff said after a half sandwich had passed.

"Thanks man," I said.

"Seriously. My dad told me this story about reincarnation. One of the gods, Indra, was building himself a huge palace to celebrate this war he won. He kept making the palace bigger and bigger, until the builder finally went to Brahma and said like, hey, get this guy off my back."

"I thought your parents were Catholic," Emily said.

"That's mostly my mom. My dad is into all kinds of stuff, religion-wise. My mom is just the pushy one. I think she tried to convert him when I was a kid, but ..."

"Okay, so Brahma decides to help out the contractor."

"Yeah, so he goes to see Indra in the form of a little boy and he starts telling Indra all kinds of things that he never knew about his ancestors. And then the boy sees a trail of ants in the corner of Indra's huge mansion and starts laughing. Indra asks why he's laughing, and the boy says that each of the ants has been Indra an infinite amount of times before," Jeff said, nodding.

"So what happened with the mansion?" Emily asked.

"Oh, I think Indra decided to forget about it and seek wisdom, or something."

"I wish my thesis advisor was so easy to placate," Emily said in her low punch-line voice.

All of Route 9 glowed as it climbed up from Lake Quinsigamond, anticipating the dusk. It grew bright with orange streetlights, white parking lot lights and a dim rainbow of back-lit plastic signs. Beyond it was a glimpse of the few tall buildings of downtown Worcester.

"Oh man, here's your present. I got it just for you," Jeff said, taking a brown paper bag from inside his coat pocket.

Inside the bag was a clay wizard with a conical cap and star-spotted cloak. The wizard held a marble for a crystal ball in one hand. The wizard had a long, white beard and his mouth was wide with joy. It was exactly the kind of gift you'd expect your mentally ill friend to give you in a time of bereavement.

"Thanks man. I like it, a lot."

Jeff leaned between the front seats to touch the wizard.

"His open hand is for incense. I just figured that, with everything going on, it might help you relax."

"Thanks. It's a great gift. I really appreciate it," I said and put the wizard on top of the dashboard.

We finished our sandwiches while the sun pressed itself into the hills. I was all cried out and all talked out. My eyes were as hollow as my cheeks. I drove Jeff and Emily to the church parking lot and said good-bye. Jeff nodded again and again with his eyes wide as we said good-bye. Emily seemed more wary.

"Call me anytime you need to—night or day. But I guess you already do that," she said.

There were still cars in the church parking lot, and I considered going inside. But by then, communal mourning had gone from being a high imperative to a poisonous form of self-abuse. I drove around Worcester as the roads filled again with rush hour traffic. Meandering in Dad's SUV, I wondered at what Jeff had said about an infinite universe, where you play every part again and again. It seemed fair, but dizzying. And it made my present anguish seem foolish.

Despite everything, I prefer the Catholic scale of things. In it, everything matters. Everything is real to everyone. Even Christ loses his patience on the cross and demands that God explain why He has forsaken His only son. Even for Christ, pain is as real as God, and even more real, for a moment. And though reality may have a happy ending in heaven, there's a lot of suffering between here and there. For the first time, the agony and struggle of Catholicism made real sense. I decided to buy some beer.

After making a hundred lefts and rights just to stay within twenty minutes of the red hot center of the pain, I pulled into the big liquor supermarket on Park Avenue. Abstracted with thoughts of suffering and God, I parked too hard into the parking lot's huge snow bank. The clay wizard rattled against the windshield and then fell down by the gas and brake pedals. In my suit, I walked fast against the cold to the liquor store. But the doors were locked. Checking the sign on the door and my cell phone, twice, I saw that it had closed three minutes ago. I knocked, but only drew the attention of a surly Puerto Rican clerk, who pointed at the sign. I held out my hands in supplication to the scratched plastic doors of the liquor store as he walked away.

Back through the orange sodium light of the parking lot, I cursed. I opened the door to Dad's SUV and hopped inside. But my feet didn't hit the mat evenly. I leaned down to see what I'd stepped on, my stubbly neck pressing against the fake wood steering wheel. I retrieved the wizard Jeff had given me, now in two pieces, the wizard, and the arm that held his crystal ball. I held up Jeff's gift, with a piece in each hand. The crystal ball caught the headlight of a car making a u-turn on Park Avenue.

"Another broken wizard," I said to no one, and wept. I went to punch the car radio, but remembered it was Dad's, and pulled back.

Eventually, I put the pieces of the wizard-shaped incense holder in the passenger seat and put the car in reverse. I took Chandler Street downtown, passing the old Worcester Market with the gorgeous terra cotta bull's head at its roof peak. I worked through the rotaries and one-way streets back to Route 9, where the snow banks had already turned their final dirty color, somewhere between gray and brown. It was the color of the long-haul portion of the winter that sends the old-timers and the short-tempered running for Florida. I drove past the Price Chopper, Papa Gino's and Newbury Comics in Shrewsbury, past the West Side Grill, which waited in the cold to go out of business again, then past the Fountainhead.

Route 9 was a profoundly unconscious stretch of the human enterprise, like so many places. The stores, the empty patches by woods and lakes, the apartment complexes, the uneven peppering of red lights—they all seemed immune to remark. I worked the gas and the brake. It was the best I could do. The night spread out forever. The earth vanished as Route 9 rushed me and my fellow travelers to the dream scenarios of parking lots, private homes, shopping centers, junkyards, interstate highways, airports and oblivion.

And death—my death and every death—was always there, just waiting. But you could lose it pretty easily, like you can lose the late afternoon sun in the downtown of a city. You only had to turn a corner, and it was gone.

From the road, I saw the lights I was looking for, and turned.

Epilogue

64.

New Haven is the line. It separates the New England and New York spheres of influence, separates Red Sox and Yankees fans, separates the dour authority of the British Puritans from the avaricious free-for-all of the Dutch merchants, separates the winter that is a way of life from the winter that is an inconvenience.

I had made the New York-to-Worcester trip hundreds of times—in a car, a train, a bus—and I always felt the changeover. This time, I crossed through the Heroes Tunnel on the Merritt Parkway. It was a few weeks after Christmas, a year after Joe was killed. I knew it was going to be a triathlon of sadness. But sadness becomes less of a good reason to do or not do something as time goes on. I got the day off work and rented a car.

New Haven and Hartford sprang up and drifted by with memories of being a teenager, knowing nothing and acting stupidly, wanting love or transcendence and not knowing how to find them. I remembered how the Hartford bus station's grimy possibility had stirred me, back when nearly every place in the world had seemed an improvement.

The intervening year had taken its toll. I lost Serena and gained twenty pounds. Dad healed. I went back to New York, and turned thirty. I held my tongue and took a job for less pay. The days rolled in and out, growing imperceptibly easier as they did. The months of living on an emotional diet of weeping, rage and exhaustion had passed, and had changed me. But I'd rejoined the living. At the end of the summer, I'd even met a special sort of girl, and I was thinking of proposing to her.

Joe was not altogether gone. He came now and then in dreams. Once I met him at Spag's, which was still open in the dream. He was working at the garden shop, by the rear parking lot. They were holding a carnival there, just like they never did. Joe was angry with me, because I'd gained so much weight. I tried to joke it off, to say how glad I was to see him. But he wouldn't let it go. After he'd harangued me for too long, I asked him what death was like.

"I can't tell you that," Joe said, his face in half a grin. "It's against the rules."

"Come on, man. It's me. Anyway, you break the rules all the time," I said.

"Not these rules," he said, his grin flattening.

"You're a dick," I said, to which he gave me his big, confrontational smile.

I was only up for the day, and only up to see Joe's grave. Dad's job had transferred him to Florida in September. I'd seen Mom over Christmas in Framingham. Olive had asked me to call her the next time I was in the area, but I didn't.

The grave was just a bronze plaque screwed into the lawn in the middle of nowhere. I had gone back because Joe mattered to me. And he still had to matter, dead or not, or else I myself would be lost. Maybe that's not perfect logic. But I am a small man in a large world, and it is the best I could do.

65.

Marissa had moved into a three-decker on Vernon Hill. She shouted my name from the second-floor balcony, waving a Budweiser and a cigarette. I got my bag out of the rental car and climbed the stairs. Her ex-boyfriend had her daughter for the night and she was having some friends over. She hugged me hard in the hallway.

"Jim, I'm so glad you're here. I miss him so much," she said, holding on.

"Me too," I said, not sure of what I meant. I'd been wary of maudlin outbursts and generally suspicious of my own emotions for a year by then. I never wanted to make mourning my vocation. But there I was.

The party started out fun—Marissa fought a guy on crutches and we all drank and drank. A Puerto Rican schoolteacher who was slurring her words got upset and ran off, leaving behind her purse and cell phone. Marissa gave me a folder of Joe's old drawings of robots and war scenes to flip through. A drunk skinny blonde kept trying to kiss me in between her crying jags. Finally some guy in a backwards baseball hat, first called her ex-husband, then her husband, showed up.

There was a lot of talk about what a fun guy, a great friend, a unique soul Joe was. He had become the perfect excuse to get bombed. There was enough weeping and toasting that it seemed impossible that Joe's grave would be so bare the next afternoon. And the grave—that was the reality. You can interpret and re-interpret what happens to you. But reality only lets you get away with so much.

After midnight, the cocaine arrived and the party got its second lease on life. People still talked about Joe's death, but only as it referred back to them. His death taught them to do this and not to do that. Or he died because, unlike themselves, he did that. Or it was this noble virtue, which they also possess, that Joe died for.

I got tired, and curled up in the small, pink bed in Marissa's daughter's room. Below the Strawberry Shortcake poster, I closed my eyes and tried to sleep. But through the door, the party kept on. Marissa and a girl who'd shown up late yelled like a coke-fueled amen corner about how the girl was going to get Marissa a job at the rent-a-car company where she worked. Then Marissa's boyfriend showed up and left with the girl to get more coke. They were gone far too long, so that Marissa started a big fight when he got back. None of it involved me, except that it kept me awake.

The next day, everyone left at Marissa's was too fucked up or too busy to make it out to the cemetery. Everyone loves the dead, right up until it costs something, I thought, bitterly.

The roads and little towns looked different from a year before. It had been a warm winter, and there was no snow on the ground. But I remembered the route to the cemetery.

It was bright and windy in the graveyard. Mild as it was, January in Massachusetts was a haunted place, full of jarring similarities to the same time a year before. I put down my flowers on the bronze plaque Joe shared with his grandfather, grandmother and mother, whose death date was blank. By that point, I knew better than to expect catharsis or relief from even prolonged weeping. But there I was.

Glad to have gone alone, I searched for an appropriate thing to say to the ground, for a proper prayer to offer. I considered my girlfriend, considered the good times I'd found in the last year, even considered the tasty egg sandwich I'd eaten on the way to the graveyard. I said a prayer of thanks that I was still alive. I stood up and thought of the party the night before. The world seemed too threadbare to stand losing a person like Joe.

I put my knee back on the ground and prayed that the universe is more efficient than it looks.

I prayed that important parts of it are not so easily lost. I prayed hard, then walked back to my rental car. It was a long drive home.

THE END

May 18, 2009
Brooklyn, NY, USA

Colin Dodds' writing has appeared in a number of periodicals, including *The Wall Street Journal Online*, *Folio*, *Explosion-Proof*, *Block Magazine*, *The Architect's Newspaper*, *The Reno News & Review* and *Lungfull! Magazine*. One of his screenplays, *Refreshment – A Tragedy*, was named a semi-finalist in 2010 American Zoetrope Screenplay Contest. Before he died, Norman Mailer wrote that one of Dodds' novels showed "something that very few writers have; a species of inner talent that owes very little to other people." He lives in Brooklyn, New York, with his wife Samantha.

Other Books by Colin Dodds

Poetry

Last Man on the Moon

The Blue Blueprint

Heaven Unbuilt

Novels

Fun's Monsters

Last Bad Job

What Smiled at Him

WINDFALL

Screenplays

Refreshment — a tragedy

Made in the USA
Charleston, SC
17 December 2011